Heaven
and Earth

Titles by Nora Roberts

HOT ICE	HOLDING THE DREAM
SACRED SINS	FINDING THE DREAM
BRAZEN VIRTUE	MONTANA SKY
SWEET REVENGE	SEA SWEPT
PUBLIC SECRETS	RISING TIDES
GENUINE LIES	INNER HARBOR
CARNAL INNOCENCE	SANCTUARY
DIVINE EVIL	HOMEPORT
HONEST ILLUSIONS	THE REEF
PRIVATE SCANDALS	JEWELS OF THE SUN
BORN IN FIRE	TEARS OF THE MOON
BORN IN ICE	HEART OF THE SEA
BORN IN SHAME	RIVER'S END
HIDDEN RICHES	CAROLINA MOON
TRUE BETRAYALS	DANCE UPON THE AIR
DARING TO DREAM	HEAVEN AND EARTH

THE VILLA

FROM THE HEART
(anthology)

ONCE UPON A CASTLE
*(anthology with Jill Gregory, Ruth Ryan Langan,
and Marianne Willman)*

ONCE UPON A STAR
*(anthology with Jill Gregory, Ruth Ryan Langan,
and Marianne Willman)*

ONCE UPON A DREAM
*(anthology with Jill Gregory, Ruth Ryan Langan,
and Marianne Willman)*

Titles written as J. D. Robb

NAKED IN DEATH	CONSPIRACY IN DEATH
GLORY IN DEATH	LOYALTY IN DEATH
IMMORTAL IN DEATH	WITNESS IN DEATH
RAPTURE IN DEATH	JUDGMENT IN DEATH
CEREMONY IN DEATH	BETRAYAL IN DEATH
VENGEANCE IN DEATH	SEDUCTION IN DEATH
HOLIDAY IN DEATH	

SILENT NIGHT
(anthology with Susan Plunkett, Dee Holmes, and Claire Cross)

OUT OF THIS WORLD
*(anthology with Laurell K. Hamilton, Susan Krinard,
and Maggie Shayne)*

NORA ROBERTS

Heaven
and Earth

BOOKSPAN LARGE PRINT EDITION

JOVE BOOKS, NEW YORK

This Large Print Edition, prepared especially for Bookspan, contains the complete, unabridged text of the original Publisher's Edition.

HEAVEN AND EARTH

A Jove Book / published by arrangement with the author

All rights reserved.
Copyright © 2001 by Nora Roberts.
Excerpt from *Face the Fire*, copyright © 2001 by Nora Roberts.
Cover art and design by Tony Greco.
This book, or parts thereof, may not be reproduced in any form without permission.
For information address: The Berkley Publishing Group, a division of Penguin Putnam Inc., 375 Hudson Street, New York, New York 10014.

Visit our website at www.penguinputnam.com

ISBN: 0-7394-2190-5

A JOVE BOOK®
Jove Books are published by The Berkley Publishing Group, a division of Penguin Putnam Inc., 375 Hudson Street, New York, New York 10014. JOVE and the "J" design are trademarks belonging to Penguin Putnam Inc.

PRINTED IN THE UNITED STATES OF AMERICA

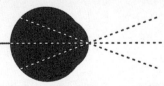

This Large Print Book carries the Seal of Approval of N.A.V.H.

To all my sisters,
not of blood but of the heart.
There's the magic.

Swift as a shadow, short as any dream;
Brief as the lightning in the collied night,
That in a spleen unfolds both heaven and earth,
And ere a man hath power to say, "Behold!"
The jaws of darkness do devour it up:
So quick bright things come to confusion.
—WILLIAM SHAKESPEARE

Prologue

THREE SISTERS ISLAND
SEPTEMBER 1699

She called the storm.

The gales of wind, the bolts of lightning, the rage of the sea that was both prison and protection. She called the forces, those that lived within her, those that dwelled without. The bright and the dark.

Slender, with her cloak streaming back like bird-wings, she stood alone on the wind-whipped beach. Alone but for her rage and her grief. And her power. It was that power that filled her now, rushed inside her in wild, pounding strokes like a lover gone mad.

And so, perhaps, it was.

She had left husband and children to

come to this place, left them under a spell-sleep that would keep them safe and un-aware. Once she had done what she had come to do, she could never go back to them. She would never again hold their much-loved faces in her hands.

Her husband would grieve for her, and her children weep. But she could not go back to them. And she could not, would not, turn from the path she had chosen.

Payment must be made. And justice, however rough, would be met at last.

She stood, arms outflung in the tempest she had conjured. Her hair flew free and wild, dark ribbons that slashed at the night like whips.

"You must not do this thing."

A woman appeared beside her, burning as bright in the storm as the fire after which she was named. Her face was pale, her eyes dark with what might have been fear.

"It is already begun."

"Stop it now. Sister, stop before it is too late. You have no right."

"Right?" She who was called Earth whirled, her eyes glowing fierce. "Who has better right? When they murdered the inno-cents in Salem Town, persecuted and hunted and hanged, we did nothing to stop it."

"Stop one flood, cause another. You know this. We made this place." Fire stretched out her arms, as if to encompass the island that rocked in the sea. "For our safety and our survival, for our Craft."

"Safety? You can speak of safety, of survival, now? Our sister is *dead.*"

"And I grieve for her, as you do." Pleading, she crossed her hands between her breasts. "My heart weeps as yours weeps. Her children are in our keeping now. Will you abandon them as well as your own?"

There was a madness in her, tearing at her heart as the wind tore at her hair. Even recognizing it, she could not defeat it. "He will not go unpunished. He will not live while she does not."

"If you cause harm, you'll have broken your vows. You will have corrupted your power, and what you send out in the night will come back to you threefold."

"Justice has a price."

"Not this. Never this. Your husband will lose a wife, your children a mother. And I another beloved sister. More, even more than that, you break faith with what we are.

She would not have wanted this. This would not have been her answer."

"She died rather than protect herself. Died for what she is, for what we are. Our sister abjured power for what she called love. And it killed her."

"Her choice." One that stayed bitter in the throat long after it was swallowed. "And still she harmed none. Do this thing, use your gift in this dark way, and you doom yourself. You doom us all."

"I cannot live, hidden here." There were tears in her eyes now, and in the storm-light, they burned red as blood. "I cannot turn from this. My choice. My destiny. I take his life for hers, and damn him for all time."

And calling for vengeance, shooting it like a bright and deadly arrow from a bow, she who was known as Earth sacrificed her soul.

One

THREE SISTERS ISLAND
JANUARY 2002

Sand, frosted with cold, crunched under her feet as she ran along the curving shore. Incoming waves left froth and bubbles lying on the crusted surface like tattered lace. Overhead, the gulls called, relentlessly.

Her muscles had warmed, and moved fluid as oiled gears in the second mile of her morning run. Her pace was a fast and disciplined jog, and her breath rushed out in white plumes. And rushed in, sharp and cold as shards of ice.

She felt fabulous.

The wintry beach held no footprints but her own, and hers were stamped, new over old, as she jogged back and forth across the gentle sweep of winter beach.

If she'd chosen to do her three miles in one straight line, she could have crossed Three Sisters from side to side at its widest point.

The idea of that always pleased her.

The little clump of land off the coast of Massachusetts was hers, every hill, every street, every cliff and inlet. Deputy Ripley Todd felt more than affection for Three Sisters, its village, its residents, its well-being. She felt responsibility.

She could see the rising sun glint against the windows of storefronts on High Street. In a couple of hours, the shops would open, people would walk along the streets going about the day's business.

There wasn't much of a tourist trade in January, but some would come over from the mainland on the ferry, poke about in the shops, drive up to the cliffs, buy some fresh fish right off the docks. For the most part, though, the winter was for islanders.

She loved the winter best.

At the end of the beach, where it bumped the edge of the seawall just below the village, she pivoted and headed back across the sand. Fishing boats plied an ocean that was the color of pale blue ice. It would change as the light strengthened, as the sky deepened. It never failed to fascinate her how many colors water could hold.

She saw Carl Macey's boat, and a figure, tiny as a toy in the stern, raised a hand. She saluted back, kept running. With under three thousand islanders year-round, it wasn't hard to know who was who.

She slowed her pace a bit, not only to cool down but to prolong the solitude. She often took her morning runs with her brother's dog, Lucy, but this morning she had slipped out alone.

Alone was another thing she liked best.

And she'd wanted to clear her mind. There was a great deal to think about. Some of which she preferred not to, so she tucked those annoyances and problems away for now. What had to be dealt with wasn't precisely a problem. You couldn't call something that made you happy a problem.

Her brother was just back from his honeymoon, and nothing could have pleased her more than to see how happy he and Nell were together. After all they'd been through, and what it had nearly cost, seeing them cozied up together in the house where she and Zack had grown up was pure satisfaction.

And over the past months, since summer, when Nell had ended her flight from fear on the island, they'd become real friends. It was a pleasure to see the way Nell had bloomed, and toughened.

But all that mushy stuff aside, Ripley thought, there was one little blight on the rose. And its name was Ripley Karen Todd.

Newlyweds didn't need to share their love nest with the groom's sister.

She hadn't given the matter a thought before the wedding, and even after, when she'd waved them both off for a week in Bermuda, she hadn't seen the whole picture.

But when they'd returned, all snuggling and flushed with a honeymoon haze, it couldn't have been more clear.

Just-marrieds needed privacy. They could hardly have hot, spontaneous sex on the living room floor if she might stroll into the house any time of the day or night.

Not that either of them had said anything about it. But they wouldn't. The pair of them might as well wear we're-nice-people merit badges plastered on their chests. And that, Ripley thought, was something she would never be pinning on her own shirt.

She stopped, used the outcropping of rocks at the far end of the beach for support as she stretched out calves, hamstrings, quadriceps.

Her body was as lean and toned as a young tiger's. She took pride in it, in her control over it. As she bent from the waist, the ski cap that she'd tugged on fell to the sand and her hair, the color of varnished oak, tumbled free.

She wore it long because it didn't require regular trims and styling that way. It was just another type of control.

Her eyes were a sharp bottle green. When she was in the mood she might fuss with mascara and eyeliner. After considerable debate, she'd decided her eyes were the best part of a face made up of mismatched features and angular lines.

She had a slight overbite because she'd despised her retainer. And she had the wide forehead and nearly horizontal dark eyebrows of the Ripley side of the family.

No one would have accused her of being

pretty. It was too soft a word—and would have insulted her in any case. She preferred knowing it was a strong and sexy face. The kind that could attract men. When she was in the mood for one.

Which she hadn't been, she mused, for several months.

Part of that was wedding plans, holiday plans, the time she'd spent helping Zack and Nell unwind legal tangles so they could be married. And another part, she was forced to admit, was her own sense of annoyance and unease that lingered from Halloween, when she'd ripped open pockets in herself that she had purposely sewn shut years before.

Couldn't be helped, she thought now. She'd done what needed to be done. And had no intention of a repeat performance. No matter how many cool, smirky glances Mia Devlin shot her way.

The thought of Mia brought Ripley back full circle.

Mia had an empty cottage. Nell had rented it, then moved out when she married Zack. As much as Ripley hated the idea of having any sort of dealings, even straight business, with Mia, the yellow cottage was the perfect solution.

It was small, private, simple.

It just made sense, Ripley decided and started up the worn wooden steps that zagged from the beach toward the house. It was irritating, but it was practical. Still, maybe it wouldn't hurt if she took a few days, let the word out that she was looking for a place to rent. Something—something that didn't belong to Mia—might drop in her lap.

Cheered by the possibility, Ripley bounded up the steps, jogged to the back porch.

Nell would already be baking, she knew, just as she knew the kitchen would smell like heaven. The biggest advantage was that she wouldn't have to hunt up breakfast. It would just be there. Delicious, delightful, and on demand.

As she reached for the doorknob, she saw, through the glass, Zack and Nell. They were wrapped around each other, she thought, like ivy on a flagpole. Wrapped around each other *and* wrapped up in each other.

"Oh, man."

Hissing out a breath, she backtracked, then came back up on the porch stomping like a horse and whistling. It would give them time to peel themselves off each other. At least, she hoped it would.

But it didn't solve her other problem. She was going to have to deal with Mia, after all.

She was going to keep it casual. To Ripley's way of thinking, if Mia knew she really wanted the yellow cottage, she would refuse to rent it.

The woman was so damn contrary.

Of course, the very best way to lock in the deal would be to ask Nell to run interference. Mia had a soft spot for Nell. But the idea of using anyone to clear the path was galling. She would just casually drop in at Mia's bookstore, the way she had almost every day since Nell had taken over the cooking and baking for the café section.

That way she could cop a righteous lunch and new digs all in one swipe.

She walked briskly along High Street, more because she wanted the business over and done than because the wind was up and blowing. It tugged playfully at the long, straight tail of hair that she habitually yanked through the opening in the back of her cap.

When she reached Café Book she paused, pursed her lips.

Mia had redone the display window. A little tasseled footstool, a soft throw of deep red, and a pair of tall candlestands with fat red candles were arranged with seemingly haphazard piles of books. Because she knew Mia never did anything in a haphazard fashion, Ripley had to admit the whole tone was one of homey warmth and welcome. And subtly—very subtly—sexy.

It's cold out, the window announced. Come on in and buy some books to take home and snuggle up with.

Whatever else Ripley could say about Mia—and she could say plenty—the woman knew her business.

She stepped inside into warmth, automatically unwinding her neck scarf. The deep-blue shelves were lined with books, parlor-tidy. Glass displays held pretty trinkets and intriguing dust catchers. The fireplace was simmering with a low golden flame, and another throw, blue this time, was tossed artfully over one of the deep, sink-into-me chairs.

Yeah, she thought, Mia knew her stuff.

There was more. Other shelves held candles of various shapes and sizes. Deep bowls were filled with tumbling stones and crystals. Colorful boxes of Tarot cards and runes were tucked here and there.

All very subtle again, Ripley noted with a frown. Mia didn't advertise that the place was owned by a witch, but she didn't hide it either. Ripley imagined the curiosity factor—both tourist and local—accounted for a healthy chunk of the store's annual profits.

None of her business.

From behind the big carved counter, Mia's head clerk, Lulu, finished ringing up a customer's purchases, then tipped down her silver-framed glasses to peer at Ripley over the top of them.

"Looking for something for your mind as well as your belly today?"

"No. I've got plenty to occupy my mind."

"Read more, know more."

Ripley grinned. "I already know everything."

"Always thought you did, anyway. Got a

novelty book in this week's shipment that's right up your alley. *101 Pick-Up Lines*—unisex."

"Lu." Ripley gave her a cocky grin as she strolled to the stairs leading to the shop's second level. "I wrote the book."

Lulu cackled. "Haven't seen you keeping company just recently," she called out.

"I haven't felt like company just recently."

There were more books on the second floor, and more browsers poking through them. But here, the café was the big draw. Already Ripley could scent the soup of the day, something rich and spicy.

The early crowd, which would have snagged Nell's muffins and turnovers or whatever treat she'd dreamed up for the day had shifted to the lunch crowd. On a day like this, Ripley imagined they'd be looking for something hot and hearty, before they treated themselves to one of Nell's sinful desserts.

She scanned the display and sighed. Cream puffs. Nobody in their right mind walked away from cream puffs, even if the other choices were equally tempting éclairs, tarts, cookies, and what looked to be a cake made up of many layers of pure gooey sin.

The artist behind the temptations rang up an order. Her eyes were a deep and clear blue, her hair a short gold halo around a face that glowed with health and well-being. Dimples flashed in her cheeks as she smiled and waved her customer off to one of the café tables arranged by the window.

Marriage, Ripley thought, agreed with some people. Nell Channing Todd was one of them.

"You look pretty bouncy today," Ripley commented.

"Feel great. The day's just flying by. Soup of the day's minestrone, sandwich is—"

"I'm just doing soup," Ripley interrupted. "Because I need one of the cream puffs to ensure my happiness. I'll take coffee with it."

"Coming up. I'm baking a ham for dinner tonight," she added. "So no grabbing pizza before you come home."

"Yeah, okay. Sure." It reminded Ripley of the second stage of business. She shifted her feet, gave the room another sweeping glance. "I didn't see Mia around anywhere."

"Working in her office." Nell ladled up

soup, added a crusty roll baked fresh that morning. "I expect she'll breeze through shortly. You were in and out of the house so fast this morning I didn't get to talk to you. Something up?"

"No, not up." Maybe it was rude to arrange for alternate living arrangements without saying something first. Ripley wondered if this fell into the area of social skills, a tricky business for her.

"Will I be in your way if I chow down in the kitchen?" she asked Nell. "That way I can talk to you while you work."

"Sure. Come on back."

Nell carried the food over to her work-table. "Are you sure nothing's wrong?"

"Not a thing," Ripley assured her. "Bitchy cold out. I bet you and Zack are sorry you didn't stay south until spring."

"The honeymoon was perfect." Even thinking of it brought on a warm, satisfied glow. "But it's better being home." Nell opened the refrigerator for the container holding one of the day's salads. "Everything I want is here. Zack, family, friends, a home of my own. A year ago I'd never have believed I'd be standing here like this, knowing that in an hour or so I'd be going home."

"You earned it."

"I did." Nell's eyes darkened, and in them Ripley could see the core of strength—a core that everyone, including Nell, had underestimated. "But I didn't do it alone." The bright *ding* of the counter bell warned her she had a customer waiting. "Don't let your soup get cold."

She slipped out, her voice lifting in greeting.

Ripley spooned up soup and sighed with contentment at the first taste. She would just concentrate on her lunch and think about the rest later.

But she'd barely made a dent in the bowl when she heard Nell call Mia's name.

"Ripley's in the kitchen. I think she wanted to see you."

Shit, shit, *shit*! Ripley scowled into her soup and got busy filling her mouth.

"Well, well, make yourself at home."

Mia Devlin, her gypsy mane of red hair tumbling over the shoulders of a long dress of forest green, leaned gracefully against the doorjamb. Her face was a miracle formed of high, ice-edged cheekbones, a full, sculpted mouth painted as boldly red as her hair, skin smooth as cream, and eyes gray as witch-smoke.

Those eyes looked Ripley over lazily, one brow lifted in a perfect and derisive arch.

"I am." Ripley continued to eat. "I figure it's Nell's kitchen this time of day. If I thought otherwise, I'd be searching my soup for wool of bat or dragon's teeth."

"And it's so hard to come by dragon's teeth this time of year. What can I do for you, Deputy?"

"Not a thing. But I did give some passing thought to doing something for you."

"Now I'm all agog." Tall and slim, she moved to the table and sat. She was wearing those needle-thin heels she was so fond of, Ripley noticed. She could never figure out why anyone would put her innocent feet in such torture chambers without a gun being held to her head.

She broke off another piece of her roll, munched. "You lost yourself a tenant when Nell and Zack tied the knot. I figured you hadn't gotten around to doing anything about renting out the yellow cottage, and since I'm thinking about getting my own place, maybe I can help you out."

"Do tell." Intrigued, Mia broke off a bite of Ripley's roll for herself.

"Hey, I'm paying for that."

Ignoring her, Mia nibbled. "A little too crowded for you at the homestead?"

"It's a big house." Ripley gave a careless shrug, then moved the rest of her roll out of reach. "But you happen to have one going empty. It's a pretty dinky place, but I don't need much. I'd be willing to negotiate a lease on it."

"A lease on what?" Nell swung back in, straight to the fridge to get out the makings for a sandwich order.

"The yellow cottage," Mia told her. "Ripley's looking for a place of her own."

"Oh, but—" Nell turned. "You have a place of your own. With us."

"Let's not make this sticky." It was too late to regret she hadn't arranged to speak to Mia privately. "I was just thinking it'd be cool to have a little place to myself, and since Mia's got one going begging—"

"On the contrary," Mia said smoothly. "Neither I nor my possessions need to beg."

"You don't want me to do you a favor?" Ripley lifted a shoulder. "No skin off mine."

"It's so considerate of you to think of me." Mia's tone was candy-sweet. Always a bad sign. "But as it happens I just signed with a tenant for the cottage not ten minutes ago."

"Bullshit. You were just up in your office, and Nell didn't say you were with anyone."

"On the phone," Mia continued. "With a gentleman from New York. A doctor. We've signed a three-month lease for the cottage via fax. I hope that relieves your mind."

Ripley wasn't quite quick enough to mask her annoyance. "Like I said, no skin off mine. What the hell's a doctor going to do for three months on Three Sisters? We've got a doctor on-island."

"He's not a medical doctor. He's a Ph.D.—and as you're so interested, he's coming here to work. Dr. Booke is a paranormal researcher, and he's eager to spend some time on an island conjured by witches."

"Fucking A."

"Always so succinct." Amused, Mia got to her feet. "Well, my work here is done. I must go see if I can bring joy into someone else's life now." She strolled to the door, waited a beat before she turned. "Oh, he'll be here tomorrow. I'm sure he'd love to meet you, Ripley."

"Keep your weirdo spook hunters away from me. Damn it." Ripley bit into her cream puff. "She's eating this up."

"Don't go anywhere." Nell lifted her order. "Peg comes on in five. I want to talk to you."

"I've got patrol."

"You just wait."

"Damn near ruined my appetite," Ripley complained, but managed to devour the cream puff.

In fifteen minutes she was stalking outside again, Nell glued to her side.

"We need to talk about this."

"Look, Nell, it's no big deal. I was just thinking—"

"Yes, you were thinking." Nell yanked her wool cap down over her ears. "And you didn't say anything to me, or to Zack. I want to know why you feel you can't stay in your own home."

"Okay, okay." Ripley put on her sunglasses, hunched her shoulders as they started down High toward the station house. "It just seems to me that when people get married, they need privacy."

"It's a big house. We're not in each other's way. If you were the domestic type, I could see you feeling displaced because I have to spend so much of my time in the kitchen."

"That's the least of my worries."

"Exactly. You don't cook. I hope you don't think I resent cooking for you."

"No, I don't think that. And I appreciate it, Nell, I really do."

"Is it because I get up so early?"

"No."

"Because I took one of the spare bedrooms for an office for Sisters Catering?"

"No. Jeez, nobody was using it." Ripley felt as though she was being systematically pounded with a velvet bat. "Look, look, it's not about cooking or spare rooms or your baffling habit of getting out of bed before the sun rises. It's about sex."

"Excuse me?"

"You and Zack have sex."

Nell stopped, cocked her head as she studied Ripley's face. "Yes, we do. I don't deny it. In fact, we have quite a lot of sex."

"There you are."

"Ripley, before I officially moved into the house, Zack and I often had sex there. It never seemed to be a problem for you."

"That was different. That was regular sex. Now you're having married sex."

"I see. Well, I can assure you the process works in almost exactly the same way."

"Har-har." Nell had come a long way, Ripley mused. There'd been a time when even the hint of a confrontation would have had her backing down.

Those days were over.

"It's just weird, okay? You and Zack are into the mister and missus thing and you've got me hanging around. What if you wanted to do the horizontal tango on the living room rug, or just have dinner naked some night?"

"We've actually done the first, but now I'll give some serious consideration to the second. Ripley." Nell touched Ripley's arm, rubbed lightly. "I don't want you to move out."

"Jesus, Nell, it's a small island. It's not like I'd be hard to reach wherever I landed."

"I don't want you to move," she said again. "I'm speaking for myself, not for

Zack. You can talk to him separately if you want and get his feelings about it. Ripley . . . I never had a sister before."

"Oh, man." She cringed, scanning the area from behind her dark glasses. "Don't get mushy, not right out on the street like this."

"I can't help it. I like knowing you're there, that I can talk to you whenever. I only had a few days with your parents when they came back for the wedding, but knowing them now and having you, I have a family again. Can't we just leave things the way they are, for now, anyway?"

"Does Zack ever say no to you once you turn those big blue headlights on him?"

"Not when he knows it's really important to me. And if you stay, I'll promise that when Zack and I have sex, we'll pretend we're not married."

"It might help. Anyway, since some jerk from New York snagged the cottage right under my nose, I'll have to let things ride." She let out a pained sigh. "Paranormal researcher, my butt. Ph.D." She sneered and felt marginally cheered. "Mia probably rented the place to him just to piss me off."

"I doubt it, but I'm sure she's enjoying

that side benefit. I wish the two of you wouldn't jab at each other so much. I'd really hoped, after . . . after what happened on Halloween you would be friends again."

Instantly, Ripley closed in. "Everybody did what had to be done. Now it's over. Nothing's changed for me."

"Only one phase is over," Nell corrected. "If the legend—"

"The legend is hooey." Even thinking of it blighted Ripley's mood.

"What we are isn't. What's inside us isn't."

"And what I do with what's inside me is my business. Don't go there, Nell."

"All right." But Nell squeezed Ripley's hand and even through the gloves that both women wore, there was a spark of energy. "I'll see you at dinner."

Ripley balled her hand as Nell walked away. Her skin still hummed from the contact. Sneaky little witch, Ripley thought.

She had to admire that.

Dreams came late in the night, when her mind was open and her will at rest. She could deny by day, close herself off, stand by the choice she'd made more than a decade before.

But sleep was a power of its own, and seduced the dreaming.

In dreams, she stood on the beach, where the waves rose like terror. They pounded, black and bitter, on the shore, a thousand mad heartbeats, under a blind sky.

The only light was the snake-whips of lightning that slashed each time she raised her arms. And the light that came from her was a furious gold edged with murderous red.

The wind roared.

The violence of it, the sheer, unharnessed *power* of it, thrilled her in some deep and secret place. She was beyond now, beyond right, beyond rules.

Beyond hope.

And part of her, still flickering, wept grievous tears for the loss.

She had done what she had done, and now wrongs were avenged. Death to death to death. A circle formed by hate. One times three.

She cried out in triumph as the dark

smoke of black magic streamed inside her, smearing and choking out what she had been, what she had vowed. What she had believed.

This, she thought as her cupped hands trembled at the force and the greed, was better. What had come before was pale and weak, a soft belly, compared to the strength and muscle of what was now.

She could do all and any. She could take and could rule. There was nothing and no one to stop her.

In a mad dance she spun across the sand, above it, her arms spread like wings, her hair falling in coils like snakes. She could taste the death of her sister's murderer, the bright copper flavor of blood she'd spilled, and knew she had never supped so well.

Her laughter shot out like bolts, cracked the black bowl of the sky. A torrent of dark rain fell and hissed on the sand like acid.

He called her.

Somewhere through the wild night and her own fury she heard his voice. The faint glow of what had been inside her struggled to burn brighter.

She saw him, just a shadow fighting

through the wind and rain to reach her. Love warred and wept in a heart gone cold.

"Go back!" she shouted at him, and her voice thundered, shook the world.

But still he came on, his hands reaching toward her—to gather her in, to bring her back. And she saw, just for an instant, the gleam of his eyes against the night, that was love, and fear.

Out of the sky came a lance of fire. Even as she screamed, as that light inside her leaped, it speared through him.

She felt his death inside her. The pain and horror of what she'd sent out springing back, times three.

And the light inside her winked out. Left her cold, cold, cold.

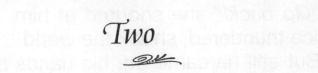

Two

He didn't look so very different from the other passengers on the ferry. His long black coat flapped in the wind. His hair, an ordinary sort of dark blond, flew around his face and had no particular style.

He'd remembered to shave and had only nicked himself twice, just under the strong line of his jaw. His face—and it was a good one—was hidden behind one of his cameras as he snapped pictures of the island using a long lens.

His skin still held the tropical tan he'd picked up in Borneo. Against it his eyes were the luminous golden brown of honey just bottled. His nose was straight and narrow, his face a bit thin.

The hollows in his cheeks tended to deepen when he lost himself in work for long periods and forgot regular meals. It gave him an intriguing starving-scholar look.

His mouth smiled easily, sensually.

He was somewhat tall, somewhat lanky.

And somewhat clumsy.

He had to grip the rail to keep a shudder of the ferry from pitching him over it. He'd been leaning out too far, of course. He knew that, but anticipation often made him forget the reality of the moment.

He steadied himself again, dipped into his coat pocket for a stick of gum.

He came out with an ancient lemon drop, a couple of crumpled sheets of notepaper, a ticket stub—which baffled him, as he couldn't quite remember when he'd last been to the movies—and a lens cap he'd thought he'd lost.

He made do with the lemon drop and watched the island.

He'd consulted with a shaman in Arizona, visited a man who claimed to be a vampire in the mountains of Hungary, been cursed by a brujo after a regrettable incident in Mexico. He'd lived among ghosts in a cottage in Cornwall and had documented the rights and rituals of a necromancer in Romania.

For nearly twelve years, MacAllister Booke had studied, recorded, witnessed the impossible. He'd interviewed witches, ghosts, lycanthropes, alien abductees, and psychics. Ninety-eight percent of them were delusional or con artists. But the remaining two percent . . . well, that kept him going.

He didn't just believe in the extraordinary. He'd made it his life's work.

The idea of spending the next few months on a chunk of land that legend claimed had been torn from the mainland of Massachusetts by a trio of witches and settled as a sanctuary was fascinating to him.

He'd researched Three Sisters Island extensively and had dug up every scrap of information he could find on Mia Devlin, the current island witch. She hadn't promised him interviews, or access to any of her work. But he hoped to persuade her.

A man who had talked himself into a ceremony held by neo-Druids should be able to convince a solitary witch to let him watch her work a few spells.

Besides, he imagined they could make a

trade. He had something he was sure would interest her, and anyone else who was tied into the three-hundred-year-old curse.

He lifted his camera again, adjusting the framing to capture the spear of the white lighthouse, the brooding ramble of the old stone house, both clinging to the high cliffs. He knew Mia lived there, high above the village, close to the thick slice of forest.

Just as he knew she owned the village bookstore and ran it successfully. A practical witch who, by all appearances, knew how to live, and live well, in both worlds.

He could hardly wait to meet her face-to-face.

The blast of the horn warned him to prepare for docking. He walked back to his Land Rover, put his camera in its case on the passenger seat.

The lens cap in his pocket was, once again, forgotten.

While he had these last few minutes to himself, he updated some notes, then added to the day's journal entry.

The ferry ride was pleasant. The day's clear and cold. I was able to take a number of pictures from different van-

tage points, though I'll need to rent a boat for views of the windward side of the island.

Geographically, topographically, there's nothing unusual about Three Sisters Island. Its area is approximately nine square miles, and its year-round inhabitants—largely in the fishing or the retail and tourist trade—number less than three thousand. It has a small sand beach, numerous inlets, coves, and shale beaches. It is partially forested, and the indigenous fauna include whitetail deer, rabbit, raccoon. Typical seabirds for this area. As well as owls, hawks, and pileated woodpecker in the forested regions.

There is one village. The majority of the residents live in the village proper or within a half-mile radius, though there are some houses and rental units farther afield.

There is nothing about the island's appearance that would indicate it is a source of paranormal activity. But I've found that appearances are unreliable documentary tools.

I'm eager to meet Mia Devlin and begin my study.

He felt the slight bump of the ferry's docking, but didn't look up.
Docked, Three Sisters Island, January 6, 2002. Glanced at his watch. *12:03 P.M. EST.*

The village streets were storybook tidy, the traffic light. Mac drove through, circled, logging various spots on his tape recorder. He could find an ancient Mayan ruin in the jungle with a map scribbled on a crushed napkin, but he had a habit of forgetting more pedestrian locations. Bank, post office, market. Ah, pizzeria, hot damn!

He found a parking place without trouble only a stop down from Café Book. He liked the look of the place immediately—the display window, the view of the sea. He fished around for his briefcase, tossed the minirecorder inside, just in case, and climbed out.

He liked the look of the store even more on the inside. The cheerful fire in a stone hearth, the big checkout counter carved with moons and stars. Seventeenth century, he decided, and suitable for a museum. Mia Devlin had taste as well as talent.

He started to cross to it and the little gnomelike woman sitting on a high stool behind it. A movement, a flash of color caught his attention. Mia stepped out of the stacks and smiled.

"Good afternoon. Can I help you?"

His first clear thought was, Wow.

"I'm, ah, hmm. I'm looking for Ms. Devlin. Mia Devlin."

"And you've found her." She walked toward him, held out a hand. "MacAllister Booke?"

"Yeah." Her hand was long and narrow. Rings sparkled on it like jewels on white silk. He was afraid to squeeze too hard.

"Welcome to Three Sisters. Why don't you come upstairs? I'll buy you a cup of coffee, or perhaps some lunch. We're very proud of our café."

"Ah . . . I wouldn't mind some lunch. I've heard good things about your café."

"Perfect. I hope your trip in was uneventful."

Up till now, he thought. "It was fine, thanks." He followed her up the stairs. "I like your store."

"So do I. I hope you'll make use of it during your stay on the island. This is my friend, and the artist of our café, Nell Todd. Nell, Dr. Booke."

"Nice to meet you."

She showed her dimples and leaned over the counter to shake his hand.

"Dr. Booke has just arrived from the mainland, and I imagine he could use some lunch. On the house, Dr. Booke. Just tell Nell what you'd like."

"I'll take the sandwich special, and a large cappuccino, thanks. Do you do the baking, too?"

"That's right. I recommend the apple brown Betty today."

"I'll try it."

"Mia?" Nell asked.

"Just a cup of the soup and the jasmine tea."

"Coming up. I'll bring your orders out."

"I can see I'm not going to have to worry

about my next meal while I'm here," Mac commented as they took a window table.

"Nell also owns and runs Sisters Catering. She delivers."

"Good to know." He blinked twice, but her face—the sheer glory of it—didn't dim. "Okay, I just have to get this out, and I hope you're not offended. You're the most beautiful woman I've seen in my life."

"Thank you." She sat back. "And I'm not the least bit offended."

"Good. I don't want things to start off on the wrong foot, since I'm hoping to work with you."

"And as I explained over the phone, I don't . . . work for audiences."

"I'm hoping you'll change your mind after you get to know me better."

He had a potent smile, she decided. Charmingly crooked, deceptively harmless. "We'll see about that. As for your interest in the island itself, and its history, you won't lack for data. The majority of the permanent residents here are from families who've lived on Sisters for generations."

"Todd, for instance," he said, glancing back toward the counter.

"Nell married a Todd, just a little under

two weeks ago, in fact. Zachariah Todd, our sheriff. While she's . . . new to the island, the Todds have, indeed, lived here for generations."

He knew who Nell was. The former wife of Evan Remington. A man who had once wielded considerable power and influence in the entertainment industry. A man who had been found to be a violent abuser. And who was now deemed legally insane and under lock and key.

It had been Sheriff Todd who'd arrested him, right here on Sisters Island, after what were reputed to be strange events on Halloween night.

The Sabbat of Samhain.

It was something Mac intended to explore in more depth.

Even as he started to bring it up, something in Mia's expression warned him to bide his time there.

"Looks great. Thanks," he said instead to Nell as she served their lunch.

"Enjoy. Mia, is tonight still good for you?"

"Absolutely."

"I'll come up about seven, then. Let me know if you need anything else, Dr. Booke."

"Nell's just back from her honeymoon,"

Mia said in a quiet voice when she was alone with him again. "I don't think questions about certain areas of her life are appropriate just now."

"All right."

"Are you always so cooperative, Dr. Booke?"

"Mac. Probably not. But I don't want to make you mad right off the bat." He bit into his sandwich. "Good," he managed. "Really good."

She leaned forward, toyed with her soup. "Lulling the natives into complacency?"

"You're really good, too. Do you have psychic abilities?"

"Don't we all, on some level? Didn't one of your papers explore the development of what you called the neglected sixth sense?"

"You've read my work."

"I have. What I am, Mac, isn't something I neglect. Neither is it something I exploit or allow to be exploited. I agreed to rent you the cottage, and to talk with you when the mood strikes me, because of one simple thing."

"Okay. What?"

"You have a brilliant and, more important, a flexible mind. I admire that. As far as trusting that, time will tell." She glanced over and gestured. "And here comes a bright enough, and very inflexible, mind. Deputy Ripley Todd."

Mac looked over, saw the attractive brunette stride on long legs to the café counter, lean on it, chat with Nell. "Ripley's another common surname on the island."

"Yes, she's Zack's sister. Their mother was a Ripley. They have long ties, on both sides of their family, to the Sisters. Very long ties," Mia repeated. "If you're looking for a cynic to weigh in on your research, Ripley's your girl."

Unable to resist, Mia caught Ripley's attention and motioned her over.

Ordinarily Ripley would merely have sneered and walked in the opposite direction. But a strange face on the island usually bore checking out.

A good-looking guy, she thought as she strolled over. In a bookish kind of way. As soon as the thought hit, her brows drew together. Bookish. Mia's doctor of freakology.

"Dr. MacAllister Booke, Deputy Ripley Todd."

"Nice to meet you." He got to his feet, surprising Ripley with his length as he unfolded himself from the chair. Most of his height, she judged, was leg.

"I didn't know they gave out degrees for the study of crapola."

"Isn't she adorable?" Mia beamed. "I was just telling Mac that he should interview you for your narrow, closed mind. After all, it wouldn't take much time."

"Yawn." Ripley hooked her thumbs in her pockets and studied Mac's face. "I don't think I'd have much to say that you'd want to hear. Mia's the goddess of woo-woo stuff around here. You have any questions about the practicalities of day-to-day life on the island, you can usually find me or the sheriff around."

"Appreciate it. Oh, I've only got a master's in crapola. Haven't finished my thesis on that one yet."

Her lips twitched. "Cute. That your Rover out front?"

"Yes." Had he left the keys in it again? he wondered, already patting pockets. "Is there a problem?"

"No. Nice ride. I'm going to grab some lunch."

"She isn't abrasive and annoying on purpose," Mia said when Ripley walked away. "She was born that way."

"It's okay." He sat again, picked up his meal where he'd left off. "I get a lot of that kind of thing." He nodded at Mia. "I imagine you do, too."

"Now and then. You're awfully well adjusted and affable, aren't you, Dr. MacAllister Booke?"

"Afraid so. It's pretty boring."

"I don't think so." Mia picked up her tea, studied him over the rim. "No, I don't think so at all."

Mac left his things in the Rover and did a solo walk-through of the yellow cottage. He'd assured Mia he didn't need her to come along. The fact was, he wanted to get a feel of the place without her. She had a strong and distracting presence.

It was small, charmingly quaint, and heads above the majority of accommodations he usually had on a research jaunt. He knew a lot of people thought he was a man more suited to a dark and dusty library. He often was, but he was just as much at home in a tent in the jungle, so long as he had enough battery power for his equipment.

The living room here was small and cozy, with a sofa that looked comfortably broken in and a little fireplace already set for lighting. He decided to take care of that first and patted his pockets absently before he saw the box of wooden matches on the narrow mantel.

Grateful for small favors, he got the fire going and continued on his tour. Because he talked to himself habitually, his voice echoed a bit.

"Two bedrooms. That one'll do for a sub-office. I think I'm going to set up primarily in the living room. Kitchen'll do if I get desperate enough to cook. Nell Todd."

He dug in his pockets again, came up with the business card for Sisters Catering that he'd taken from the café counter. He laid it in the middle of the stove where he would see it if he thought about cooking.

He looked out the windows, appreciating the woods that tucked in close and the lack of other houses. He often worked odd hours. Here he didn't have any neighbors close enough to complain.

He tossed the single bag he'd brought in

with him on the bed in the larger of the two bedrooms, dropped his butt on the bed to give it a test bounce.

The image of Mia drifted into his mind. "Down, boy," he warned himself. "No carnal thoughts about a woman who might be able to pluck them out of your head, and who's also your primary research target."

Satisfied with his living arrangements, he headed outside to unload the Rover.

On his second trip he stopped to watch the sheriff's cruiser pull up, and Ripley climb out.

"Deputy Todd."

"Dr. Booke." She was feeling vaguely guilty about giving him a hard time on their first encounter. Which she wouldn't have felt, she thought resentfully, if Nell hadn't scolded her about it. "You've got a lot of stuff here."

"Oh, this is only part of it. I've got more being sent in tomorrow."

Nosy by nature, she looked in the back of the Rover. "More than this?"

"Yeah. Lots of neat stuff."

She turned her head. "Neat?"

"Lots of it. Sensors, scanners, and

gauges and cameras and computers. Cool toys."

He looked so pleased with the idea that she didn't have the heart to smirk. "I'll give you a hand hauling what you've got inside."

"That's okay. Some of it's pretty heavy."

Now she did smirk, and hefted a large box out of the back. "I can handle it."

No question about that, he decided and led the way inside. "Thanks. You work out? What do you bench-press?"

Her brows lifted. "I do twelve reps of ninety pounds in a set." She couldn't get a good gauge of his body type in the long coat and the thick sweater under it. "You?"

"Oh, about the same, considering body weight." He walked out again, leaving her following and trying to get a sense of his shoulders. And his ass.

"What do you do with all this . . . neat stuff?"

"Study, observe, record, document. The occult, the paranormal, the arcane. You know, the different."

"Freak shows."

He only smiled. Not just his mouth, she noted, but his eyes as well. "Some people think so."

They hauled the rest of the boxes and bags in together.

"It's going to take you a week to unpack."

He scratched his head, scanned the piles now crowding the living space. "I never mean to bring so much, but then, you never know what you might need. I was just in Borneo and could've kicked myself for not packing my backup energy detector—like a motion detector, but not," he explained. "You just can't find one of those on Borneo."

"I bet."

"I'll show you." He shrugged out of his coat, tossed it carelessly aside before hunkering down to paw through a box.

Surprise, surprise, Ripley thought. Dr. Weird had one excellent butt.

"See, this one's handheld. Completely portable. I designed it myself."

It put her in mind of a little Geiger counter, though she didn't think she'd ever seen an actual Geiger counter.

"It detects and measures positive and negative force," he explained. "Simply put, it reacts to charged particles in the air, or in a solid object, even water. Except this one isn't submersible. I'm working on one that will be. I can hook this up, when I need to, to my computer and generate a graphic printout of the size and density of the force and other pertinent data."

"Uh-huh." She gave a quick glance at his face. He looked so earnest, she thought, so pleased with his little handheld gadget. "You're really a total geek, aren't you?"

"Yeah, pretty much." He flipped his unit on to check the batteries. "I've always been into the paranormal and electronics. I found a way to indulge myself on both levels."

"Whatever floats your boat." But she scanned the piles of boxed equipment. It looked like Radio Shack had exploded. "All this high-tech junk. Lots of dough, I bet."

"Mmm." He wasn't giving her his full attention. His activated sensor was giving off a low but definite reading.

"Do they give you grants for stuff like this?"

"Umm, maybe, but I never needed one. I'm a really rich geek."

"No kidding? Don't let Mia know or she'll jack up the rent." Curious, she wound her way through the boxes. She'd always liked the little cottage well enough, and was still a bit steamed that she wasn't the one moving in. But things with MacAllister Booke weren't adding up for her.

"Look, usually I'm big on minding my own business, and I've got less than no interest in the stuff you do, but I've just got to say, you just don't seem to fit. Professor of strange, geeky rich guy, little yellow cottage. What are you after?"

He didn't smile now. His face went quiet, almost eerily intent. "Answers."

"What answers?"

"All of them I can get. You've got great eyes."

"Huh?"

"I was just noticing. Nothing but green. No gray, no blue, just intense green. Pretty."

She angled her head. "You coming on to me, Dr. Geek?"

"No." He very nearly flushed. "I just noticed, that's all. Half the time I don't realize I'm saying something that's in my head. Comes from spending a lot of time on my own, I guess, and thinking out loud."

"Right. Well, I've got to get going."

He stuck the sensor in his pocket, neglecting to turn it off. "I appreciate the help. No offense before, okay?"

"Okay." She offered her hand to shake.

The instant their fingers clasped, the sensor in his pocket beeped madly. "Wow! Wait. Hold on."

She tried again to tug her hand free, but his grip turned surprisingly strong. With his free hand, he dragged the sensor out of his pocket.

"Look at this." Excitement rippled through his voice, deepened it. "I've never had it measure anything this strong. Almost off the scale."

He began to mutter numbers as if memorizing them while he tugged her across the room.

"Hold on, pal. Just what do you think—"

"I need to record these numbers. What time is it? Two twenty-three and sixteen seconds." Fascinated, he passed the gauge over their joined hands. "Jesus! Look at that jump. Is that cool or what?"

"Let go. Right now—or I'm taking you down."

"Huh?" He looked back at her face, blinked once to orient himself. The eyes he'd admired were hard as stone now. "Sorry."

He released her hand immediately, and the sensor's beeping began to slow.

"Sorry," he repeated. "I get caught up, especially with a new phenomenon. If you could just give me a minute to record this, then interface the portable with my computer."

"I don't have time to waste while you play with your toys." She shot the sensor a furious look. "I'd say you need an equipment check."

"I don't think so." He held out the palm that had clasped hers. "It's vibrating. How about yours?"

"I don't know what you're talking about."

"Ten minutes," he said. "Give me ten to put the bare essentials together, and let's try it again. I want to test our vital signs. Body temperature, ambient temperature."

"I don't let guys test my vital signs until they've bought me dinner." She jerked her thumb. "You're in my way."

He stepped to the side. "I'll buy you dinner."

"No, thanks." She headed straight for the door without looking back. "You are *so* not my type."

Rather than waste time on annoyance when she slammed the door behind her,

Mac searched for his recorder and began relaying the data.

"Ripley Todd," he finished. "Deputy Ripley Todd, late twenties, I'd guess. Abrasive, suspicious, casually rude. Incident occurred on physical contact. A handshake. Personal physical reactions were a tingling and warmth along the skin, from point of contact, up the right arm to the shoulder. An increase of heart rate and a temporary feeling of euphoria. Deputy Todd's physical reaction is unsubstantiated. Impressions are, however, that she experienced the same or similar reactions, which resulted in her anger and denial."

He sat on the arm of the sofa, considering. "Early hypothesis reached upon previous research, current observations, and recorded data is that Todd is another direct descendant of one of the three original sisters."

Pursing his lips, Mac switched off the recorder. "And I'd say the idea of that really ticks her off."

It took Mac the rest of the afternoon and all of the evening to unpack and set up. By the time he surfaced, the living room looked like a high-tech science lab, with monitors and keyboards and cameras and sensors arranged precisely to his preferences.

It left very little room to maneuver, but he didn't expect to be entertaining.

He moved what little furniture there was into one corner, and tested every piece of equipment. When he was finally finished, the fire had long since burned out and he was starving.

Remembering the pizzeria, he grabbed his coat and started outside.

He was greeted by almost unrelieved darkness. There was a splinter of moonlight, a scatter of stars. The village, which according to his best memory was about a quarter mile south, was nothing more than vague silhouettes shadowed under the pretty march of streetlights.

Baffled, he looked at his watch. Swore. It was after eleven at night, outside a small village on a knuckle of land.

There would be no pizza tonight.

His stomach, wide awake now, protested crossly. He'd gone hungry before, often because of his own forgetfulness. But he didn't have to like it.

Without much hope, he went back inside to search for crumbs in the kitchen. Maybe he had an old bag of trail mix or candy in his briefcase. But he hit the jackpot in the freezer. He found a container labeled "clam chowder," with instructions for heating. Compliments of Sisters Catering.

"I love Nell Todd. I'm her slave." Deliriously pleased, he set it in the microwave at the time and temperature directed. The first wisps of scent nearly had him crying.

He ate the entire container, standing up.

Sated, refreshed, and revived, he decided to take a walk down to the beach.

Two minutes later, he came back and dug out a flashlight.

He had always liked the sound of the sea, especially at night when it seemed to fill the world. The cold wind was bracing, the smooth velvet dark soothing.

As he walked he made mental notes of chores and tasks he would need to see to the following day. The knowledge that most if not all of his list would be forgotten didn't stop him from making it.

He would need to stock up on supplies. Transfer some money to the local bank for convenience. Arrange for phone service. A post office box. He wanted to do more in-depth research on the Todd ancestry, and the Ripley family history as well.

He wondered how much information he could pump out of Mia. Definite tension between her and the deputy. He'd be interested to know what caused it.

He needed to spend more time with both of them, though neither one would be easily nudged.

A prickling on the back of his neck made him stop, slowly turn.

She was glowing. A faint aura of light outlined her body, her face, the long coils of her hair. Her eyes were green as a cat's against the dark. And watched him, just as steadily, just as patiently.

"Ripley." He wasn't easily spooked, but she'd managed it. "I didn't know there was anyone else out here."

He started back toward her. A ripple of air shivered over him. The sand shifted under his feet. He saw a single tear, diamond bright, slide down her cheek. Before she vanished like smoke.

Three

Three Sisters Island was still and white and perfect, like, Ripley thought, one of the snow globes on the shelf at Island Treasures. The storm that had swept through during the night had covered the beach, the lawns, the streets. Ermine-draped trees stood still as a painting, and the air was church quiet.

She hated to mar it.

Even now Zack was calling Dick Stubens and telling him to start up his plow. Soon the world would move again. But for now it was still and silent. Irresistible.

A few feet of snow was one of the only things that kept her from her morning run on the beach. She tossed her gym bag over her shoulder, took one last whiff of whatever it was her sister-in-law was baking, and slipped out of the house.

For now, for the length of her walk to the hotel and its health club, the island belonged only to her.

Smoke pumped from chimneys. Lights gleamed behind kitchen windows. Oatmeal was being stirred, she imagined, bacon was sizzling. And inside those warm, snug houses, children were doing a dance of joy. No school. Today was for snow battles and snow forts, for sledding and mugs of hot chocolate at the kitchen table.

Her life had been just that simple once.

She trudged toward the village, leaving a trough in the snow. The sky was a soft, waiting white, as if it was considering shaking out a few more inches just for good measure. Either way, she thought, she would take her hour at the gym, then head back home to help Zack shovel out the cruiser and Nell's car.

As she crossed into the village, she looked down and frowned. The snow wasn't pristine here, as she'd expected, as she'd wanted it to be. Someone else had been out and about early, too, and had left a narrow path.

It irritated her. It was a tradition, almost a ritual, that she be the first to break the field of snow on this part of the island. Now someone had spoiled her routine and pricked her contentment bubble.

She kicked at the snow and kept walking.

The path led, as hers did, toward the Gothic stone hotel, the Magick Inn.

Some mainlander, she decided, who'd come out of his hotel room early to see a genuine New England village in the snow. Hard to blame him, she admitted, but he might have waited another hour. She stomped up the short flight of steps, bumped the bulk of the snow off her boots, and went inside.

She waved to the desk clerk, hitching up her gym bag, and jogged up the lobby steps to the second floor. She had a long-standing pay-as-you-go deal with the hotel for health club privileges. She preferred working out on her own, and during the summer she used the sea as her pool, so an official membership wasn't worth her while.

Turning left, she headed straight into the women's locker room. As far as she could remember, only a handful of guests were in residence this week. More than likely she would have the gym and the pool to herself.

After dumping her outerwear in the locker that the hotel kept for her, she stripped down to her black sports bra and bike pants, tugged on her socks and cross-trainers.

Her mood was up again at the prospect of a good sweaty bout with the resistance machines and free weights. Since she despised the treadmill she would save the aerobic portion of her workout for the hotel pool.

She circled around the locker room for the door leading to the gym. She heard the clang of metal on metal before she saw anyone. Her mood wavered again. The TV was on, tuned to one of the early-morning shows full of chatter and cheer.

She preferred blasting music when she worked out.

But her glance toward the bench press turned her scowl into interesting speculation. She couldn't see much of him, but what she could see was superior.

Long legs, toned and muscled and already sheened with sweat. Long arms, sleek biceps rippling on the lift and set. She approved of his shoes, a good brand, basic style and far from new.

He was bench-pressing 120 in smooth, steady reps. Better and better.

This wasn't a weekend warrior but a regular. And if the rest of him lived up to his limbs, he was *hot.*

If she was going to have to share the equipment with someone, he might as well be hot, buff, and sweaty.

Just the way I like 'em, she thought with delight. She was missing men—at least missing sex. She would just check out Mr. Fitness here and see if he lived up to the advertising.

She snagged a towel, hooked it around her shoulders, and wandered his way.

"Need a spotter?" she began, then nearly choked as she looked down into Mac's face.

He grunted, lowered the bar. "Hey, how's it going? Some snow last night, huh?"

"Yeah, some snow." In disgust she turned away to begin her warm-up stretches. Wouldn't you just know it? Just as she starts to get stirred up, Mr. Fitness turns out to be Dr. Geek.

"Nice club," he commented, grunting a little as he pressed the bar up. "I was surprised to find it empty."

"Not much traffic in the hotel this time of year." She spared him a look. He hadn't shaved, and that shadow of stubble turned the attractive bookworm face into something edgy. Sexy.

Damn it, he *was* hot.

"Did you get a membership?" she asked him.

"Yeah. Damn, lost count. Well." He hooked the bar on the safety, scooted up. "You work out here regularly?"

"No. I've got a setup at home. Free weights, a Bowflex. But when I can't run outside, I like to use their stuff, and the pool. Are you watching this junk?"

He adjusted the weight and pressure on another machine, glanced at the television. "Not especially."

Taking this for a no, she switched it off while he settled into leg presses. She turned the music on, and up to blasting to discourage any conversation.

Unfazed, Mac worked through his routine while she worked through hers. He watched her, mostly out of the corner of his eye. He didn't ogle women in health clubs. It wasn't, well, polite. But he was human. It was only the two of them, and she had one beautiful, tight body.

Shame about the attitude.

He thought about what he'd seen on the beach two nights before, that instant when he'd thought it was Ripley standing there. Of course it hadn't been. He'd realized that almost immediately. The eyes had been *almost* the same. That sharp, intense, and pure green. But the woman, or the vision, or whatever it had been on the beach, hadn't had that taut, disciplined body. And her hair, while dark and long, had been curling coils where Ripley's was straight as rain.

And the face, though there'd been some resemblance, had been softer, sadder, rounder.

Added to all that was the fact that he didn't think Ripley Todd would stand on a dark beach, weeping, then vanish into the air.

It had been one of the sisters, he was sure. And from the research he'd done, he was betting on the one called Earth.

Still, Deputy Todd was a part of it all. He was sure of that, too.

He just wasn't sure how to chip through that flinty attitude and work on—that is, work *with* her. Since he intended to do just that, it wasn't a coincidence that they picked up free weights at the same time.

She started with flies. He followed suit.

Despite the music, they were close enough now for him to speak without shouting and feeling like a moron.

"How's the food in the restaurant here?"

"Two restaurants. Fine. Fancy one's pricey."

"You up for breakfast after this? I'm buying."

She slanted him a look. "Thanks, but I've got to get back."

He saw her gaze at his weights. He was pumping twenties. She was using tens. But between the beat of the music and the mirrored motions, they were lifting in unison.

"I've got my equipment set up." He set it casually as they both switched motions. "You'll have to come by and take a look."

"Why would I do that?"

"Curiosity. If you're uneasy about what happened last time, I can promise not to touch you."

"I'm not uneasy about anything."

There was just enough bite in her voice to show him exactly how to chip away. Some women were vain about their looks, or their brains. Ripley was vain about her spine.

"I couldn't blame you for being reluctant to come around, or even to talk to me after that." His smile was back, easygoing, edging toward sheepish. "I tend to forget that laypeople aren't used to paranormal events. It can be scary."

"You think I'm afraid?" She gritted her teeth, continued her reps. "You don't scare me, Booke, and neither do your stupid toys."

"I'm glad to hear that." Voice cheerful, face pleasant, he finished off the mat routine and got up to do bicep curls. "I was a little worried, the way you took off."

"I didn't take off." She snapped it out and began to work on her triceps. "I left."

"Whatever."

"I had work to do."

"Okay."

She sucked in a breath and imagined what would happen to that dopey grin of his if she smashed her barbell in his face. "You may be the idle rich, buddy, but I work for a living."

"Absolutely. If you're not worried about the energy spike the other day, I'd really like you to come back. Now that I'm up and running, it'll help to re-create the event, or see if it can be re-created."

"Not interested."

"I'll pay you for your time."

"I don't need your money."

"That doesn't make it less useful. Think about it." He decided to cut his routine short and give her the time to do just that. "By the way," he added as he replaced the weights. "Nice abs."

She merely peeled back her lips to show her teeth as he strolled out.

Imagine, she thought as she finished out her routine, a dork like that accusing her of being afraid. If it hadn't been so laughable, it would've been insulting. Then thinking he could buy her time for his ridiculous experiments or study or whatever the hell he called what he did.

It was a shame, a damn shame that he was the best-looking and certainly the best-built guy she'd run across in months. If he hadn't been such an irritating moron, they could have enjoyed some workouts of an entirely different nature.

Instead, she was going to have to make the effort to avoid him whenever possible. It wouldn't be easy, but she would make it her winter project.

With her muscles comfortably fatigued, she went back in the locker room, showered off, pulled on her tank suit, and headed into the pool area.

And realized, immediately, she should have known. He was already in the pool, doing laps with slow, almost lazy strokes. It surprised her to see that his tan covered every inch of him, or every inch she could see. The black Speedo he wore wasn't hiding much.

She wasn't giving up her swim, even if it meant sharing the water with him. Tossing her fresh towel aside, she dived in.

When she surfaced he was an arm-span away, casually treading water. "I've got an idea."

"I bet you're just full of them." She dipped her head and slicked the hair back from her face. "Look, I want to get in my laps and go. It's a big pool. You stay on that side, I'll stay on this one."

"Let's not call it an idea, let's call it a proposition."

"Booke, you're going to piss me off."

"I didn't mean—"

He did flush now, a perfectly gorgeous combination with that manly stubble. The little twist of lust in her belly really put her off.

"I didn't mean to imply—" He took two careful breaths, knowing he would stutter otherwise. "I meant a race."

He knew he'd caught her competitive streak by the way her eyes glinted just before she turned in the water and swam to the side. "Not interested."

"I'll give you a quarter-length handicap."

"Yeah, no question, you're going to piss me off."

"Four lengths," he continued, clamping onto the idea like a hound onto a bone. "If you win, I don't bother you again. If I win, I get one hour of your time. One hour, against three months. Those are pretty favorable odds for you."

She started to brush him off. Wanted to brush him off. He couldn't bother her if she didn't let him bother her. There was only one slight hitch. She couldn't resist a dare.

"Four lengths, head to head." She pulled swim goggles over her head, adjusted them. "When I win, you keep your distance, you don't mention your project or whatever you call it to me again, and you don't try hitting on me on a personal level."

"Now that last part stings, Deputy, but agreed. If I win, you come to the cottage, assist me in some tests. One hour's work, with your full cooperation."

"Deal." When he held out a hand, she simply stared at it blandly. "Forget it."

She waited for him to join her at the wall, prepared herself with long, slow breaths. "Freestyle?"

"Okay. On three?"

She nodded. "One, two . . ."

They pushed off together on three, cut through the water. She didn't intend to lose, didn't even consider it a possibility. She swam nearly every day of her life, and she was the home team.

She noted his form as they paced each other on the first lap. It wasn't bad, but hers was better.

They slapped the far wall, pushed off for the second lap.

She was beautiful to watch, and he hoped he had the opportunity to do more of it. Under less intense circumstances. It wasn't just strength, he noted. She had the fluid, disciplined grace of the true athlete.

He'd never deluded himself that he quali-
fied in that area. But if there was one thing
he could do, it was swim. He had to admit
he hadn't expected them to be so evenly
matched. He had a longer reach and a
good seven inches on her in body length,
but the woman had a powerful kick.

He picked up the pace, testingly, on the
third length. She matched it. He found himself both challenged and amused. She was
toying with him. He put on more speed and
admitted it was a damn good thing she'd
tossed his handicap back in his face.

The sonofabitch was like an eel, Ripley
thought. When they shoved off for the final
lap in tandem, she realized she'd seriously
misjudged his abilities. Gathering herself,
she poured it on, nipped past him by a
quarter of a body length, felt her adrenaline
kick in for that final push.

And was struck with shock and dazed
admiration when he streamed by her and
slapped the wall two strokes ahead.

Chest heaving, she surfaced, shoved
back her goggles. No one, not even Zack,
could beat her at four lengths. It was demoralizing.

"So." He panted, shoved his hair back. "Any time today good for you?"

The bastard hadn't even had the *courtesy* to rub it in. It only made the taste of defeat more sour. He'd been so, so damn pleasant about the whole thing. She began to wonder if he was on drugs. Surely no one could stay so even-tempered without chemical assistance.

She worked off part of her mad shoveling snow, soothed her bruised ego with some of Nell's famous cinnamon buns. But it picked at her, a restless fingernail at a scab, throughout the day.

There were a number of calls to keep her busy: cars sliding off the road, a smashed window due to a poorly aimed snowball, and the usual variety of mischief that liberated kids could create on a snow day.

Still, it worried her mind and spoiled her mood.

In the station house, Zack listened to her muttered curses, watched her pour yet another cup of coffee. He was a patient man, and he knew his sister. He'd crossed paths with her several times that day on patrol and had recognized the signs of her temper brewing.

But since it hadn't passed, he was going to have to poke it out of her.

Now seemed like a good time.

He was enjoying a coffee break of his own, with his feet propped up on the desk.

"Are you going to keep chewing on whatever's got your goat, or spit it out?"

"Nothing's got my goat." She slurped at coffee, burned her tongue, cursed.

"You've been in a stew since you got back from the gym this morning."

"I don't stew. You stew."

"I brood," he corrected. "Which is a solitary and thoughtful process involving finding the solution to a conflict or situation. Stewing is stirring a bubbling pot until it boils over and spills on someone. As I'm the only one currently in harm's way, I have a vested interest about the contents of this particular pot."

She turned back to him with a dangerous sneer. "That's the stupidest thing I ever heard."

"See." He wagged his finger at her. "You're trying to figure out how to take it out on me. Tell me who pissed you off, and we'll go whip their asses together."

He had a way about him, Ripley admitted, that could make her laugh in the worst of times. She walked over to the desk, sat on the edge. "Have you met this Booke character?"

"The big brain from New York? Yeah, I met him yesterday when he was out walking the village, getting his bearings. Seems nice enough."

"Nice." She snorted. "Do you know what he's here for?"

Zack grunted an assent. She only had to mention MacAllister Booke for Zack to clue in to the source of her mad. "Rip, we deal with variations of this theme off and on all the time. We can't live on Sisters and avoid it."

"This is different."

"Maybe it is." He was frowning himself when he got up to replenish his coffee. "What happened with Nell last fall raises eyebrows. And not just because she came back, figuratively, from the dead, or that that bastard Remington was exposed as someone who got his rocks off knocking her around during their marriage. Not even because he threatened to kill her once he tracked her here."

"And stabbed you." She said it quietly because she could still see the blood on his shirt, the way it had gleamed dark in the shadows of the forest.

"All of that made good press copy," Zack continued. "A big, juicy scandal. But you add how it all went down—"

"We kept a lid on that."

"As best we could," he agreed.

He stopped beside her, touched her face. He knew she'd broken a promise to herself that night. Linking hands with Mia, using what she had inside her to save Nell, to save him.

"Enough got out," he said quietly. "Rumor and speculation, and the babblings of a madman. Enough to build more, to spark interest. You had to expect something along these lines."

"I expected the weirdos," she admitted. "Maybe an increase in the gawking tourists, that sort of thing. This Booke is different. He's the serious article, a kind of, I don't know, crusader. And he's got credentials. A lot of people may think he's just another nutcase, but a lot won't. Added to all that,

Mia might get it into her head to talk to him. To cooperate with him."

"Yeah, she might." He didn't want to add that he was all but sure Nell would as well. They'd already had a discussion about it. "It's her choice, Rip. It doesn't have to weigh on yours."

She gave her coffee a disgusted look. "He won an hour from me."

"What?"

"Sneaky sonofabitch conned me into a bet this morning. I lost, so I have to give him an hour with his voodoo crap."

"Ouch. How'd you lose?"

"Don't wanna talk about it," she muttered.

But he was already trying to work it out. "You didn't go anywhere but the gym this morning, did you? I heard he picked up a membership there. Is that where you ran into him?"

"Yeah, yeah, yeah." She pushed off the desk, paced. "Who'd have thought he could *move* like that? At a sprint, okay, I could see it because of his height advantage. But not at a hundred sixty foot freestyle."

"A swim race?" Zack voiced his surprise. "He took you in a swim race?"

"I said I don't want to talk about it. I was off my rhythm, that's all." She whirled back with a slanted look. "Was that a laugh I heard?"

"You bet. No wonder you're stewing."

"Just shut up. I don't know what he thinks he can prove in an hour anyway. With his energy detectors and spirit sensors. It's a waste of time."

"Then you've got nothing to worry about. How much he take you by?"

"Shut up, Zack."

She decided to get it over with, the way you would a root canal. And she'd decided to walk, leaving Zack with the cruiser, because that postponed the getting-it-over-with stage just a little longer.

It was full dark when she made the turn to the yellow cottage, and the moon was new and black. Another three inches of snow had fallen since morning, but the clouds had passed by evening. The clear wash of sky and stars sucked out any hope of warmth in the air. The cold was clean and sharp as a razor, slicing keenly against any exposed skin.

She walked fast, using her flashlight to guide the way.

She shook her head when she ran the beam over Mac's Rover. He hadn't bothered to dig it out. Typical Nutty Professor behavior, she decided. Ignoring the practical.

She stomped up to the door, pounded with a wool-covered fist.

He answered wearing a gray sweatshirt that had seen better days and jeans that looked equally well used. She caught the unmistakable scent of Nell's beef-and-barley soup and quickly decided it was that, and that alone, that made her mouth water.

"Hi. Jesus, it's freezing out there. Must be down around zero." Even as he stepped back to let her in, he looked outside. "No car? You walked in this? Are you crazy?"

She studied the equipment jammed cheek by jowl into the tiny living room. "You live like this, and you ask if *I'm* crazy?"

"It's too cold to be out for an evening stroll." Instinctively, he took her gloved hands, rubbing them between his own.

"You get grabby, we're on the clock."

"Check the attitude." His voice wasn't mild and easygoing now, but hot as a bullet. It had her eyeing him speculatively. "Have you ever seen frostbite?"

"As a matter of fact—hey!" She yanked back when he pulled off her gloves to examine her fingers.

"I was with a group in Nepal a few years ago. One of the students got careless." Ignoring her resistance, he wiggled her fingers. "He lost two of these."

"I'm not careless."

"Okay. Let me take your coat."

She shrugged out of it, the neck scarf, the wool cap, the insulated vest, piling each layer she peeled off into his arms. "I guess you're not careless." Then he glanced around, looking for a place to dump everything.

She couldn't help it—she grinned. "The floor's good enough."

"No, we'll just . . . the bed," he remembered, and carted them out down the narrow path he'd made to the bedroom.

"Are you afraid of the dark?" she called out.

"Huh?"

"You've got every light on in this place."

"I do?" He came out again. "I'm always forgetting to turn things off. I bought a quart of Nell's soup today, I just nuked it. Do you want some?" He waited a beat, reading her perfectly. "Eating's off the clock."

"I'm not hungry," she quickly responded, and felt a good sulk coming on.

"Okay, I'll have it later so we can get started. Where did I put . . ." He patted his pockets, circled. "Oh, yeah." And found his mini-recorder beside a monitor. "I want to get some basic personal data first, so we'll just—"

He broke off again, brow furrowed. He'd piled old files, clippings, research books, photographs, and other tools on the sofa. Even the floor didn't offer enough room for two people to sit.

"Tell you what, we'll do this part in the kitchen."

She shrugged her shoulders, stuffed her hands in her pockets, and followed him back. "I'm going to go ahead and eat, since it's here." He took down a bowl, then decided to take pity on her. "Why don't you change your mind so I don't feel rude eating in front of you?"

"Fine. Got a beer?"

"No, sorry. Got a pretty decent Merlot, though."

"That'll work." She stood while he dumped soup in bowls, poured wine.

"Have a seat."

He settled down across from her, got up immediately. "Damn it, one more minute. Go ahead and eat."

Ripley picked up her spoon as he hurried back out. She heard muttering, papers rattling, and a small crash as something hit the floor.

He came back with a spiral notebook, two pencils, and a pair of metal-framed glasses. The minute he slipped them on, her stomach clutched.

Oh, man, she thought, an incredibly sexy geek.

"I'm going to take notes," he explained. "Back up the tape. How's the soup?"

"It's Nell's," she said simply.

"Yeah." He began to eat. "She saved my life the other night when I lost track of time. I found a container of chowder in the freezer and nearly broke down and cried. Your brother's a lucky man. I met him yesterday."

"So he said." She began to relax, thinking that as long as he made small talk, the clock was ticking. "They're great together."

"I got that impression. How old are you?"

"What?"

"Your age—for the record."

"I don't know what the hell that has to do with anything. I turned thirty last month."

"What day?"

"Fourteenth."

"Sagittarius. You know the time of birth?"

"I wasn't paying a lot of attention at the time." She picked up her wine. "I think my mother said it was about eight at night, after sixteen hours of sweating in the Valley of the Shadow and so on. Why do you need that?"

"I'll input the data and run an astrological chart. Give you a copy if you want."

"That stuff's totally bogus."

"You'd be surprised. You were born on the island?"

"Yeah, at home—doctor and midwife in attendance."

"Have you ever experienced any paranormal activity?"

She didn't mind lying, but she hated the

fact that it always made her throat feel tight. "Why would I?"

"Do you remember your dreams?"

"Sure. I had a doozy the other night about Harrison Ford, a peacock feather, and a bottle of canola oil. What do you think that means?"

"Since a cigar is sometimes just a cigar, sexual fantasies are sometimes just about sex. Do you dream in color?"

"Yeah, sure."

"Always?"

She moved her shoulders. "Black and white's for Bogart movies and art photography."

"Are your dreams ever prophetic?"

She nearly answered in the affirmative before she caught herself. "So far Harry and I haven't gotten it on. But I have hope."

He switched tactics. "Got any hobbies?"

"Hobbies? You mean like . . . quilting or birdwatching? No."

"What do you do with your free time?"

"I don't know." She nearly squirmed before she caught herself. "Stuff. TV, movies. I do some sailing."

"Bogart movies? Top pick?"

"Maltese Falcon."

"What do you sail?"

"Zack's little day cruiser." She tapped her fingers on the table, let her mind drift. "I think I'm going to get my own, though."

"Nothing like a day on the water. When did you realize you had power?"

"It was never a . . ." She straightened, carefully wiped all expression off her face. "I don't know what you mean."

"Yes, you do, but we can let that slide for the moment if it makes you uncomfortable."

"I'm not uncomfortable. I just don't understand the question."

He set his pencil down, nudged the bowl of soup aside, and looked directly at her. "Let's put it this way, then. When did you realize you were a witch?"

Four

She heard the blood rush and roar in her head, pulsing in time with the gallop of her heart. He sat calmly, studying her as if she were some mildly interesting lab experiment.

Her temper began to tick like a bomb.

"What kind of a stupid question is that?"

"With some, it's an instinct—hereditary knowledge. Others are taught the way a child is taught to walk and talk. There are some who come into it at the onset of puberty. Countless others, I believe, who go through life without ever realizing their potential."

Now he made her feel as though she was a slightly dim-witted student. "I don't know where you get this stuff—or where you've come up with the half-baked idea that

I'm . . ." She wasn't going to say it, wasn't going to give him the satisfaction of saying it. "This hocus-pocus area is your deal, not mine, Dr. Weird."

Intrigued, he cocked his head. "Why are you angry?"

"I'm not angry." She leaned forward. "Want to see me angry?"

"Not particularly. But I'm willing to bet that if I put a sensor on you right now, I'd get some very interesting readings."

"I'm finished betting with you. In fact, I'm finished with you period."

He let her get to her feet, continued to make notes. "You still have forty-five minutes on your time. If you're going to renege . . ." He swept his gaze up, met her furious stare. "I can only assume you're afraid. It wasn't my intention to frighten or upset you. I apologize."

"Stuff your apology." She strained against pride, always her most fretful war. She'd made the damn bet, she'd accepted the terms. With a bad-tempered jerk, she scraped her chair back out and sat again.

He didn't rub it in, only continued to make notes, as if, Ripley thought, grinding her teeth, he'd known all along he would win.

"I'm going to take a wild leap here. You don't practice."

"I have nothing to practice."

"You're not a stupid woman. And my impression is you're very self-aware." He watched her face. She was trying to remain steady. But there was something beneath the calm veneer, some strong, even passionate emotion.

He wanted desperately to dig in. Discover it. Discover her. But he would never get the chance, he realized, if he alienated her so quickly. "I'm assuming this is a sensitive area for you. I'm sorry."

"I've already told you what you can do with your apology. You can do the same with your assumptions."

"Ripley . . ." He lifted a hand, spread his fingers in a gesture of peace. "I'm not a reporter looking for a story. I'm not a groupie looking for a show or a neophite searching for a mentor. This is my work. I can promise to respect your privacy, keep your name out of my documentation. I won't do anything to hurt you."

"You don't worry me, Booke. You're going to have to look for your guinea pig elsewhere. I'm not interested in your . . . work."

"Is Nell the third?"

"You leave Nell alone." Before she could think, she reached across, gripped his wrist. "You mess with her, I'll take you apart."

He didn't move, didn't even breathe. Her pupils had gone so dark they were nearly black. Where her fingers gripped were points of heat so intense he wouldn't have been surprised to see his skin smoke. "Bring harm to none," he managed in a voice that somehow remained steady. "That's not just Craft philosophy. I believe it. I won't do anything to hurt your sister-in-law. Or you, Ripley."

Very slowly, watching her as he might a guard dog who had snapped its chain, he brought his hand up to cover hers. "You can't control it, can you?" His voice was soft. "Not completely." He gave her hand a squeeze that was almost friendly. "You're burning my wrist."

With that statement she lifted her fingers, spread them. But her hand wasn't steady as she looked down, saw the red welts where her fingers had been.

"I won't do this." She struggled to bring her breathing back to normal, to close off that violent spike of energy. To be herself again.

"Here."

She hadn't heard him get up, or go to the sink. In an instant he was standing beside her, offering her a glass of water.

After she'd taken it, gulped it down, she was no longer sure whether she was angry or embarrassed. But she was sure it was his fault. "You've no right to come here, prying into people's lives."

"Knowledge, and truth, save us from chaos." His tone was quiet, reasonable. And made her want to bite him. "Tempering them with compassion and tolerance makes us human. Without those things, fanatics feed on fear and ignorance. The way they did in Salem, three hundred years ago."

"Not hanging witches anymore doesn't make the world tolerant. I don't want to be part of your study. That's the bottom line."

"Okay." She looked so tired all at once, he noted. Bone-weary. It stirred him, a mixture of guilt and sympathy. "All right. But something happened the other night that might make that difficult for both of us."

He waited a moment, while she shifted in

her chair then gave him her reluctant attention. "I saw a woman on the beach. At first I thought it was you. Same eyes, same coloring. She was very alone, and brutally sad. She looked at me, for one long moment. Then vanished."

Ripley pressed her lips together, then picked up her wine. "Maybe you've been drinking too much Merlot."

"She wants redemption. I want to help her find it."

"You want data," she tossed back. "You want to legitimate your crusade, maybe cop a book deal."

"I want to understand." No, he admitted, that wasn't all of it. That wasn't the core of it. "I want to know."

"Then talk to Mia. She loves attention."

"You grew up together?"

"Yeah. So?"

It was easier, he decided, even more pleasant, to deal with her when she had her attitude back in place. "I caught some . . . tension between the two of you."

"I must repeat myself. So?"

"Curiosity is the scientist's first tool."

"It also killed the cat," Ripley said with a glimmer of her former sneer. "And I don't call bopping around the globe playing witch-hunter science."

"You know, that's just what my father says." He spoke cheerfully as he rose to take their soup bowls to the sink.

"Your father sounds like a sensible man."

"Oh, he is that. I'm a constant disappointment to him. No, that's unfair," Mac decided as he came back, topped off their wine. "I'm more a puzzle, and he's sure some of the pieces have gone missing. So. Tell me about your parents."

"They're retired. My father was sheriff before Zack, my mother was a CPA. They took their life on the road a while back, in a big Winnebago."

"Hitting the national parks."

"That, and whatever. They're having the time of their lives. Like a couple of kids on an endless spring break."

It wasn't what she said so much as how she said it that told him the Todd family was tight and happy. Her problem with her power didn't stem from family conflict. He was sure of that.

"You and your brother work together."

"Obviously."

There was no doubt about it, she was

back. "I met him the other day. You're not much like him." He glanced up from his notes. "Except for the eyes."

"Zack got all the nice-guy genes in the family. There weren't any left over for me."

"You were there when he was injured while arresting Evan Remington."

Her face went very still again. "Do you want to read the police report?"

"Actually, I have. It must've been a rough night." And let's just circle around that for now, he decided. "Do you like being a cop?"

"I don't do things I don't like."

"Lucky you. Why *The Maltese Falcon*?"

"Huh?"

"I was wondering why you picked that instead of, say, *Casablanca*?"

Ripley shook her head, adjusted her thoughts. "I don't know. Because I figure Bergman should've told Bogart, 'Paris, my butt' instead of getting on the plane. In *Falcon* he did the job. He turned Astor over. That was justice."

"I always figured Ilsa and Rick got together after the war, and Sam Spade . . . Well, he just kept being Sam Spade. What kind of music do you like?"

"What?"

"Music. You said you like working out to music."

"What does that have to do with your project?"

"You said you didn't want to be involved in my work. We might as well pass the rest of the time getting to know each other."

She blew out a breath, sipped her wine. "You're a really strange individual."

"All right, then, enough about you. Let's talk about me." He sat back and, when her face blurred out of focus, remembered to remove his reading glasses. "I'm thirty-three, embarrassingly rich. The second son of the New York Bookes. Real estate. The MacAllister branch—we have that surname as first name in common—they're corporate law. I got interested in preternatural subjects when I was a kid. The history, variations, the effect on cultures and societies. My interest caused my family to seek the advice of a psychologist, who assured them this was just a form of rebellion."

"They took you to a shrink because you liked spooky?"

"When you're a fourteen-year-old college freshman, someone's always calling the shrink."

"Fourteen?" She pursed her lips. "That had to be strange."

"Well, it was pretty hard to get a date, let me tell you." The slight twitching of her lips pleased him. "I channeled the energy from what would have been those first sexual rumbles into study and my personal interest."

"So you got off on books and research."

"In a manner of speaking. By the time I was eighteen, my parents had given up on trying to box me into one of the family firms. Then I hit twenty-one and came into the first lap of my trust fund and could do what I wanted."

She angled her head. She was interested now, couldn't help herself. "Did you ever get a date?"

"A couple. I know what it is to be pushed in a direction you don't want to go, or one you're not ready for. People say they know what's best for you. Maybe sometimes it's true. But it doesn't matter if they keep pushing until they take your choices away."

"Is that why you're letting me off the hook tonight?"

"That's one reason. Another is because you're going to change your mind. Don't get steamed," he said quickly when her mouth thinned. "When I first came here, I thought it would be Mia I needed to work with. But it's you—at least primarily it's you."

"Why?"

"That's something I'd like to find out. Meanwhile, you've paid off your bet. I'll drive you home."

"I'm not going to change my mind."

"Then it's a good thing I've got plenty of time to waste. I'll get your coat."

"And I don't need you to drive me home."

"We can arm-wrestle over that," he called back. "But I'm not letting you walk home in the dark, in subzero temperatures."

"You can't drive me home. You didn't dig out your car."

"So I'll dig it out, then drive you home. Five minutes."

She'd have argued with that, but the front door slammed and she was left stewing in the house alone.

Curious, she eased open the back door, stood shivering while she watched him attack the snow around the Rover with a shovel. She had to admit those muscles she'd seen that morning in the gym weren't just for show. It appeared that Dr. Booke knew how to put his back into the job at hand.

Still, he wasn't particularly thorough. She nearly called out to say so when it occurred to her that any comment she made would prove she'd been interested enough to watch him. Instead she shut the door and rubbed the warmth back into her hands and arms.

When the front door slammed again, and she heard him stomping his feet, she was leaning against the kitchen counter, looking bored.

"Bitching cold out there," he called back. "Where did I put your stuff?"

"In the bedroom." And since she had a minute, she scurried around the table to flip through his notes. Hissed when she saw they were in shorthand, or what she assumed was shorthand. In any case, the notes were odd symbols, lines and loops that meant nothing to her. But the sketch in the center of a page had her gaping.

It was her face. And a damn good likeness, too. A quick pencil sketch, full face. She looked . . . annoyed, she decided. And watchful. Well, he was right about that, too.

There was no doubt in her mind that MacAllister Booke bore watching.

She was standing a foot away from the table, her hands innocently in her pockets, when he came back. "Took me a few minutes longer because I couldn't find my keys. I still can't figure out what they were doing in the bathroom sink."

"Poltergeist?" she said sweetly and made him laugh.

"I wish. I just never seem to put anything in the same place twice." He'd tracked snow through the house. Rather than point it out, Ripley slipped on her vest and scarf.

He held her coat, made her shake her head when she realized he intended to help her on with it.

"I can never figure that out. How do you guys figure we get our coats on when you're not around?"

"We have no idea." Amused, he set her cap on her head, then pulled her hair through the back as he'd seen her wear it. "Gloves?"

She pulled them out of her pocket. "Are you going to put them on for me, too, Daddy?"

"Sure, honey." But when he reached out, she slapped his hand away. And was grinning until she saw the welts on his wrist.

Guilt churned in her. She didn't mind hurting someone, when they deserved it.

But not that way. Never that way.

Still, what was done could be undone, even if it did mean swallowing pride.

He saw a change in her expression as she stared at his wrist. "It's no big deal," he began and started to pull his cuffs down.

"It is to me." She didn't bother to sigh, but took his wrist again. Her gaze shot up, held his. "This is off my time, off the record. Off everything. Understood?"

"All right."

"What in anger I have harmed, I regret and spin this charm. Heal this hurt caused by me by the power of one times three. As I will, so mote it be."

He felt the mild pain, the heat lift away from his skin. The flesh where her fingers lay was now cool, as if they'd drawn the burns out. There was a jump in his belly, not so much from the physical change as from the change in her eyes.

He had looked into power before, and knew he looked into it now. It was something he never forgot to respect.

"Thanks," he told her.

"Don't mention it." She turned away. "I mean that."

When she reached for the doorknob on the kitchen door, his hand, its wrist un-marked, closed over it first. "We don't know how you open doors either," he said. "They're so heavy and complicated."

"Funny guy." When they stepped out, his hand slid under to cup her elbow. The long, baleful look she sent him only brought on a shrug.

"It's a little icy. I can't help it. It's very diffi-cult to resist early childhood training."

She let it go, and didn't have the heart to jab at him when he walked her around the Rover and opened the passenger door for her.

It wasn't much of a drive, but as she di-rected him she realized she was, indeed, grateful for the lift. Even in the hour she'd been inside, the temperature had dropped. The heater wouldn't have time to kick in, but at least they were out of the open air— air that seemed cold enough to break.

"If you're looking for more firewood, Jack Stubens sells it by the cord," she told him.

"Stubens. Can you write that down?"

Steering one-handed, he dug in his pocket. "Got any paper?"

"No."

"Try the glove compartment."

She opened it, and felt her jaw drop in shock. There were dozens of notes, countless pens, rubber bands, a half-empty bag of pretzels, three flashlights, a hunting knife, and several unidentified objects. She pulled one out that looked to be made up of red twine, various beads, and human hair.

"What's this?"

He glanced over. "Gris-gris. It was a gift. No paper?"

She stared at him another moment, then put the charm back and pulled out one of the many scribbled notes. "Stubens," she repeated, scrawling it on the scrap of paper. "Jack, over on Owl Haunt Lane."

"Thanks." He took the paper, stuffed it in his pocket.

"Turn here. It's the two-story, wraparound porch."

As the police cruiser was in the drive, he could've figured it out for himself. Lights were glowing cheerfully in the windows, and smoke puffed out of the chimney.

"Nice house." He got out, and though

she'd already hopped down before he could come around and open her door, he took her arm again.

"Look, Mac, it's kind of cute and all that, but you don't need to walk me to the door. This wasn't a date."

"It's a compulsion. Besides, we had a meal, and conversation. And wine. So that's several date elements."

She stopped on the porch, turned. He'd pulled a ski cap on, and his dark blond hair escaped here and there. He couldn't help but look at her intensely. "So, what, you want a kiss good night now?"

"Okay."

The response was so cheerful, so harmlessly cheerful, she grinned. But only for an instant.

He had . . . moves. Smooth, unexpected, incredible moves.

It wasn't fast, but it was so slick, so silky, she had no time to readjust. To think.

His arms came around her, *slid* her against him, body to body so that without any real pressure she was molded to him. He dipped her back, just the slightest bit, and somehow conjured the illusion that they were horizontal instead of vertical.

The intimacy of it jolted through her, sent her head on a dizzy spin even before his mouth took hers.

Soft. Warm. Deep. His lips didn't brush or nibble, but simply absorbed. Now the dizziness was joined by a shimmering wave of heat that seemed to start in her toes and rise until it melted every bone.

A little sound—stunned pleasure—hummed in her throat. Her lips parted in welcome. Oh, more! It took two tries to lift her boneless arms and circle his neck.

Her knees buckled. It wouldn't have surprised her to feel her body simply dissolve and slide in little liquid drops into a pool at his feet.

When he eased back, gently set her away, her vision was blurred, her mind blank.

"We'll have to do this again sometime," he said.

"Uh." She couldn't quite remember how to form words.

He gave her hair a friendly tug. "Better get inside before you freeze."

"Ah." She gave up, turned blindly and walked into the door.

"Let me get that for you." He spoke quietly, quite soberly, and turned the knob, nudged the door open. "Good night, Ripley."

"Mmm."

She stepped inside, then had no choice but to lean back against the door he closed until she got her bearings and her breath back.

Harmless? Had she actually thought he was harmless?

She managed to stagger a few steps, then lowered herself to the bottom tread of the staircase. She would just wait until her legs were back under her, she decided, before she tried to make it upstairs to her room.

January 8, 2002
9–10 P.M. EST

I'll transcribe my notes and the tape from my initial interview with Ripley Todd shortly. I didn't make as much progress with her as I'd hoped. However, there were two specific incidents that will be set down in more detail in my official log. My personal reaction, however, belongs here.

Ripley's temperament and her protective attitude toward her sister-in-law,

Nell Todd (data on Nell Todd cross-referenced under her name), can and will overpower her reluctance to discuss her gift. Or, as I learned tonight, to demonstrate that gift. It's my impression that her warning to me when I mentioned Nell was instinctive, and the result was unplanned. Harming me was a by-product rather than a goal. The burns on my wrist, from visual examination, matched the grip and shape of her fingers. It wasn't a flash burn, but more a steady increase in heat. As you might experience when turning up a flame.

Her physical changes during this phenomenon were a dilation of pupils, a flush under the skin.

Her anger turned inward immediately.

I believe this lack of control, and a fear of what she is capable of, are what cause her reluctance to discuss, and explore, the nature of her talents.

She's an interesting woman, one obviously close to her family. In all areas but this, I sense and observe a complete confidence, an ease of self.

She's beautiful when she smiles.

He stopped, nearly crossed out his last observation. It wasn't even accurate. She wasn't beautiful—attractive, intriguing, but not beautiful.

Still, he reminded himself, the journal was for impressions. The thought that she was beautiful must have been in his mind for him to note it down. So it stayed.

The second incident occurred just before we left, and was, I have no doubt, more difficult for her. The fact that she would remove the burns, deliberately demonstrate her ability, indicates a strong sense of right and wrong. That, as with her instinct to protect who and what she loves, overcomes her need to block off her gift.

I hope, as time goes on, to discover what event or events influenced her to deny or abjure her powers.

I need to see her again, to verify my suppositions.

"Oh, hell," he muttered. If he couldn't be honest here, where?

I want to see her again, on a completely personal level. I've enjoyed being with her, even when she's rude and insulting. It worries me, a bit, that I might enjoy being with her because she's rude and insulting. Beyond that, there's a strong sexual attraction. Unlike the sheer admiration for beauty I felt on first meeting Mia Devlin—and the completely natural and human fantasy that resulted—this is more basic, and therefore, more compelling. I want, on one level, to carefully take this complex woman apart, piece by piece, and understand what she is. On the other, I just want to . . .

Nope, Mac decided, even a personal journal needed some censoring. He couldn't write down just what he wanted to do with Ripley Todd.

I find myself wondering what it would be like to be her lover.

There, he thought, that was acceptable. No point in going into graphic detail.

I drove her home tonight, as the temperatures are hovering at zero Fahrenheit. The fact that she had walked here, and would have walked home under such conditions, demonstrates her stubbornness as well as her independence. She was, very obviously, amused at simple courtesies such as helping her with her coat, holding the door. Not insulted, but amused, which I found disarming.

I wouldn't have kissed her if she hadn't brought it up. I certainly had no intention of doing so at this early stage of our relationship. Her response was unexpected and . . . arousing. She's a strong woman, body and mind, and to feel her going almost limp . . .

He had to stop, take a breath, guzzle some of the water he'd poured.

To feel the reaction of her body to mine, and the heat . . . Knowing the chemical and biological causes for the increase of body heat during such an event doesn't diminish the wonder of the experience. I can still taste her— strong again, a strong and sharp flavor. And hear the kind of purr she made down in her throat. My legs went weak, and when her arms came around my neck, it was like being surrounded by her. Another minute—another instant, and I would have forgotten that we were standing on an open porch on a bitterly cold night.

But since I had—despite her teasing— initiated the embrace, it was my responsibility. At least I had the satisfaction of seeing her face, and the dazed, dreamy expression in her eyes. And of watching her walk straight into the door.

That was a good one.

Of course, I nearly ran off the road twice coming back to the cottage—and got lost, but that part isn't atypical without the stimuli.

Yes, I want to see her again, on a number of levels. And I don't expect to sleep particularly well tonight.

Five

Nell iced the last batch of cinnamon buns and bided her time. She had an hour before she needed to load up her car with the café stock. Today's soup was porcini mushroom, and it was already sealed in the kettle. The three salad selections were prepared, the muffins baked. She'd finished the napoleons.

She'd been up and at it since five-thirty.

Diego, her sleek gray cat, was curled on one of the kitchen chairs, watching her. Lucy, the big black Lab, sprawled in a corner, watching Diego. They had come to terms—Diego's terms—and lived together in an acceptable state of distrust and suspicion.

While her cookies baked, Nell kept the radio on low and waited.

When Ripley entered, bleary-eyed, wearing the sweatpants and football jersey she'd slept in, Nell simply held out a mug of coffee.

Ripley grunted, as close to a thank-you as she could manage before caffeine, and plopped into a chair.

"Too much snow for your morning run."

Ripley grunted again. She never felt completely herself without her three miles. But the coffee was helping. She sipped, idly patted Lucy's head when the Lab came over to greet her.

She'd have to use the damn treadmill. Hated that. But she couldn't go two days without a run. Zack was taking the first shift—where the hell was Zack?—so she could wait until midmorning before popping into the gym.

She didn't want to run into Mac.

Not that he worried her or anything. She'd already reasoned out a number of very plausible excuses for her reaction to that good-night kiss.

She just didn't want to deal with him, that was all there was to it.

Nell set a bowl in front of her. Ripley blinked at it. "What?"

"Oatmeal."

Suspicious and far from enthusiastic, Ripley leaned over and sniffed. "What's in it?"

"Nutrition." Nell took a batch of cookies from the oven, slid in another tray. "Try it before you make icky faces."

"Okay, okay." She had been making icky faces behind Nell's back. It was sort of lowering to be caught at it. She sampled, pursed her lips, took another spoonful. There didn't seem to be anything Nell put together that didn't go down well. "It's good. My mother used to cook oatmeal in the winter, but it looked like gray glue. Tasted worse."

"Your mother has other talents." Nell poured herself a cup of coffee. She'd all but shoved Zack out of the house early so she could grab this time with Ripley. She didn't intend to waste it. She sat. "So, how did it go?"

"What?"

"Your evening with Mac Booke."

"It wasn't an evening. It was an hour."

Defensive, Nell thought. Cranky. Well, well. "How did your hour go?"

"It came and it went, which wraps up my obligation."

"I was glad he drove you home." At Ripley's lifted brows, Nell blinked her baby blues innocently. "I heard the car."

And had looked out the window. Had seen Mac walk Ripley to the door. There'd been quite the little time lag before he'd walked back to the car.

"Yeah, he was all 'It's too cold out. You'll get frostbite and die before you get home.' " She shoved oatmeal into her mouth, then wagged her spoon. "Like I don't know how to take care of myself. Guys like that burn me. He can't even find his keys half the time, but I'm going to wander off and turn into a Popsicle. Please."

"I'm glad he drove you home," Nell repeated.

"Yeah, well." Ripley sighed, toyed with her oatmeal by putting little crescent-shaped dents on it with the tip of her spoon. She decided it looked sort of like a moonscape.

If he hadn't driven her home, she'd have been fine, but she'd have missed one whale of a kiss. Not that she was obsessing about it or anything.

"You wouldn't recognize the cottage," she went on. "It looks like the den of some mad scientist. All this electronic and computer junk shoved in there. No place to sit down except the kitchen. The guy's totally wrapped up in his spook show. He's even got some voodoo charm in his glove compartment. He knows about me," she finished in a rush, and lifted her gaze to Nell's.

"Oh." Nell drew in a quiet breath. "Did you tell him?"

Ripley shook her head. Her insides jittered, infuriating her. "He just knew. Like I had a sign on my forehead, saying 'Local Witch.' It's all real academic with him. 'Well, this is interesting, Deputy Todd, perhaps you could conjure something for me for the recorder.' "

"Did he ask you to do magic?"

"No." Ripley rubbed her hands over her face. "No," she said again. "But I . . . Damn it, he pissed me off, and I . . . I burned him."

"Oh, my God." Coffee sloshed at the rim as Nell set her cup down.

"I didn't set him on fire or anything. I burned his wrist with my fingers." She stared down at them now. Harmless, ordinary, maybe a little on the long side, with short, unpainted nails.

Nothing special.

Lethal.

"I didn't think about it, not consciously. All the mad went to heat and the heat went to my fingers. I haven't needed to think about it, to worry about it, in so long. The last few months . . ."

"Since you opened back up to help me," Nell finished quietly. She rose at the buzz of the oven timer.

"I don't regret that, Nell, not for an instant. It was my choice, and I'd do it again. It's just that it's been harder to lock everything down again. I don't know why—"

Wouldn't admit why, she thought, and ground that thought to dust. "It just is. I caused physical harm. I had to fix it, but that doesn't make up for causing it."

"How did he deal with it?"

"Like it was no big deal. Got me a glass of water, practically patted me on the head and went back to conversation like I'd done nothing more than spill some wine on the tablecloth. The man's got *cajones,* I'll give him that."

Nell walked back, stroked Ripley's hair as she might have stroked a child. "You're too hard on yourself. I can't even count the mistakes I've made in the past few months, even with Mia guiding me step by step."

"It's not a good time to bring her name up." Ripley leaned over again, began to eat as if the food would ease the clenching in her stomach. "If she hadn't brought him here—"

"She didn't bring him, Ripley." The faint but unmistakable edge of impatience in Nell's voice had Ripley hunching her shoulders. "And if she hadn't rented him the cottage, he'd have found another, or stayed at the hotel. Did it ever occur to you that by renting him her cottage, by agreeing to talk to him, she controls the situation to an extent that she couldn't otherwise?"

Ripley opened her mouth, shut it again. "No, it didn't. It should have. She never misses a trick."

"I'm going to talk to him, too."

The spoon clattered into the bowl. "That's just a bad idea. All-round bad idea."

"I've thought about it. He's promised Mia that he won't use real names without permission. I'm interested in his work," she continued, scooping cookies off the tray and onto the cooling rack. "I'd like to know more about it myself. I don't have the same feelings for what I am as you do."

"I can't tell you what to do." But Ripley

would make certain Mac didn't push too hard, or in the wrong direction. "How does Zack feel about it?"

"He's left it up to me. He trusts me, respects me. That's every bit as wonderful as knowing he loves me. I'm not worried about Dr. Booke."

"He's sneakier than he looks," Ripley muttered. "He sort of lulls you into thinking he's like this harmless puppy dog. But he's not."

"What is he?"

"Smart, slick. Oh, he's got those puppy-dog qualities in there, and the combination throws you off. One minute he's looking around with that lost look, wondering where he put his head last time he took it off. And the next . . ."

Nell sat again. "And the next?"

"He kissed me."

Nell's fingertips tapped together before she laced them. "Really?"

"It was supposed to be like a joke. Guy has to walk you to the door like you're coming back from prom night. Then he just sort of . . ." She trailed off as she tried to mime the way his arms had slid around her. "And you know, reeled me in. Taking his time about it, and everything got blurry and hot. Then it was like being gulped down, slow."

"Oh, my."

"I didn't have any bones left, so I was just, like, fused against him while he's doing all these incredible things to my mouth." She blew out a breath, sucked another in. "I've kissed a lot of men, and I'm damn good at it. But I couldn't keep up."

"Wow. Well." Nell scooted her chair an inch closer. "What happened next?"

"I walked into the door." Ripley cringed. "It was mortifying. I walked right into the door. *Blap.* And Dr. Romeo just politely opens it for me. It's the first time a kiss ever made me feel like an idiot, and it's going to be the last."

"If you're attracted to him—"

"He's cute, he's built, he's sexy, of course I'm attracted to him." Ripley gave a quick shake of her head. "But that's not the issue. He shouldn't have been able to dissolve my brain with one kiss. The problem is I haven't been going out in a while. It's been more than four months since I had, you know. . . ."

"Ripley." Nell gave a quick laugh.

"I figure this was just like, I don't know,

spontaneous combustion or something. He's got good moves, boom. Now that I know what's up, I can handle it."

Feeling better, she polished off the oatmeal. "I can handle him."

Mac browsed the bookstore, flipping pages, scanning covers. He'd already acquired and read material on Three Sisters, but there were a couple of books here he'd yet to come across.

He tucked them under his arm and continued to wander.

The store had a nice eclectic selection. He found a pretty volume of Elizabeth Barrett Browning's *Sonnets from the Portuguese*; the latest in a vampire hunter series he liked; two books on local sites, flora and fauna; and a handbook for solitary witches. And two other books on the paranormal to replace those he'd misplaced . . . somewhere.

Then there was a really cool Arthurian Tarot deck.

Not that he collected them or anything.

Never one to miss an opportunity to indulge in books, he took them all. They would, he thought, entertain him in his free time and give him the opening he wanted to talk to Lulu.

He carried the books to the checkout counter, offered his most innocent smile. "Terrific bookstore. You don't expect to see this kind of selection in a small town."

"Lots of things around here people don't expect." Lulu glared at him over the top of her glasses to let him know she'd yet to make up her mind about him. "Cash or charge?"

"Uh, charge." He dug out his wallet, tilted his head to see the title of the book she'd been reading. *Serial Killers: Their Hearts, Their Minds.* Oh, boy. "How's the book?"

"Too much psychobabble, not enough blood. Intellectual types don't cut much mustard."

"A lot of intellectual types don't get out in the world enough. Too much classroom, not enough fieldwork." He leaned companionably on the counter, as if she were handing him roses instead of thorns. "Did you know one theory is Jack the Ripper had preternatural powers, and while his period in London was the first documented case of serial killing, he'd lived before, and killed before, in Rome, Gaul, Brittany."

She continued to watch him over the top of her glasses as she rang up the books. "I don't hold with that."

"Me, either. But it makes a good story. *The Ripper—Murder Through Time*. The way I read it, he was the first to use the hornless goat—human sacrifice," he explained when Lulu's eyes narrowed—"in ritual magic. Black magic. Very black."

"Is that what you're looking for around here? Blood sacrifices?"

"No, ma'am. Wicca uses no blood sacrifice. The white witch harms none."

"Lulu. Don't call me ma'am." She sniffed at him. "Pretty clever, aren't you?"

"Yeah. Sometimes it irritates people."

"You're barking up the wrong tree with me, pretty boy. I'm not a witch."

"No, you just raised one. It must've been interesting watching Mia grow up. And Ripley." He began to shuffle his purchases idly. "They're about the same age, aren't they?"

Yes, she thought. Very clever boy. "What of it?"

"You know how it is with intellectual

types. We're full of questions. I'd like to interview you, if Mia doesn't mind."

Caution warred with delight. "What for?"

"Call it human interest. Most people don't understand the ordinary, the everyday pattern of an extraordinary woman. Even if they open their minds to the extraordinary they tend to think there's no usual, no simple. No math homework, or getting grounded for coming in after curfew, or having someone's shoulder to lean on."

Lulu swiped the credit card he handed her. "Have you got personal designs on Mia?"

"No. But I sure like looking at her."

"I don't have time to talk to some college boy for his term paper."

Mac signed the credit slip without, Lulu noted, looking at the total. "I'll pay you."

She heard the faint sound—*ca-ching*—in the back of her mind. "How much?"

"Fifty an hour."

"What, are you stupid?"

"No. Loaded."

Shaking her head, Lulu handed him his sack of books. "I'll think about it."

"Okay. Thanks."

When he walked out, she shook her head again. Pay her to talk. Could you beat that?

She was still wondering over it when Mia glided down the stairs. "Too quiet in here today, Lu. I think I'm going to run a cookbook sale upstairs, get people in. Nell could make some samples from some of the books."

"Whatever. College Boy was just in."

"Who? Oh." Mia handed Lulu the cup of tea she'd brought her from the café. "The interesting and yummy MacAllister Booke."

"Shelled out over a hundred fifty for books without batting an eye."

Mia's businesswoman's heart went pitty-pat. "Bless him."

"Looks like he can afford it. He offered me fifty an hour to talk to him."

"Really?" Sipping her own tea, Mia lifted an eyebrow. She knew Lulu had an ongoing love affair with profit, an affection she'd learned at Lulu's knobby knee. "I should've charged him more rent. What does he want to talk to you about?"

"You. Said it was like human interest. How many times I had to swat your butt when you were growing up, that sort of thing."

"I don't think we need refer back to the unfortunate incidents of butt-swatting," Mia said dryly. "But this is interesting *and* unexpected. I'd thought he'd be pestering and pressuring me to discuss and demonstrate. Instead he's letting all that sit to one side and offering you a consultant fee to discuss my formative years."

She tapped a fingertip on her bottom lip. Both were painted bold red. "Very clever of him."

"He admitted he was, and that it irritated some people."

"I'm not irritated. I'm intrigued, which is just what he'd hoped for, I imagine."

"Claims he doesn't have any designs on you of a personal nature."

"Now, I'm insulted." With a laugh, Mia kissed Lulu's cheek. "Still watching out for me?"

"You could do worse than take a look in his direction. He's polite, rich, and has brains—and he's not tough to look at."

"He's not for me." With a little sigh, she rested her cheek on Lulu's hair. "I'd know if he was."

Lulu started to speak, then kept her

tongue still, hooked an arm around Mia's waist.

"I'm not thinking of Samuel Logan," Mia said, though she had been. The only man who'd ever held her heart. The only man who'd ever crushed it. "I'm just not romantically attracted to the interesting, clever, and yummy Dr. Booke. Are you going to talk to him?"

"Depends."

"If you're worried that I have an objection, I don't. I can protect myself if I need protecting. And I won't, not from him."

There was something else, something not quite clear, that slithered around the edges of home. But it didn't come from MacAllister Booke.

She drew away, picked up her tea again. "In fact, I may agree to talk to him myself. Fifty dollars an hour." She let out a low, delighted laugh. "Fascinating."

Loaded down with portable equipment, Mac plowed through the snow piled on the floor of the narrow forest beside his cottage. The police report and the newspaper stories he'd read cited this as the place Nell had run to when Evan Remington attacked her and Zack Todd.

He'd already completed scans of the kitchen area, the site of the attack. He'd found no negative energy there, no remnants of violence. Which had surprised him until he'd reasoned out that either Nell or Mia would have cleansed the house.

He hoped to find something in the woods.

The air was still and cold. Ice gleamed on the dark trunks and branches of trees. Snow lay on them like fur.

He saw, and was charmed by, what he recognized as deer tracks, and automatically checked his camera to be certain he'd loaded film.

He passed a little brook where trickles of water forced their way over rocks and ice. Though his gauges didn't register any anomaly, he felt something. It took him a moment to realize it was simply peace. Simply pleasure.

A bird called, flashed by like a bullet. Mac just stood, happy and content. It felt *good* here, he thought. A place where the mind could be quiet. A place for picnics or contemplation.

With some reluctance, he continued to walk, but promised himself he would come back and just enjoy.

He wandered, and though he hated to spoil the mood, he tried to imagine what it had been like to run, fleeing in the dark from a man bent on violence. A man armed with a knife already bloody.

Bastard, he thought. The bastard had hunted her down. A rabid wolf after a doe. Because he could. Because he would rather have seen her dead than free of him. Prepared to swipe the knife over her throat rather than lose what he considered his possession.

Fury raged in him, hot, roiling fury. He could almost smell the blood, the hate. The fear. Steeped in it, he needed several moments to realize that his sensors were going wild.

"Jesus!" He jolted back, shook himself, and was abruptly the cool-headed scientist again.

"Here. Right here."

He swept with scanners, dragging out his tape recorder, muttering data into it. He paced off the area, using another gauge to measure distance, radius, diameter. Down on his knees in the snow, he recorded, calculated, documented. Considered, while the numbers and needles on his tools swung wildly.

"Highest charge, almost pure positive energy encompasses an area of twelve feet, in a perfect circle. Most rites of paranormal origin involve protective circles. This is the most powerful I've found."

Pocketing his tools, he used his hands to dig, to clear. A light sweat covered his back before he uncovered a reasonable portion of the energy circle.

"There are no markings under the snow. No symbols. I'll need to come back with a shovel to clear the entire circle. If this was made on the night Evan Remington was arrested, it was cast more than two months ago and would have been ritualistically closed on that same night. Yet there is a positive echo registering a steady six-point-two on my scale."

Six-point-two! His mind leaped at the data. Hot dog!

"My previous experience, with an active

circle during an initiation rite, registered no more than five-eight. Check those data."

He got to his feet again, snow clinging everywhere as he took photographs. He dropped his tape recorder, cursed, and spent some time scooping it out of a pile of snow, then worrying that he'd damaged it.

But nothing could diminish the thrill. He stood in the silent wood and wondered if he had stumbled across the heart of the Sisters.

An hour later, without bothering to go back to the cottage, Mac was trudging along the snowy beach. The tide had moved in, moved out and swallowed some of the snow with it. But the damp and the cold had packed what remained like bricks in a wall.

The air was far from still here, shivering in from the sea in icy streams. Despite the layers he wore, his fingers and toes were beginning to feel it.

He thought idly about a steaming-hot shower, steaming-hot coffee, as he examined the area where he remembered seeing the woman on his first night on the island.

"What the hell are you doing?"

He looked up and saw Ripley standing at the seawall. And was mildly embarrassed that looking at her turned his thoughts, immediately, to steaming-hot sex.

"Working. How about you?"

She set her hands on her hips. He couldn't see her eyes, as she wore dark glasses. It made him wish he'd remembered his own, for the sun bouncing off the snow was blinding.

"Working at what? Becoming the Abominable Snowman?"

"The yeti isn't indigenous to this part of the world."

"Take a look at yourself, Booke."

He did, glancing down. He was, indeed, covered with snow. It was, he knew, going to be a damn mess when he peeled everything off for that shower. "I guess I'm really into my work." He shrugged.

Since it didn't appear that she would come to him, he started toward her. It wasn't an easy process, and he managed to find a couple of snowdrifts that hit above his knees. But he trudged to the seawall, hitched himself up on it, and caught his breath.

"Ever hear of frostbite?" she said dryly.

"I can still feel my toes, but thanks for thinking of me. How about some coffee?"

"I don't happen to have any on me."

"Buy you a cup."

"I'm working."

"Maybe I do have frostbite." He turned his head and sent her a soulful look. "Wouldn't it be your duty as a civil servant to assist me to a warm and sheltered location?"

"No, but I'll call the health clinic."

"Okay, strike one." He swung over the wall, remembering in the nick of time to protect his dangling camera, and stood beside her. "Where are you headed?"

"Why?"

"I thought wherever it was, there'd be coffee."

She sighed. He looked frozen and ridiculously adorable. "All right, come on. I'm heading in, anyway."

"Didn't see you at the gym this morning."

"I got a late start."

"Didn't see you around the village either."

"You're seeing me now."

She had a long stride, he noted. He barely had to check his to keep pace with her.

She stopped in front of the station house, took a good look at him. "Stomp that snow off your boots."

He obeyed, sent a little flurry of snow from his coat and pants.

"Oh, for God's sake. Turn around." She slapped and brushed at the snow that clung to him, scowling as she worked her way around to the front. Then her eyes flicked up, caught his grin.

"What are you smiling at?"

"Maybe I just like being handled. Want me to do you?"

"You'll watch your step if you want that coffee." She shoved the door open and was bitterly disappointed that Zack wasn't in.

She peeled off her gloves, her coat, unwinding her neck scarf as he did the same. "What the hell were you doing crawling around in the snow?"

"Do you really want to know?"

"I guess I don't." She walked to the coffeepot, poured the last of the thick brew into two cups.

"I'll tell you anyway. I was in the woods

earlier, and found the area where you . . . dealt with Remington that night."

Her stomach did a quick jerk and clench, a sensation he seemed to cause regularly. "How do you know you found it?"

He took the coffee she held out. "It's my job to know. You closed the circle, didn't you?"

"Talk to Mia about that."

"Just yes or no, it's not a hard choice."

"Yes." Curiosity needled her. "Why?"

"Because there's an energy echo. Unprecedented in my experience. Strong magic."

"Like I said, that's Mia's area."

Patiently, he blew on the hot coffee. "Is there a specific reason the two of you don't get along, or is it more general?"

"It's specific and general, and none of your business."

"Okay." He sipped. It tasted like hot mud, but he'd had worse. "Want to have dinner tonight?"

"Yes, I do, and I plan to."

His lips twitched. "I meant with me."

"Then no."

"It's going to be hard to work my way

around to kissing you good night again if we don't have dinner first."

She leaned on the little table that held the coffeepot. "That was a one-time deal."

"You might change your mind after we split a pizza."

She was already changing her mind. Just looking at him whetted her appetite. "Are you as good with the rest of the routine as you are with kissing?"

"Now how am I supposed to answer that without sounding like an idiot?"

"Good point. Let's say I'll think about splitting a pizza at some later date. If and when that event occurs, your work, as it involves me, is off the table."

"I can agree to that." He held out a hand.

She considered ignoring it, but it seemed cowardly. She clasped his hand, shook, and felt great relief that there was nothing there but the casual meeting of palms.

But he didn't let go.

"This is really terrible coffee," he said.

"I know." What was happening now was completely natural, she told herself. That stirring of the blood, woman for man. The anticipatory thrill, the memory of just what that mouth of his was capable of.

"Oh, hell." She moved into him. "Do it."

"I was hoping you'd say that." He set his coffee down. This time he took her face, a light framing with his hands, a slight skim of fingers that made her skin hum.

His mouth touched hers, sank in, and sent her brain tumbling.

"Oh, man. Man! You are really good at this."

"Thanks." He slid one hand to the base of her neck. "Now be quiet, okay? I'm trying to concentrate."

She linked her arms around his waist, plastered herself against him, and enjoyed.

Through her lashes, she saw that his eyes were open, focused on her. It made her feel like the only woman in the world. Another first. She'd never needed that from a man, but being given it was a silky stroke.

The fingers at the base of her neck began to knead, lightly, softly, finding odd little points she hadn't known existed. He changed the angle of the kiss, as if experimenting, and toppled her from pleasure to need.

She nearly crawled over him, crawled into him. Her heart rate bounded, her blood flashed.

He held her there a moment, had to hold her there, trembling, until he found his own balance again and drew her away with hands that were no longer steady.

"Okay." She sucked in a breath. "Wow. I've got to give it to you. What, did you study exotic sexual techniques or something?"

"Actually . . ." He cleared his throat. He really, *really* needed to sit down. "In a manner of speaking, and merely as an offshoot of research."

She stared at him. "I don't think you're kidding."

"Sexual rites and customs are often an important part of . . . Why don't I just show you?"

"Uh-uh." She held up a hand to ward him off. "I'm on duty, and you've already managed to get me stirred up enough. I'll let you know if and when I'm ready for that pizza."

"Give me five minutes, and you'll be ready." He stepped forward until her palm met his chest.

"No deal. Put your coat back on and go away."

For a moment she didn't think he was going to do as she asked. Then, like magic, he stepped back. "When the time comes, I like my pizza large and loaded."

"Funny, so do I."

"That keeps it simple." He dragged on his coat, picked up his camera. "It was nice running into you, Deputy Todd. Thanks for the coffee."

"We're here to serve, Dr. Booke."

Outside, he pulled on his ski cap. He would go back to the beach, he decided, throw himself bodily into the icy water. If he didn't drown, he would cool off.

Six

It took a lot of fast talk, a lot of grease for a lot of palms, and the tenacity of a bulldog. But Jonathan Q. Harding was willing to invest all of those elements when it came to a hot story.

His instincts, which he considered the best in the business, told him that Evan Remington was going to be his funnel to the story of the decade.

Not just the sizzle of scandal that was still shooting out a few sparks. All the angles on Remington himself—how he had hidden that violent face from the world, from his fancy Hollywood clients, from the upper crust of society—had been done to death as far as Harding was concerned. Even most of the details on how his pretty young wife had escaped him, risked her life to get free of his abuse and his threats, were common fodder now.

Harding didn't bother with the common.

He'd dug around a bit, and he had enough confirmed information on where she'd run, how she'd run, where she'd worked, lived, during the first eight months after she'd ditched her Mercedes over a cliff. It was decent stuff—the former society wife, the pampered princess living in cheap, furnished rooms, working as a short-order cook or a waitress, moving from town to town. Dyeing her hair, changing her name.

He could get some ink out of it.

But it was the period of time from after she'd landed on that bump of land out in the Atlantic to when Remington had been dragged into a cell that had his nose twitching.

Things just didn't add up there, not tidily enough for Harding to close the book. Or maybe it was just too tidy.

Remington tracks her down. Pure coincidence. Knocks her around. Enter the hero, the local sheriff and new love interest.

Got himself stabbed for his trouble, Harding thought now, but he kept on riding to the rescue. Took Remington into custody in the woods, talking him out of slitting the pretty heroine's throat. Hauled him to jail, and got himself sewed up.

Good boy saves girl. Bad boy goes into a padded cell. Good boy marries girl. Happy days.

That story, with all its angles, had been four-walled in the media for weeks after Remington's arrest. And had, as most did, pretty much petered out.

But there'd been whispers. The kind no one could confirm, that more had gone on in the woods that night than an in-the-nick-of-time arrest.

Whispers of witchcraft. Of magic.

Harding had been willing to dismiss that idea, maybe play on the angle for a few column inches, but just for the novelty. After all, Remington was a raving lunatic. His statement about that night, which Harding had paid good money for, could hardly be taken without a truckload of salt.

And yet . . .

Dr. MacAllister Booke, the Indiana Jones of the paranormal, had taken up temporary residence on Three Sisters Island.

Didn't that prick up the ears?

Booke wasn't one to waste his time,

Harding knew. The man hacked his way through jungles, hiked over miles of desert, climbed mountains to do research in his unlikely chosen field. And mostly on his own nickel, of which he had plenty.

But he didn't waste his time.

He debunked more so-called magic than he verified, but when he verified, people tended to listen. Smart people.

If there wasn't something to those whispers, why would he have gone? Helen Remington, excuse me, Nell Channing Todd, wasn't making any claims. She'd spoken to the police, of course, but there was no mention of witchcraft phenomena in her statement. None in the press release funneled through her attorneys either.

But MacAllister Booke had deemed Three Sisters worth his time. And that interested Harding. Interested him enough that he'd read up on the island, its lore, its legends himself.

And his reporter's nose had scented a story. A big, fat, and potentially juicy story.

He'd tried, unsuccessfully, to pry interviews out of Mac before. The MacAllister-Bookes were eye-crossing rich, influential, and staunchly conservative. With a little cooperation he could have generated a series of solid features on the family and their spook-chasing son.

But nobody, particularly Booke himself, cooperated.

And that stung.

Still, it was just a matter of finding the right crowbar and knowing the correct amount of pressure to apply. Harding was confident that Remington himself would help him ease the lid off.

After that, he could take care of the rest.

Harding walked down the corridor of what he thought of as the loony bin. Remington had been judged legally insane, which had saved the taxpayers the cost of a long, detailed trial and cheated them out of the meaty morsels the media could have dispensed had there been one.

The fact was, the weapon used against the island sheriff had Remington's fingerprints on it. The sheriff, and two witnesses, including the island's deputy, had given statements that Remington had held that knife to his wife's throat and had threatened her life.

Even more damning, Remington hadn't simply confessed, he'd screamed about murdering her, babbled about till death do us part, and carried on about the need to burn the adulterous witch.

Of course, he'd screamed about a lot of other things, too. About glowing eyes, blue lightning, snakes crawling under his skin.

Between the physical evidence, the witness statements, and his own rantings, Remington had copped himself a room in the barred and guarded section of the nuthouse.

Harding's visitor's badge flapped on the lapel of his tailored suit jacket. His tie, the exact shade of charcoal as the suit, was perfectly knotted.

His hair was dark, shot with silver and meticulously cut to suit his square, ruddy face. His features were blocky, and his eyes, a dark brown, tended to vanish when he smiled. His mouth was thin, and when annoyed he appeared to be lipless.

If his face, and his speaking voice, had been marginally more appealing, he might have wormed his way into television news.

He'd once wanted that, the way some boys want that first touch of female breast. Lustfully, gleefully. But the camera was not his friend. It accented his features and made his short, stocky build resemble a tree stump.

His voice, as some smart-mouthed tech had once told him, sounded like a wounded goose when miked.

The cruel loss of that childhood dream had helped turn Harding into the kind of print reporter he was today. Ruthless and iceberg-cold.

He listened to the echo of locks being released, heavy doors opening. He would remember to describe them when he wrote of this visit, of the eerie clang of metal on metal, the impassive faces of the guards and medical staff, the oddly sweet smell of madness.

He waited outside yet another room. There was a final check here, an attendant beside the door with a bank of monitors on his desk.

The inmates in this section, Harding had been told, were under twenty-four-hour surveillance. When he stepped in with Remington, he himself would be watched as well. That was, he admitted, a comfort.

The last door was opened. Harding was reminded he had thirty minutes.

He intended to make the most of it.

Evan Remington didn't look like the man Harding was used to seeing in the glossy pages of magazines, or in sparkling color on the television screen. He sat in a chair, dressed in a violently orange coverall, his posture ruler-straight. There were restraints on his wrists.

His hair, once a golden crown, was dull yellow and cut short. His handsome face was puffy now, from the institutional food, from medication, from lack of salon treatments. The mouth was slack, the eyes dead as a doll's.

They had him sedated, Harding imagined. Take your average sociopath, toss in a few psychoses and violent tendencies, and drugs were everyone's best friend.

But he hadn't counted on trying to wend his way through the chemical maze to Remington's brain.

There was a guard at the door to Remington's back who was already looking bored. Harding sat on his side of the counter, looked between the bars. "Mr. Remington, I'm Harding, Jonathan Q. Harding. I believe you were expecting me today?"

There was no response. Harding cursed inwardly. Couldn't they have waited to give him his zoning pills until after the interview?

"I spoke with your sister yesterday, Mr. Remington." Nothing. "Barbara, your sister?"

A thin line of drool slid out the corner of Remington's mouth. Fastidiously, Harding looked away from it.

"I was hoping to talk to you about your ex-wife, about what happened on Three Sisters the night you were arrested. I work for *First Magazine.*"

Or he did for the moment. His editors were becoming entirely too delicate, and penny-pinching, for his taste.

"I want to do a story on you, Mr. Remington. To tell your side. Your sister is eager for you to talk to me."

That wasn't entirely true, but he had convinced her that an interview might lead to a sympathetic story, which might in turn give weight to her legal action to have her brother moved to a private facility.

"I might be able to help you, Mr. Remington. Evan," he corrected. "I *want* to help you."

He got nothing but that dead and silent

stare. And the sheer emptiness of it scuttled along his skin.

"I'm planning to talk to everyone involved, to get a fully rounded story. I'm going to talk to your ex-wife. I'm going to arrange to interview Helen."

At the sound of the name, the dark, dull eyes flickered.

Someone's at home after all, Harding thought and edged slightly forward. "Is there anything you'd like me to tell Helen for you? Any message I can take to Helen?"

"Helen."

The voice was raspy, hardly more than a whisper. Harding told himself that was why a cold finger tickled down his spine at the sound of it. "That's right. Helen. I'm going to see Helen very soon."

"I killed her." The slack mouth bowed up into a stunning and brilliant smile. "In the woods, in the dark. I kill her every night, because she keeps coming back. She keeps laughing at me, so I kill her."

"What happened that night in the woods. With Helen?"

"She ran from me. She's mad, you know. Why else would she run, would she think she could get away? I had to kill her. Her eyes burned."

"Blue lightning? Did they burn like blue lightning?"

"It wasn't Helen." Remington's eyes darted, black birds on the wing. "Helen was quiet, and obedient. She knew who was in charge. She knew." As he spoke his fingers began to scrabble on the arms of the chair.

"Who was it?"

"A witch. Came out of hell, all of them. So much light, so much light. They blinded me, they cursed me. Snakes, under my skin. Snakes. Circle of light. Circle of blood. Can you see it?"

For a moment he could. Clear as glass, and terrifying. Harding had to force back a shudder. "Who are 'all of them'?"

"They're all Helen." He began to laugh, a high, keening sound that shivered along Harding's skin until the fine hairs on his arm stood up. "All Helen. Burn the witch. I kill her every night. Every night, but she comes back."

He was screaming now, so that Harding, who'd seen his share of horrors, pushed away, leaped up even as the guard surged forward.

A lunatic, Harding told himself as attendants hustled him out of the room. Mad as a hatter.

But . . . but . . .

The smell of the story was too strong to resist.

Some people might have been nervous at the prospect of spending an evening in the home of a witch. Being nervous, they might have stocked up on wolfsbane or carried a pocket full of salt.

Mac went armed with his tape recorder and notebook and a bottle of good Cabernet. He'd waited patiently through his first week on the island, hoping for this initial invitation.

He was about to dine with Mia Devlin.

It hadn't been easy to resist driving up to her house on his own, hiking through her woods, poking around in the shadows of the lighthouse. But that would have been, by his standards, rude.

Patience and courtesy had paid off, and she'd casually asked him if he would like to come up for dinner. He'd accepted, just as casually.

Now, as he drove up the coast road, he was filled with anticipation. There was so much he wanted to ask her, particularly since Ripley shut down each time he tried to question her. He had yet to approach Nell.

Two warnings by two witches made a definite point. He would wait there, until Nell came to him or the path was cleared.

There was plenty of time. And he still had that ace in the hole.

He liked the look of her place, the old stone high on the cliff, standing against time and the sea. The art of the gables, the romance of the widow's walk, the mystery of the turrets. The white beam from the lighthouse cut through the dark like a wide blade, swept over sea, the stone house, the dark stand of trees.

It was a lonely spot, he thought as he parked. Almost arrogantly alone and undeniably beautiful. It suited her perfectly.

The snow had been neatly cleared from her drive, from her walk. He couldn't imagine any woman who looked like Mia Devlin hoisting a snow shovel. He wondered if that was a sexist opinion.

He decided it wasn't. It had nothing to do with her being a woman, and everything to do with beauty. He simply couldn't imagine her doing anything that wasn't elegant.

The minute she opened the door, he was certain that he was right.

She wore a dress of deep forest green, the sort that covered a woman from neck to toe and still managed to tell a man that everything under it was perfect. Was fascinating.

Stones glittered at her ears, on her fingers. On a braided silver chain a single carved disk glinted almost at her waist. Her feet were seductively bare.

She smiled, held out a hand. "I'm glad you could come, and bearing gifts." She accepted the bottle of wine. It was her favorite, she noted. "How did you know?"

"Huh? Oh, the wine. It's my job to dig up pertinent data."

With a laugh, she drew him inside. "Welcome to my home. Let me take your coat."

She stood close, let her fingertips graze his arm. She considered it a kind of test, for both of them. "I'm tempted to say come into my parlor." Her laugh came again, low and rich. "So I will." She gestured to a room off the wide foyer. "Make yourself comfortable. I'll open the wine."

Slightly dazed, he walked into a large room where a fire burned brightly. The room was full of rich color, soft fabrics, gleaming wood and glass. Old, beautifully faded rugs were spread over a wide-planked floor.

He recognized wealth—comfortable, tasteful, and somehow female wealth.

There were flowers, lilies with star-shaped petals as white as the snow outside, in a tall, clear vase.

The air smelled of them, and of her.

Even a dead man, Mac imagined, would have felt his blood warming, his juices flowing.

There were books tucked on shelves among pretty bottles and chunks of crystals and intriguing little statues. He gave those his attention. What a person read gave insight into the person.

"I'm a practical woman."

He jumped. She'd come in silently, like smoke.

"Excuse me?"

"Practical," she repeated, setting down

the tray that held the wine and two glasses. "Books are a passion, and I opened the store so I could make a profit from my passion."

"Your passion's eclectic."

"Single channels are so monotonous." She poured the wine, crossed to him, her eyes never leaving his. "You'd agree, since your interests are varied as well."

"Yes. Thanks."

"To a variety of passions, then." Her eyes laughed as she touched her glass to his.

She sat on the low sofa, smiling still as she patted the cushion beside her. "Come, sit. Tell me what you think of our little island in the sea."

He wondered if the room was overwarm or if she simply radiated heat wherever she went. But he sat. "I like it. The village is just quaint enough without being trite, and the people friendly enough without being obviously nosy. Your bookstore adds a touch of sophistication, and the sea adds glamour, the forests mystery. I'm comfortable here."

"Handy. And you're comfortable in my little cottage?"

"More than. I've gotten considerable work done already."

"You're a practical soul, too, aren't you, MacAllister?" She sipped, red wine against red lips. "Despite what many would consider the impracticality of your chosen field."

It felt as though the collar of his shirt had shrunk. "Knowledge is always practical."

"And that's what you seek under it all. The knowing." She curled up, and her knees brushed his leg, lightly. "A seeking mind is very attractive."

"Yeah. Well." He drank wine. Gulped it.

"How's your . . . appetite?"

His color rose. "My appetite?"

He was, she decided, absolutely delightful. "Why don't we move into the dining room? I'll feed you."

"Great. Good."

She uncurled, trailed fingertips down his arm again. "Bring the wine, handsome."

Oh, boy, was his only clear thought.

The dining room should have felt formal, intimidating with its huge mahogany table, the wide sideboards and high-backed chairs. But it was as welcoming as her parlor. The colors were warm here, too, deep burgundy shades mixed with dark golds.

Flowers in the same hues scented this air as well and speared out of cut crystal. A fire crackled, like an accompaniment to the quiet music of harps and pipes.

The trio of windows along the wall was left uncovered to bring the contrast of black night and white snow into the room. Perfect as a photograph.

There was a succulent rack of lamb and the light of a dozen candles.

If she'd been intending to dress a stage for romance, she had succeeded, expertly.

As they ate she steered the conversation into literature, art, theater, all the while watching him with flattering attention.

It was almost, he thought, hypnotic. The way she looked at a man, fully, directly, deeply.

Candlelight played over her skin like gold on alabaster, in her eyes like gilt over smoke. He wished he could do better than rough pencil sketches. Hers was a face that demanded oil and canvas.

It surprised him that they had so much common ground. Books enjoyed, music appreciated.

Then again, each of them had spent considerable time learning of the other's background. He knew she'd grown up here, in this house, an only child. And that her parents had given most of her day-to-day care into Lulu's hands. She'd gone to college at Radcliffe and had earned degrees in literature and business.

Her parents had left the island before she'd graduated, and rarely returned.

She came from money, as did he.

She belonged to no coven, no group, no organization, and lived quietly and alone in the place of her birth. She had never married, nor had she ever lived with a man.

He wondered that a woman so obviously, so elegantly sexual, had not done so.

"You enjoy traveling," she said.

"There's a lot out there to see. I guess I enjoyed it more in my twenties. The kick of packing up, taking off, whenever I wanted, or needed to."

"And living in New York. The excitement, the stimulation."

"It has its advantages. But my work can be done anywhere. Do you get to New York often?"

"No. I rarely leave the island. I have all I need and want here."

"Museums, theater, galleries?"

"I don't have much of a thirst for them. I prefer my cliffs, my forest, my work. And my garden," she added. "It's a pity it's winter, or we could take a stroll through my garden. Instead we'll have to settle for coffee and dessert in the parlor."

She treated him to delicate profiteroles, which he enjoyed. Offered him brandy, which he declined. A clock from somewhere deep in the house bonged the hour as she once again curled herself on the sofa beside him.

"You're a man of great personal restraint and willpower, aren't you, Dr. Booke?"

"I'm not sure that's ever come up. Why?"

"Because you've been in my home, alone with me, for more than two hours. I've plied you with wine, candlelight, music. And yet you haven't brought up your professional interest in me, nor have you tried to seduce me. Is that admirable, I wonder, or should I be insulted?"

"I thought about both those things."

"Really? And what did you think?"

"That you invited me into your home, so

to bring up my professional interest was inappropriate."

"Ah." She tilted her head, deliberately giving him the opening to lean in, take her mouth. "And the seduction?"

"If there's a man who's been within a half a mile of you and hasn't imagined seducing you, he needs therapy immediately."

"Oh, I do like you. More than I'd counted on, actually. Now, I'll apologize for baiting you."

"Why? I liked it."

"Mac." She leaned over, touched her lips lightly to his. "We're going to be friends, aren't we?"

"I hope so."

"I might have enjoyed being more, but it would have been brief, and it would have complicated destinies."

"Yours or mine?"

"Both, and more. We're not meant to be lovers. I didn't know you'd already realized that."

"I hope you don't mind if I regret it a little."

"I'd be annoyed if you didn't." She tossed back her curling flood of dark-red hair. "Ask the professional question that's most on your mind. I'll answer if I can."

"The circle in the woods by the cottage. How did you cast it?"

Surprise had her pursing her lips. She rose to give herself a moment to think. "That's a good one," she said, wandering to the window. "How did you find it?" Before he could answer, she waved a hand. "No, never mind. It's your job. I can't answer a question that involves others who may not wish it."

"I know about Ripley, and Nell."

She glanced back over her shoulder. "Do you?"

"From research, process of elimination, observation." He shrugged his shoulders. "From being good at what I do. I haven't approached Nell because both you and Ripley objected."

"I see. Are you afraid what we'd do if you ignored our objections?"

"No."

"No. Just that simple and quick. A courageous man."

"Not at all. You wouldn't use your gift to punish or harm—not without cause or provocation—and then only to protect. Ripley doesn't have your control or dedication, but she has her own code, possibly more strict than yours."

"You read people well. And you've approached Ripley? You've spoken to her?"

"Yes, I have."

The corners of her mouth bowed up, but there was little humor in the smile. "And you say you're not courageous."

There was enough bite to the words to intrigue. "What happened between the two of you?"

"That's a second question, and I've yet to decide if I'll answer the first. Until Ripley confirms your supposition—"

"It's not a supposition, it's fact. And she has confirmed it."

"Now you surprise me." Puzzling it out, Mia paced to the fireplace, from there to the coffeepot to pour, though she had no desire for coffee.

"You'd protect her, too," Mac said quietly. "She matters to you, a great deal."

"We were friends, as close as friends can be, for most of our lives. Now we're not." She said it simply, though it was anything but simple. "But I haven't forgotten what we were, or what we shared. Even so, Ripley can protect herself. I can't think why she'd have admitted to you, so quickly, what she has. What she is."

"I boxed her in."

He hesitated only a moment, then told Mia of the energy burst, the woman on the beach, the hour he'd spent with Ripley in the cottage.

Mia took his wrist, examined it herself. "Her temper was always a problem. But her conscience is even stronger. She'll suffer for having harmed you. She'd have transferred the burns, you know."

"Pardon?"

"That would have been her way to do penance, to make it right and just again. Taking the burns from your flesh onto her own."

He thought of the heat, the pain. Swore. "Damn it, that wasn't necessary."

"For her, it was. Let it go." She released his wrist, wandered about the room, and settled her mind. "You want her, sexually."

He shifted on the sofa. The blush wanted to creep up his neck. "I'm not entirely comfortable getting into that subject with another woman."

"Men are so often squeamish about sex.

Discussing it, not having it. That's all right."
She came back, sat again. "Now to answer
your question—"

"I'm sorry. Would you object if I recorded
your answer?"

"Dr. Booke." Amusement sang in her
voice as he took the little tape recorder out
of his pocket. "Such a Boy Scout. Always
prepared. No, I don't suppose I'd object,
but we'll just put it on record as well that
this goes into no publication without my
written permission."

"You're a Boy Scout yourself. Agreed."

"Nell had taken precautions, and so had
I. Legal action was about to begin as further
protection. Zack, who is also good at his
job and very much in love with Nell, was
also protecting her. Yet Evan Remington
came to the island, and he found her. He
hurt her and terrorized her. He nearly killed
Zack and would have killed Nell. Despite
everything, he would have taken her life that
night. She ran to the woods to keep him
from killing Zack, who was already
wounded. Ran there knowing he would follow her."

"She's a courageous woman."

"Oh, indeed. She knew the woods,

they're hers, and it was the dark of the moon. Yet still he found her, as part of her knew he would. There are fates that nothing can turn—no magic, no intellect, no effort." Her eyes were deep and intense as they met his now. "Do you believe that?"

"Yes, I do."

She nodded as she studied his face. "I thought you would, and on some level, you even understand it. He was meant to find her. This . . . test that held her life in the balance was written centuries ago. Her courage, and faith in self, were key."

She paused a moment, gathering herself. "Even knowing that, I was afraid. As a woman is afraid. He held a knife to her throat. Her face was already bruised from his hand. I abhor those who prey on others, who deliberately cause fear and pain in those they see as weaker."

"You're a civilized woman," he said.

"Am I, Dr. Booke? Do you also understand that it was within my power to have caused Evan Remington's heart to stop, to have stopped his life, given him unspeakable pain, in the instant he threatened my sister?"

"A curse of that magnitude, that violence,

requires the belief of the one being cursed. And a complex ritual with . . ." He trailed off because Mia was sipping coffee and smiling—pure amusement now. "All my research confirms that."

"As you like." She said it lightly, and the back of his neck prickled. "What I could have done is one thing. I'm bound by my own beliefs, my own vows. I can't break faith and be what I am. We stood, the five of us, in that wood. Both Zack and Ripley had weapons. But using them would certainly have ended Nell's life as well as Remington's. There was only one path, one answer. The circle of three. We cast it that night, without the ceremony, the tools, the chants that are most often required. We cast the circle through will."

Fascinating, he thought. Amazing. "I've never seen that done."

"Nor had I, until that night, ever attempted it. Needs must," she murmured. "A link, mind to mind to mind. And power, Dr. Booke, ran in a ring like fire. He couldn't harm her when she would *not* be harmed. He couldn't stay sane when forced to face what lived inside him."

She spoke quietly, but something—the

word *magic* seemed almost too ordinary—shimmered in the room, stroked over his skin. "Ripley told me you closed the circle."

"Ripley is uncharacteristically chatty with you. Yes, we closed the circle."

"The energy's still there. Stronger than any open circle I've documented."

"The three are very strong when linked. I suspect the energy will be there long after we're just memories. Nell found what she needed. The first step toward the balance."

The air cooled again, and she was just a beautiful woman holding a china pot. "More coffee?" she asked.

Seven

The slick-handed son of a bitch.

First he puts the moves on her, then he worms his way past her better judgment with that cute, trust-me act, then he makes it clear he wants to have sex.

Ripley ground her teeth as she jogged along the beach.

Then, *then,* at the first chance, he cozies up to Mia.

Men, she decided, were slugs.

She might not have gotten wind of it either if Nell hadn't casually commented about Mia having Mac up to her house for dinner.

Dinner? she snorted. Right, dinner.

She just bet he had his mind on his stomach when he bought a bottle of Mia's favorite fancy French wine at Island Liquors. She'd heard about that, too, after the fact.

He'd even *asked* the clerk which type—vintage—Mia preferred.

Well, he was free to put the make on Mia and on every female on the island. But *not* when he'd put it on Ripley Todd first.

Bastard. City-slicker bastard getting her all stirred up and twitchy, then sneaking off to nibble on Mia. Mia had probably cast out lures just to get her goat.

It would be just like her.

She swung around at the end of the beach, pounded in the opposite direction.

No, damn it, it wasn't. However much she would have enjoyed jabbing her elbow in Mia's face on principle, she couldn't delude herself. Mia never went sniffing after someone else's man. The fact was, she didn't sniff after men at all, which was probably why she was such a moody, irritating woman. A little recreational sex would improve her attitude.

But it wasn't Mia's style, and however much at odds they were, Mia Devlin was entirely too loyal, and too damn classy, to poach.

Which brought Ripley back full circle to Mac.

His fault, completely and totally. All she

had to do now was figure out the most satisfying way to make him pay for it.

She finished her run, showered, dressed for the day in dark wool slacks and a turtleneck, buttoning a flannel shirt over it. She laced up her boots. Then took a good long look at herself in the mirror.

She could never compete with Mia in the looks department. Who could? Then again, she'd never wanted to. She had her own style and was comfortable with it. Still, she knew just how to bump up the package when she was in the mood.

Toying with the outline of an idea for vengeance, she slicked on lipstick, smudged on eyeliner and shadow, brushed on mascara. Satisfied that she'd made the best use of what she had to work with, she sprayed on some of the perfume Nell had put in her Christmas stocking.

It was a deep, earthy scent and suited her more than anything floral or airy.

After some debate, she ditched the flannel shirt. She might be a bit chilly before end of day, but the turtleneck and slacks showed off her curves. Pleased with the results, she strapped her holster to her belt and headed out to work.

Pete Stahr's mutt had gotten off the leash, again. He'd nosed out a goodly pile of frozen fish guts, feasted on same. Then had sicked them up, along with his morning ration of kibble, on Gladys Macey's pristine front stoop.

It was the sort of neighborhood crisis Ripley preferred leaving to Zack. He was more diplomatic, more patient. But Zack was on the windward side helping to deal with a couple of downed trees. That left her stuck.

"Ripley, I'm at the end of my patience."

"I don't blame you for that, Mrs. Macey." They stood, hunched against the cold, and several steps downwind from the mess on the front stoop.

"That dog—" She pointed to where the unrepentant hound sat tied to a tree trunk by a length of clothesline. "He's got no more sense than a block of wood."

"No arguing there, either." Ripley watched the dopey-faced dog grin and loll his tongue. "But, you know, he's affable."

Gladys merely puffed her cheeks full of air, blew it out. "Why he's taken such a shine to me I don't know, but the fact is, every blessed time he gets loose he's over here doing his business in my yard, burying some mangy bone in my flower beds, and now this."

She set her hands on her hips and scowled at her stoop. "Just who's going to clean up that awful mess?"

"If you're willing to wait, I'll see that Pete does it. It's coming up to lunchtime, and I'll root him out and make him come over and deal with it."

Gladys sniffed, nodded sharply. Justice, she thought, was justice, and the Todds usually found a way to meet it. "I want it done soon and I want it done right."

"I'll see to that. Pete's going to get slapped with a fine, too."

Gladys folded her lips. "Been fined before."

"Yes, ma'am, he has." Okay, Ripley thought, what would Zack do? The dog was harmless, puppy-friendly and dumb as a turnip. His major flaw was his obsession with dead fish parts, which he either joyfully rolled in or greedily consumed. Each with revolting results.

As inspiration struck, Ripley hardened her

face. "The fact is, that dog's a public nuisance, and Pete's been warned." She tapped her fingers on the butt of her weapon. "We'll have to impound the dog this time."

"Well, I should think . . ." Gladys trailed off, blinked. "What do you mean, impound?"

"Don't you worry about that, Mrs. Macey. We'll take care of the dog. He won't be coming around your yard to do any kind of mischief in the future."

The little clutch in Gladys's throat had her voice quavering. "Now wait just a minute."

As Ripley had counted on, Gladys gripped her arm. "Do you mean to take that dog in and . . . and have it put down?"

"He can't be controlled . . ." Ripley let the sentence, and its implication, hang. The dog cooperated by sending out a pitiful whine.

"Ripley Todd, I'm ashamed of you for suggesting such a thing. I'm not having it, not for a minute."

"Now, Mrs. Macey—"

"Don't you Mrs. Macey me." Incensed, she wagged her finger in Ripley's face. "That's the most heartless thing I've ever heard! Putting that harmless dog down just because he's stupid."

"But you said—"

"I said he pooped in my yard!" Gladys waved her arms, currently covered in the shocking-pink wool of her sweater. "What are you going to do, pull that gun and put a bullet in his ear?"

"No, I—"

"Oh, I can't even talk to you right now. You go on, and you leave that dog be. I want my stoop cleaned, and that's the end of it."

"Yes, ma'am." Ripley hung her head, let her shoulders droop as she walked away. And winked at the dog.

Zack, she decided, couldn't have done it any better.

She tracked down Pete, read him the riot act. He would go without lunch, the Macey stoop would sparkle, and the dog, who already laid claim to a snazzy red doghouse complete with a heated blanket, would get a stronger chain to keep him on the Stahr property when no one was home.

And that, Ripley thought, would likely

wrap up the keeping of the peace of Three Sisters Island for the day.

On her way back to the station house, she spotted a small figure climbing through the first-floor window of a clapboard saltbox.

Okay, she decided with her hands on her hips, maybe there was a bit more peace to be kept.

Her brows lifted, then knit. It was the home of one of her cousins, and the bright blue jacket on the B and E man was very familiar.

"Dennis Andrew Ripley, what the hell do you think you're doing?"

She heard his yowl of pain when he bumped his head on the window, and felt no sympathy. He was twelve, and any boy of twelve who didn't own a hard head should, in her opinion, develop one.

He went still for a moment, half in, half out, battle-scarred hightops dangling. Then, slowly, he wiggled to the ground. His hair was pale blond and stuck out in tufts around his ski cap. Freckles exploded over his face and stood out in sharp relief against his bright flush.

"Ah . . . hi, Aunt Ripley," he said innocently.

He was, Ripley thought with admiration, an operator. "That's Deputy Todd to you, you little weasel. What're you doing crawling in the window?"

"Um. I don't have a key?"

"Dennis."

"Well, I don't. Mom and some of her lady friends went over to the mainland to shop and stuff. She must've locked the door."

"Let's try the question this way. Why are you crawling in the window of your own house instead of sitting at your desk at school?"

"Because I'm sick?" he answered hopefully.

"Is that so? Come on, then, I'll take you over to the clinic right now. Your mother has her cell phone, doesn't she? We'll just give her a call and let her know her sweet baby boy's feeling poorly. I bet she'll come home on the next ferry."

Ripley had the satisfaction of watching his face blanch. "Don't call her. Okay? Please? I'm feeling a lot better. It musta been something I ate is all."

"I just bet. Spill it, kiddo, and if you try to bullshit me again, I'm hauling you to the clinic and telling them to get out their biggest, dullest needle."

"We're having a history test," he blurted out, and talked very fast now. "History's the pits, Aunt Rip. It's all about dead people, anyway. So, you know, who cares? And it's like European history crap, and we don't even *live* there. I mean, hey, do you know the capital of Liechtenstein?"

"Didn't study, did you?"

He shifted from foot to foot—Jeez, what was it with boys and their big clown feet, she wondered—and attempted a pitiful look from under his lashes. "I guess maybe not."

"So you decided to blow off the test and hook school."

"Just one stupid day. I could take the test later. I was going to hang out in the woods today, and study," he added, with quick inspiration. "But it's too cold."

"So you were going to go inside . . . and study."

"Um. Yeah! Yeah, I was going to hit the books. Couldn't you just pretend you didn't see me?"

"No."

"Aw, Aunt Rip." He sighed, recognizing the look on her face. "Deputy Todd."

She hooked him by the ear. "You're getting a police escort to school."

"Mom's going to kill me."

"That's right."

"I'm going to fail the test."

"Should've studied for it."

"I'll get in-school suspension."

"Kid, you're breaking my heart."

When he muttered "shit" under his breath, she gave the back of his head a quick tap. "Watch the mouth, peewee. We're going to pay a visit to the assistant principal, you'll make a full confession, and take your lumps."

"Like you never hooked school."

"When I did, I had enough brains not to get caught. Therein, young Skywalker, is the power of the Force."

He snorted out a laugh. And because he did, because he was hers, she walked him the rest of the way to judgment with her arm companionably around his shoulders.

The morning's work and her replay of both incidents for Zack put her in a much better frame of mind. She strolled into the bookstore, looking for lunch, and gave a quick wave at Lulu.

"Put your belly on hold a minute and come over here."

"About a minute's all my belly can wait." But Ripley detoured and walked to the counter. "What's up?"

"I got a letter from Jane."

"Yeah?" Ripley thought of the café's former chef. She and her man had taken off for New York so he could have a shot at a part in an Off Broadway play. "How're they doing?"

"Well enough. Sounds to me like they mean to stay." Lulu glanced toward the stairs, lowered her voice. "Guess who strolled, big as life, into the bakery where Jane's working?"

"Harrison Ford." At Lulu's steely stare, Ripley shrugged. "I've had a thing for him lately. Okay, who?"

"Sam Logan."

"No shit?" Ripley's voice dropped as well. "What does Jane say about him? How's he look? What's he doing?"

"If you'd shut up for five seconds I'll tell you. He looks, so Jane says, better than ever. Tall, dark, and dangerous. That's Jane

speaking. She got all giddy because he recognized her. She never had two licks of
sense. I don't suppose he said what he was
doing, or she didn't ask, otherwise she'd
have put every word of it down. But she did
say he asked after Mia."

"What do you mean, 'asked after'?"

"Just that, casual, according to Jane.
'How's Mia?' "

"And?"

"And nothing. That was it, that was all. He
bought a box of pastries, wished Jane good
luck, and walked out again."

Considering, Ripley pursed her lips, juggled the angles in her mind. "Funny coincidence. Of all the bakeries in all the city, he
walks into the bakery where Mia's ex-cook
works."

"I don't think it was coincidence. I think
his curiosity took him there."

"I won't disagree. Are you going to tell
her?"

"No." Lulu sucked air through her nose. "I
thought about it, chewed on it, twisted it
around, and I don't see the point."

"Are you asking my opinion?"

"Do you think I'm telling you all this to
give my tongue a workout?"

"Okay, then I agree with you. There's no point in it. It still hurts her." She sighed because it could still hurt, just a bit, to know that Mia hurt. "Besides, if Mia wanted to know what he's up to, she could find out."

Lulu nodded. "Just feels better to have somebody agree with me. Go eat. Soup's black bean today."

"That'll hit the spot. Oh, Lu?" Ripley paused on her way to the stairs. "If you write Jane back, tell her not to say anything about this. You know."

"Already done."

That, Ripley told herself, was that. Three good deeds in one day. What more could anyone ask? She strolled up to the counter, started to ring the bell. Then saw, through the kitchen door, Nell serving soup and a sandwich to Mac.

He was sitting at the kitchen table, a place reserved for friends. She'd taken two long strides toward the end of the counter before she stopped herself.

This wasn't the way, she thought. Going in guns blazing—metaphorically—wasn't the way to deal with the man, the situation, or her own annoyance.

She gave herself a moment to calm, then walked around the counter, into the kitchen.

"Hi, Nell. Mac." Doing everything she could to radiate goodwill, she sniffed the air. "Smells great. I'll have what he's having. Okay if I eat back here?"

"Of course. Coffee with that?" Nell asked her.

"Let's jazz it up and go with a latté." Ripley unbundled her coat, hung it on the back of a chair. And sent Mac a slow, warm smile. "Don't mind a little company, do you, Professor?"

"No. You look great today."

"Thanks." She sat across from him. "What're you up to?"

"I asked him to come back, Ripley." Nell squeezed Ripley's shoulder before setting down a bowl of soup. "To talk."

Annoyance clawed up in her throat, and was dutifully swallowed. "If you're all right with it, I'm all right with it."

"Actually, Mac's been entertaining me with some stories of his travels, and his work. It's fascinating. I'm going to order those books you recommended," Nell added, tossing him a glance as she made Ripley's sandwich.

"I hope you'll tell me what you think, after you've read them."

"I will." She served the sandwich. "I'll get your latté."

When she was out of earshot, Mac leaned forward. "I'm not pushing her."

Ripley held up a hand. "Truce. Nell's in charge of her own life, makes her own decisions." You miserable son of a bitch.

"Okay. But I want you to understand that I know she's been through more than anyone should ever have to go through. I won't push, whatever the circumstances."

The fact that she believed him didn't change a thing.

She ate with him, listened to his laugh when she told him about the dog, the boy. It irritated her to realize she liked talking to him, hearing him laugh.

The man was good company, even if he was a slug.

Under other circumstances she'd have enjoyed spending time with him. Getting to know him better. Finding out all the *stuff* that went on inside of that high-voltage brain.

His smarts weren't boring. She'd already figured out that much. Then there were those terrific brown eyes, the long, slow smile, the really superior body. To say nothing of the moves—which were past excellent.

Then she imagined him using those moves on Mia only hours, *hours* after he'd danced with her.

There was only one recourse. He must be annihilated.

"So," she said, "you must be keeping pretty busy, hunting spooks and searching for, what is it, vortexes or whatever."

"Busy enough. I'm getting my bearings, getting to know the island."

"And the natives," she said. Sweetly.

"Sure. You know, my day's still pretty flexible," he told her. "I can wander over to the gym almost anytime. I'd enjoy the workout more with company."

Why don't you ask Mia to come sweat with you? she thought. "What time do you usually go over in the morning?" She knew, of course. She knew everything that went on under her own damn nose.

"About seven-thirty."

"That could work for me."

In fact, she decided, it would be perfect.

She walked into the gym at seven-forty-five. He was already on the stepper, and just working up a sweat. He hadn't shaved again. When he shot her a quick grin, she could only think it was too damn bad she had to crush him like a bug.

He was working out to music instead of TV. Wasn't it just like him to try to be obliging?

She set the weight on a leg machine, slithered onto the bench on her belly, and began to work on her hamstrings. The added benefit was to give him a good view of her butt.

Look and dream, pal, she thought. Look and dream.

"I heard we're in for more snow."

She counted off reps. "The sky's full of it. Did you get that wood?"

"Not yet. I lost the name."

"It's in your coat pocket."

"It is?"

He looked cute when he was baffled. "That's where you stuck it after I wrote it down for you. Right pocket of your long black coat."

"Oh."

"Nobody seems to be thinking of health and fitness this morning," she commented.

"Actually, there was a guy in here before. He finished up right before you came in. Great legs you've got there, Deputy Todd."

"You think?" She slid a flirtatious smile onto her face, gave him a deliberate once-over. "Yours aren't so bad, either, Dr. Booke."

"You should've seen me at eighteen. Well, twenty," he corrected. "Any time up to twenty I was the model for the guy who gets sand kicked in his face at the beach."

"Skinny, were you?"

"A toothpick with a sign on his back saying 'Please, pick on me.' "

There was a little tug of sympathy for the skinny, undoubtedly awkward boy. Remembering her mission, she ignored it. "So you decided to get cut." She switched to work her calf muscles.

"A guy with my body type doesn't get cut unless he devotes his life to it. I just wanted to get in shape. I read up on bodybuilding."

She couldn't stop the laugh. "Read up on it?"

"That's my approach," he said with a

shrug. "Then I experimented with different programs until I found what I could do." Obviously amused at himself, he grinned over at her. "I made charts."

"No joke?"

"No joke," he admitted. "Charts, graphs. A computer analysis, before and after. A merging of the intellect and the physical. Worked for me."

"I'll say."

He flushed a little. "Well, it didn't take long to figure out that if I was going to be hiking trails, climbing into caves, hacking through the occasional jungle, I'd better be able to handle the physical part of the job. Walk a few miles in a hundred percent humidity, carrying a full pack and sensitive equipment, you realize you'd better put in a few hours a week at the gym."

"Whatever the reason, the results are fine."

She rose to change machines and gave him a quick pinch on the butt as she passed. When he only stared at her, she laughed. "You can pinch me back anytime, cutie."

She worked her quads, pleased to note that she'd ruined his rhythm.

"Have you taken a tour of the island yet?"

"Not complete." He lost count of his reps, and struggled to get his pacing back. "I've been working, more or less, inch by inch."

"Next time the two of us have a couple of hours free, I'll show you around."

He was starting to heat up, and it wasn't just the exercise. "I can be free anytime."

"Now, that's a dangerous thing to say to a woman. I like it." She all but purred. "I like a man willing to take risks." She licked her lips. "Have you been thinking about me?"

"Only ten or twelve times a day."

"Ah." She wriggled off the bench as he picked up free weights. "Another risky statement. Not to be outdone, I've given you considerable thought as well."

She walked to the weights, but instead of selecting hers, skimmed a fingertip over his arm. "Mmm. All slicked up, aren't you? Me, too." She shifted closer, brushed bodies. "Wouldn't we just slither and slip all over each other right now?"

Maybe, just maybe, if all the blood hadn't drained out of his head, he'd have caught the hard-edged glint to her eyes when she smiled. But even the best man often stopped thinking with his brain when a hot, sexy, willing woman was rubbing herself against him.

"Let me put these down," he managed. "Before I drop them on my foot. Or yours."

"I like lean muscles on a man." She squeezed his biceps. "Long . . . lean . . . limber."

The weights clanged like a pair of anvils against the stand. He fisted a hand in her hair, drew her up, had his mouth a breath from hers.

Then her elbow rammed straight into his gut.

"Back off!"

He coughed. It was the only way his body could gather air. "What? What the hell?" He was too shocked for anger, too busy trying to breathe normally again to do anything but stare into her suddenly furious face.

"You think I want your hands on me?"

He managed the breath, rubbed gingerly at his stomach. "Yes."

"Well, think again. Nobody juggles me with another woman."

"What the hell are you talking about?"

"And don't pull that innocent act. Maybe you think you can pretend you forget you've been hitting on me when you decide to hit on her, and vice versa, but that's taking the absentminded professor act one step too far."

"Who? What?"

She bunched both fists and nearly used them. Very nearly used them. "You're not worth it."

She turned on her heel and stalked into the women's locker room.

She kicked the wall, just because it felt good, then limped to her locker. She was just about to strip off her sports bra when Mac swung in after her.

"You turn around and march straight out of here," she ordered. "Otherwise I'm arresting you for lewd and lascivious behavior."

He didn't turn, he didn't march. He stalked, seriously surprising her, until he stood toe-to-toe with her.

"I'm entitled to an explanation of what just went on in there."

"You're not entitled to anything from me. Now beat it."

"If you think you can sashay in there, tease me half to death, punch me in the stomach—"

"It was an elbow jab. And I've never sashayed in my life."

"You deliberately came on to me with the express purpose of slapping me back. I want to know why."

"Because I don't like cheats, I don't like sneaks. And I don't like men who try to see how many women they can sleep with at one time, especially when they're trying to add me to the list."

"I haven't slept with anyone. I haven't even gone out with anyone since I've been here."

"Let's add 'I don't like liars' to that list."

He took her firmly by the elbows, lifted her straight off her toes. "I don't lie. And don't even think about spitting any magic at me."

She opened her mouth, shut it again. When she spoke, it was dead calm. "Take your hands off me."

He set her on her feet, took a full step back. "I've made it clear I'm interested in you on a personal level. It happens that I'm not interested, at the moment, in anyone else on that same level. I haven't juggled anyone. I don't have the reflexes for it."

"You bought a bottle of fancy wine and spent an evening snuggled up to Mia."

"Where the hell do you get this?" Flustered, he dragged his hands through his hair. "I went to Mia's for dinner, though that's completely my business. She's one of the main reasons I'm here. That's a professional interest. However, I also happen to like her very much. I didn't sleep with her, don't intend to sleep with her."

"Fine." Because she'd started feeling like a fool even before he'd released her, she turned to her locker. "It's your business, like you said."

"You're jealous." He paused a moment, as if to gather his wits. Or his temper. "After I get over being seriously pissed off, I might find that flattering."

She whirled back. "I'm not jealous."

"Replay that little scene," he suggested, jerking a thumb toward the gym. "See what you come up with. Now, I'm going to go soak my head. I suggest you do the same."

He strode out, sending the swinging door slapping.

Eight

There was one thing Ripley hated more than feeling guilty. It was feeling ashamed. It took her a while to get there, as her temper wasn't of the flash-and-fade variety.

She wallowed in anger, enjoyed the way it bubbled and churned inside her and kept clear, rational thinking at bay.

She rode on that blissful annoyance most of the day, and it felt good. It felt just. The energy it gave her had her whipping through a backlog of paperwork at the station house and taking Zack's turn at cleaning the premises. She did her patrol on foot, then, still raring to go, volunteered to take her brother's cruise shift.

She drove all over the island, looking for trouble. Hoping for it.

When trouble didn't cooperate, she spent

an hour at home, beating the hell out of her punching bag.

Then common sense began to trickle through. She hated when that happened. That trickle opened a crack, and through the crack she was able to view her own behavior with distressing clarity.

She'd been stupid and that was hard to swallow. She'd been wrong and that was a bigger, nastier gulp. Feeling like an idiot made her depressed, so she skulked down to the kitchen when no one was around and ate three of Nell's brownies.

She could hardly believe she'd worked herself up into that sort of a *state* over a man in the first place. Not that it had been jealousy, she thought, contemplating a fourth brownie. He was completely wrong about that. But she had overreacted, big time.

And she, she decided as the feeling of stupidity began to slide toward the first sticky edge of guilt, had treated him shabbily.

She'd teased him. She had no respect for women who used sex as a weapon, or a bribe. Or a reward, for that matter. But she'd used it as bait and punishment.

That shamed her.

Replaying her actions in the gym drove her to brownie number four.

Even if he had been interested in Mia, which she was now convinced he hadn't been, he was a free agent. A couple of lip locks with her didn't make them exclusive, or oblige him to fidelity.

Though she firmly believed that if you were nibbling on one cookie, you finished it off before you picked up another.

But that was neither here nor there.

The best thing to do, she thought, rubbing her now slightly unsettled stomach, was nothing. Stay out of his way, nip any personal connection in the bud, though it was probably a little late for the bud stage, she admitted.

They would just pretend nothing had ever happened—which, of course, it shouldn't have.

She crept back up to her bedroom, closed herself in, and decided it would be wise to avoid all human contact for the next eight hours.

Sleep didn't come easily, but she put that down to overdosing on chocolate and deemed it fair punishment for her crimes.

The dreams, when they came, seemed harsher than she deserved.

The winter beach was deserted. Solitude weighed like chains around her heart. The moon was full, ripely white so that its light washed over the shore and sea. It seemed you could all but count every grain of sand that glittered in that beam.

The sound of the surf drummed in her ears, a constant sound that reminded her she was alone. Would always be alone.

She flung up her hands, called out in pain, in fury. The wind answered, and spun those sparkling grains of sand. Faster. Faster.

Power sliced through her, a blade so cold it burned hot. The storm she called roared and built until it blocked the light of that pure white moon.

"Why do you do this?"

She turned in the torrent and looked at her lost sister. Golden hair shimmered, blue eyes were dark with sorrow.

"For justice." She needed to believe that. "For you."

"No." The one who had been Air didn't reach out but stood quiet, hands folded at her waist. "For vengeance. For hate. We were never meant to use what we are for blood."

"He spilled yours first."

"And should my weakness, my fears, excuse yours?"

"Weak?" Magic dark boiled inside her. "I am stronger now than ever I was. I have no fears."

"You are alone. The one you loved sacrificed."

And she could see, like a dream within the dream, the man who had held her heart. She watched him, watched again, as he was struck down, taken from her and their children by the bitter edge of her own actions.

The tears that swam into her eyes burned like acid.

"He should have stayed away."

"He loved you."

"I am beyond love now."

Air turned over her hands, hands that gleamed as white as that blinding moonlight. "There is no life without love, and no hope. I broke the first link between us, and lacked the courage to forge it back again. Now you break the second. Find your compassion, make your amends. The chain grows weak."

"I would change nothing."

"Our sister will be put to the test." Urgently now, Air stepped closer. "Without us, she may fail. Then, our circle is broken once and forever. Our children's children will pay. I have seen it."

"You ask me to give up what I have tasted. What I can now call with a *thought*?" She flung out a hand and the great sea rose to rage against the shimmering wall of sand—a thousand voices, screaming. "I will not. Before I am done with this, every man, every woman, every child who cursed us, who hunted us like vermin, will writhe in agony."

"Then you damn us," Air said quietly. "And all who come after us. Look. And see what may be."

The wall of sand dissolved. The furious sea reared back, froze for one throbbing moment. The moon so white, so pure, split and dripped cold blood. Across the black sky, lightning slashed and whipped, stabbed down toward the earth to smoke and to burn.

Flames erupted, fed by the wild and greedy wind, so that the dark was blinded with light.

The night became one long, terrified scream as the island was swallowed by the sea.

However upsetting the dream, Ripley could convince herself it was a result of guilt and chocolate. In the light of day she could shrug off the anxiety it had caused and expend her energy shoveling the latest snowfall.

By the time Zack joined her, she'd finished the steps and half the walk. "I'll do the rest. Go in and get some coffee, some breakfast."

"Couldn't eat. I gorged on brownies last night, so I can use the exercise."

"Hey." He caught her by the chin, lifting her face for a long study. "You look tired."

"Didn't sleep very well."

"What's gnawing at you?"

"Nothing. I ate too many sweets, didn't sleep well, and now I'm paying for it."

"Baby, you're talking to somebody who knows you. When you've got a problem you march through work—physical and mental drudgery—until you come out the other side. Spill it."

"There's nothing to spill." She shuffled her feet, then finally just sighed. Her brother could simply stand and wait through an entire geological era for an answer. "Okay, I'm not ready to spill it. I'm working it out."

"All right. If all this shoveling's helping you with that, I'll just leave you to it."

He started back in. She didn't just look tired, he thought. She looked unhappy. At least he could take her mind off that. He scooped up a handful of snow, smoothed it into a ball. What were big brothers for? And let it fly.

It hit the back of her head with a solid *whomp.* He wasn't leadoff pitcher for the island's softball team without reason.

Ripley turned slowly, studied his cheerful grin. "So . . . want to play, do you?"

She grabbed up snow as she side-stepped. The instant he bent down for ammo, she fired straight between his eyes. She played third, and it was a brave or foolish runner who tried to steal home against her arm.

They pummeled each other, winging snowballs across the half-shoveled walk, slinging insults and taunts after them.

By the time Nell came to the door, the

once pristine blanket over the lawn was bi-
sected with messy paths, dented with fur-
rows where bodies had temporarily fallen.

Lucy, with high, delighted barks, shot
through the door like a bullet and dived into
the action.

Amused, Nell hugged her arms against
the chill and stepped out on the porch. "You
children better come in and get cleaned
up," she called out. "Or you'll be late for
school."

It was instinct more than plan that had
brother and sister doing instant and identi-
cal pivots. The two snowballs hit Nell dead
center. The resulting squeal had Ripley
laughing so hard she had to drop to her
knees, where Lucy leaped on her.

"Oops." Zack swallowed the grin as he
caught the dangerous glint in his wife's
eyes. "Sorry, honey. It was, you know, a reflex."

"I'll show you a reflex. It's comforting to
know the entire island police force will
shoot the unarmed." She sniffed, shot her
chin into the air. "I want that walk cleared
off, and you can clean off my car while
you're at it, if you can spare a moment from
your hilarity."

She sailed back inside, slammed the door.

"Ouch," Ripley said, then dissolved into laughter again. "Looks like you may be bunking on the sofa tonight, hotshot."

"She doesn't hold a grudge." But he winced, hunched his shoulders. "I'll go take care of her car."

"Got you whipped, doesn't she?"

He merely burned her with a look. "I'll kill you later."

Still chuckling, Ripley hauled herself to her feet as her brother and Lucy plowed through the snow toward the back of the house. Nothing, she thought, like a good snow fight to put everything back on an even keel. As soon as she finished the walk, she would go inside and make nice to Nell.

Still, she'd counted on Nell's having a little more sense of humor. What was a little snow between friends? Brushing herself off, Ripley picked up the shovel, then heard the pained howl, the wild barks.

Gripping the shovel like a bat, she raced around the side of the house. As she cleared the corner, she was greeted by a face full of snow. The shocked gasp caused her to swallow some of it, choke. As she spit it out, rubbed it off her face, she saw her brother, covered to his shoulders with snow.

And Nell, standing with a smug smile, and two empty buckets. She banged them together smartly to shake out any remaining snow. "That," she said with a nod, "was reflex."

"Boy." Ripley tried to dig under her collar where snow was dribbling, cold and wet. "She's good."

She was able to maintain the good, even mood through most of the day. She might've stayed there if Dennis Ripley hadn't come shuffling into the station house.

"It's my favorite delinquent." As he rarely failed to entertain her, Ripley propped her feet on the desk and prepared to enjoy the show. "What's up with you?"

"I'm supposed to apologize for causing trouble, and to thank you for taking me back to school, and blah blah."

"Gosh, Den." Ripley dabbed at an imaginary tear. "I'm touched."

The corner of his mouth turned up. "Mom said I had to. I got two days ISS, I'm grounded for three weeks, and I have to write essays on responsibility and honesty."

"Essays? That's the worst, huh?"

"Yeah." He plopped down in the chair across from her, sighed weightily. "I guess it was pretty stupid."

"Guess it was."

"No point in hooking school in the winter," he added.

"No comment. How about the history test?"

"I passed."

"No kidding? You are a jackass, Den."

"Well, it wasn't as hard as I thought it was going to be. And Mom didn't wear me out like I figured she would. Dad either. I just got the lecture."

"Oh." Ripley obliged him with a shudder and made him grin. "Not the lecture!"

"I can use most of it in the essays. I guess I learned my lesson, though."

"Do tell."

"Well, besides planning better so you don't freeze your ears off in the woods when you ditch school, it's less trouble to

just do what you're supposed to—mostly—
in the first place."

"Mostly," she agreed. And because she
loved him, she rose to make him a cup of
instant hot chocolate.

"And because you made me go in and
say what I did, right out, I didn't have to
sweat it out, you know? Dad said how when
you mess up, you have to face up to it,
make it right. Then people respect you, and
even more, you can, you know, respect
yourself."

She felt a twinge in her gut as she
dumped chocolate powder in a mug.
"Man," she muttered.

"Everybody makes mistakes, but cow-
ards hide from them. That's a good one,
doncha think, Aunt Rip? I can use that in
the essay."

"Yeah." She cursed under her breath.
"That's a good one."

If a twelve-year-old boy could face the music, Ripley told herself, then a thirty-year-
old woman had to be able to do the same.

Maybe she'd rather be grounded, maybe

she'd rather write the dreaded essay than knock on Mac's door. But there was no option. Not with guilt, shame, and the example of a twelve-year-old crowding her.

She thought Mac might just slam the door in her face, and she couldn't find it in herself to blame him if he did. Of course, *if* he did, then she could just write a polite note of apology. Which was almost like an essay when you thought about it.

Face-to-face had to be the first move, though. So she stood in front of his cottage door as the light dimmed with dusk, and prepared to eat crow.

He opened the door. He was wearing his glasses, and a sweatshirt that carried an emblem from Whatsamatta U and a picture of Bullwinkle. Under any other circumstances, it would have been amusing.

"Deputy Todd," he said. Very coolly.

"Can I come in for a minute?" She swallowed the first stringy morsel of crow. "Please."

He stepped back, gestured.

She could see he'd been working. A couple of the monitors were booted up. One of them had zigzagging lines that put her in mind of hospital equipment.

He had a fire going, and she could smell stale coffee.

"I'm interrupting," she began.

"That's all right. Let me take your coat."

"No." Defensively, she pulled it tighter. "This won't take long, then I'll get out of your hair. I want to apologize for the other day. I was wrong. Totally wrong, and completely out of line. There's no excuse for what I did, what I said, or how I behaved."

"Well, that about covers it." He'd wanted to stay angry with her. He'd been very comfortable in that groove. "Accepted."

She jammed her hands in her pockets. She didn't like it when things were too easy. "I overreacted," she said.

"I'm not going to argue there."

"I'd like to finish." Her voice frosted.

"Go right ahead."

"I don't know why I overreacted, but that's what I did. Even if you had been with Mia in a . . . in an intimate fashion, it was none of my business. I'm responsible for my own actions, my own decisions, and my own choices, and that's the way I like it."

"Ripley," he said, gently now. "Let me take your coat."

"No, I'm not staying. I got myself worked

up about it, way more than it warranted, considering. That pisses me off. And the fact is, I'd talked myself into thinking that you'd put the moves on me—then put them on Mia—to try to soften both of us up so we'd help you out with your work."

"Well." He took his glasses off, dangling them by the earpiece. "That's insulting."

"I know it," she said grimly. "And I'm sorry for it. More, I'm ashamed that I let myself use that to justify me using sex—you know, getting you worked up like I did—as a punishment. Women who do that give sex a bad name. So—"

She blew out a breath, tested herself. No, she didn't feel better, damn it. She felt mortified. "So, that's all. I'll let you get back to what you were doing."

She turned to the door, and he moved with her. Braced a hand on it. "Digging beneath the surface, which is something I like doing, there's a small, specific area of your overreaction that I find satisfying. In a strictly shallow, egotistical manner."

She didn't look at him. Refused to. Why bother when she could hear the smirk in his voice? "That just makes me feel more like an idiot."

"I'm not opposed to that result." He ran his hand down her long tail of hair. "I'm taking your coat." He tugged it off her shoulders. "Want a beer?"

"No." It surprised her that what she wanted was a hug. Just a quick little cuddle. And she'd never been the cuddling type. "No, I'm on call."

He touched her hair again, a quick dance of his fingers down the soft stream of it. "Want to kiss and make up?"

"I think we'll just take a break from the kissing part of the agenda." She took the coat from him, sidestepped and dumped it on the floor by the front door. She nodded at his sweatshirt. "Your alma mater?"

"Hmm?" He glanced down, focused. "Yeah. I did some postgrad work there. You haven't lived till you've seen spring in Frostbite Falls."

She smiled and felt better. "I can't peg you, Mac."

"Me either. Do you want—" He broke off as the phone rang, then stood looking blankly around the room.

"Sounds like the telephone to me," Ripley said helpfully.

"Yeah. Which one? Bedroom," he decided and loped away.

She reached down for her coat. It would probably be best if she just eased out while he was busy. Then she heard him, speaking what she thought was Spanish.

What was it about foreign languages, she wondered, that stirred the juices? She left her coat where it was and strolled casually toward the bedroom.

He was standing by the bed, his glasses now hooked by the earpiece in the front pocket of his jeans. The bed was made; she appreciated that basic tidiness in a man. Books were stacked, piled, spread everywhere. He paced as he spoke, and she noticed he wasn't wearing shoes. Just thick socks—one black, one navy. It was so cute.

He seemed to be talking very quickly. Whenever she heard a foreign language, it seemed to be rapid, just a flood of incomprehensible words in fascinating accents.

She cocked her head. He seemed to be concentrating fiercely, but not, she thought, on the Spanish. It came too fluently to be anything but second nature.

Then he began searching the room, patting his shirt with one hand.

"Right front pocket," she said and caused him to turn and blink at her. "Glasses?"

"Uh, no. Yes. *Qué? No, no, uno momento.* Why don't I have a pen?"

She walked over, picked up one of the three that lay on his nightstand. When he still looked frustrated, she offered a pad to go with it.

"Thanks. I don't know why they always— *Como? Sí, sí.*"

He sat on the side of the bed and began to scribble. Since she'd already poked her nose in this far, Ripley didn't see any reason to stop now. She angled her head to read his notes, only to be confounded when they were, again, in shorthand.

Probably in Spanish, too, she decided, and took the opportunity to study his bedroom.

There weren't any clothes strewn around. There wouldn't have been much room for them with the books, the magazines, the stacks of paper. No personal photographs, which she thought was too bad.

There was the usual pile of loose change on the dresser, along with a Saint Christopher's medal. She remembered the gris-gris in his glove compartment and wondered how many other bases he'd covered.

There was a Leatherman knife, a set of small screwdrivers, a few unidentifiable bits of plastic and metal that might have been some sort of fuse, and some kind of glassy black rock.

She touched it and, feeling a low, vibrating hum, decided not to touch it again.

When she turned back, he was still sitting on the side of the bed. He'd hung up the phone and was staring into space with an expression both distracted and dreamy.

She cleared her throat to get his attention. "So, you speak Spanish."

"Mmm."

"Bad news?"

"Huh? No. No, interesting. A colleague in Costa Rica. Thinks he may have a line on an EBE."

"What's that?"

"Oh, EBE—extraterrestrial biological entity."

"A little green man?"

"Sure." Mac set the note aside. "It goes with all the broom-riding witches I've documented."

"Ha."

"Anyway, it's interesting. We'll see how it goes. If nothing else it got you in my bedroom."

"You're not as fog-brained as you look."

"Only about half the time." He patted the bed beside him.

"That's a really thrilling offer, but I'll pass. I'm going to head home."

"Why don't we grab some dinner?" He took off his glasses, tossed them carelessly on the bed. "Out. We'll go out and get some dinner. Is it dinnertime?"

"It could be. Take your glasses off the bed. You'll forget and sit on them or something."

"Right." He picked them up, laid them on the nightstand. "How did you know I do that?"

"Wild guess. Mind if I call home, let my family know I won't be home for dinner?"

"Go ahead."

When she stepped to the phone, he took her hand, turned her, nudging her in until she stood between his legs. "I'd like to discuss that break from kissing you talked about. And I think since you're the one who apologized, you should be the one to kiss me."

"I'm thinking about it." She picked up the phone first, kept her eyes on his as she called, spoke briefly to Zack, then replaced the receiver. "Okay, here's the deal. Hands on the bed. And you keep them there. No touching, no grabbing."

"That's very strict, but okay." He placed his palms down on the edge of the bed.

It was time, she decided, to show him he wasn't the only one with moves. She leaned over, slowly, letting her hands run through his hair before they rested on his shoulders. Her mouth paused an inch from his, curved.

"No hands," she said again.

A brush of lips, a slight scrape of teeth, a hint of tongue. She nibbled one corner of his mouth, then the other, let her breath come out on a long sigh.

She eased back, a breath away—held the moment suspended. Then her fingers dived into his hair, fisted, and she plunged.

Instant heat, enough to burn a man alive from the inside out. His hands tightened like vises on the edge of the bed, and his heart spiked straight into his throat.

It was like being devoured, with merciless greed.

She took him over, pumped into his system like a fast-acting drug, one that scraped nerve endings raw rather than numbing them. He could feel . . . too much, and waited for his system to simply implode.

She nearly shoved him back, nearly gave in to the need plunging inside her and pushed him back on the bed. Something happened to her, every time she was with him, that jangled her brain, shocked her body, squeezed her heart. Even now, when she'd demanded and taken control, she was losing.

She felt him tremble, and her own shiver of response.

It took every ounce of will for her to end the kiss, to draw back.

He let out a ragged breath. She could see the pulse beating in his throat like a jackhammer. Yet he hadn't touched her. That kind of control was something to respect, she thought. To admire, and to challenge.

She dabbed a fingertip at the corner of her mouth. "Let's eat," she said and strolled out of the room.

Point for point, she decided as she scooped up her coat, they were dead even.

Nine

Jonathan Q. Harding knew how to get people to talk. It was a matter, first of all, of knowing that under the veil of dignity and discretion or reluctance, people *wanted* to talk. The seamier or more bizarre the subject, the more they wanted to gab about it.

It was a matter of persistence, patience, and occasionally palming over a folded twenty.

The story had its teeth in him every bit as much as he had his teeth in it. He started back at the cliff on Highway 1, where a desperate woman had faked her own death. It was a picturesque spot—sea, sky, rock. He imagined stark black-and-white photographs, the drama of them.

He was no longer thinking just a feature in

a magazine. Harding had upped the bar to a big, juicy, best-selling book.

The seeds of that ambition had been planted during his first visit with Remington. It was odd, he thought, that it hadn't occurred to him before. That he hadn't realized how, well, *hungry* he was for the fame, for the fortune.

Others had done it, turned their expertise or their hobby into a book with a glossy cover and fast sales. Why couldn't he?

Why was he wasting his time and his considerable skill on magazine bylines? Instead of him pursuing Larry King for an interview, this time around Larry King would come to him.

A voice he hadn't known was inside him had awakened, and it continually whispered, *Cash in.*

That's just what he intended to do.

Gathering tidbits of information, morsels of speculation and hard bites of fact from police records, he began to follow Helen Remington's, now Nell Channing Todd's, trail.

He had an interesting conversation with a man who claimed to have sold her the secondhand bike she'd used as her initial transportation, and after various questions asked at the bus station in Carmel confirmed the bike's description.

Helen Remington had started her long journey pedaling a blue six-speed.

He imagined her riding up and down the hills. She'd been wearing a wig—some reports said red, some brown. He was going with the brunette. She wouldn't have wanted to be flashy.

He spent more than two weeks tracking, backtracking, rapping into the wall of false leads until he hit his first jackpot in Dallas, where Nell Channing had rented a cheap motel room with kitchenette and taken a job as a short-order cook in a greasy spoon.

Her name was Lidamae—it said so on the name plate pinned to the candy-pink bodice of her uniform. She'd been waiting tables for thirty years and figured she'd poured enough cups of coffee to fill the whole of the damn Gulf of Mexico. She'd been married twice and had kicked both sons of bitches out on their lazy asses.

She had a cat named Snowball, a tenth-grade education, and a Texas twang so sharp you could've cut diamonds with it.

She didn't mind getting off her dogs for a

few minutes to talk to a reporter. And didn't scruple to refuse the offer of a twenty for her time and trouble. Lidamae tucked the bill just where you'd suppose she would. Into the generous cup of her bra.

The sheer perfection of her, the over-bleached hair teased into an enormous cascade, the blowzy body, the staggering blue of the eyeshadow that covered her lids almost to her eyebrows, had Harding wondering who might play her in the film based on his book.

"I told Tidas—Tidas, he runs the kitchen back there—I told Tidas there was something odd about that girl. Something spooky."

"What do you mean by 'spooky'?"

"A look in the eye. A rabbit look. Scared of her own shadow. Always watching the door, too. 'Course, I knew right off she was on the run." With a satisfied nod, Lidamae took a pack of Camels out of her apron pocket. "Women, we sense these things about our own kind. My second husband tried to kick me around a time or two." She dragged in smoke like breath. "Hah. It was his ass got kicked. A man raises his hand to me, he'd better have a good health policy, 'cause he's gonna spend some quality time in a medical-type facility."

"Did you ever ask her about it?"

"Wouldn't say boo to a goose, that one." Lidamae snorted, sending a dragon-stream of smoke out of her nostrils. "Kept to herself. Did her work, you can't say different, and never was anything but polite. A lady, I said to Tidas, that Nell's a lady. Got quality written all over her. Thin as a rail, her hair all whacked off any which way and dyed mongrel brown. Didn't matter, quality shows."

She took another drag, then wagged the cigarette. "I wasn't the least bit surprised when I saw the news report. Recognized her right off, too, even though she was all polished up and blond in the picture they showed. I said to Suzanne—Suzanne and me were working the lunch shift—I said, 'Suzanne, look at that on the TV set.' That one there, over the counter," she added for Harding's benefit. "I said, 'That's little Nell who worked here a few weeks last year.' Coulda knocked Suzanne over with a feather, but me, I wasn't surprised."

"How long did she work here?"

"Right about three weeks. Then one day, she just doesn't show for her shift. Didn't see hide nor hair of her again till that news report on the TV. Tidas was pissed, let me tell you. That girl could cook."

"Did anyone ever come looking for her? Pay more attention to her than seemed natural?"

"Nope. Hardly ever poked her head out of the kitchen anyway."

"Do you think Tidas would let me see her employment records?"

Lidamae took a last drag on her cigarette, studying Harding through the curtain of blue smoke. "Don't hurt to ask, does it?"

It cost him another twenty to look at the paperwork, but it gave him the exact date of Nell's departure. Armed with that, and a reasonable assessment of her finances, Harding scouted out the bus station.

He tracked her to El Paso, nearly lost her, but then dug up the man who'd sold her a car.

He followed her trail by day, read, over and over, every news article, interview, statement, and commentary that had been written since Remington's arrest.

She'd worked in diners, hotel restaurants, coffee shops, rarely staying in one spot longer than three weeks during the first six months of flight. There seemed little rhyme and no reason to her route.

And that, Harding thought, had been the point. She would head south, then east, then overlap her own tracks and drive north again. Even so, she'd always, eventually, headed east again.

Though he didn't put much credence in Lidamae's opinion of her own insight, he did find a thread of consistency throughout his interviews with employers and coworkers.

Nell Channing was a lady.

How much more she was, he'd have to judge for himself. He couldn't wait to meet her face-to-face. But before he did, he wanted more. He wanted Evan Remington's story.

Unaware that her life was currently under a microscope, Nell took advantage of her day off and a break in the weather. The February thaw offered a teasing hint of spring, with warmth that required no more than a light jacket.

She took Lucy for a walk on the beach and toyed with the idea of going into the village to buy something foolish and unnecessary. The fact that she could toy with the idea was one of her daily miracles.

For now, she was content with the beach, the sea, and the big black dog. While Lucy entertained herself chasing gulls, Nell sat on the sand and watched the waves.

"Lucky for you I'm in a good mood, or I'd have to write you up for having that dog off the leash."

Nell glanced over as Ripley dropped down beside her. "You'd have to write yourself up, too. I didn't see a leash when the two of you went for a run this morning."

"I used the invisible leash this morning." Ripley wrapped her arms around her up-drawn knees. "God, what a day. I could take a few hundred of these."

"I know. I couldn't stay in the house. My to-do list is as long as your arm, but I ran away."

"It'll keep."

"It's going to."

When Nell continued to stare at her, Ripley tipped down her sunglasses, peered over them. "What?"

"Nothing. You look . . . pleased with yourself," Nell decided. "I haven't seen much of you in the past couple weeks, but whenever I have you've looked quite smug."

"Is that so? Well, life's good."

"Uh-huh. You've been spending some time with MacAllister Booke."

Ripley trailed her fingers through the sand, drawing little curlicues. "Is that your polite way of asking if we're doing it?"

"No." Nell waited a beat, exhaled. "Well, are you?"

"No, not yet." Content, Ripley leaned back, braced her elbows in the sand. "I'm enjoying this pre-sex interlude more than I figured I would. Mostly, I've always figured if you're going to dance, just get up and dance. But . . ."

"Romance is a dance of its own."

Ripley's look was sharp and quick. "I didn't say we were having a romance. Like hearts and flowers and cow eyes. He's an interesting guy to hang out with, that's all— when he's not caught up in spook patrol. He's been all over the place. I mean, to places I didn't even know *were* places."

He'd known the capital of Liechtenstein, she remembered. Imagine that.

"Did you know he graduated from college when he was sixteen?" she continued. "Is that brainy or what? Even with all that, he gets into regular stuff. Like movies and baseball. I mean he's not snooty about, what is it, popular culture."

"No intellectual snobbery," Nell commented, enjoying herself.

"Yeah, that's it. He's into Rocky and Bullwinkle, and he listens to regular music. It's like he's got this enormous brain capacity so it can hold on all the E-equals-MC-squared junk, but it still has room for the Barenaked Ladies. Plus, he's totally buff, and he's got excellent form in the water, but sometimes he just trips over his own feet. It's kind of cute."

Nell opened her mouth to comment again, but Ripley was already plowing on. "Sure, he's a complete geek, but it's sort of handy. He fixed my headset when I was going to pitch it. And the other day . . ." She frowned when she caught Nell's wide grin. "What now?"

"You're smitten."

"Oh, please. What kind of a word is

that?" She snorted, crossed her legs at the ankles. "Smitten. Jesus."

"It's the perfect word from where I'm sitting. And I think it's wonderful."

"Don't get on that romance boat of yours and sail, Nell. We're just hanging out. Then we'll have sex and hang out. We'll keep it friendly as long as he doesn't shove the witch angle down my throat. Then he'll go back to New York and write his book or paper or whatever. We're not stuck on each other."

"Whatever you say. But in all the months I've been on the Sisters, I haven't seen you spend this much time with anyone else, or look as happy doing it."

"So, I like him better than most." Ripley sat up again, shrugged. "And I'm more attracted to him than most."

"Smitten," Nell said under her breath.

"Shut up."

"Bring him to dinner?"

"Huh?"

"Bring him home to dinner tonight."

"Why?"

"Because I'm making Zack's favorite, and there'll be plenty."

"We're having Yankee pot roast?" Ripley's mouth began to water.

"I'm sure Mac would appreciate sitting down to a home-cooked meal instead of eating takeout or eating in a restaurant, or heating up one of my deliveries." Nell stood up, brushed sand off her pants.

"Sure, he likes to eat. Nell, you're not going to try any matchmaking deal, are you?"

Her blue eyes widened with innocence. "Of course not. Tell him six-thirty, and let me know if that's not convenient."

She clapped her hands, called for Lucy, then started for home.

She had a great deal to do in a short amount of time.

"I'm not doing a spell."

Mia angled her head, smiled sweetly as Nell scowled at the potato she was peeling. "Then why did you ask me to come by and discuss your plans for tonight's dinner?"

"Because I admire your taste."

"Try again."

"Because you know Ripley better than I do."

"Keep going."

"Oh, all right." Grimacing in disgust, Nell snatched up another potato. "It's not a spell. That would be wrong . . . wouldn't it?" she added with a quick sidelong glance.

"Yes, that would be wrong. You have neither party's permission. Added to that, interfering with anyone's personal life crosses a line."

"I know it." Nell's shoulders slumped, just for a minute. "Even when you have their best interest at heart?" She let the statement hang as a question, though she knew the answer. "She looks so happy. You've seen it for yourself. You should have heard her. She was absolutely bubbling about him."

"Deputy Dawg bubbling?" Mia chuckled. "I'd have paid to see that one."

"She was, and it was adorable. All I wanted was to give her a little nudge. Not with a spell," she added quickly, before Mia could speak. "A nice friendly family dinner. And if I added a little of this, a bit of that, just something to encourage clear vision. Something that would lower the boundaries just a tiny inch or two."

"And if they're seeing what they need to

see, feeling what they need to feel, at this moment? Can you be sure your . . . nudge won't be in the wrong direction?"

"You're so frustrating when you're practical. Worse when you're right. It's hard not using what's available to help."

"Power's a tricky business. If it wasn't, it wouldn't mean anything. You're in love yourself," Mia said. "Still riding on that lovely rush of it all, and you're seeing everyone coupled and cozy and content. Not all of us are meant for what you have with Zack."

"If you could have heard the way she babbled about him before she caught herself." Shaking her head, Nell scrubbed her peeled vegetables. "She's halfway in love with him and doesn't even know it."

Mia indulged herself in one moment of pleasure and envy at the thought of her childhood friend taking the fall. "And if she did know it, if you helped her see what may be happening inside her, she might scramble back from that edge before she falls. It would be just like her."

"You're right again. I hate that. Tell me what you think of him. You've talked to him more than I have."

"I think he's a very clever man, very astute and very focused. He's not pushing Ripley with his research because he knows she'll balk. So he circles around that."

Mia wandered to the cookie jar, dipped in. "Chocolate chunk. I'm doomed."

"That's calculation." Automatically Nell moved to the stove to brew tea to go with Mia's cookie. "If he's using her—"

"Wait." Mia held up a finger, swallowed. "Of course he's using her. That isn't always wrong. She refuses to let him be direct in this area, so he's indirect. Why should he ignore what she is because she does, Nell?"

"To spend time with her, to play on her feelings. That's wrong."

"I didn't say that, and I don't think he is. He's too well mannered. And I think besides being smart, he's also a very good man."

Nell sighed. "Yes. So do I."

"I imagine he's quite attracted to her, despite the fact that she's abrasive, annoying, and hardheaded."

Nell nodded. "That makes sense. You care about her a great deal, despite those facts."

"I once did," Mia said flatly. "Your kettle's boiling."

"She matters to you. You matter to each other, no matter what happened between you." Nell turned to deal with the tea and missed Mia's soulful expression.

"She'll have to deal with me again, and I with her. Until she accepts who she is, what she is, and what she's meant to do, she'll never be open to what you have. You had fear. So does she. So do we all."

"What's your fear?" As soon as she asked, Nell turned back. "I'm sorry, but I look at you and see only confidence, such incredible assurance."

"I fear feeling my heart break a second time, because I'm not sure I could survive it. I'd rather live alone than risk the pain."

The statement, the quiet truth in it, made Nell's own heart ache. "You loved him that much?"

"Yes." It hurt, Mia thought, just to say it. As much as it ever did. "I had no barriers where he was concerned. So you see, it could be dangerous to nudge at Ripley's. MacAllister Booke is part of her destiny."

"You know that?"

"Yes. Looking isn't interfering. They're

connected to each other. But what they do about it, the choices made, are for them alone."

There was no arguing with Mia's logic. But . . . there was no reason *not* to choose pink candles for the table. She neither charmed nor inscribed them. The color being that used for love spells could be purely coincidental.

She already had rosemary potted on the windowsill, for cooking, of course. And also to absorb negative energy. It was true that that particular herb was used in love charms, but that was neither here nor there.

Nor was the rose quartz tumbled in a bowl, nor the amethyst crystals that stimulated intuition.

It wasn't as if she'd made a charm bag.

She'd used Zack and Ripley's grandmother's china, the silver candlesticks she'd unearthed weeks before and polished to a gleam, an antique lace tablecloth that had been a wedding present, and a centerpiece of lily of the valley that she'd forced to keep the winter gloom away.

The wineglasses had been another wedding gift, and their garnet stems went well, she thought, with the pale pink candles and the rosebuds on the china.

She was so intent on judging the results that she jumped when Zack came up behind her and wrapped his arms around her waist.

"Pretty fancy." He rubbed his lips over her hair. "The table hasn't looked like that in . . . Come to think of it, I've never seen it look like that."

"I want it to be perfect."

"I don't see how it could look better. Or smell better. I nearly fell to my knees in reverence when I passed through the kitchen. How come Rip's not helping you out? It's her date, isn't it?"

"I chased her out half an hour ago. She was in my way. And so"—she turned, kissed him briefly—"are you."

"I figured you needed somebody to sample some of those little canapé things you've got in the kitchen."

"No."

"Too late." He grinned at her. "They're great."

"Zack. Damn it, I had them arranged."

"I scooted everything in," he told her as he followed her back into the kitchen. "No gaps."

"Keep your fingers out of the food or I won't make beef stew and dumplings with the leftovers."

"Nell, honey, that's downright mean."

"No sulking. Now, let me look at you." She stepped back, skimmed her gaze over him. "My, aren't you handsome, Sheriff Todd."

He hooked a finger in the belt of her slacks. "Come over here and say that."

She obliged, was just lifting her mouth to his when she heard the knock on the front door. "That's him." She broke free, dragged off her apron.

"Hey, come back here. Ripley can get the door."

"No, she can't. She needs to make an entrance. Oh, just—" She waved a hand at him as she hurried out. "Go put on some music or something."

Mac brought wine and flowers, and earned Nell's approval. Three times, that Nell counted, he touched Ripley's hand as they enjoyed appetizers in the living room.

It was comfortable, as she'd wanted, casual as she'd planned. And watching the two of them together she felt a nice warm glow. By the time they settled down in the dining room, Nell was already patting herself on the back.

"Of all the places you've been," she asked Mac, "which is your favorite?"

"Wherever I am is always my favorite. Three Sisters is like this perfect little slice of the world."

"And the natives are friendly enough," Zack added.

"They are." Mac sent Ripley a grin as he ate his roast. "Mostly."

"We discourage munching on missionaries and explorers these days." Ripley stabbed a potato. "Mostly."

"Lucky for me. I've had some interesting interviews. Lulu, the Maceys."

"You talked to Lulu?" Ripley interrupted.

"Mmm. She was top of my list. She's lived here a long time, but she wasn't born here. And there's her close association with Mia. It's intriguing to me the easy, almost casual way Lulu accepts the metaphysical. She accepts Mia's gifts the way another might accept a child's hair color. It would be different for you," he said to Nell. "Coming into your talents as an adult."

"I suppose." She didn't mind talking about it. In fact, Nell thought she might enjoy discussing the entire matter on an intellectual, scientific plane. But she recognized the warning signals in Ripley's stiff shoulders. "More beef?" she asked brightly.

"Thanks. It's great. Zack, I wonder if I could schedule some time with you? Get your perspective as someone who's lived here all his life, and who married a woman of considerable talents."

"Sure. My time's fairly flexible." He wasn't oblivious to his sister's reaction, but he considered it her problem. "You're going to find that most of us don't think about the history of the island on a daily basis. We save that for the tourists. Most of us just live here."

"That's one of my points. You live with it, go about your business, create and maintain normal lives."

"We are normal," Ripley said softly.

"Exactly." Mac lifted his wine, studied her coolly. "Power doesn't alter, doesn't have to alter, elemental human needs. Home, family, love, financial security. The close, familial relationship between Lulu and Mia, for example, isn't based on what Mia is, but on who she is."

He looked at Zack. "I don't imagine you married Nell because she's a witch, or despite it, but because she's Nell."

"True. Then there was her pot roast."

"Which can't be discounted. Strong emotion feeds power. I've been pretty emotional about Nell's cooking since my first bowl of soup."

Zack chuckled as he topped off everyone's wine. "Good thing I saw her first."

"Timing is key. If Lulu hadn't landed here when she landed here, she might not have had the major role in Mia's upbringing. And as I understand it, Nell, if you hadn't walked into the bookstore at the exact moment that Mia's former café chef was quitting, you might not have made that connection—or not that precise connection. That connection led to one with Zack, and to Ripley, and in a winding, indirect way, to me."

"I don't have anything to do with it." Ripley's voice remained soft, but the barbs were poking through.

"Your choice," Mac said easily. "Choice is another key. In any case, since you're reluctant to show me around the island when I'm working, I wanted to ask you about a place on the south point. Great old house. Lots of gingerbread, wide covered porch. There's not much else around it. It's just up from a cove that has a shale beach. There's a terrific little cave."

"The Logan place," she said shortly. "The family that owns the hotel."

"It looked empty."

"They don't live here anymore. They rent it out now and then during the season. Why do you care?"

"First, because it's a beautiful spot and an appealing old house. Next, because I got particularly strong readings in that area." He watched Ripley's gaze flick to her brother's face, hold a moment. "I haven't heard much about the Logans. They show up in my research, of course, but no one has much to say about them in the village. How long since any of the family lived in the house?"

"More than ten years," Zack answered when Ripley remained silent. "Mr. Logan, or one of his representatives, comes back now and then to look things over, but they stay at the hotel."

"Shame to let a beautiful house like that sit empty. Is it haunted?"

Zack's lips twitched at the muttered rumble his sister made. "Not that I know of."

"Too bad." And he meant it. "How about the cave? I got the strongest readings there."

"The cave's a cave," Ripley shot. There was a little twist in her heart, and it annoyed her.

"We used it as boys," Zack began. "To play pirate and hunt for treasure. Teenagers have been known to treat it as a kind of lovers' lane." He stopped abruptly as it struck home.

Sam Logan, and Mia. They'd been teenagers once, and the cave would surely have been theirs. One look at his sister's face told him she'd known. And was trying to protect a childhood friend's privacy.

"Wouldn't surprise me if your equipment's picking up on all those hormones," Zack said cheerfully. "What's for dessert, honey?"

At sea, Nell rose. "I'll get it. Ripley, mind giving me a hand?"

"No, fine. Sure." Annoyed, Ripley pushed away from the table and stalked into the kitchen.

"What is it?" Nell demanded. "What don't you want to say about the Logan place?"

"It's just an old house."

"Ripley, I can't help if I'm in the dark."

With her hands in her pockets, Ripley paced the kitchen. "Sam and Mia—they were a major item."

"I know that much. He left, and hasn't been back. It still hurts her."

"Yeah, well, she ought to get the hell over it." With a sigh, Ripley bent down to stroke Diego the cat. "They were lovers. Mia and I, we were still . . . we were friends. We knew everything about each other. The first time she was with Sam, the first time they were together, was in the cave. It was one of their meeting places."

"I see."

"It's still a raw spot with her, and she doesn't need some jerk asking questions and taking energy readings."

"Ripley, don't you think if Mac knew he'd be less likely to rub against that sore spot?"

"I don't know what to think about him." Disgusted, Ripley straightened. "One minute he's a nice guy, and the next he's trying to wheedle data out of you over your own pot roast. He's got no business coming here as a guest and pressuring you and Zack."

"I didn't feel pressured." Nell took a Boston cream pie out of the refrigerator. "I'm sorry it upsets you, Ripley, but I've already decided to talk to Mac. I'm interested in his work, and I'm interested in contributing to it."

"You want to be one of his lab rats?"

"I don't feel that way. I'm not ashamed of what I am, and I'm not afraid of what I've been given. Not anymore."

"You think I'm afraid?" Ripley's temper flared. "That's bullshit. As big a pile of bullshit as this idiotic project of his. I don't want anything to do with it. I've got to get out of here."

She turned on her heel and shoved out the back door.

She couldn't think, but she knew she needed to walk off the anger before she said or did anything regrettable. Nell's business was Nell's business, she tried to tell herself as she jogged down the beach steps in the pearl glow of moonlight. And if

Nell wanted to make an exhibition of herself, expose herself to gossip, to ridicule, to God knew what, she was entitled to do so.

"In a pig's eye," Ripley called out, kicking at sand as she hit the beach.

What Nell said or did had a direct link to her. There was no avoiding it. Not only because they were related by marriage, but because they were connected.

And that son of a bitch MacAllister Booke knew it.

He was using her to get to Nell, using Nell to get to her. She'd been stupid to let her guard down these past few weeks. Stupid. And there was little she hated more than realizing she'd been a fool.

At the barking behind her she turned, just as the big black shape leaped out of the dark. Lucy's exuberance knocked Ripley on her butt.

"Damn it, Lucy!"

"Are you hurt? Are you okay?" Mac rushed up behind the dog, started to lift Ripley to her feet.

"Get off me."

"You're freezing. What the hell's wrong with you, running out without a coat? Here."

Even as she slapped at his hands, he bundled her into the jacket Nell had given him.

"Fine. You've done your good deed. Now beat it."

"Your brother and Nell are probably used to your spontaneous displays of rudeness." He heard the scolding tone of his own voice, but the closed and stubborn look on her face told him that she deserved it. "However, I'd like an explanation."

"Rude?" She used both hands to shove him back two full steps. "You've got the nerve to call me rude after that interrogation at dinner?"

"I recall a conversation at dinner, not an interrogation. Just hold on." He grabbed her arms as Lucy, wanting to play, wiggled between them. "You don't want to talk to me about my work, and I haven't pressed you. That doesn't mean I'm not going to talk to anybody else."

"You hook Nell, and you know it's going to involve me. You talked to Lulu, and you damn well asked her questions about me."

"Ripley." Patience, he warned himself. She wasn't just angry, she was scared. "I never said I wouldn't ask questions. I'm just not asking you. If you want control of what involves you, then talk to me. Otherwise, I have to use what I get secondhand."

"All of this was just to corner me."

He was a patient man by nature, but that patience had its limits. "You know better, just as you know saying that is an insult to both of us. So just can it."

"Just—"

"I have feelings for you. It makes it complicated, but I'm dealing with it. And that aside, Ripley, you're not the center of this. You're only part of it. I'll work around you or with you. It's your choice."

"I won't be used."

"Neither will I, as a target for your emotional storms."

He was right, bull's-eye right, and she wavered. "I won't be ogled like a sideshow."

"Ripley." His voice gentled. "You're not a freak. You're a miracle."

"I don't want to be either. Can't you understand that?"

"Yeah, I can. I know exactly what it's like to be looked at as one or the other, or both at the same time. What can I tell you? All you can be is who and what you are."

Temper was gone. She couldn't even find

the pieces of it. He'd talked her down not because he wanted something but because he got it. At the core, he got it.

"Maybe I didn't think you'd understand, you'd know. Maybe I should have. I guess being the big brain is a kind of magic, and it's not always comfortable. How do you do it?" she demanded. "How do you stay so goddamn balanced?"

"I'm not . . . Cut it out, Lucy." Still gripping Ripley's arms, he shifted as the dog barked and vibrated between them. Then he saw what had caught Lucy's attention.

She stood on the beach, as she had before. And she watched them. Her face was pale in the moonlight, her hair dark as the wind teased it. Her eyes seemed to glow against the night. Deeply green, deeply sad.

The surf foamed up, spilled over her feet and ankles, but she made no sign of feeling the cold or wet. She simply stood, watched, and wept.

"You see her," Mac whispered.

"I've seen her all my life." Tired now, Ripley stepped away from him because it would be too easy, frighteningly easy, to step toward him. "I'll let you know what I decide when I decide it. And I want to apologize for being rude and swiping at you, for mucking things up. But right now . . . I need to be by myself."

"I'll walk you back."

"No. Thanks, but no. Come on, Lucy." Mac stayed where he was, between two women. Both of them pulled at him.

Ten

Nell found it strange to knock on the door of a house where she'd once lived. Part of her still thought of the yellow cottage as hers.

She had lived much longer in the white palace in California, and had never considered it hers. Unless it was to think of it as her prison, one she'd risked her own life to escape.

But the little cottage by the wood had been hers for only a few months, and had given her some of the happiest moments of her life.

Her first home, the place where she had begun to feel safe, and strong. The place where she and Zack had fallen in love.

Even the terror she'd known there, the spilled blood, couldn't spoil the sense of belonging that the little yellow cottage with its dollhouse rooms gave her.

Still, she knocked, and waited politely on the front stoop until Mac opened the door.

He looked distracted. He was unshaven, his hair sticking up in wild spikes.

"Sorry. Did I wake you?"

"What? No. Up for hours. Um." He dragged a hand through his hair, tousling it further. What was she doing there? Did they have an appointment? Jeez, what time *was* it? "Sorry. My mind's . . . come on in."

The peek past him showed her the room jammed with equipment. Lights were glowing, and something was beeping steadily. "You must be working. I won't disturb you. I just wanted to bring you some of last night's dessert. You missed it."

"Dessert? Oh, right. Thanks. Come in."

"Actually, I'm on my way to work, so I'll just . . ." Since she was now talking to his retreating back, Nell shrugged and stepped inside, closed the door behind her. "Why don't I just put this in the kitchen for you?"

"Uh-huh. Look at this. Wait, wait." He held up one hand, making notes with the other as he studied a printout that put Nell in mind of a seismograph.

After a moment he looked over at her again and beamed. "You just sparkle, don't you?"

"Excuse me?"

"The readings changed the minute you came into the house."

"Really?" Fascinated, she stepped a little closer. And realized that no matter how close she got, she would never understand a thing about it.

"It's different with Ripley," Mac went on. "Her readings are all over the chart, and you never know. But you, you're a dependable soul."

Her lips pursed, the beginnings of a pout. "That makes me sound boring."

"On the contrary." He took the plate from her, lifting the protective wrap to break off a piece of the pie. Scattering crumbs. "You're a comfort. I'd say you're a woman who's found her place and is happy there. I'm sorry I messed up dinner last night."

"You didn't. If you're going to eat that now, let me get you a fork."

When she walked back to the kitchen, he followed her, watched her go to the right drawer, take out a fork. "Does it . . . sorry."

"Does it bother me to be in here?" she finished for him, and handed him the fork. "No. This house is clean. I cleansed it myself. I needed to do it myself."

"A strong comfort. Sheriff Todd's a very lucky man."

"Yes, he is. Sit down, Mac, I've got ten minutes. Do you want coffee with that?"

"Well . . ." He glanced down at the pie. He couldn't quite remember if he'd eaten any breakfast. Besides, the pie was here. "Sure."

"You said it was different with Ripley," Nell said as she measured out coffee. What was already in the pot looked nearly as hideous as it smelled, and she poured it straight down the drain. "You're right. I don't know all the reasons why, but she doesn't talk about it. And if I did, *I* wouldn't talk about it. It's for her. But she's my sister, so I'm going to ask you straight out. Is your interest in her only to do with your work?"

"No." He shifted a bit, seeking comfort. He was a man more used to asking the questions than answering them. "In fact, it would probably be easier for me, and certainly easier for her, if she wasn't involved in the work. But she is. Was she all right when she got home last night?"

"She wasn't angry anymore. Unsettled, but not angry. I'm going to confess and get this out of the way. I set things up last night."

"You mean the pink candles, the rose quartz, sprigs of rosemary, and so on?" Relaxed again, Mac shoveled another bite of pie into his mouth. "I noticed."

"So much for subtlety." Irked, Nell got down a mug. "I didn't do a spell."

"Appreciate it," he said with his mouth full. "I also appreciate knowing you *thought* about doing one. I'm flattered you'd consider me someone you'd like to see with Ripley."

"Are you making fun of me?"

"Not exactly. I upset her last night, and I'm sorry for that. But it's something we're both going to have to come to terms with. She is what she is. I do what I do."

Angling her head, Nell studied him. "She wouldn't be attracted to you—not for long, anyway—if you were a pushover."

"Good to know. Will you talk to me on the record?"

"Yes."

"Just like that? No qualifications?"

She set his coffee on the table. "I won't tell you anything I don't want you to know. I'm still learning, Mac. I may learn as much from you as you do from me. But now I have to get to work."

"One question. Does the power make you happy?"

"Yes. Happy and centered and strong. But I could be all those things without it." Her dimples winked. "Now ask me if I could be this happy without Zack."

"I don't have to."

After she'd left, Mac sat thinking about her for a while, about how she seemed to fit so comfortably into the rhythm of the island, the rhythm of her power.

It couldn't have been easy for her, yet he thought she made it seem like the most natural thing in the world to have started a new life out of the horrors of another.

What had happened to her hadn't scarred her. She'd been able to trust again, to love again. To become. That, he decided, made her the most admirable woman of his acquaintance.

He could also see why Ripley was so determined to protect her. Somehow he would have to make the hardheaded deputy see that Nell was in no danger from his direction.

He packed up the equipment he wanted to take with him on his planned field trip. And spent ten frustrating minutes searching for his glasses before realizing that he'd hooked them onto his shirt pocket.

He found his keys in the bathroom medicine cabinet, scooped up a few extra pencils, and was on his way to the south point of the island.

The Logan house pulled at him. He could think of no other way to describe the almost physical tug he experienced when he stood on the edge of the narrow shale road and studied it. It was big and rambling. He wouldn't have said it was particularly grand, particularly charming.

Compelling, he decided as he dragged out his recorder to log his thoughts.

"The Logan house sits on the south point of the island, and is accessible by a narrow crushed-shale road. There are other houses nearby, but this one sits on the highest rise and is closest to the sea."

He paused a minute, let himself feel the wind, taste the salt in it. The water was a hard blue today, a hue that made him wonder why the sea didn't slice itself open with its own waves.

When he turned a circle, he studied the other houses. More rentals, he deduced. There was no sound, no movement except the sea and the air, and the gulls that swooped over this quiet stretch to cry.

Mia's cliffs—and wasn't it odd that they were at nearly the precise opposite end of the island—were more picturesque, he thought. More dramatic. More everything. Yet this spot seemed . . . right somehow. Right for him.

"It's three stories," he continued with recording his observations. "It looks as though several additions have been made to the original structure. It's wood—cedar at a guess, faded to silver. Someone must maintain it, as the paint, a grayish blue, is fresh on the shutters and trim. The porches, front and back, are deep and wide, with a section of the back area screened off. It has narrower balconies off many of the second- and third-story windows, with curling . . . maybe they're called valances—I'll look it up—along the overhangs. It's a lonely spot, but it doesn't feel lonely. More like it's waiting. It's odd that it feels as if it's waiting for me."

He walked across the sandy patch of lawn, around the side of the house, to the back, where he could stand just above the beach and study the quiet cove. There was a dock, again well maintained, but no boat tied to it.

He would want a sailboat, he decided. Maybe a motor launch as well.

And the masculinity of the house needed to be softened a bit with some flora. He would have to research what grew best in this type of soil. He wondered if both the chimneys were in working order, and what it would be like to sit in the winter with a fire roaring while he watched the sea.

Shaking off the daydreams, he went back to his Land Rover and unloaded his equipment. It was only a short hike to the cave. He noted that the shadowed mouth of it was hidden from the house by the slight curve of the land. Making it more private, more mysterious. A perfect spot for kids' adventures and young lovers, he decided.

But if it was still used for such purposes, there was no sign. He could see no litter, no footprints, no markings as he walked across the shale.

He had to make two trips, and though the air in the cave was cool and slightly damp, he shed his jacket. He set up his equipment to the pretty music of lapping water and the echoes of the underground chamber.

The cave wasn't large. He measured it at just over eleven feet long and just under eight wide. He was grateful that the heart of it was more than seven feet high. He'd spent time in others that had forced him to squat or hunch or even explore on his belly.

Armed with a halogen flashlight—something he hadn't had along with him on his first trip—he studied every inch of the cave while his equipment ran.

"Something here," he mumbled. "I don't need the machines to tell me, there's something here. Like layers of energy. New over old. Nothing scientific about that, but there you go. It's a strong sense, gut sense. If this is the cave mentioned in my research, it means—What's this?"

He paused, shining his light on the wall of the cave. He had to squat after all to see it clearly.

"Looks like Gaelic," he said, reading the words carved into the stone. "I'll have to translate it when I get back."

For now he copied down the words in his notebook, and the symbol beneath them.

"Celtic knot, Trinity pattern. This carving

isn't that old. Ten years, twenty maximum. Another guess. I'll test and verify."

Then he ran his fingers along the carvings. The indentations filled with lights that lanced out in narrow beams. His fingertips warmed with the heat of them.

"Holy shit! Is that cool or what?"

He sprang up to get his gauge and his video camera, forgetting the curve of the cave ceiling. And he rapped his head hard enough to see stars.

"Idiot! Son of a bitch! Damn it! God!" With one hand clamped on his head, he paced and cursed until the sharpest edge of the pain dulled to a vicious throb.

Pain was replaced by disgust when he noted the wet smear of blood on his palm. Resigned, he dug out a handkerchief, dabbed gingerly at the knot that was forming. He held the cloth in place while he gathered his camera and gauge.

This time he sat on the ground.

He took measurements, logged them, then, prepared to document the changes, ran his fingers over the carving again. And nothing happened.

"Come on, now, I saw what I saw, and I have the minor concussion to prove it."

He tried again, but the carving stayed dark, and the stone cool and damp.

Undeterred, he stayed where he was, cleared his mind. He ignored the nasty headache already full blown. As he lifted his hand again, his monitors began to beep.

"What the hell are you doing? Holding a séance?"

Ripley stood at the mouth of the cave, the sun throwing a nimbus around her body. Too many thoughts jumbled in his mind, and all of them involved her. He gave up, for now, on the carving and just looked at her.

"Are you on cave patrol today?"

"I saw your car." She scanned his equipment as she stepped into the cave. It was still madly beeping. "What are you doing sitting on the ground back there?"

"Working." He scooted around to face her, then sat back on his heels. "Got any aspirin on you?"

"No." She played her flashlight over him, then rushed forward. "You're bleeding. For God's sake, Mac!"

"Just a little. I hit my head."

"Shut up. Let me see." She yanked his head forward, ignoring his yelp of protest, pawed through his hair to get to the scrape.

"Jeez, Nurse Ratched, have a heart."

"It's not too bad. You won't need stitches. If you didn't have all this hair to cushion your lame brain, it'd be a different story."

"Are we on speaking terms again?"

She sighed a little, then lowered herself to the cave floor, sitting as he was, back on her heels. "I did some thinking. I don't have any right to interfere with your work. I don't have any business resenting it, either. You were up front about it, right from the start, and what you said last night was true. You haven't pushed me."

She was wearing earrings. She didn't always. These were tiny dangles of silver and gold. He wanted to play with them, and the pretty curve of her ear. "That sounds like a lot of thinking."

"I guess it was. Maybe I've got to do some more. But for right now, I'd like to put things back the way they were."

"I'd like that, but I need you to know I'm going to talk to Nell. On the record."

Ripley pressed her lips together. "That's up to Nell. It's just that she's . . ."

"I'll be careful with her."

Ripley looked in his eyes. "Yeah," she said after a moment. "You will."

"And with you."

"I don't need you to be careful with me."

"Maybe I'd enjoy it." He slid his arms around her waist, rising to his knees. Drawing her up to hers.

In the back of his mind he could hear the monitors pick up again. He could have cared less. He wanted one thing at that moment, and only one thing. His mouth on hers.

As their lips met, her arms wound around him. Her body fit to his, like the last piece of a complex and fascinating puzzle.

For a moment, it was soft, and it was warm. And it was everything.

Shaken, she drew back. Something inside her was trembling. "Mac."

"Let's not talk about it." His mouth brushed her cheeks, her temples, skimmed down to graze her neck. "After a while talk just intellectualizes everything. I ought to know."

"Good point."

"It has to be soon." His lips crushed down on hers. "Soon. Or I'm going to lose my mind."

"I need to think about it a little more."

He let out one ragged breath before he gentled his grip. "Think fast, okay?"

She laid her palm on his cheek. "I'm pretty sure I'm about done with that section of our program."

"How odd," Mia said as she strode into the cave. "And how awkward." As she watched Ripley and Mac draw apart, she tossed her hair back. "I don't mean to interrupt."

Even as she spoke, Mac's equipment began to shrill. Needles slashed like whips. As one of his sensors began to smoke, he scrambled up.

Saying nothing, she spun around and walked back into the sunlight.

"Jesus, it fried it. It fucking fried it."

Since he sounded more excited than distressed, Ripley left Mac to his equipment and followed Mia outside.

"Hold up."

As if she hadn't heard, Mia continued over the shale to where the water of the cove lapped and retreated, where small tidal pools teemed with life.

"Mia, wait a minute. I didn't think you walked over this way anymore."

"I walk wherever I please." But not here, she thought, staring blindly across the water. Never here . . . until today. "Did you bring him here?" She spun around, hair flying, eyes brimming with a terrible grief. "Did you tell him what this place is to me?"

The years fell away between them, for that moment. "Oh, Mia. How could you think that?"

"I'm sorry." One tear escaped. She'd sworn never to shed another over him, but one escaped. "I shouldn't have. I know you wouldn't." She dashed the tear away, turned to face the water again. "It was just seeing you in there together, holding each other, and in that particular spot."

"What—Oh, God, Mia." Ripley pressed her fingers to her forehead as she remembered the carving. "I didn't realize. I swear, I wasn't thinking."

"Why should you? It shouldn't matter, anyway." She crossed her arms over her breasts, hugged the elbows tight. Because it did matter, and it always would. "It was long ago when he wrote that. Long ago when I was foolish enough to believe he meant it. To need him to."

"He's not worth it. No man's worth it."

"You're right, of course. But I believe, unfortunately, that there's one person for each of us who's worth everything."

Rather than speak, Ripley laid a hand on Mia's shoulder, left it there when Mia reached back, held it.

"I miss you, Ripley." The grief of it trembled in her voice, like tears. "The two of you left holes in me. And neither of us will be pleased tomorrow that I said that today. So." Briskly she released Ripley's hand, stepped away. "Poor Mac. I should go make amends."

"You smoked one of his toys, I think. But he seemed more jazzed by it than upset."

"Still, one should have more control," she replied. "As you well know."

"Bite me."

"Ah, we're back. Well, then, I'll go see what I can do to patch things up." She started back toward the cave, glanced over her shoulder. "Coming?"

"No, you go ahead." Ripley waited until Mia disappeared into the shadow of the cave before she let out a long breath. "I miss you, too."

She stayed there, crouching at a tidal pool until she pulled herself together. Mia had always been better, she thought, at smoothing her ruffles. And Ripley had always envied her that degree of self-control.

She watched the little world in the water, a kind of island, she supposed, where each depended on the others for survival.

Mia was depending on her. She didn't want to think about it, didn't want to accept her connection or the responsibility it put on her shoulders. Refusing to believe it had given her a decade of normality, and cost her a cherished friend.

Then Nell had come, and the circle had formed again. The power of that had been so brilliant, so strong. As if it had never been locked away.

It had been hard, very hard, to turn the key again.

Now there was Mac. She had to decide if he was the next link in a chain that would drag her down, or the key to another lock.

She wished with all her heart he could be just a man.

Mia's laughter drifted out of the cave, and Ripley straightened. How did she do that? Ripley wondered. How did she turn herself around in such a short span of time?

She started toward the cave just as Mia and Mac stepped out. For an instant she saw another woman, hair bright as flame, sweep out of that dark mouth. Bundled in her arms was a sleek black pelt.

The vision wavered, blurred, then slid away, like a painting left out in the rain. It left behind the vague headache that those images always brought with them.

Ten years, she thought again. For ten years she'd blocked it all. Now it was seeping back, liquid through cracks in a glass. If she didn't shore up those cracks it would all break free. And never be contained again.

Though her knees had jellied, she strode forward. "So, what's the joke?"

"Just enjoying each other's company." Mia wrapped her arm around Mac's, sent him a slow, warm look from under her lashes.

Ripley just shook her head. "Get the goofy grin off your face, Booke. She does it on purpose. What is it about you and men, Mia? You get within two feet of one, and his IQ drops below his belt."

"Just one of my many talents. Don't look so flustered, handsome." She rose to her toes to kiss Mac's cheek. "She knows I never poach."

"Then stop teasing him. He's starting to sweat."

"I like him." Deliberately Mia cuddled against Mac's side. "He's so cute."

"Is there any way I can enter this conversation," Mac wondered, "without sounding like a moron?"

"No. But I think we're done now." Ripley hooked her thumbs in her jacket pockets. "How's your head?"

"Nothing a bottle of aspirin won't cure." When he reached up to probe gingerly at the knot, Mia asked, "Did you hurt yourself? Let me see." She was a great deal more gentle than Ripley had been, but just as firm. After she took a look, she hissed out a breath. "You might have had some compassion," Mia snapped at Ripley.

"It's just a scratch."

"It's seeping blood, swollen and painful. None of which is necessary. Sit," she ordered Mac and gestured at a tumble of rocks.

"Really, it's nothing. Don't worry about it. I'm always banging into something."

"Sit." Mia all but shoved him down, then drew a small bag out of her pocket. "I have . . . a connection to the cave," she said as she took some cayenne out of her bag. "And so a connection to this. Be still."

She stroked her fingers over the cut. He felt a gathering of heat, a focus of the pain. Before he could speak, she was chanting quietly.

"With herb and touch and thought to heal, this wound under my care to seal. From illness and pain let him now be free. As I will, so mote it be. There, now." She bent over, touched her lips to the unmarked top of his head. "Better?"

"Yes." He blew out a long breath. The ache, the throbbing had vanished before she'd finished her chant. "I've seen cayenne work on minor cuts, but not like that. Not instantly."

"The herb's a kind of backup. Now be more careful with that handsome head of yours. Friday night, then?"

"I'm looking forward to it."

"Wait." Ripley held up a hand. "What?"

"I thought it only fair that I make it up to Mac for damaging his equipment. I've invited him up on Friday to observe a ritual."

Ripley was speechless for a moment, then she grabbed Mia's arm. "Can I talk to you?"

"Of course. Why don't you walk me to my car?" Mia sent Mac an easy smile. "Friday, after sunset. You know the way."

"Obviously you've lost your mind," Ripley began as she accompanied Mia across the shale. "Since when do you perform for an audience?"

"He's a scientist."

"All the more. Listen . . ." Ripley broke off as they started up the rise to the road. "Okay, listen," she started again. "I know you're probably a little shaken up right now, and not thinking straight."

"I'm fine, but I appreciate your concern."

"Fine, my ass." Ripley took three long strides away, three long strides back. Waved her arms. "Why don't you sell tickets?"

"He's not a gawker, Ripley, and you know it. He's an intelligent man with an open mind. I trust him." Mia angled her head, and those witch-smoke eyes were both amused and puzzled. "I'm surprised you don't."

"It's not a matter of trust." But she rolled her shoulders as though she felt a twinge. "Just take some time, think it through before you do something you can't take back."

"He's part of it," Mia said quietly. "You already know that. I feel something for him. Not sexual," she added. "But intimate, nonetheless. A warmth without heat. If there'd been heat, I'd have acted on it. He wasn't for me."

She said the last pointedly. "What you feel for him is different, and it unsettles you. If it was just sexual attraction, you'd have had sex with him."

"How do you know I haven't?" When Mia merely smiled, Ripley cursed. "And this has nothing to do with anything."

"It has all to do with everything. You'll make your own choices, in your own time. I'm going to ask Nell to join us, if she'd like." Mia opened the car door as Ripley stood and steamed. "You're welcome, of course."

"If I wanted to join the circus, I'd have learned how to juggle."

"Your choice, as I said." She climbed in, then lowered her window. "He's an exceptional man, Ripley. I envy you."

That statement had Ripley's mouth dropping open as Mia drove away.

Mac was packing up when Ripley came back. He'd gotten all he believed he was going to get that day, but he intended to return when the atmosphere wasn't quite so volatile.

In any case, he needed to do some repairs and needed to settle himself as well.

When Ripley's shadow crossed the opening of the cave, he tucked his Palmcorder into its bag. "You tried to talk her out of meeting with me."

"That's right."

"Is that how you refrain from interfering in my work?"

"This is different."

"Why don't you give me your definition of interference?"

"Okay, you're pissed off. I'm sorry, but I'm not going to keep my mouth shut when someone I . . . someone I know makes a decision because she's whacked out emotionally. It isn't fair."

"You think I'd take advantage of whatever it is that upset her?"

"Wouldn't you?"

He was quiet for a moment, then shrugged. "I don't know. She has several days to change her mind."

"She made the deal, she'll keep it. That's how she works."

"So do you. You're like two pieces of the

same puzzle. What caused the rift between you?"

"It's old news."

"No, it's not. She hurt and you bled for her. I watched you. Now you'd protect her if you could." He picked up two of his bags, straightened. "You're the same with Nell. You're a shield for those who matter to you. Who stands for you, Ripley?"

"I can take care of myself."

"I don't doubt it, but that's not the point. They stand for you, and that's what you don't quite know how to handle."

"You don't know me well enough to know what I can handle."

"I've known you all my life."

She reached out to stop him before he walked outside again. "What is that supposed to mean?"

"I asked you once about your dreams. One day, I'll tell you about mine."

He'd put dreams in her mind, that's what she told herself even as she was sucked into them. Knowing it was a dream didn't stop the action.

She was on the beach with a storm charging in like a runaway train. And the storm was her fury. There were others with her, shadows and lights. Love, and the barbed trap of its opposite.

A bolt sliced out of the sky, a silver blade that cleaved the earth in two. The world around her was madness, and the taste of it wildly tempting.

The choice is yours, now and always.

Power snapped. And stung.

The choice, now and always. She could reach out, clasp the hand that beckoned, that offered a bridge to the light. Or she could stay in the dark and feed.

She was hungry.

Ripley awoke weeping, with images of destruction still reeling in her mind.

Eleven

She rarely sought counsel. In her experience advice was never easy to swallow. But
the dream had broken her back.

Half a dozen times during the day she'd
nearly dumped it all on Zack. He'd always
been there for her, and their friendship was
as solid and true as their blood tie. But she
was forced to admit she wanted a woman's
shoulder. Mia and Nell were out of the
question. They were too tightly connected.

But there was one who was linked to all
of them, and who could always be counted
on to speak her mind. Whether or not you
cared to hear it.

She went to Lulu.

She waited until she thought that Lulu had
had time enough to get home from the bookstore but not enough to settle in too com-

fortably. After she'd waded through the lawn art, adjusted her eyes to the virulent colors that Lulu habitually selected to paint her house, and knocked on the back door, Ripley was pleased to see her timing was good.

Lulu had changed out of her work clothes into a sweatshirt that read, "Coffee, Chocolate, Men . . . Some things are just better rich." She had an unopened bottle of wine in her hand and was wearing ratty red slippers and the faintly irritated look of a woman who'd been interrupted.

"What's up with you?" she demanded.

It wasn't the warmest of welcomes, but it was Lulu. "Got a minute?"

"I guess I do." She turned away and clomped back to the counter for her corkscrew. "Want a glass of this?"

"Wouldn't mind it."

"Good thing I didn't light that joint."

Ripley winced. "Damn, Lu."

Lulu let out a cackling laugh and popped the cork. "Just kidding. Always could get you. Haven't had a toke in . . ." She sighed nostalgically. "Twenty-six years. Your daddy was the first and last to bust me. Confiscated my pretty little plant, and my stash. Told me he knew I could get more where that came from if I had a mind to, or I could keep on working for Mia's grandmother— and tending Mia, and he figured I had the good sense to know which I needed more. Always liked your daddy."

"That's a heartwarming story, Lu. Just chokes me up."

Lulu poured wine into two glasses, then sat and propped her feet on one of the kitchen chairs. "What brings you to my door, Deputy?"

"Can we start with some light conversation, so I can work up to it?"

"Okay." Lulu sipped, savoring the first taste of the end of the workday. "How's your sex life?"

"That's sort of part of what I'm going to work up to."

"Never thought I'd see the day when Let-'Er-Rip came to my door for a sex talk."

Before she could stop herself, Ripley squirmed. "Jeez, Lu, nobody calls me that anymore."

Lulu grinned. "I do. Always did admire your up-front approach to things. Got man trouble, baby doll?"

"Sort of. But—"

"Nice-looking man. PhDee-licious." Lulu

smacked her lips. "Not your usual type, of course. Kinda slow and thoughtful, and a little on the sweet side. Not so sweet he hurts your teeth or anything. Just a nice flavor. If I were thirty years younger—"

"Yeah, yeah, you'd have a taste of him yourself." Sulking, Ripley propped her chin on her fists.

"Don't smart-ass me. Anyway, it's nice to see you realize brains are sexy. So, how's he rate in the sack?"

"We haven't been there."

Rather than surprising her, the statement confirmed Lulu's recent observations. She set down her glass, pursed her lips. "Figured, and that tells me one thing. He scares you."

"I'm not scared of him." Accusations of that nature always put Ripley's back up, especially when they were true. "I'm just being cautious and taking my time. It's . . . complicated."

Lulu pressed her fingertips together in a kind of prayer tent. "Here is some wisdom of the ages, grasshopper."

Despite herself, Ripley grinned. "Who's the smart-ass?"

"Shut up and listen. The wisdom is this: sex is better when it's complicated."

"Why?"

"Because. When you can snatch the pebbles out of my hand, you will know the answer for yourself."

"I really like him. I mean *really*."

"What's bad about that?"

"Nothing. I just wish, sort of, that we'd gone ahead with it right off the bat so there wouldn't be all these jitters and wondering and buildup so it all seems so . . ."

"Important."

The breath whizzed out of Ripley's lungs. "Okay, yeah. Important. Worse, I think he knows it's important, and if he does, it means when it all comes down I'm not going to be really, you know, in charge."

Lulu just sipped. And waited.

"And that sounds really stupid, doesn't it? Okay." Ripley nodded, oddly settled on one very important level. "I think maybe I've got that now."

"There's more."

"Yeah. Mia's going to let him observe a ritual on Friday," Ripley blurted out. "And if Mia's involved, Nell will be, too. She's only doing it because she was upset yesterday. At the cave . . . you know, the cave. She got all twisted up, and it doesn't matter how quick she manages to untwist again, it shakes her. She's just doing this to prove she can handle everything."

"She can handle it," Lulu said quietly. "If you'd stuck with her all those years ago, you'd have a better grip on what she can handle."

"I couldn't."

"That's done. Matters more what you're going to do now."

"I don't know what to do. That's the whole thing."

"Are you looking for me to tell you?"

Ripley lifted her glass. "I guess I wanted to know what you'd say, what you thought. This messes me up, Lu. It's coming back on me, in me. Oh, fuck, I don't know how to explain it. I wanted it to go away. I *made* it go away. Now it's like there are these little openings all over the place, and I can't plug them all."

"It never did sit comfortable on you. Some things aren't meant to be comfortable."

"Maybe I was worried it would get too comfortable. I don't have Mia's control, or Nell's compassion. I don't have those things."

Circles, Lulu thought. They always came around. "No, what you've got is passion, and an innate sense of right and wrong—and a need to see it served up. That's why the three of you make the circle, Ripley, bringing to it the best of yourselves."

"Or the worst." And that was her fear. Her terror. "That's the way it went down three hundred years ago, if you buy into it."

"You can't change what was, but you can what's coming. But you can't hide from either. It sounds to me like you're thinking you've been hiding out long enough."

"I never thought of it as hiding. I'm not a coward. Even after we dealt with Remington I could pretty much pull it back, maintain the status quo. But since Mac, it keeps slipping out of my fingers."

"So you're worried that if you're with him, you won't be able to pull anything back. Not just what you are, but what you feel."

"That's about it."

"So you're going to tiptoe around." Lulu let out a huff of breath, shook her head. "Worry and fret and whatnot about what might be instead of swinging into the saddle and finding out what is."

"I don't want to hurt the ones who matter to me."

"Doing nothing sometimes hurts more than doing something. Life doesn't come with a guarantee, which is just as well, because most guarantees are bullshit."

"Well, when you put it that way." There was nothing and no one like Lulu, Ripley thought, for clearing out the murk. "I guess I've been on the edge of doing something for a while now, and not doing it is making me crazy. And stupid," she added, as she would have said to few others.

"You gonna take that last step now?"

Ripley drummed her fingers on the table, then sighed. "Let's say I'm going to take a step and see what happens next. Can I use the phone?"

"What for?"

"I need to call in a pizza order."

It took Mac most of the day to fix the sensor, and even then it was only jury-rigged. It would take a day or two to get the replacement parts, and with Friday looming, he was in a crunch.

I'm not sure what to expect on Friday, he wrote. *It's better that way. It's a mistake to go into an experience anticipating specific results. Closes off the mind to possibilities. I do, now, have a theory on the events in the Logan cave. The Gaelic phrase carved into the cave wall translates to "My heart is your heart. Ever and always." While it will take time to ascertain the age of the carving (send rubbing and scraping to lab, ASAP) I continue to believe it was made within the last twenty years. Based on that, the location of the cave, and Mia Devlin's reaction to finding me and Ripley there, it's a logical assumption that the cave has particular and personal meaning for her. The carving, I believe, was done by her or for her.*

The Logans had a son, Samuel, who was raised on the island. No one speaks of him in connection with Mia. It's a studied, deliberate omission, which naturally leads me to conclude that he and Mia Devlin were involved, most probably were lovers before he moved off-island.

This, in turn, may be the foundation for the last step of the legend, which is mirrored by the descendants of the original sisters.

Nell to Zack being the first, and hypothetically, Mia to Logan being the last.

Which leaves Ripley in the middle. Ripley and . . .

His fingers fumbled, so he stopped, sat back, rubbed his eyes under his glasses. He reached absently for his coffee mug and knocked it off the table. The obligatory cleanup gave his system time to settle.

I'm connected to the pattern, he continued. I sensed it before I came here, and with the documents I've yet to share with the others, I've formed certain theories. But theories and reality are different matters, with different effects on those involved. On me. It's more difficult than I'd imagined to maintain objectivity, to stay in the role of observer, documenter when . . .

I can't stop thinking about her. Trying to separate feelings from professional judgment is hard enough, but how can I be sure those feelings don't stem from professional interest?

"And glands," he muttered, but he didn't write that down.

Does Deputy Ripley Todd fascinate me because she has a preternatural gift that has come down to her over three centuries? Or because she's a woman who has managed to attract me on every possible level?

I'm beginning to think it's both, and that I'm already in too deep to care where these feelings come from.

He sat back again, and as his concentration level dipped, he tuned in to the beeps and buzzes of his equipment in the living room. He shoved away from the little desk, rapping his knee sharply on its underside, then limped cursing out of his office.

Ripley stood inside the door, scowling at his machines.

"Don't you ever turn these things off?"

"No." He had to resist rubbing his stomach. It ached, just looking at her.

"I knocked."

"I was in the office, working. Didn't hear you."

"You're lucky I'm persistent." She held up the cardboard box she carried. "Pizza delivery. Large and loaded, as requested. In the mood?"

His mouth watered, and his belly tightened. "It so happens I've been craving a pizza for weeks now."

"Me, too." She set it down, on top of what happened to be a machine that cost in the high six figures. She shrugged out of her coat and let it fall on the floor. She pulled off her cap, tossed it in the general direction of her coat as she walked toward him. "Hungry?"

"Oh, yeah."

"Good. I'm starved." She leaped, hitching herself up, wrapping her legs around his waist and crushing her mouth down on his.

He stumbled back two full steps. Every rational thought slipped out of his brain and drained out of his ears.

"Sex now," she said, breathless as she

raced her lips over his face, bit his neck. "Pizza later. Good for you?"

"Excellent." He staggered toward the bedroom, made it as far as the doorway before he had to brace her against the jamb. "Just . . . let me . . ." He changed the angle of the kiss, sinking deep until her moan echoed his.

"I taste you all the time." He scraped his teeth along her throat. "All the time. Drives me crazy."

"Me too. I want you naked." She began to tug at his sweatshirt.

"Wait. Slow down."

"Why?" Laughing, she did tormenting things to his ear with her tongue.

"Because . . . Jesus. Because I've been thinking about this a while." His fingers dug into her hips as he started toward the bed. "Feels like centuries. I don't want to rush it." He managed to get a handful of her hair, to draw her head back until their eyes met. "I want to savor it. Savor you. I want . . ." He leaned in, nibbled at her mouth. "To take years to make love with you. To touch you," he continued as he lowered her to the bed. "Taste you." Gently, he lifted her arms over her head.

She quivered beneath him. "You talk a good game," she managed, "for a geek."

"Let's see how it plays." He traced the exposed line of her belly when her sweater rode up. "With a little teamwork."

He lowered his head, and at the last instant angled away so his lips rubbed over her jaw.

Her body was taut under his, pumping off energy in almost visible waves. He wanted that, all of that. But first he wanted her limp, weak and stunned from pleasure.

Her hands flexed under his, but she didn't struggle. Her heart pounded against his, and her lips yielded when he asked for them. That alone was arousing, knowing she would let him set both pace and tone.

She was strong enough, what she felt was strong enough, to give him that gift. Now, he would show her he treasured it.

She'd never known a man who could light so many fires with his mouth alone. Even as she yearned for his hands, her bones, her muscles, melted under the heat. She sighed, and surrendered to it.

Her pulse thickened. Her mind blurred.

When he released her hands, her arms felt soft, heavy. She lifted them, slipping off his glasses, tossing them aside so she could frame his face to bring his mouth back to hers again.

He touched her now, a skim and glide of fingers as he inched her sweater up, off. A lazy journey over her breasts just at the edge of her bra, then a teasing dance over the center clasp.

She tugged his sweatshirt off, let her hands roam in turn.

Then his mouth came to hers again and brought out a quiet sound of pleasure. Weightless, she floated on the kiss. She nuzzled, stroked, contented as a cat when his mouth skimmed the curve of her shoulder. Shivered lightly in anticipation as his tongue trailed down the side of her neck. Moaned when it dipped under cotton to tease her nipple.

Then cried out, arching helplessly as his mouth closed, hot and hungry, over her breast.

She fought for breath, for balance. Her fingers dug into the bedclothes as her system was plunged abruptly from contentment to desperation.

It was like throwing open a door to a furnace, he thought. A man could be consumed by all that heat. Still he craved more. He snapped open her bra, found flesh. He felt her gather beneath him—storm clouds merging into one electric mass—and shuddered at her strangled cry of release.

As she went limp again, he moved down her, down the lean, taut lines of disciplined female form. Angles and curves, dips and lovely, lovely lines. He wanted to wallow in them, exploit them, absorb them. The jump of her pulse here, then here, matched the leap of his own. And the taste of her grew warmer. Stronger. Until he wondered how he'd ever lived without it.

She was helpless. Had never been helpless. Had never been taken with such ruthless patience. He owned her, and there was a thrill in it. In knowing she would let him do anything he pleased. In knowing she would enjoy it.

Her skin was damp, hot. It seemed he knew every nerve in her body and would send each quivering, one by one. She reached for him, opened to him, gave to him with a freedom she'd never felt for another.

Every move seemed impossibly slow, as

if they swam through water. His body trembled for hers, his heart raced. She felt it all, and the tensing bunch of his muscles under her stroking hands.

When his senses were full of her, the scent, the flavor, the texture, he rose over her. Waiting, waiting until those eyes, clouded now with pleasure, opened.

He slid into her. Deep, deeper.

He took her, long, slow thrusts until her breath began to sob and his blood to pound. He watched the pulse in the lovely line of her throat rage as she came again.

Her arms slid bonelessly from around him. "I can't."

"Just let me," he replied as he pressed his mouth to hers again. "Let me."

As if spellbound, she rose with him, fell with him, and felt the impossible need build yet again.

"Go with me." She gripped his hips, groaned as she felt herself being swept up one more time.

He already was. His world wavered. Burying his face in the dark spread of her hair, he lost himself.

She felt . . . perfect. As if her skin had turned to velvet dusted with gold. Every ounce of tension had drained away. In fact, she didn't see how she could possibly worry about anything ever again.

Great sex, she decided, was the best of all possible drugs.

She wasn't much of a cuddler afterward, and had never been big on pillow talk. But here she was, wrapped cozily around Mac, snuggled in because it felt exactly right. Her legs were tangled with his, her head cradled on his shoulder, her arm hooked around his neck.

What made it even better was the way he held on to her, as if he was just as content to stay there for the next two or three years himself.

"Did you learn some of those moves by studying the sexual habits of primitive societies?"

He rubbed his cheek against her hair. "I like to think I put my own spin on them."

"You do good work."

"Right back at you."

"I threw your glasses on the floor. You want to watch out you don't step on them."

"Sure. I meant to tell you something before."

"What?"

"You're beautiful."

"Get out. You're in a sexual haze."

"You have all this dense, dark hair. And I keep wanting to bite that heavy top lip of yours. Add that really swell body, and it's a great package."

When she tipped her head up and stared at him, he blinked until he had her in focus. "What?" he asked.

"I'm just trying to think when's the last time I heard anyone use the word 'swell' that way in a sentence. You're really weird, Mac. Cute, but weird." She lifted her head just enough to nip at him. "Need fuel," she said. "Want pizza."

"Okay, I'll get it."

"Nope, I brought it, I'll get it. You just stay where you are. And stay naked," she added as she rolled over him and off the bed. "By the way, you've got a really swell body, too."

She strolled into the other room, stretched luxuriously. Limber and naked, she went into the kitchen for a couple of beers to go with the pizza. She grabbed a pile of napkins, then did a quick spin.

Could she feel any better? she wondered.

Not just the sex, she thought with a dreamy sigh that would have embarrassed her if she hadn't been so loose. It was Mac. He was so sweet and smart, so steady without being boring or stuffy about it.

She loved listening to him, watching the way his mouth quirked just a little higher on the left corner than the right when he grinned. And the way his eyes got all blurred and unfocused when he was thinking. The way his hair, all dark blond and thick, was never quite tidy.

Then there was all that fascinating intensity balanced by the easy humor.

He was the first man she'd ever let herself be involved with, she admitted, who had so many layers. He wasn't simple, and didn't expect her to be.

And wasn't that lovely?

With the bottles clanging cheerfully together, she wandered back into the living room to retrieve the pizza. Happiness soared through her, and before she realized what was happening, her heart did a slow turn, a kind of waltz, then suddenly fell.

Her eyes popped wide. "Oh, my God!"

Before she could react to the abrupt and

slightly terrifying realization that she'd fallen in love, every machine in the cottage went into action.

Her head rang with the sound of them. Beeping, squealing, buzzing, humming. Needles whipped, lights flashed. And she stood frozen in shock.

Mac gave a shout and leaped out of bed. He sprinted toward the living room, tripped over a pair of sneakers and went sprawling. Cursing, he scrambled up and ran naked into the room.

"What'd you touch? What'd you do?"

"Nothing. Nothing." Ripley gripped the bottles like lifelines. Later, she told herself— much later—she would look back at this and it would all be so ridiculous she'd crack a rib laughing.

But for now she could only stare as Mac rushed from machine to machine, calling out readings, actually patting his naked body as if he might find a pocket in his skin where a pencil was hiding.

"Man! Man! Would you look at this?" He pulled up sheets of paper, holding them almost to his nose as he scanned the printout. "Major events. The first one nearly an hour ago. I think. I can't read the time. Can't see a fucking thing on the graphs. Where the hell are my glasses? Holy cow, fried another sensor. This is *great*!"

"Mac."

"Yeah, uh-huh." He waved a hand at her as if she were a vaguely annoying fly. "I just want to rewind the videotape, see if there were any visible manifestations."

"You'd better put some clothes on because you're a little . . . vulnerable to injury at the moment."

"Hmm? What was that?" he asked distractedly.

"Why don't we both get dressed, and I'll let you get back to your work."

Only an idiot, he thought, would turn a naked woman away to play with toys. Especially when the woman was Deputy Ripley Todd.

Dr. MacAllister Booke was no idiot.

"No. Let's have pizza." He picked up the box, and the scent of it, of her, stirred his appetite again. "I'll go over the data tomorrow. It's not going anywhere." He went to her, skimmed his knuckles over her cheek. "I don't want you going anywhere either."

Fair enough, she decided. She would go over her internal data tomorrow, too.

"Watch your step this time. I don't want you falling on the box and smashing dinner."

Ordering herself to settle down, she walked with him back to the bedroom. "How'd you get the scar on your butt?"

"Oh, I sort of fell off a cliff."

"Jesus, Mac." They settled on the bed, the pizza between them, and she handed him a beer. "Only you."

She hadn't meant to stay. Sleeping over was entirely different, in Ripley's view, from sleeping with. It added another layer of intimacy that, too often, got sticky.

But somehow, without her being entirely sure how he managed it, she ended up squeezing into the tiny shower with him the next morning.

He proved to be very adept in tight places.

As a result she was feeling loose, a bit muggy in the brain, and vaguely embarrassed when she let herself into her own house. Her hope was to sneak upstairs, change into sweats for a run on the beach, and act as if nothing much had happened.

That hope was dashed as Nell called out from the kitchen.

"Is that you, Ripley? Coffee's fresh."

"Damn it," she muttered under her breath and reluctantly changed directions. She was mortally afraid there was about to be a girl talk and hadn't a clue how she should handle it.

There Nell was, working in the kitchen that was alive with the homey scents of baking, looking daffodil-fresh as she filled another round of muffin tins.

One look and Ripley felt bedraggled, awkward, and ravenous.

"Want breakfast?" Nell asked cheerfully.

"Well, maybe. No." She sucked it in. "I really want to get a run in first. Ah . . . I guess I should've called last night to let you know I wouldn't be home."

"Oh, that's all right. Mac called."

"I just didn't think . . ." In the act of reaching into the fridge for a bottle of water, she froze. "*Mac* called?"

"Yes. He thought we might worry."

"He thought," Ripley repeated. Which made her, what? An inconsiderate idiot. "What did he say?"

"That the two of you were having hot

monkey sex and not to worry." She glanced up from her muffins, dimples flashing as she laughed uproariously at the horrified shock on Ripley's face. "He just said you were with him. I inferred the hot monkey sex."

"Aren't you a laugh riot in the morning?" Ripley countered and twisted the top off the water bottle. "I didn't know he'd called you. I should have done it."

"It doesn't matter. Did you ... have a good time?"

"I'm walking in at, what, seven forty-five in the morning. You should be able to infer something from that."

"I would, except you seem a little cranky."

"I'm not cranky." Scowling, Ripley glugged down water. "Okay, it just seems to me that he could have told me he was going to call you, or suggested *I* call you, but either way that would've been assuming I intended to stay the night, which I didn't, but which he obviously decided I was going to, which is pretty pushy if you ask me because it wasn't as if he actually *asked* me to stay in the first damn place."

Nell waited a beat. "Huh?"

"I don't know. I don't know what I just said. God." Irritated with herself, she ran the cold bottle over her forehead. "I'm just weirded out over stuff."

"Over him?"

"Yes. I don't know. Maybe. I've got all these feelings piling up and I'm not ready for them. I need to run."

"I've done a lot of running myself," Nell said quietly.

"I mean on the beach." At Nell's sympathetic nod, Ripley sighed. "Okay, I get you, but it's too early for metaphors."

"Then let me ask one straight question. Are you happy with him?"

"Yeah." Ripley's stomach tied itself into slippery knots. "Yeah, I am."

"It wouldn't hurt to just go with that for a while, and see what happens next."

"Maybe I would. Maybe I could. But I've figured out that he's always one step ahead of me. Sneaky bastard." She gave up, sat. "I think I'm in love with him."

"Oh, Ripley." Nell leaned down, took Ripley's face in her hands. "So do I."

"I don't want to be."

"I know."

Ripley hissed out a breath. "How do you know so damn much?"

"I've been where you are, and not so long

ago. It's scary and exciting, and it just changes everything."

"I liked things the way they were. Don't tell Zack," she said, then immediately regretted it. "What am I saying? Of course you'll tell Zack. It's like a rule. Just maybe give it a few days first. I may get over this."

"Okay." Nell walked over to transfer baking trays.

"It could be I've just got the hots for him and it's messing me up."

"I suppose."

"And if last night's any indication, we'll probably burn each other out in a couple of weeks, max."

"It happens."

Ripley tapped her fingers on the table. "If you're just going to stand over there and humor the fool, I'm changing. I'm going for my run."

Nell set the muffins on the rack to cool, totally content with herself as Ripley stormed out. "Go ahead and run," she said softly. "Bet he catches you."

Twelve

Considering that he was criminally insane, Evan Remington had his good days. He could, depending on what pictures were wheeling through his mind, be fairly lucid, even momentarily charming.

There were moments, according to one of the nurses Harding interviewed, when you could see the sly intellect that had made him a top Hollywood power broker.

Other times, he just sat, and drooled.

To Harding he had become a fascination that was edging toward an obsession. Remington was a man in his prime, by all accounts a brilliant operator of the entertainment machine, one who had come from wealth and privilege. And yet he'd been brought to nothing. By a woman.

The woman was also a fascination. A

quiet, biddable little mouse, if you accepted the opinion of many who'd known her during her marriage. A courageous survivor who had escaped a nightmare, if you went with the popular feminist take.

Harding wasn't convinced that she was either. But he was willing to consider she was something more.

There were so many angles there. Beauty and the beast, destroyed by love, the monster behind the mask.

Already he had mountains of notes, reams of tape, photographs, copies of police and medical reports. He also had the beginnings of a rough first draft of the book he was certain would make him very rich and very famous.

What he didn't have, as yet, were solid personal interviews with the key players.

He was willing to invest a lot of time and effort into acquiring them. While he followed Nell's trail across the country, forming impressions, gathering data, he flew back to visit Remington regularly.

And each time he did, he was fueled with more purpose, more ambition, and an underlying anger that baffled him. The anger would fade, but it came back stronger every time.

Most of the travel was dumped on his expense account, and though he shot off stories to the magazine, he was well aware that there would come a day of reckoning. He was already dipping into his personal funds, couldn't seem to stop himself.

Whereas once he had been proud of his magazine work, had enjoyed, even thrived on, the pace and demands of it, he now found himself resenting every hour he had to spend fulfilling his professional obligations.

The Remington/Todd story was like a fever burning in him.

On Valentine's Day—and he would always find that wonderfully ironic—he made his first real connection with Evan Remington.

"They think I'm crazy."

It was the first time Remington had spoken to him without prompting. It took everything Harding had not to jump at the quiet, *reasonable* sound of his voice. He gazed at the recorder to be sure the tape was running.

"Who thinks that?"

"The people here. My traitorous sister. My adulterous wife. Have you met my wife, Mr. Harding?"

Something icy seemed to slick the inside of Harding's gut at being called by name. He had introduced himself on every visit, but he'd never believed, never really considered, that Remington had heard, or understood.

"No, I haven't. I was hoping you would tell me about her."

"What can I tell you about Helen?" There was a sigh, a sound of patient amusement. "She deceived me. She's a whore, a cheat, a liar. But she's my whore. I gave her everything. I made her beautiful. She belongs to me. Has she tried to seduce you?"

The spit in Harding's mouth dried up. Ridiculous as it seemed, it felt as if Remington could see into his mind. "I haven't met . . . your wife, Mr. Remington. I hope to have the opportunity to meet her. When I do, I'd be happy to take her a message from you."

"Oh, I have plenty to say to Helen. But it's *private*," he said, whispering the last word as a slow smile curved his lips. "Many things between a man and his wife should be private, don't you agree? What happens between them in the sanctity of their home is no one's concern."

Harding offered a sympathetic nod. "It's difficult, isn't it, to balance that privacy when you're a man who has the public's attention."

Remington's eyes clouded, fog over ice, and began to dart around the room. The intelligence, the crafty humor in them, had vanished. "I need a phone. I seem to have misplaced my phone. Where's the damn concierge?"

"I'm sure he'll be right here. Could I ask you what it was about Mrs. Remington that first attracted you to her?"

"She was pure, simple, like clay waiting to be formed. I knew immediately she was meant to be mine. I sculpted her." His hands flexed at the ends of his restraints. "I didn't know how deeply flawed she was, how much work would be involved. I devoted myself to her."

He leaned forward, his body vibrating as it strained. "Do you know why she ran?"

"Why?"

"Because she's weak, and stupid. Weak and stupid. Weak and stupid." He said it again and again, like a chant as his fisted hands pounded. "I found her because I'm not." He turned his wrist as if checking the Rolex that was no longer there. "It's time I left here, isn't it? Time I fetched Helen and took her home. She has a lot of explaining to do. Call the bellman for my bags."

"He's . . . on his way. Tell me what happened that night on Three Sisters Island."

"I don't remember. Anyway, it's not important. I have a plane to catch."

"There's plenty of time." Harding kept his voice low and soothing as Remington began to squirm in his chair. "You went to find Helen. She was living on the island. You must have been pleased to find her alive."

"Living in a hovel, hardly more than a tool shed. Little bitch. Pumpkins on the porch, a cat in the house. Something wrong with the house." He licked his lips. "It doesn't want me to be there."

"The house didn't want you?"

"She cut her hair. I didn't give her permission to do that. She whored herself. She has to be punished, has to be taught. Has to remember who's in charge. She makes me hurt her." Remington shook his head. "She begs for it."

"She asked you to hurt her?" Harding asked cautiously. Something stirred in him, something ugly and unrecognizable. Something that was *aroused* by the thought.

It shocked and appalled him, nearly made him pull back once more. But then Remington was speaking.

"She doesn't learn. Can she be that dense? Of course not. She enjoys punishment. She ran when I killed her lover. But he came back from the dead," Remington went on. "I had a right to kill him for trying to take what belonged to me. A right to kill them both. Who are all those people?"

"What people?"

"In the woods," Remington said impatiently. "The women in the woods. Where did they come from? What business is this of theirs? And him! Why didn't he die when I killed him? What kind of world is this?"

"What happened in the woods?"

"The woods." He rubbed his lips together as his breath began to rush through them. "There are monsters in the woods. Beasts hiding behind my face. Crawling inside me. Light, in a circle. Fire. Too many voices. Screaming? Who is that screaming? Hang the witch. 'Thou shalt not suffer a witch to live.' Kill them all, before it's too late!"

He was screaming now, howling like a madman. As aides rushed in, ordered Harding to leave, he picked up his tape recorder with a trembling hand.

And didn't see the crafty gleam in Remington's eyes.

Ripley slogged her way through paperwork. She'd lost the coin toss with Zack, which still irritated her, since the false spring was hanging on. It would be close to sixty degrees by afternoon, and she was stuck on desk duty.

The only good part was that he wasn't around, so she was free to sulk and call him nasty names under her breath. When the door of the station house opened, she prepared to launch a few at him, face-to-face. But it was Mac who walked in, behind what looked to be most of Holland's supply of tulips.

"What're you doing, going into the florist business?"

"No." He crossed to her, held out the

rainbow of spring flowers. "Happy Valentine's Day."

"Oh, well. Wow." Even as her heart went soft as putty, her stomach jumped. "Um."

"You say thanks, and kiss me now," Mac told her helpfully.

"Thanks."

There were so many of them, she had to hold them out to the side before she could manage the kiss. And when she would have kept that part of the ritual light, he simply slid his arms around her, drew her closer, sucked her down into that soft, slippery world.

"There are a lot of flowers." He rubbed his lips over hers, stirring them both. "Say thanks again."

"Th—" He took the kiss deeper until her skin was humming and she'd risen to her toes.

"That ought to cover it." He ran his hands up and down her sides.

"I guess." She had to clear her throat. "They're really pretty." She felt silly holding them, sillier still because she wanted to bury her face in them and sniff like a puppy. "But you didn't have to bring me flowers. I don't really go in for the whole Valentine's gig."

"Yeah, crass commercialism and blah, blah. So what?"

He made her laugh, and she stopped feeling silly. "There's a hell of a lot of them— the florist must have fallen weeping to his knees when you walked out. Let me see if we've got something around here to hold them."

She had to settle for a plastic scrub bucket—but did indulge herself with some sniffing and sighing as she filled it with water from the bathroom tap.

"I'll do better by them when I take them home," she promised as she carried them back out. "I didn't know tulips came in so many colors. I guess I haven't paid attention."

"My mom goes for tulips. She—what do you call it—forces the bulbs in little glass jars every winter."

Ripley set the makeshift vase on the desk. "I bet you sent your mother flowers today."

"Sure did."

She looked at him, shook her head. "You're a hell of a sweetheart, Dr. Booke."

"Think so?" He dug in his pocket, frowned, dug in the other. And came up with a little candy heart, then dropped it into Ripley's palm.

Be Mine, she read, and felt that little jitter in the belly again.

"So, how about it?" He reached around to tug on her ponytail. "Are you going to be my valentine?"

"Boy, you're really into this. Looks like you've got me. Now I'm going to have to go buy you a mushy card."

"It's the least you can do." He continued to play with the sleek tail of hair. "Listen, about tonight. I didn't realize it was Valentine's Day when I made the arrangements with Mia. If you want, I can reschedule that and we can go out to dinner, take a drive, whatever you'd like."

"Oh." It was Friday, she remembered. She'd done her best to block that particular fact out of her head. Now he was giving her the perfect way to put it all off. To put off something that was important to his work.

Yep, she thought with an inward sigh, the man was a sweetheart.

"No, don't worry about it. It's already set up."

"You could come with me."

When she started to turn away, he kept her in place with his hand on her hair, turning a tender gesture into a no-nonsense one with a simple flexing of fingers.

"I don't know what I'm going to do. Don't count on me."

"Whatever you say." He hated to see her struggle, but knew of no way to smooth it all away. "There are some things I want to talk to you about. If you decide to give the session at Mia's a pass, can you come by the cottage afterward?"

"What things?"

"We'll talk about it." He gave her hair a last tug before walking to the door. "Ripley." He paused, his hand on the knob and looked at her. A gun at her hip, a pail of tulips at her side. "I know we're standing on opposite sides of a line in one area. As long as we understand why, and accept that, accept each other, we're okay."

"You're so damn stable."

"Hey, my parents spent a lot of money to make sure of it."

"Shrinks," she said and worked up a sneer for him.

"Damn right. See you later."

"Yeah," she murmured when the door closed behind him.

Problem was, she wasn't quite so stable. Not quite so okay. Because she was crazy about him.

It was difficult for a woman to maintain her dignity and reputation as somewhat of a hard-ass when she was walking around with a bucket full of tulips. It was damn near impossible when that same woman got caught perusing a dwindling display of sentimental Valentine's Day cards.

"I like this one." Gladys Macey reached around her and tapped a huge card with an enormous pink heart. Ripley did her best not to squirm.

"Yeah?"

"I picked it out for Carl a week ago, and he liked it fine when I gave it to him this morning. Men like big cards. Must make them feel more manly."

Having no doubt that Gladys knew more about such matters than she did, Ripley plucked the card out of the slot.

"Last one," she commented. "Lucky me."

"Lucky you, indeed." Gladys bent down to admire the tulips. "Must be four dozen tulips in there."

"Five," Ripley corrected. Okay, she'd counted. She couldn't help it.

"Five dozen. Mmm. And they cost the earth this time of year. Pretty as a picture, though. You get candy, too?"

Ripley thought of the little heart that she'd tucked in her pocket. "Sort of."

"Candy, too." Gladys nodded wisely. "The man's smitten."

Ripley nearly bobbled the bucket. "What did you say?"

"I said the man's smitten."

"Smitten." Something tickled Ripley's throat, but she wasn't sure if it was panic or humor. "That word's getting around these days. Why do you think that?"

"Well, for heaven's sake, Ripley, a man doesn't buy a woman flowers, give her candy and so forth on Valentine's Day because he wants a canasta partner. What makes young people so thickheaded about these things?"

"I just figured he was one of those people who make Hallmark stand up and cheer."

"Men don't make grand gestures unless

they're reminded to, in trouble, guilty, or smitten." Gladys ticked these possibilities off on her fingers, with nails newly polished in Valentine Red. "Not in my experience. Did you remind him what day it was?"

"No, I forgot about it myself."

"You have a spat?"

"No," Ripley conceded.

"Anything you can think of for him to be guilty about?"

"No, there's nothing in particular for him to feel guilty about."

"Well, then, where does that leave him?"

"According to your lineup, smitten." She'd have to think about it. She studied the card in her hand. "So, they like the big ones?"

"Absolutely. You put those flowers in something pretty now. They're too sweet to stay in that old bucket." She gave Ripley a pat on the shoulder, then wandered off.

As soon as she could manage it, Gladys would be spreading the word that the village deputy was sweet on the mainlander. And vice versa.

The mainlander was back at work. He'd studied, organized, and logged the varied data that had come through on the night he and Ripley had been together. He was formulating theories, hypotheses, and working toward logical conclusions.

He hadn't noted the time when he and Ripley had made love. His mind had been on more important matters. Nor had he clocked the duration. But his printouts, assuming that his theories on energy dispersal were correct, pinned it down for him.

The machines had picked up burst after burst, spikes, long, steady rises, fluctuations. Wasn't it interesting that he hadn't heard the clatter of them as they recorded? He'd been so completely absorbed in her.

Now he could look at the tangible record of what they'd brought to each other. It was oddly arousing.

He measured distances between the spikes and rises, calculated the valleys between energy peaks and the output of each.

Then he had to get up and walk around until he could stop imagining her naked and concentrate on science.

"Long steady holding pattern here. Low-grade energy levels." He crunched on an apple, pushed up his glasses. "Afterglow period. We're just lying there now. Languor, pillow talk. Makes sense. So why does it start building again here?"

It was almost like steps, he noted. A rise, a plateau, a rise, a plateau.

He tried to think. She'd gotten up, gone for the pizza, into the kitchen for a couple of beers. Maybe she'd been thinking about making love again. He didn't mind thinking she was. It was a nice boost to the ego.

But it didn't explain the abrupt and violent energy flash. Nothing steplike there. It had been like a rocket going off. Nothing he could find indicated that it came from an outside source or an underlying well of energy.

To his best recollection, he'd been in a kind of twilight sleep, just sort of floating while he waited for her. He'd been thinking about the pizza, about eating it in bed with her. Naked. It had been a pleasant image, but he hadn't been the cause of this.

Therefore, Ripley had. But how and why were the puzzles.

An aftershock sort of thing? That was possible. But aftershocks were rarely as powerful as the initial quake, and this one punched right through the ceiling.

If he could re-create the event. . . . That was a thought. Of course, he would need to find a delicate way to propose that to her.

They had a lot to talk about.

He bit into the apple again, and felt happy just remembering the stunned look on her face when he'd walked in with all those flowers. He liked surprising her that way, then watching her deal with it.

He just liked watching her.

He wondered how much work it was going to be for him to talk her into taking a trip with him, maybe in the spring. Before he had to buckle down and turn his data and theories and conclusions into a book. They could make a quick stop in New York. He wanted her to meet his family.

Then they could take a few days somewhere, anywhere she wanted. He wasn't particular.

Some time alone with her, away from work. It might help him evaluate another hypothesis he was working on. That he was falling in love with her.

Ripley decided to keep her distance from whatever was going to happen at Mia's that evening. Since Zack had chosen to go along, she would have the house to herself for a change. She could take advantage of that by turning the TV up too loud, eating junk food, and watching a really bad action movie on cable.

She'd been spending nearly all her free time with Mac, and maybe that was part of the problem. A little alone time in her own space was just what she needed.

She would work off some energy lifting weights, take a long, hot shower, then settle in with popcorn, loaded with salt and butter, and watch TV with her pals Lucy and Diego.

She turned the music up to earsplitting in the spare room she used for workouts, then with the dog and cat trailing her, walked into the bedroom to change into her gear.

And there were the tulips, the charming explosion of them, taking over her dresser. The air was sweet with them.

"Valentine's Day's just a racket," she said out loud, then gave up. "But it really works."

She picked up the card she'd bought for Mac. It wouldn't take her very long to run over to the cottage, slip it under his door. In fact, it would probably be better if she didn't have to give him something so, well, mushy face-to-face.

And she could add a little note saying that she would see him tomorrow. The more she'd thought about it, the less she wanted to talk about whatever it was he wanted to talk about when he was still pumped from his witch session.

She didn't care if it was unfair or unrealistic, or even stupid. For now, for a while longer, she wanted to keep whatever it was they felt for each other separate from his work and her . . . gift.

She'd never been in love before. What was wrong with holding on to that for a while, and putting off the rest?

"Okay, back in ten," she told Lucy and Diego. "No smoking, drinking, or making long distance calls while I'm gone."

She grabbed the card and headed toward the door leading out to the deck.

And stepped out onto the beach, into a rising storm. The wind slashed, the icy tip of a whip. The air was blue with lightning. She was spinning, spinning through it, flying on a current of power that pulsed in a thousand heartbeats over her skin.

The circle was a white flame on the sand. She was in it, and above it, outside it.

Three figures ringed inside it. She saw herself, who was not herself, link hands with her sisters. And the chants that rose up hummed inside her.

She saw herself, yet not herself, standing alone, beyond that bright circle. Arms lifted, hands empty. And the grief shot up out of that lonely heart into her own.

She saw herself, as she was, as she could be, alive in that storm. Beyond the circle where her sisters waited. Rage and power twisted inside her.

One man cowered at her feet, and another ran toward her in the violent dark. But she could not be reached. Would not be reached. In her hand was the bright silver sword of justice. With a cry, she brought it down.

And destroyed them all.

She awoke sprawled on the deck, shuddering helplessly in the balmy night. Her skin was damp and there was the electric smell of ozone stinging the air. Her stomach spasmed as she pushed herself to her hands and knees.

Too weak to stand, she stayed there,

rocking gently, taking gulping breaths to feed her starved lungs. The roaring in her head subsided and became the endless rolling of the sea.

It had never come on her like that, never so abruptly, so physically. Not even when she was practicing, when she had willingly sought such things.

She wanted to crawl back into her room, to curl up on the rug in the dark and whimper like a baby. It was the small, pitiful sounds coming from her own throat that made her force herself up until she was kneeling, until she was breathing deep and steady again.

With the vision still pounding at her, she scrambled to her feet and ran.

Thirteen

"Are you sure you want to do this?" Nell linked her hand with Zack's, deliberately slowing the pace. Thin clouds sailed overhead, filtering the starlight. The fat curve of moon was a soft and waiting white. She knew her way in the dark, through Mia's gardens, past her jutting cliffs and into the winter forest. With her hand warm in Zack's, she let Mia and Mac pull ahead.

She could hear Mia's voice, like a light trail of music, slip back through the trees and shadows.

"Would you rather I stayed behind?"

"No. It's just that you've never come with me before."

"You never asked me before."

Her fingers curled in his, she stopped. She could see him clearly enough. She could always see him clearly. "It wasn't that you weren't welcome." In the starlight, she saw his brows arch, and she smiled. "Exactly."

In a slow, easy movement, he lifted their joined hands to his lips. "Does my being here make you uncomfortable?"

"Not uncomfortable. A little nervous, maybe." Because she was, she touched him, just a skim of her fingers over his arm. "I'm not sure how you might react, how you'll feel about this part of me."

"Nell." He put his hands on her shoulders, gave them a little rub. "I'm not Darren."

"Who?"

"You know—Darren. *Bewitched.* You twitch your nose and I get all grumpy about it."

It took her a minute, then she wrapped her arms around his waist. Nerves, doubts, worries, were completely swamped by joy. "I really love you."

"I know. There is one thing. I was going to be open-minded and not bring it up, but . . ." He glanced over to where Mac had disappeared into the dark with Mia. "I've read up on rituals and magic and that sort of thing, and I know that sometimes they involve getting naked. I don't care how stupid it sounds, but I want you to keep your clothes on when Mac's around."

She tried to hide her amusement. "He's a scientist. Like a doctor."

"I don't give a rat's ass. In this particular area, I'm Darren."

"Well, Darren, it's not warm enough to go skyclad. And to be perfectly frank, I keep my clothes on even when it's just me and Mia. Apparently I'm a very prudish witch."

"Suits me."

They began to walk again, with him letting her lead the way. "So . . . does Mia get naked?"

"Skyclad," Nell corrected. "And I don't see why you'd be interested."

"Purely from an academic standpoint."

"Yeah, right."

They were still teasing each other as they stepped into the clearing.

Shadows, gray as smoke, ringed the edges. Hanks of dried herbs and chains of crystals hung from the bare branches of the trees. A trio of stones rose up in a kind of altar. Mac crouched in front of it, busily taking readings.

Mia had denied him his video camera and tape recorder. No amount of persuasion had moved her on that point. But she had permitted his sensors and his notebook.

And his mind.

Mia had already set down the bag she carried, and now walked over to Zack to take the one he'd brought for Nell. "Let's give our scientist a moment to play, shall we?" She gestured toward Mac. "He's so happy."

Then she slipped an arm around Nell's shoulders. "There's no need to be nervous, little sister."

"It just feels a little odd. And I'm still new to all this."

"Your man stands with you. You come here already more powerful than you were the first time, and more aware of self." She shifted her gaze to Zack, studied his face. "Can't you feel his pride in you? In all that you are? There are some who never have that vital magic. Without it, the light's never quite bright enough."

As much to bolster herself as Nell, she gave Nell's shoulders a little squeeze before going to join Mac.

"She's so lonely," Nell confided to Zack.

"She doesn't think it, and she's so confident, so complete, no one sees it. But there are times she's so lonely it makes me ache."

"You're a good friend, Nell."

Mia laughed at something Mac said, then spun away from him. It wasn't quite a dance, Mac would think later. But still somehow balletic. Her long gray dress billowed, then settled as she lifted her arms. And her voice, rich and full, was the music.

"This is our place, the place of the Three. It was conjured from need and knowledge, from hope and despair. From power turned away from death and fear and ignorance. This is our place," she repeated, "passed down to us, the Three to the Three. For tonight, we are two."

Mac got slowly to his feet. She was changing in front of him. Her hair was more vivid, her skin sheening like marble. Her already staggering beauty increased, as if some thin veil had been lifted.

He wondered if she used her magic to enhance what she had now, or if she used her gift to dim it at other times. And he cursed the lack of recording equipment.

"We come here to give thanks, to honor

those who came before, to offer, and re-member. This ground is sacred. You are welcome here, MacAllister Booke, when you're invited. I won't insult you by asking for your promise not to come here other-wise."

"You have it anyway."

She inclined her head, a regal acknowl-edgment.

"Zack, you are Nell's, and this place is hers as much as mine. So it's yours. You can ask questions if you like," she added as she bent to open her bag. "I imagine Dr. Booke has most of the answers."

Because the request was implied, Mac crossed over and stood with the other man. "The candles they're getting out are ritual candles. I imagine they've already been consecrated and inscribed. They're using silver, representing the goddess. Female power. The symbols on them . . ."

He edged a little closer, squinted. "Ah, yeah. The four elements. Earth, Air, Fire, Water. Mia wouldn't tell me what ritual they'd do tonight, but from the setup, it's probably a call to the four elements. An of-fering of respect," he continued. "Maybe a request for dream interpretation or clairvoyance. Those are represented by the silver candles, too. It's an attractive ritual."

"You've seen it before." Zack watched his wife remove a knife with a curved handle, a goblet, a wooden wand with a crystal tip from her bag.

"Yeah. If the ritual generates enough power, you may feel a little tingle in the air. Even without that, my sensors will pick up the energy increase. They'll cast a circle and light the candles with wooden matches."

"Matches?" Zack felt his face split into a grin. "Brother, keep watching." Amused now, and fascinated by his wife, Zack slipped his hands into his pockets, rocked back on his heels.

Mac scribbled in his notebook as they cast the circle. It was a fairly standard casting, little variation on the other chants and movements he'd observed.

"Too bad it's cloudy," he commented as he checked the new reading on his sensor. "We could use more light."

Even as he spoke, a thin line of silver shimmered over the ground, a perfect circle of light.

"Jeez." With equal parts shock and fascination, he took a step forward, notebook forgotten.

From the center of the circle, Mia and Nell set the candles alight, with no more than a sweep of arm.

"I thought you'd seen this deal before," Zack said.

"Not like this. Never like this." Catching himself ogling, he pulled himself back. And got to work.

"We are two," Mia said. "And we bring two more. One for love, and one for knowledge. One to be cherished, the other to be sought." She picked up her wand. "Such things are tools," she said, conversationally now. "Tools are to be respected." She opened a small jar and took out a handful of petals. "Iris, for wisdom."

From another, Nell took a sprig of rosemary. "And this for love." She took up her ritual knife and used the tip to draw symbols on the earth. "And here we twine them, here we bind them, love and knowledge blessed with hope, within the circle and without, sought and cherished they conquer fear and vanquish doubt."

"Hearts and minds, open and free," Mia continued, sprinkling herbs and flowers into a wide bowl. "Only then can we meet our destinies. Because these things we both hold dear, we allow two to witness what we do here. In this place and on this night, we open our ritual to their sight. This I do willingly."

"As do I," Nell responded.

"All right, then. Any questions, Professor?"

"I've never seen that particular ritual."

"Just a little precaution. We wouldn't want you to be taken as Peeping Toms. Consider it a kind of warm-up act for the main performance. Still, you're not to attempt to enter the circle, or even approach it, once we begin. Understood?"

"Oh, yeah."

"Then . . ."

"One more?" Mac lifted a finger.

"Ask," Mia said with a nod.

"What is this place?"

Mia held out a hand, palm up, fingers gently cupped, as if she held something precious. The air—Mac would have sworn it—pulsed.

"It is," she said quietly, "the heart."

Then she lowered her hand. Mia nodded at Nell. "Blessed be, little sister."

Nell drew in breath, held it as she lifted her arms. "I call to Air, both restless and sweet. On her breast my wings will beat. Rise and turn and blow your breath warm, come stir the wind, but do no harm. I am Air," she called out as the hanging crystals began to sing, "and she is me. As I will, so mote it be."

The wind swirled, dancing in the once still night. Mac could smell the sea in it, feel it whisper, then rush over his face and hair.

"Amazing," was the best he could do, and watched Mia mirror Nell's gesture before she picked up the chant.

"I call to Fire, her heat and light. In her heart life burns strong and bright. Flame like the sun, bring harm to none. I am Fire, and she is me. As I will, so mote it be."

The silver candles sprang like torches, and the shimmering circle rose like a flaming wall.

Mac's sensors rang like alarms. For the first time in his long career, he gave them not a thought. The pencil he held slipped unnoticed out of his fingers. He could feel the heat, see through it. The women behind that sheer, fiery curtain glowed just as brightly.

And the wind sang like a woman in love.

Within the circle, Nell and Mia turned to each other, clasped hands.

Ripley rocketed out of the woods. Mac caught only a glimpse—her pale, pale face, dark eyes, then she was diving into the fire.

"No!"

With images of her burning, he leaped forward.

"Stay back!" Mia snapped out the order even as she knelt beside Ripley.

"Damn it, she's hurt." Mac lifted one unsteady hand, pressed against an invisible barrier. It sparked, hissed, but wouldn't give way. Nothing he'd seen or done had prepared him to stand helpless behind magic, unable to reach the woman he loved.

"Break the circle," he demanded. "Let me through."

"This isn't for you."

"She is." He curled his fists against the shield, ignoring the heat that radiated from it.

"Nell." Zack strained at the edge of the fire. He felt the scorch of its power, and for the first time a ripple of fear.

"It's all right. She's safe here. I promise."

Watching her husband, she cradled his sister's head. "Please."

"You know better." Mia's voice was steady even as she brushed back Ripley's hair. Even as she watched Ripley's eyes clear, her heart thudded. "I wasn't prepared for you, nor you for this."

"Don't scold her. She's shaking. What is it, Ripley?" Nell asked. "What happened?"

Shaking her head, Ripley struggled to her knees. "I can't control it. I couldn't stop it. I don't know what to do."

"Tell me," Mia insisted as she gave a worried glance toward the men. Her will and her wall wouldn't hold them out much longer. No defense lasted against love. "And be quick."

"A vision. Hit me like a fist. What was, what might be. It's bad. It's me." She moaned and sank into a ball. "It hurts."

"You know what needs to be done."

"No."

"You know," Mia repeated and ruthlessly dragged her up again. "You came, you're here, and you know what you have to do for this, for now. The rest comes when it comes."

Her stomach pitched, cramped. "I don't want this."

"And still you came. To save us? Well, save yourself first. Do it. Now."

Her breath was coming in ragged gasps, and the look she shot Mia was anything but friendly. But she held out a hand. "Well, damn it, help me up. I won't do it on my knees."

Nell took one hand, Mia the other. And when Ripley stood on her feet, they let her go.

"I don't remember the words."

"Yes, you do. Stop stalling."

Ripley hissed out a breath. Her throat was so tight it stung, and her stomach was alive with cramps. "I call to Earth, generous and deep, in her we sow that we may reap . . ."

She felt the power rising, swayed with it. "Mia—"

"Finish."

"Give us your charm and bring no harm. I am Earth and she is me. As I will, so mote it be."

Power gushed into her, flooded out the pain. The ground at her feet sprang with flowers.

"And the last." Mia gripped her hand firmly, took Nell's. They were linked, a circle within a circle. "We are the Three. We call to Water, stream, and sea."

"Within her great heart," Nell continued, "life came to be."

"With your soft rain, bring no harm, no pain." Ripley lifted her face and joined her sisters in the last of the chant.

"We are Water, and she is we. As we will, so mote it be."

Rain fell soft as silk and bright as silver.

"We are the Three," Mia said again, quietly so that only Nell and Ripley could hear.

Because he had no choice, Mac waited until the ritual was complete and the circle closed. The minute he could reach her he grabbed Ripley's arms. A shock of electricity jolted through his hands, but he held on.

"Are you okay?"

"Yes. I need to—"

"Don't pull away from me." His voice carried an undertone of steel.

"I wouldn't pull if you didn't grab."

"I beg your pardon," he said and released her.

"Look, damn it." She poked at his arm as he turned away. "I'm a little churned up right now. I could use a few minutes to settle down."

"Take all the time you need. I've got plenty to do."

He walked back to pick up his notebook, check his equipment.

"That was unkind of you," Mia scolded.

"Don't hassle me now."

"Suit yourself. We're going back to the house. You're welcome, of course. Or you can go to the devil, which often suits you as well."

She shot her nose in the air and walked off to join Mac.

"Hey." Zack stepped to her, ran a hand through her hair, then framed her face. "Scared me."

"Scared me, too."

"Keeping that in mind, you might want to cut the guy some slack. I've seen a little of what the three of you can pull off together before. He hasn't. Rip." He pulled her close a moment. "You go running through fire, it shakes a man up some."

"Yeah, okay." Nothing, she thought, ever felt quite as solid and steady as her brother. "I'll talk to him. Why don't you take Nell and Mia back to the house? We'll be along in a minute."

"You got it."

She gathered herself, picked up one of Mac's scattered pencils and took it to him. "I'm sorry I snapped at you."

"No problem."

"Look, don't go sulky on me. You don't know what it's like to . . ."

"No, I don't," he shot back. "And you don't know what it's like to just stand there, fucking *stand* there, when I don't know if you're hurt."

"Okay, I'm sorry. I couldn't . . ." To her horror, her voice broke, and her vision wavered with tears. "Damn it, I told you I was churned up."

"Okay. Whoa." He drew her into his arms, stroked her hair. "Why don't you just hold on here a minute?"

"Crying pisses me off."

"I bet. Just hold on."

She gave in, gave up and wrapped her arms around him. "I'll get it together in a minute."

"That's okay, because I want to hold on, too. I thought you were . . ." He saw it again, that flash of her face that was white as bone as she leaped into a wall of golden flame. "I don't know what I thought. I'm prepared for a lot of this kind of thing. I've seen magic. I believe in it. But nothing I've seen or imagined comes close to what the three of you did tonight."

"I didn't want to be here."

"Then why were you? What scared you enough to bring you here?"

She shook her head. "I only want to tell it once. Let's go back to Mia's."

He hitched his equipment bag onto his shoulder. "You were in pain. I saw that."

"The circle wasn't prepared for me, and I wasn't prepared for it."

"No, before that. Before you did your death-defying leap."

"You see a hell of a lot, don't you, for a guy who's always losing his glasses."

"They're just for reading and close work." He wanted to stroke, to tend, to cuddle. And was afraid if he did, they'd both fall apart. "Is there any pain now?"

"No." She sighed. "No. I took the power,

called my element, made the circle of Three. There's no pain now."

"But you're not happy about it."

Like Nell, she knew her way through the forest, through the dark. Already she could see the glimmer of light from Mia's windows. "It brings Nell joy, and gives Mia a kind of, I don't know, foundation. For Nell it's an exploration, for Mia it's like breathing."

"And for you?"

"For me it's a goddamn stampede."

"So you chose to fence it in."

"And I didn't use strong enough nails," she finished, with just a hint of bitterness, and shook her head to ward off any more questions.

Mac supposed the food and wine were another kind of ritual, one used as a bridge between the fantastic and the ordinary. Though he doubted he would forget even the smallest detail about the night, he scribbled in his notebook as Mia played hostess.

"Is it all right to ask questions?"

She smiled at him.

"Of course," she replied, as she curled cozily in a chair. "But they may or may not be answered."

"What you did tonight . . . your preparations, your ceremonial tools and ritualistic, well, trappings, were very simple, very basic for such extraordinary results."

"Too many trappings and too much ceremony is usually a cloak to disguise a lack of power, or used to feed the ego, perhaps to impress an audience."

"Do you need them at all?"

"What an interesting question, Mac. What do you think?"

"I think not." And even he, before tonight, wouldn't have believed it. "I think the gift in each one of you is beyond them. I think you could light the fire in your hearth without moving from that chair, without casting a circle, without ritual."

She sat back, regarding him. What was it about him, she wondered, that tugged at her? That made her want to share with him what she'd shared with no outsider? "There's a reason for traditions, even for superstition. For ceremony. It helps focus power, and pays respect to the source. But, of course . . ." Behind her, the fire leaped to life in the hearth. "You're quite right."

"Show-off," Ripley muttered.

She laughed, and the fire damped down to a soft and pleasant glow. "You're right, too." She sipped her wine, and her eyes met Ripley's over the rim of her glass. "You used to have more of a sense of humor about it."

"And you used to lecture that I should take more responsibility."

"I suppose I did. How tedious of me."

"Oh, don't start pinching at each other," Nell ordered. "You wear me out."

"We could have used her as a mediator years ago." Mia sipped her wine again. "We are the Three. It can't be changed, avoided, or ignored. You know the legend," she said to Mac.

"Very well. The one called Air left the sanctuary of the island. She married a man who couldn't accept her, wouldn't cherish her, and in the end destroyed her."

"She destroyed herself," Nell said, disagreeing. "By not believing in who she was, by lacking the courage to."

"Maybe." Mac nodded. "The one called Earth refused to accept what had happened. It ate through her until she used her power to avenge her sister."

"She wanted justice." Ripley rose to prowl. "She needed it."

"Her need caused her to break trust." Mia's hand lifted an inch off the chair, then lowered again. It wasn't time to reach out. "To turn from everything she was and had been given and use power to harm."

"She couldn't control it," Ripley said in a shaky voice. "She couldn't stop it."

"She didn't control or stop it, and doomed herself and what she loved."

"And the third," Ripley spun back. "She who was Fire found a silkie in human form sleeping in a cave near a cove. And taking his pelt, she hid it and bound him to her."

"It's not against the laws of magic to do so." In a casual move that cost her a great deal, Mia leaned over and selected a cube of cheese from a tray. "She took him as lover, as husband, raised her children with him, then the children of her lost sisters."

The food tasted like chalk in her throat, but she nibbled casually. "She gave him her heart. But the day came when she was less than vigilant, and he found his pelt. And though he had loved her, when a silkie has his pelt, the sea beckons. He forgot her, their life, their love, their children—as though they had never existed—and left her for the sea."

Mia lifted a shoulder. "Without sister, without lover, without husband she pined, and pining, despaired. She cursed her magic for bringing her love, then stealing it away. And abjuring it, leaped from the cliffs to the sea where her lover had gone."

"Death isn't the answer," Nell added. "I know."

"It was, at that moment, hers," Mia stated. "So three hundred years later, the descendants of the sisters, of the Three, must make restitution, must turn back each key. One by three. Or the island they made will tumble forever into the sea."

"If you believe that, why do you live here?" Ripley demanded. "Why are you in this house, why the bookstore, why anything?"

"This is my place, and my time. The same as it's yours, and Nell's. If you don't believe it, why are you here tonight?"

Mia could feel her temper begin to snap, and yanked it back. She also saw the misery on Ripley's face. It was hard, after so many years, to reach out. But she got to her feet, held out a hand.

"Tell me. Let me help."

"I saw—it was painful, like being ripped open, head to gut. And so fast there was no time to react."

"You know it doesn't have to be that way. You know it doesn't ask for pain, nor want harm."

"Threefold." A single tear spilled over before she could stop it. "What you send comes back, times three. She destroyed them."

"Not alone. Each of them had responsibility. Tell me." She wiped the tear from Ripley's cheek herself. "What did you see?"

"I saw . . ." She replayed the vision, her voice calming as she spoke. "I don't know who he was, or what he represented, but he'll come. None of you could stop me, no more than I could stop myself. It was my sword, Mia. My ritual sword. I killed him with it—and killed us all."

"You won't. You won't," she repeated before Ripley could protest. "You're stronger than that."

"I wanted to hurt him. I could feel the rage. I've never had control over power when my emotions take over. Why the hell do you think I stopped?"

"Because you were afraid?" The temper came bubbling back, a decade of fury. "You turned away from me, from what you are, because you were afraid of what you might do? You're just *stupid*!"

She whirled away, then yelped when Ripley grabbed her by the hair and yanked. "Who the hell are you calling stupid, you skinny, snotty, self-serving bitch?" Her eyes narrowed when Mia lifted a bunched fist, then she let out a laugh. "Yeah, like that scares me. Hit me with your thumb tucked in that way, you're going to hurt yourself more than me. You're such a damn girl, Mia."

"That's an interesting observation, since you're the one doing the hair pulling."

With a shrug, Ripley let go. "Okay, we're even." She blew out a breath, blinking when she realized that all the other people in the room had gotten to their feet. She'd forgotten they were there. "Sorry."

After smoothing her hair, Mia slid into her chair again. "Pissed you off when I called you stupid, didn't I?"

"Damn right. So watch it."

"But you didn't use power to strike at me when my back was turned." Mia lifted her glass again. "You didn't even consider it."

Tricky witch, Ripley thought with reluctant admiration. She'd always been tricky. "I wasn't that mad."

"Yes, you were," Zack commented, and settled down again. "You really hate being called a coward or stupid. She did both. And all you did was pull her hair."

"It's not the same thing."

"Close enough." Zack took his wife's hand, studied his sister. "There are two things you're not, Rip. You're not a coward and you're not stupid. Everyone in this room can handle themselves. I don't know as much about all this as the rest of you, but I know you. And it's time you stopped thinking everything hinges on you. Nobody's alone here."

"I couldn't stand to hurt you, to be responsible for it. I couldn't live with it. Mom and Dad, Nell. Answer me this," she demanded, turning back to Mia. "And no bullshit. What if I leave the island, if I pack up, get on the ferry, and just don't come back? Could it break the chain?"

"You already know the answer. But why

don't we ask Mac to give it? This is his field, as an academic, an observer, and someone who has done considerable research into such matters. Your objective opinion, Dr. Booke?"

"The island itself has power. In sort of a holding pattern until it's stirred up or applied."

"Then if I leave it, I take away my, what, conduit to it? Can I do that?"

"On some level, yes, but that would only decrease, potentially decrease, your personal focus of energy. It wouldn't change a thing. I'm sorry. Where you go isn't the point. What you do is."

He could see she wasn't satisfied, so he spread his hands and tried to explain his theory. "Okay. If, for the purposes of this discussion, we take legend as fact, you'll have a choice to make. Something to do or not to do. You're here."

He used a napkin as the island, placed three olives on it. Then he plucked one olive up and set it on a tray. "You leave. All you do is change the location of the choice, the act, the restraint. Wherever you go, the four elements exist. You can't defy basic natural law. What you are doesn't change, and what you do carries back—by earth, air, fire, water."

He jabbed a fingertip onto the napkin. "Right back to the source. Inevitably. Staying is your only logical choice. You're stronger here, and the three of you together make the difference."

"He's right." Nell spoke and brought Ripley's attention around. "We've already changed the pattern once. We're three, when before there were only two left. Without you and Mia, without you," she said to Zack, "there would only be two now. Their circle was broken by this point. Ours isn't."

"But it is rusty," Mia said and chose another cube of cheese. "You'll need to get back in shape, Deputy."

Ripley snagged an olive, popped it into her mouth. "The hell I will."

Fourteen

"How about, for tonight, you turn those things off?"

Ripley stood on the threshold of the yellow cottage. She wasn't willing to go in and have a bunch of damn machines start scanning her, not after the evening she'd had.

"Sure." Mac slipped by her, set down his equipment bag, then began shutting down.

He hadn't expected her to come back with him. Though she didn't look it, he imagined she was tired. Or at the least had had enough of people in general. Perhaps him in particular.

She'd bounced back, that was certain. Back to trading sharp little barbs with Mia, to behaving as if what had happened in the clearing had been nothing major.

It was an unbelievable shield that she

hefted, he thought. Nearly as impressive as the one that had kept him out of the circle in the clearing. He wondered just how vulnerable she felt when her grip on that shield slipped.

"You want to sit?" he asked when she stepped inside and shut the door. "Or just go to bed?"

"Well, that's cutting to the chase."

His color rose. "I didn't mean sex. I thought you might want some sleep."

She saw now that was exactly what he'd meant. Yeah, he was a damn sweetie all right, she decided, and prowled what she could of the room. "It's a little early to bunk down. I thought you had stuff you wanted to talk to me about."

"I do. I didn't figure you'd be up for it tonight."

"I'm not tired. It doesn't work that way."

"How . . . Here, let me take your jacket."

She stepped back before he could, and shrugged out of it herself. "If I know you're thinking the question, you might as well ask it. How does it work? I feel like I've got a tanker load of caffeine in my system. Energized," she continued, crossing to him to give him a quick, firm shove. "Edgy." And another. "So yeah, I want to go to bed." The last shove pushed him through the bedroom doorway. "And nobody's going to sleep."

"Okay, then. Why don't we just—"

She shoved him again, then slapped on the lights. "I don't want conversation, and I don't want the dark."

"Right." For some reason he felt as if he'd just opened the door to a very hungry she-wolf. Her eyes were different. Greener, sharper. Predatory. His blood began to pump, quickly, helplessly. "I'll just . . . close these curtains."

"Leave them."

"Ripley." His laugh was a little strangled. "We're pretty isolated, but nonetheless, with the lights on—"

"Leave them." She yanked her sweater off in one quick move. "If you like that shirt, you'd better strip it off, and now. Otherwise, it's toast."

"You know"—he let out a breath, tried to work up an easy smile—"you're scaring me."

"Good. Be afraid."

She leaped at him, knocking him back on the bed. Hunching over him like a sleek cat.

She made some primitive sound in her throat as she bared her teeth. Then set them on his neck.

"Christ!" He went hard as rock.

"I want it fast," she panted, tearing open his shirt. "And rough. And now."

He reached for her, but she fisted her hands in his hair, yanked, then ravished his mouth. The sheer heat of her seared through him, scorching the nerves, stealing the breath, boiling the blood.

He spiraled down into the dark where pain and pleasure were twins, equally vital, equally irresistible. In response, the animal inside him lunged, straining at the end of its tether. Snapping it.

His body reared up beneath hers, and his hands were hard and bruising as they tore, and took. He yanked her hair, dragging her head back to expose her throat for his teeth.

It wasn't desperation that filled him. But appetite.

They rolled over the bed, fighting for more flesh, more heat.

She was alive with need, and all of it feral. Energy pumped through her, and all of it savage. Her nails raked at him, her teeth nipped. And when his fingers drove into her, her cry was one of fierce and greedy triumph.

Higher, was all she could think. Faster. She wanted peak after violent peak. Lights danced in her mind, a blinding silver shower. And the storm that fueled them, fueled her.

She slithered over him like a snake, straddled him. And filled herself.

It was like being consumed. Devoured whole. She closed over him like a fist, trapping him in hot, wet heat, holding him there by the power of her own climax. Staggered, he watched it rip through her, watched her body, pearled with sweat, bow back. And shudder, shudder.

And she began to move. Lightning fast. Her hair fell forward, a tangle of dense brown, as she leaned down, chewed restlessly on his bottom lip.

He pistoned himself into her, hard, fast strokes while his hands gripped her hips like a vise.

Then she leaned back, rode him ruthlessly to the barbed edge of peak.

"Not yet. Not yet," she panted.

Even as his vision blurred, as his system

strained toward that blessed release, she lifted her arms above her head, as she had done when she'd called her power. He felt the shock of it, like a red-tipped arrow through the haze of mad pleasure. Clean, sharp, and stunning as it pierced through her, and into him.

He lay like a dead man, but it didn't seem to matter. Dying for such an experience didn't seem too high a price to pay right at the moment.

He felt as though he'd been hulled out. Every care, every worry, every spare thought carved away to be replaced by pure sensation.

He might not be able to walk or speak or think again, but those were minor inconveniences. He was going to pass out of this world a very happy man.

Ripley made a little purring sound. Aha, he thought vaguely. He could still hear. That was a nice bonus. Then her mouth closed over his. His body could still register sensation. Better and better.

"Mac?"

He opened his mouth. Some sound came out. It wasn't words, but there were a great many forms of verbal communication. He'd make do.

"Mac?" she said again, and slid her hand down his body, closed her fingers over him.

Oh, yeah, he was definitely able to feel sensation.

"Uh-huh." He cleared his throat, managed to open one eye. He wasn't blind, after all. Another plus. "Yeah. I wasn't asleep." His voice was rusty, but there. And he realized his throat was desperate with thirst. "I was having a near-death experience. It wasn't bad."

"Now that you're back from beyond . . ." She slithered up his body again, and rendered him speechless when he saw she still had that gleam in her eye. "Again."

"Hey, well." He had some trouble breathing when her lips trailed down his chest. "You're going to have to give me a little time to recover, you know. Maybe a month."

She laughed, and the wicked sound of it rippled over his skin. "In that case, you're just going to have to lie there and take it."

Her mouth kept going. He melted into the bed. "Well, if I have to, I have to."

Ripley knew she was in trouble. She'd never shared power with a man before. Never felt the need or desire to do so. With Mac, it had been a kind of compulsion, a deep, drowning need to extend that intimacy, link that part of her with him.

There was no longer any doubt that she was in love with him, or any hope that she could rationalize it away.

Traditionally, Todds waited a long time to fall in love, and when they did it came hard and fast, and it was forever. It looked as if she was upholding the family name.

But she didn't have a clue what to do about it.

Right at the moment, she couldn't seem to care.

As for Mac, he felt slightly drunk and saw no reason to fight the sensation. The wind had started to rise. The sound of it shivering against the windows only made the cottage cozier. It was as if they were the only two people on the island. As far as he was concerned, it could stay that way.

"What was that stuff you wanted to tell me?"

"Hmm." He continued to play with her hair and thought he could happily stay under those tangled sheets with her for the rest of his life. "It can wait."

"Why? I'm here, you're here. I'm thirsty." She sat up, scooped her hair back. "Didn't you say something about wine?"

"Probably. You sure you're up for wine and conversation?"

She angled her head. "It's that, or you'll have to get up for something else."

As lowering as it was to admit it, he was certain if she jumped him again, he would never live through it. "I'll get the wine."

She laughed as he rolled out of bed. "Here." He pulled open a drawer, tossed her some sweats. "Might as well be comfortable."

"Thanks. Got any food?"

"Depends on your definition."

"Just some munchies. I've got a craving."

"Tell me about it. I've got potato chips."

"That'll do." She tugged on the sweatpants, adjusting the drawstring until she was reasonably sure they'd stay up.

"I'll dig them out."

When he was gone, she pulled on the sweatshirt and indulged herself by sniffing at the sleeves, exploring the sensation of wearing something that was his. It was foolish and female, she admitted, but nobody had to know about it but her.

When she walked into the kitchen, he already had the wine open, two glasses out, and a bag of chips on the counter. She snagged the chips, plopped down in a chair, and prepared to gorge.

"Let's not, ah . . . do this in here," Mac began. Nerves pricked at his bubble of contentment. He had no idea how she would react to what he had to tell her. That was just one of her fascinations for him—her unpredictability.

"Why?"

And there was another, he thought. She asked why nearly as often as he did himself. "Because we'll be more comfortable in the other room."

"The living room? We'll sit on your equipment?"

"Ha-ha. No, there's the couch, it's still in there. And we can get a fire going. Are your feet cold? Want some socks?"

"No, I'm fine." But he wasn't, she noted. Something was making him jumpy. She pondered it as she followed him back into the living room. Since they had to squeeze their way through to get to the sofa, she doubted he'd used it for its intended purpose since he'd taken over the cottage.

He put the wine on the floor, then began to move stacks of books off the cushions and set them aside. She opened her mouth to protest the trouble, then shut it again with an almost audible snap.

Wine, conversation, a cozy fire. Romantic. Just the sort of romantic setup, she imagined, a man might want when he told a woman he loved her.

Her heart began to beat thickly.

"Is this an important conversation?" she asked him through lips that felt trembly and soft.

"I think so." He hunkered down in front of the hearth. "I'm a little nervous about it. I didn't expect to be. I'm not sure how to start."

"You'll figure it out." Her legs wobbled a little, so she sat down.

He set logs, kindling, then glanced back at her. It took her a minute to clue in to his speculative look. What she thought of as his scientist look. "Yes, I could start it from here," she told him. "But I won't."

"Just wondering. Ah, lore holds that making fire is the basic form of magic, usually the first learned and the last lost. Would that be accurate?"

"I guess if you're talking about a tangible form, one that requires direction, focus, control." Because she felt hot and itchy, she shifted. "Mia's better than I am at explaining that sort of thing. I don't—haven't been—thinking about it for a long time. She never stops."

"That's probably why the control and philosophy come more naturally to her." He struck a long wooden match, set it against the starter. "Your power's more—I don't know—explosive, while hers is more centered."

He got to his feet as the flames began to lick, rubbed his hands on the hips of his jeans. "I'm trying to think how to approach what I want to tell you."

A flock of sparrows dive-bombed in her stomach. "You could just say it."

"I work better with a buildup." He bent down to pour the wine. "I had it pretty well set in my head before tonight. But, first seeing you, understanding to some extent what you went through, what you feel, then being with you. Ripley."

He sat beside her, handed her the wine, then touched the back of her hand. "I want you to know that it's never been like it is with you. Not with anyone else."

There were tears in her throat, and for the first time in her life she found the taste of them lovely. "It's different for me."

He nodded, felt a little hitch in his heart as he took that to mean she experienced intimacy differently because of what she was. "All right. Well, what I'm trying to say here is that because of what's—" He dragged a hand through his hair. "Because you matter, because what's between us matters to me, the rest of it is a little more complicated. I guess I'm concerned that, especially after I get into the rest, you might think you matter to me only because of my work. That's not true, Ripley. You just matter."

Everything smoothed out inside her, like silk brushed with a loving hand. "I don't think that. I wouldn't still be here if I did. I wouldn't want to be here, and I do."

He took her hand and, kissing her palm, sent a long, slow ripple sliding from her toes to her throat. "Mac . . ." she whispered.

"Originally I was going to tell Mia first, but I want to tell you."

"I—you—Mia?"

"Theoretically, she's the main connection. But it's all linked, anyway. Plus I realized I needed to tell you first." He kissed her hand again, somewhat absently this time, then sipped his wine like a man wetting his throat before preparing to lecture.

Her lovely mood went ragged at the edges. "I really think you'd better spit it out, Mac."

"Okay. Each one of the sisters had children. Some stayed on the island, others left, never to return. And others traveled, married, then came back to the island to raise their families. I imagine you know all that, and that their children did the same, and so on down the generations. As a result, some of their descendants have always remained on Three Sisters. But others scattered over the world."

"I don't know what you're getting at."

"I'd probably be better off showing you. Hold on a minute."

She watched him get up, then wind his way through the equipment. Hearing him curse lightly when he stubbed his toe gave her small, but vicious, satisfaction.

The son of a bitch, she thought, rapping her fisted hand on the cushion. He wasn't about to pledge his undying love, to pour out his heart, to beg her to marry him. He'd circled right back around to his stupid research while she'd been sitting there starry-eyed.

And whose fault is that? she reminded herself. She was the one who'd gotten it all twisted up. She was the one who'd left herself open for the clip on the jaw. *She* was the stupid one, the one who'd gone all mushy with love and stopped thinking clearly. She would just have to fix that.

Not the love. She was a Todd and accepted that she loved him and always would. But she certainly could get her head on straight again and start thinking.

He was the one meant for her, so he was going to have to deal with it. Dr. MacAllister Booke wasn't just going to study witches. He was damn well going to marry one. As soon as she figured out how to make him.

"Sorry." He skirted the equipment more carefully this time. "It wasn't where I thought I put it. Nothing ever is." His expression changed with the glittering look she sent him. "Ah . . . Something wrong?"

"No, not a thing." Playfully, she patted the cushion beside her. "I was just thinking it's a waste to sit alone in front of the fire." When he sat, she slid her leg intimately over his. "Much better."

"Well." His blood pressure began a steady rise as she leaned in and rubbed her lips over his jaw. "I thought you'd want to read this."

"Mmm. Why don't you read it to me?" She nibbled lightly on his earlobe. "You have such a sexy voice." She took the glasses out of his pocket. "And you know how turned on I get when you wear these."

He made some sound, then fumbled the glasses on. "These are, ah, photocopied pages. I have the original journal in a vault, because it's old and fragile. It was written by my great . . . well a number of greats, grandmother. On my mother's side. The first entry was made September 12, 1758, and written on Three Sisters Island."

Ripley jerked back. "What did you say?"

"I think you should just listen. 'Today,' " he read, " 'my youngest child had a child. They have named him Sebastian, and he is hale and healthy. I am grateful Hester and her fine young man are content to remain on the island, to make their home and family here. My other children are so far away now, and though from time to time I look into the glass to see them, my heart aches that I am unable to touch their faces, or the faces of my grandchildren.

" 'I will never leave the island again.

" 'This, also, I have seen in the glass. I have time yet on this earth, and I know death is not an end. But when I see this beauty of life in this babe of my babe, I am saddened that I will not be here to see him grown.' "

He risked a quick glance at Ripley, saw she was staring at him as if she'd never seen him before. Best to finish it all, he told himself. Just get it all out at one time.

" 'I am saddened that my own mother did not choose life,' " he continued, " 'that she denied herself the joy I have felt this day on seeing a child come from one of my own.

" 'Time moves swiftly. What comes from this boy will one day balance the scales, if our children remember and choose wisely.' "

Though she'd forgotten she held it, Ripley's knuckles were white on the stem of her glass. "Where did you get this?"

"Last summer I was going through some boxes in the attic of my parents' house. I found the journal. I'd been through those boxes before. I used to drive my mother crazy because I was always pawing through the old stuff. I don't know how I missed it, unless you subscribe to the theory that it wasn't there for me until last June."

"June." When a shudder worked through her, Ripley got to her feet. Nell had come to the island in June—and the three had linked. She sensed that Mac started to speak, and she held up a hand. She needed to focus.

"You're assuming this was written by an ancestor."

"Not assuming. I've done the genealogy, Ripley. Her name was Constance, and her youngest daughter, Hester, married James MacAllister on May 15, 1757. Their first child, a son, Sebastian Edward MacAllister, was born on Three Sisters Island. He fought in the Revolutionary War. Married, had children, settled in New York. The line runs down through my mother, and into me."

"You're telling me you're a descendant of . . ."

"I have all the documentation. Marriage records, birth records. You could say we're really distant cousins."

She stared at him, then turned to stare into the fire. "Why didn't you tell us when you first came here?"

"Okay, that's a little sticky." He wished she would sit back down, cuddle up against him again. But he didn't think that was going to happen until they got through this. "I thought I might have to use it as an incentive, a kind of bargaining chip."

"Your ace in the hole," she remarked.

"Yeah. If Mia put up roadblocks, I figured this information would be a good way to knock some of them down. But she didn't, and I started to feel uncomfortable about withholding it. I was going to tell her tonight. But I needed to tell you first."

"Why?"

"Because you matter. I realize you're ticked off, but—"

She shook her head. "Not really." Unsettled, she thought, but not angry. "I'd've done the same thing to get what I wanted."

"I didn't know you'd be here. You know

what I mean. You. I didn't know we'd be involved like this. I'm in what most people consider an illogical field. It's only more essential to approach it logically. But under it, on a personal level, I've been pulled to this place all my life without knowing where it was that I was being pulled. Last summer I finally knew."

"But you didn't come."

"I had to gather data, research, analyze, fact-check."

"Always the geek."

She sat on the arm of the couch. It was, he thought, a step. "I guess. I dreamed of the island. Before I knew where it was—or if it was—I dreamed of it. I dreamed of you. All of that was so strong, so much a part of my life, that I needed to approach it the way I'd been trained. As an observer, a recorder."

"And what do your observations tell you, Dr. Booke?"

"I've got reams of data, but I don't think you'd be interested in reading it." She shook her head at his questioning look. "Right. But I've also got one simple feeling. That I'm where I'm supposed to be. I have a part in this. I just don't know, yet, exactly what it is."

She was up again. "A part in what?"

"Balancing the scales."

"Do you believe, in that detail-filing brain of yours, that this island is doomed to fall into the sea? How can you buy some centuries-old curse? Islands don't just sink like swamped boats."

"There are a number of respected scholars and historians who would argue that point, using Atlantis as their example."

"Of which you would be one," she said sourly.

"Yeah, but before you get me started on that and I bore you senseless, let me just say that there's always room for less-than-literal interpretations. A force five hurricane, an earthquake—"

"Earthquake?" She'd felt the earth tremble under her feet. She'd *made* the earth tremble. And didn't want to think of it. "Jesus, Mac!"

"You don't want me to start on plates and pressure and shifts, do you?"

She opened her mouth, shut it again, and settled for shaking her head.

"Didn't think so. I've got degrees in geology and meteorology, and I can get really boring. Anyway, put simply, Nature's a bitch and she barely tolerates us."

She studied him consideringly. Earnest, sexy, quiet. Somehow unshakably confident. Hardly a wonder that she'd fallen for him.

"You know what? I bet you're not as boring when you get going as you think."

"You'd lose." Because he thought she would accept it now, he reached out to take her hand. "Heaven and Earth, Ripley, do more than hold us between them. They expect us to deserve it."

"And we have to decide how far we'll go."

"That pretty much wraps it up."

She puffed out her cheeks, blew out a breath. "It gets harder to tell myself this is all crap. First Nell, then you, and now this," she added glancing down at the copies of journal pages. "It starts to feel like somebody's added bars to a cage, so there's less and less chance of squeezing out again."

She frowned down at the pages as another thought sprang into her head. "You've got a blood connection to the Sisters." Her gaze flashed up to his. "Do you have magic?"

"No. Seems like a rip-off to me," he said.

"I may have inherited the interest, the fascination, but none of the practical usage."

She relaxed and slid down on the seat beside him. "Well, that's something at least."

Fifteen

Mia read the first journal entry while sitting at her desk in her office. A freezing rain had come in behind the wind and was now battering her window.

She'd dressed in bright, bold blue to dispel the gloom and wore the little stars and moons Nell had given her for her last birthday at her ears. As she read, she toyed with them, sending star colliding with moon.

When she'd finished the entry, she leaned back and studied Mac with amusement. "Well, hello, cousin."

"I wasn't sure how you'd take it."

"I try to take things as they come. May I keep these a while? I'd like to read the rest of them."

"Sure."

She set the pages aside, picked up her latté. "It's all so nice and tidy, isn't it?"

"I realize it's quite a coincidence," he began, but she stopped him.

"Coincidence is often what tidies things up. I can trace my family back to its start on the Sisters. I know some stayed, some scattered. And I remember now, there was a MacAllister branch. The one son, among three daughters. He left the island, survived a war, and began to make his fortune. Odd, isn't it, that I didn't think of that until now, or connect it with you? I suppose I wasn't meant to. Still, I felt something for you. A kinship. That's nice and tidy, too. And comforting."

"Comfort wasn't my first reaction when I put it all together."

"What was?"

"Excitement. Descended from a witch and a silkie. How cool is that?" He broke off a piece of the applesauce muffin she'd urged on him. "Then I was pretty irked that I didn't get any power out of the deal."

"You're wrong." The affection and admiration in her voice nearly made him flush. "Your mind is your power. The strength and the openness of that mind make very strong magic. Stronger yet because it doesn't close off your heart. We'll need both." She waited a beat. "She'll need you."

It gave him a jolt. Mia had said it so quietly, so simply. "Do me a favor and don't mention that to Ripley. It'll just piss her off."

"You understand her, recognize all of her various flaws, numerous shortcomings, and irritating habits. But you love her anyway."

"Yes, I . . ." He trailed off, set the muffin aside. "That was very sneaky."

"I'd apologize, but I wouldn't mean it." Her laughter was too warm and soft to sting. "I thought you were in love with her, but I wanted to hear you say it. Can you be happy living on the island?"

He said nothing for a moment. "You really know her, don't you? Ripley would never be happy anywhere else. So, yes, I can be happy here. I've been heading here all my life, in any case."

"I like you, very much. Enough to wish, just a little, that it had been me you were meant for. And you," she added when he looked slightly panicked, "who'd been meant for me. Since neither of those things is, I'm glad we can be friends. I think you'll help each other find the best you can be."

"You really love her, don't you?"

For an instant, Mia's calm ruffled. Color washed her cheeks, a rare occurrence. Then she shrugged. "Yes, nearly as much as I'm irritated by her. Now, I trust you'll keep that to yourself as I keep your feelings to myself."

"Deal."

"And to seal it—" She rose and turned to the shelves behind her. She took down a carved wooden box and, opening it, removed a star-shaped pendant of silver, set with a sunstone.

"This has been in my family—our family," she corrected, "since we began here on the Sisters. It's said that she who was mine forged the pendant from a fallen star and the stone from a sunbeam. I've kept it for you."

"Mia—"

But she only kissed him lightly and slipped the chain over his head. "Blessed be, cousin."

Harding paid one more visit to Evan Remington. His plans were set, his schedule outlined. But he felt it imperative to see Remington again before he left.

He felt an odd kinship with the man. The realization of it was both appalling and alluring to him. Remington was a kind of monster. And yet . . .

Didn't all men have that beast lurking inside them? The sane, the civilized—and Harding considered himself both—restrained it. Controlled it.

He supposed it only made those who did neither—who indulged it, kept it fed and ready—more fascinating.

He told himself that his regular visits to Remington were research. Business. But in truth, he had come to find those frequent brushes with evil thrilling.

We were all one step away from the pit, Harding thought, composing notes in his head as he waited to be admitted. Only by observing, by learning from those who had fallen, would we understand what waited for us on the other side of sanity.

Harding stepped into the visitation room, heard the echo of the lock. Is that the last sound we hear as we fall? he wrote in his head. The hopeless shooting of the bolt?

Remington wasn't restrained this time. Harding had already been told that as part of his treatment and rehabilitation, Remington had been taken off full restraints. He'd exhibited no violence to others or himself and had been responsive and cooperative in recent sessions.

The room was small, and nearly empty. One table with two chairs. While the restraints were missing, Harding heard the bright jingle of chain from the cuff on Remington's right wrist. There was a third chair in the corner, occupied now by a broad-shouldered, pasty-faced guard.

Security cameras recorded every sound and movement.

The pit, Harding thought, whatever name we gave it, offered no privacy and little comfort.

"Mr. Remington."

"Evan." Today you could hardly see the madness. "After all this, we can hardly be formal. I'll call you Jonathan. Do you know, Jonathan, you're the only one who comes to talk to me? They tell me my sister's been here. But I don't remember. I remember you."

The voice was quiet but perfectly clear. Harding experienced a small inward shudder as he remembered just how Remington had looked and sounded on his first visit.

He was still thin, and too pale, his hair lank.

But Harding thought if you put him back in a designer suit and shipped him off to L.A., his associates would take a look and simply think he'd been working a bit too hard.

"You're looking well. Evan."

"Hardly my best, but one must take the facilities into account." A muscle twitched in his cheek. "I don't belong here. My attorneys bungled the entire business. But I've taken care of that. Dealt with that. Stupid, incompetent bastards. I've fired them. I expect to have new representation within the week. And my freedom shortly after."

"I see."

"I think you do." Remington leaned forward, then he gazed up toward the security cameras. "I think you do see. I was defending myself and mine." His eyes stayed on Harding's now, and something dark seemed to swim behind their colorless surface.

"I was betrayed and misused. Those who stood against me, they belong in here. Not I."

Harding couldn't look away, couldn't break the connection. "Your ex-wife?"

"My wife," Remington corrected, then in barely a whisper mouthed, "Till death do us part. Tell her I'm thinking of her when you see her, won't you?"

"I beg your pardon?"

"You can't finish what you've started, you can't get what you want, until you deal with her, and the rest of them. I've thought about it." Remington nodded slowly and his eyes, pale as water, stayed locked on Harding's. "I have plenty of time for thinking. I need someone to remind her I haven't forgotten. I need someone to show them all that I can't be ignored. An agent, if you will."

"Mr. Remington. Evan. I'm a reporter. A writer."

"I know what you are. I know what you want. Fame, fortune, recognition. Respect. I know how to get those things for you. I made it my business to get those things for others. You want to be a star, Jonathan. I make stars."

Something seemed to move behind his eyes again, like sharks swimming in a deep pool. Harding shuddered, but couldn't look away. And as his skin crawled cold, he could feel himself being pulled in. His breath came short beneath a terrible pressure in his chest.

"I'm going to write a book."

"Yes, yes. An important book. You'll tell it as it's meant to be told. End it as it needs to be ended. I want them punished." He reached over with his free hand, clasped Harding's limp fingers. "I want them dead."

Something snapped in the air, sizzled, and brought the guard to his feet. "No contact."

"Thou shalt not suffer a witch to live," Harding said dully as a fierce grin flashed on Remington's face.

"No physical contact," the guard ordered and strode toward the table. But Remington was already breaking his grip.

"I'm sorry." Remington kept his gaze averted, his head lowered. "I forgot. I just wanted to shake his hand. He comes to visit me. He comes to talk to me."

"We were just saying good-bye." To his own ears, Harding's voice sounded tinny with distance. "I have to take a trip, and won't be able to visit for a while. I have to go now." Harding got unsteadily to his feet. A headache blasted in his temples.

Remington lifted his gaze one last time. "I'll see you again."

"Yes, of course."

Remington allowed himself to be led away. He kept his head lowered, shuffled obligingly back to his cell. In his heart, black glee bloomed like a fetid flower. For he had discovered that there was power in madness.

By the time Harding was on the ferry for Three Sisters, he could barely remember his last visit to Remington. It irritated him, made him worry that he was coming down with something. His memory for details was one of his most polished skills. And now an event less than eight hours old was like some sketchy scene behind foggy glass.

He couldn't remember what they'd spoken of, only that he'd been suddenly struck with a blinding headache. It had made him so ill, he'd been forced to stretch out on the front seat of his car and wait for the chills, the pain, the nausea to pass before he'd dared drive away.

Even now, just thinking of it gave him the shakes. His condition wasn't helped by the fact that the seas were rough and a needle-sharp icy rain was pounding. He had to huddle inside his car, dry-swallow more seasickness pills.

He was terrified that he would have to

race through that vicious rain and vomit into the pitching sea.

In defense, he once more lay down across the seat, fighting to breathe slowly and evenly. He began to count the minutes until he reached solid land again.

And must have fallen asleep.

He dreamed of snakes sliding under his skin, the slither of them ice cold.

Of a woman with blue eyes and long gold hair who cried out—all pain and pleas—as he brought a cane down, again and again, to batter her.

She's quiet now. Quiet now. Spawn of Satan.

Of a bolt of blue lightning that shot like an arrow out of the sky and into his heart.

He dreamed of terror and vengeance and hate.

He dreamed of a lovely woman in a white dress who wept as she curled on a marble floor.

Of a wood, dark under a new moon, where he stood holding a knife to a smooth white throat. And this time, when it sliced clean and her blood covered him, the world erupted. The sky split and the sea opened its mouth wide, to swallow all who had stood against him.

He awoke with screams strangling in his throat, slapping at himself as if to kill whatever was crawling inside him. For an instant he stared horrified in the rearview mirror.

And eyes that weren't his, eyes pale as water, stared back.

Then the ferry let out its blasting note to herald the docking on Three Sisters. The eyes that stared back at him as he dragged out his handkerchief to wipe his damp face were red-rimmed, haunted, and his own.

Just caught a little bug, he assured himself. He'd been working too hard, traveling too much. Crossing time zones too often. He would take a day or two to rest, to let his system catch up.

Bolstered by the idea, he snapped on his seat belt, started his car. And drove off the ferry ramp and onto Three Sisters Island.

The storm turned into a gale. On the second day of it, Mac surfaced from his work and took a good look around. He'd had another shipment of books sent in, and replacement parts for some of his equipment. Right now he had pieces of a sensor spread all over the little kitchen table. A monitor that was acting up stood on the counter with its guts spilling out.

The kitchen still smelled of the eggs he'd burned that morning—which, he had to admit, he'd had no business making when his mind was elsewhere.

He'd broken a glass, too. And had a nice slice in his heel, since he'd gotten distracted before he swept it all up.

He'd turned the entire cottage into a lab, which wasn't so bad. But without a lab assistant cleaning things up behind him, he'd also turned it into a disaster.

He really didn't mind working in a disaster area, but it certainly wouldn't do as a permanent living arrangement.

If the cottage was too small to accommodate him and his work on more than the short term, it was certainly too small to accommodate a . . .

Ripley, he thought quickly. He wasn't quite ready to use the term "wife," even in his thoughts.

Not that he didn't want to marry her, because he did. And not because he doubted she would marry him. He would just wait her out in that area until she caved. He'd match his patience against her stubbornness any day of the week.

But first things first.

When a man wanted to settle down permanently, he had to find a place to settle. However much affection he had for the cottage, it wouldn't fill the bill. And he doubted seriously if Mia would sell it.

He rose, and managed not only to tread on a screw but to step on it at the exact point of his recent cut. He spent a little time on some inventive cursing and hobbled out to find the shoes he'd thought he'd already put on.

He found a pair in the bedroom doorway, where they had obviously planted themselves, cagily waiting for him to trip over them.

And holding them, took a look at the bedroom. Winced.

He didn't usually live like a slob. Okay, he admitted, he didn't usually *intend* to live like a slob. It just happened.

Forgetting the shoes, he pushed up his sleeves. He would shovel out the bedroom and use the manual labor to clear his mind. He needed to think about a house.

It needed to be a pretty good size so his equipment didn't get in everybody's way. He would need an office, too.

Not entirely sure when he might have changed his sheets last, he decided to err on the side of caution and stripped them off.

It would be good if there was space to set up weights and exercise equipment. Ripley would want some space of her own, too, he imagined, and started gathering up socks, shirts, underwear. Somewhere she could get away from him when he started to drive her crazy.

His mother called hers an escape hatch, he remembered, and reminded himself to phone home.

He carted the laundry to the tiny room off the kitchen, missed stepping on the same screw by a hair, and stuffed everything that would fit into the washing machine. He added soap, then deciding he should write down some of the basic house require-ments, wandered out to find a pad and for-got to turn on the washing machine.

Three bedrooms minimum, he thought. Four would be better.

Someplace close to the water. Not that anywhere on the island was far from it, but

Ripley was used to living right on the beach so . . .

"Booke, you idiot! It's staring you right in the face. You knew the first time you saw it."

He dashed to the phone and dialed long distance information. "New York City," he told the operator. "I need the number for Logan Enterprises."

An hour later, to celebrate what he considered the first step in becoming a homeowner, he braved the elements. Thaddeus Logan hadn't jumped at the offer, but he hadn't dismissed it out of hand, either.

It hadn't hurt that Logan was acquainted with Mac's father. Connections within connections, Mac thought as he hissed in his breath and decided to walk to Café Book rather than risk the iced-over roads in his Rover.

He had a good feeling about it, and he was certain Logan would negotiate. Which reminded Mac—he should call his father for advice in that area. The one thing he was sure of was if you wanted something too much, and the other party knew it, you were asking to get skinned.

He needed to do some research on real estate values in the area, and he patted his pockets absently, hoping for a handy piece of paper to make a note to himself.

Not that the money mattered all that much, but the principle did. And he imagined that if he let himself get taken, Ripley would get torqued about it. That would start the whole process off on a bad note.

Tomorrow, Mac promised himself, he would take a drive and get another good look at what was going to be theirs.

Delighted with the idea, he strolled along, head down, as the wind screamed in his ears and the ugly mix of ice and snow swirled and spat.

Just look at him, Ripley thought. Out in this mess when he doesn't have to be. Not looking where he's going and bopping along as if it's a sunny day in July.

The man needs a keeper.

She would just have to take on the job.

She started toward him, then judging time and distance, planted herself. And let him walk straight into her.

"Jeez." Since she was braced and he

wasn't, he went skidding. Reflexively he grabbed her, and that took them both on a fast slide. "Sorry."

But she was laughing, and the little elbow jab she gave him was friendly. "How many walls do you walk into on your average day?"

"I don't count. It's demoralizing. Gosh, you're pretty." He grabbed her again, but was steady this time. Lifting her to her toes, he planted a long, warm kiss on her mouth.

Her system tilted, sweetly. "What I am is cold and wet. My nose is red, and my toes are ice cubes. Zack and I just spent a miserable hour out on the coast road. We've got power lines down, and cars off the road, and the best part of a tree through Ed Sutter's workshop roof."

"Nice work if you can get it."

"Very funny. I think the worst of it'll blow out by tomorrow," she said, looking, as islanders had for centuries, out to sea and sky. Both were gray as pewter. "But we're going to be cleaning up after this one for a while yet. What the hell are you doing out here? You lose power?"

"It was on when I left. I wanted some decent coffee." He clued in to the direction from which she'd come, and the direction she'd been going. "Were you coming to check on me?"

"It's my job to check on the residents of our happy little rock."

"That's really considerate of you, Deputy Todd. How about I buy you a cup of coffee?"

"I could use it, and someplace warm and dry for ten minutes."

He took her hand as they headed into the wind up High Street. "How about if I buy a quart of soup and whatever, take it home? We can have dinner at my place later."

"Chances of the power lasting in the cottage through the night are slim. We've got a generator at our place. Why don't you pack what you need and plan on staying there tonight?"

"Is Nell cooking?"

"Is grass green?"

"I'm there." He pulled open the door for her.

Like magic, Lulu popped out from behind a bookshelf. "I should've known it was a couple of lunatics. Sensible people are home whining about the weather."

"Why aren't you?" Ripley asked.

"Because there are just enough lunatics

on this island to keep the store open. Got a few of them up in the café right now."

"That's where we're heading. Did Nell go home?"

"Not yet. Mia cut her loose, but she's sticking. Didn't see why Peg should have to come out in this when she was already here. We're closing early, in an hour, anyhow."

"Good to know."

Ripley pulled off her soaked cap as she started up the stairs. "Do me a favor?" she said to Mac.

"Sure."

"Can you hang around till closing, make sure Nell gets home safe?"

"Glad to."

"Thanks. It'll be a load off. I can let Zack know, and he won't worry."

"I'll ask her to come by my place, help me get my stuff together."

Ripley shot him a smirk. "Pretty smart, aren't you?"

"People are always saying so." He kept her hand in his as they walked to the café counter.

"Zack just called," Nell told them. "You've had a hell of a day, haven't you?"

"Goes with the territory. You can give me

two large coffees to go, and I'll take one back to him. This guy's springing for them," she added, jerking a thumb at Mac.

"A large for me, too, but I'll have it here. And . . . is that apple pie?"

"It is. Want a slice warm?"

"Oh, yeah."

Ripley leaned on the counter, idly scanning the café. "I better tell you I invited Mac's appetite to dinner, and to bunk over."

"We're having chicken pot pie."

Mac's face lit up. "Homemade chicken pot pie?"

Nell laughed as she fit tops on the takeout cups. "You're too easy."

Ripley shifted her body away from the table area. "Who's the guy sitting by himself?" she asked Nell. "Brown sweater, city boots."

"I don't know. It's the first time he's been in. I got the impression he was staying at the hotel. He came in about a half hour ago."

"Did you chat him up?"

Nell cut a generous slab of pie for Mac. "I spoke with him in a friendly manner. He came in on the ferry a couple of days ago, just beat the nor'easter. People do come here, Ripley."

"It's just an odd time for a slicker to head over. No business groups at the hotel now. Anyway." She took the cups Nell set on the counter. "Thanks. See you later," she said to Mac, and might have warded off the kiss if her hands hadn't been full.

"Be careful out there." He yanked her cap out of her pocket and tugged it onto her head.

Harding watched the byplay from behind the newspaper he'd brought over from the hotel. He'd recognized Ripley Todd from his files. Just as he'd recognized Nell. It didn't explain his reaction to both.

He'd expected to feel a nice zing of anticipation as he lined up the players on the stage. Instead, in each case he'd felt nearly ill. A kind of white-hot fury had pumped through him when he'd topped the steps and seen Nell back at the café counter.

He'd been forced to turn away, to walk behind bookshelves until he had himself under control. There he'd sweated like a pig. And had imagined his hands closing around her throat.

The violence of the experience had nearly caused him to turn around and leave. But it had passed, almost as swiftly as it had come. And he'd remembered his purpose.

The story, the book. Fame and fortune.

He'd been able to approach the counter, to order lunch, with his usual calm. He wanted a day or two to observe her and the others before he attempted to interview them.

He'd already lost some time. For the first twenty-four hours on the island, whatever bug he'd picked up had plagued him. He had been able to do little more than lie in bed, sweating his way through vivid and unpleasant dreams.

But he'd felt better by that afternoon. Nearly himself again.

He was still shaky, Harding told himself. There was no doubt about that. But a little food and a little exercise would help right him.

The soup had certainly soothed his system, at least until the brunette had walked in.

Then the clamminess had come back. The headache, the unexplained rage. He had the strangest image of her, pointing a gun at him, shouting at him, and he'd wanted to leap up and pummel her face with his fists.

Then another, fast on its heels, where she loomed over him in a storm, her hair blowing and tipped with light, and a sword that gleamed like silver gripped in her hands.

He thanked God she was leaving, and that the strange mood was leaving with her.

Still, his hand trembled as he picked up his spoon again.

Ripley brought Zack his coffee and sipped her own while he finished a phone call. As she paced she heard him reassuring someone about the storm, emergency procedures, medical aid.

Had to be a new resident, Ripley thought. Probably the Carters, who'd moved on-island in September. There was no one else new enough to the Sisters to panic over a midwinter storm.

"Justine Carter," Zack confirmed when he hung up. "Storm's making her buggy."

"She'll get used to it, or head back to the mainland before next winter. Listen, I told

Mac to come to our place tonight. Power's bound to go."

"Good idea."

"And I asked him to hang at the book-store until Nell leaves, to make sure she gets home okay."

"And an even better one. Thanks. What's up?"

"Maybe the storm's making me buggy. I got an itch over this guy I saw at the café. Can't pin it down. City. New boots, mani-cure, upper-end-department-store clothes. Late forties. Strong build, but he looked a little sickly to me. Pale, sweaty."

"Flu runs around this time of year."

"Yeah, well. I thought I'd go by the hotel, see if I can wheedle some information on him."

Because he trusted Ripley's instincts, Zack pointed to the phone. "Call them and save yourself another trip out in this mess."

"No, I'll get more in person. He gave me the jitters, Zack," she admitted. "The guy was just sitting there reading his paper and eating his lunch, but he gave me the jitters. I want to check it out."

"Okay. Let me know."

Sixteen

Procedures, taken in planned steps after calculations and hypotheses. The tools of his work. Science, even that still considered out of the mainstream. These were all familiar to him. They were, had always been to Mac, a kind of comfort as well as a path to discovery.

For the first time since he'd started on that path, he was uneasy.

He'd never worried overmuch about taking risks, as nothing worthwhile could be gained without them. But each step he took now pushed him farther down a strange and fascinating road. One he wasn't traveling solo.

"Are you sure you want to do this?"

Nell shifted her gaze up to where Mac leaned over the top of her head. "I'm sure."

"It's just that I don't want you to feel obliged." He attached the next electrode. "Don't think you have to be polite to the crazy man. You can just tell me to forget it."

"Mac. I don't think you're crazy, and I don't feel polite. I feel interested."

"That's good." He skirted around the sofa where she was stretched out, looked down at her. As he'd told her once before, she sparkled. She was also, he sensed, very open. "I'm going to be careful. I'm going to go slow. But anytime you want to stop, you just say so. And that's it."

"Got it, and I will." Her dimples fluttered. "Stop worrying about me."

"It's not just you." At her questioning look, he dragged a hand through his hair. "Everything I do now, even somehow what I don't do, affects Ripley. I don't know how I know that. It's not really logical. But I know it."

"You're connected," Nell said softly. "As I am. Neither of us will do anything to hurt her." She touched a hand to the back of his. "But both of us will, more than likely, do things that will annoy her. I guess we'll just have to handle it."

"I guess we will. Okay, well . . ." He gestured vaguely with the two electrodes in his hands. "I need to put these . . . You see, we'll need to monitor your heart rate, so . . ."

She looked at the little white adhesive, back up at his face. "Ah."

"If you feel uncomfortable or weird about that, we'll just skip that part."

She studied his expression and decided the only man she trusted more than the one currently trying not to look embarrassed was her husband. "In for a penny," she said and unbuttoned her blouse.

He was quick, efficient, and gentle.

"Just relax and be comfortable. We'll get your resting rates."

He turned away from her to work with the machines that he'd hauled over from the cottage. He hadn't intended to bring them, or to do the test—not yet. But when Nell had come back to the cottage with him, she'd asked questions. Polite interest at first, he thought, then more direct, more detailed.

Before either of them realized it, they were discussing physical reactions of magic. Brain-wave patterns, lobes, pulse rates. And she was agreeing to participate in a series of tests.

"So, where'd you learn to cook?"

"My mother. That's where my interest started. After we lost my father, she started her own catering business."

He adjusted dials, watched the graph. "Ever think about opening a restaurant?"

"I gave it a passing thought, but I don't want the structure or the limitations. I like my catering operation, and working in Mia's café. Though I am toying with ideas there. I think we—she," Nell corrected, "could expand a bit. Outdoor seating in the season. Maybe a cooking club. I'm going to talk to her about it when I have it more formulated in my mind."

"You've got a head for business."

"Oh, absolutely." And she said it with no small sense of pride. "I ran that end of my mother's operation. I like to organize."

"And create. You create with your cooking."

She dimpled again, with sheer pleasure. "That's a nice thing to say."

"It's a gift, like your power is a gift." Her vital signs were steady and stable. He checked the readout on the EKG, made some quick notes on his laptop.

"I wonder when you knew you were gifted. It seems to me Mia was born knowing."

"She was. We've talked about it."

"And Ripley."

"She doesn't talk about it as much, but I think it was almost the same. A knowing, always."

And a burden? he wondered. Always? "For you?"

"A discovery, and a learning process. I had dreams when I was a child, of this place, of people I'd yet to meet. But I never thought of them as—I don't know—memories or foretelling. Then, after Evan . . ." Her hands tensed, deliberately relaxed again. "I forgot them, or blocked them. When I left, my only clear thought was to run, to get away. But the dreams started coming back."

"Did they frighten you?"

"No, not at all. They were a comfort at first, then a kind of need. One day I saw a painting—the lighthouse, the cliffs, Mia's home—and I needed to be there. It was a . . . a destination. Do you know what it's like to find out where it is you finally need to be?"

He thought of the house near the cove. "Yes. I do exactly."

"Then you know it's not just a relief, but a thrill. I drove onto the ferry that day in June, and when I caught my first glimpse of the Sisters, I thought—there. *Finally.* I could belong there."

"You recognized it."

"Part of me did. Another part just yearned. Then I met Mia, and everything began."

He continued to monitor her, one part of his brain ruthlessly calculating changes, peaks, dips. "Would you say she tutored you?"

"Yes, though she would say she just reminded me." Nell turned her head so she could look at Mac. How cool he looks, she realized. Cool and controlled. And yet his voice was warm, friendly. "The first time she helped me try magic, I stirred the air."

"How did it feel?"

"Amazing, exciting. And, somehow, familiar."

"Could you do it now?"

"Now?"

"If you're comfortable with it. Nothing major. I don't want you to spin your furniture around. A little ripple for my readings."

"You're such an interesting man, Mac."

"Excuse me?"

"Just a little ripple for your readings," she said with a chuckle. "No wonder Ripley's crazy about you."

"What?"

"Here, then. A little ripple in the air, just a stir from here to there. A quiet breeze, this man to please."

Even before it began, the readings popped. Like a gathering, Mac thought, noting the rise of heart rate, the fluctuation in brain-wave patterns.

Then they jumped again as the air, well, rippled.

"Fabulous! Look at this pattern! I knew it. It's not just an increase in brain activity. It's like an expansion, almost fully right brain. Creativity, imagination. Really neat."

Nell chuckled again, and stilled the air. Not so cool now, Dr. Booke. "Is it what you were looking for?"

"It goes a long way toward confirming some of my theories. Could you do something else? Something more complicated.

Not that what you just did was small potatoes," he added quickly. "Something that requires more effort."

"More of a punch?"

"There you go."

"Let me think." Her lips bowed up as she considered. Because she wanted him to be surprised, she did the chant in her head, a call to the senses that was both sweet and stunning.

This time the gathering came faster, and bigger. The needle on the EKG graph whipped in wide, rapid sweeps. Suddenly, the room was alive with music—harps, pipes, flutes. It was drenched in a rainbow of colors and tender with the scent of spring.

He could barely keep up with the changes. Desperate to be certain that he had it all on record, he checked his camera, his monitors, nearly danced around the EKG.

"You like it?" Nell asked playfully.

"It's fucking great! Sorry, beg your pardon. Can you just keep it going another minute?" he asked as he checked his energy sensor. "It's really pretty, by the way."

"I'm eager for spring."

"Me, too, after the last two days. Respiration's up, but not that much. Pulse strong, steady. Physical exertion appears to be minimal. Hmm, heart rate's actually back at rest. Did the use of power calm her, or the result?"

"The result," Nell answered.

He blinked and focused on her again. "What?"

"You were talking to yourself, but I think I know the answer." She laughed lightly when she saw Diego prance into the room to bat playfully at her rainbows. "It's a soothing spell. It relaxes me."

"Yeah?" Interested, he sat down on the floor beside her while harp strings wept. "Would you say your physical reactions reflect the nature of the spell or charm?"

"Exactly."

"So, for example, the other night, in the clearing, it was more powerful, maybe edgier, because of what you were doing, and the fact that the three of you were together."

"It's always stronger with the three of us. I feel like I could move mountains. Afterward, I stay energized for hours."

He remembered just how Ripley had

channeled her energy and cleared his throat. "Okay. How are you able to sustain this spell while I'm distracting you with conversation?"

She looked completely blank for a moment. "I never thought about it. That was clever of you. I didn't know you were distracting me. Let me think . . . It's just there?" she suggested. "No, that's not completely accurate. It's more like the way you're able to do two different things at one time."

"Like patting your head and rubbing your stomach."

"No," she responded. "More like . . . cooking a roast and setting the table. You can keep your mind on the one so you don't burn it and still manage the other easily enough."

"What's nine times six?"

"Fifty-four. Oh, I see, left-brain function. I'm good with numbers."

"Recite the alphabet backward."

Concentrating, she began. Twice she fumbled, backtracked, hesitated, but the music and color never faltered.

"Are you ticklish?"

Suspicion flickered over her face. "Why?"

"I want to try a physical distraction." He squeezed a hand on her knee, made her yelp and jolt, just as Ripley and Zack came through the door.

"What the hell is going on?"

Hearing Ripley's voice made Mac wince and curse himself for not paying attention to the time. Then, realizing he still had his hand on Nell's knee—and her husband was armed—he quickly removed it.

"Um."

"From the looks of it," Zack said with a wink at Nell, "this guy's making time with my wife." As Lucy had come into the house with him, he leaned down casually to rub her head as she sniffed the air and batted her tail. "I guess I have to take him outside and kick his ass."

"Get in line," Ripley said and reminded Mac that she was armed as well.

"I, ah . . . Nell agreed to participate in a couple of tests," he began.

"That's not quite true," Nell corrected, and succeeded in making all the blood drain out of Mac's face. His sudden stricken look made her whoop with laughter. "I *volunteered* to participate."

"Would you mind turning off the entertainment portion of your little program?" Ripley said coolly.

"All right." Nell closed the spell, and there was a moment of complete silence.

"So . . ." Zack began to strip off his coat. "What's for dinner?"

"You can help me with that." Nell spoke brightly. "As soon as I'm unhooked from these things."

"Oh, sorry. Let me . . ." Mac started to reach for the electrodes monitoring her heart rate, then pulled his hands back as if he'd burned them. "Nobody's going to shoot me in the back, are they?" he asked Nell.

"I can promise Zack won't. He was just teasing you."

"He's not who I'm worried about." As delicately as possible, he unhooked her, and kept his gaze discreetly averted as she buttoned her blouse again.

"That was fun," Nell said as she got up. "And informative. Zack, why don't you give me a hand in the kitchen? Now!"

"All right, all right. I hate missing the fun," he complained as she dragged him off.

"Okay, Booke, why don't you try explaining to me why I shouldn't start swinging?"

"Because violence is never a sensible solution?"

Her answer to that was a low, dangerous growl. He stopped shutting down his equipment and turned to her. "Okay, I figure you're ticked off on a couple of levels, so I'll pick one to start. There was no funny business going on between me and Nell. It was completely professional."

"Son, if I thought otherwise you'd be braying like a jackass."

"Right." He took his glasses off, to see her more clearly, and because if she decided to try to deck him, he didn't want them broken. "You're angry because I brought equipment here and ran tests on Nell."

"Bingo. I invited you here, to my home. It's not a goddamn lab."

"It's also Nell's home," he pointed out. "I wouldn't have brought anything if she hadn't agreed."

"You wheedled her."

"I can wheedle when I have to," he said equably. "I didn't have to. The fact is, she was interested. She's exploring herself, and this is part of it. I'm sorry it upsets you; I was afraid it would. And if I'd been paying more attention to the time, I'd have shut it all down before you got home."

"So you'd have hidden it from me? That's a nice touch."

His own temper rumbled. "Tough to win with you, Deputy. No, I've never hidden my work from you, and I wouldn't have done so now. But I'd have tried to respect your feelings about it, as I've tried to do from the start."

"Then why—"

He cut her off by holding up one finger. "The simple fact is, this *is* my work, and you have to deal with that. But this is your home, and my being here under these circumstances upsets you. I'll apologize for that. It'll only take me about fifteen minutes to break this down and get it out. I'll tell Nell I'll take a rain check on dinner."

"Oh, stop being such a jerk."

"You know, Ripley, you just keep pushing and pushing until nobody wins."

When he turned away to remove his camera from the tripod, she reached up, pulled her own hair until the sharp pain cleared her head. "Maybe I do. I didn't ask you to leave."

"What are you asking?"

"I don't know! I come home after a pisser of a day, I'm tired and I'm irritable, and I walk in on you doing your mad scientist routine with Nell, who's obviously not only cooperating but enjoying the hell out of it. I wanted a damn beer and a hot shower, not a confrontation."

"Understandable. I can only apologize for the timing. It doesn't change the fact that this is what I do."

"No, it doesn't." Nor, she realized with a twinge, did it change the fact that she'd jumped down his throat because of it. That he'd *expected* her to.

Not only was she being a bitch, she was being a predictable bitch. It was lowering.

"You missed a level."

He packed his camera, closed up his laptop. "Which is?"

"I want to know why you didn't ask me."

"I couldn't ask you if you'd mind if I ran tests with Nell because you weren't here to be asked."

"No, why didn't you ask me to run them with you?" As he stopped unhooking cables to stare at her, she shrugged. "I think it's rude that you went to Nell before you came to me."

Just when he thought he had her pegged, she changed the pattern on him. "Would you have agreed?"

"I don't know." She huffed out a breath. "Maybe. I'd have thought about it, anyway. But you didn't ask."

"Are you serious, or are you just using this angle to twist things up so I come out being a jerk?"

There was no arguing that however geeky he might be from time to time, his mind was a scalpel that cut through all the bullshit in one swipe. "The jerk part's just a side benefit. I shouldn't have jumped on you that way. Taken jabs at you and your work. I'm sorry for it."

"Now you're apologizing. I have to sit down."

"Don't milk it, Booke." But she went to him, laid her hands on his arms. "Why don't you get us those beers, then while I'm taking that hot shower you can explain to me what all this stuff's for. Maybe I'll let you use it on me."

"I can do that." He reached up to take her hands before she could slide them away. "But I have a question first. Why are you considering it now?"

"Because it's like you said. It's your work, your deal. I respect you, Mac. So it looks like I'm going to have to start respecting what you do."

Not one of his professional or academic accolades had ever given him such pleasure as that one hard-won statement did. He stepped closer to her, framed her face with his hands. "Thank you."

"You're welcome. You're still a jerk."

"Understood." He felt her lips curve into a smile under his when he kissed her.

"Paranormal science—"

"Now, see, there you lose me, right at the kickoff," Ripley complained. "Because to me that's an oxymoron."

They were in her bedroom, with her sitting cross-legged on the bed while he set up his equipment.

"There was a time when astronomy was considered outside the mainstream. If science doesn't push the accepted scope, study the possibilities, it stagnates. We don't learn anything by standing still."

"Science and education are part of what

turned magic from the acceptable into the condemned, then into the dismissed."

"You're right, but I would add ignorance, intolerance, and fear to that mix. It's science and education that may, in time, turn the tide back again."

"They hunted us down, slaughtered us and countless others."

It was in her voice, he thought. Cold rage, hot fear. "You can't forgive that?"

"Could you?" She moved her shoulders restlessly. "I don't dwell on it, but it pays to remember what can happen when fingers start to point."

"You're worried about what might happen to you if outsiders look too close."

"I can take care of myself. Just as the sisters took care of themselves. Do you know how many witches were hanged in Salem Town, Mac? None," she said before he could speak. "All were innocent, powerless victims."

"So you're a cop," he said, "because you've chosen to protect the innocent and the powerless as others once weren't protected."

She started to speak, then just hissed out

her breath. "You don't have to be a super-hero to keep order on Three Sisters."

"That's not the point, though, is it? You protect, Mia educates—books—and Nell nurtures. You've all chosen to do what you can to heal old wounds. To balance."

"That's all a little deep for me."

He ran his hand gently over her hair before he bent down to hook up cables.

The gesture, the simple gentleness of it, loosened every muscle in her body.

"Have you ever been hypnotized?"

Just as that question tightened all her muscles up again. "No. Why?"

He glanced back at her. Briefly, casually. "I'd like to try it. I'm licensed."

"You didn't do that weird stuff with Nell."

"I'll ignore the word *weird*. No, I didn't use hypnosis with Nell. I didn't want to push it. But you and I have a different relationship and, I like to think, a different level of trust. I wouldn't hurt you."

"I know that. It probably wouldn't work on me, anyway."

"That's part of what I'd like to see. It's a simple process, based on relaxation techniques, and perfectly safe."

"I'm not afraid—"

"Good. Why don't you lie down?"

"Just wait." Panic ticked at her throat. "How come you can't just follow the same routine you did downstairs with Nell before dinner?"

"I could. I'd like to add a few tests, if you're willing. First, I'm interested in seeing if your gift makes you more, or less, susceptible to hypnosis. And if you can be hypnotized, if you're able to demonstrate power in that state."

"Have you considered that in that state I might not have perfect control?"

He nodded absently while he nudged her back on the bed. "That would be interesting, wouldn't it?"

"Interesting. Jesus. You'll recall that Mia fried one of your toys when she was a little miffed."

"That was cool. But she didn't hurt me," he reminded Ripley. "And neither will you. I'm just going to hook you up now. I explained what the machines are for."

"Yeah, yeah."

"You need to lose the sweater."

She glanced toward the camera, smirked. "So do you and your fellow geeks watch these tapes at stag parties?"

"Absolutely. Nothing like watching a video of a half-naked woman to break up the tedium of lab work." He kissed her forehead before affixing the first electrode. "But I'll keep this one in my private collection."

He took her through the same steps as he had Nell. Casual questions, monitoring and recording her resting vital signs. There was a slight shift when he asked her to do a small, basic spell. Anxiety, he noted. She wasn't completely comfortable opening herself to power.

But she obliged, and the lights in the adjoining bath switched off and on rapidly.

"I used to do that when Zack was in the shower, when we were kids," she said. "Just to piss him off."

"Give me something bigger, more demanding." Her heart rate was up more than Nell's had been. Anxiety again, he decided. But the brain-wave patterns were remarkably similar.

She cupped her hands, lifted them. He saw the ball of light glow, then shoot up to the ceiling. Another followed, still another. As he watched them take position, he grinned.

"It's a baseball field. Infield, outfield, nine players."

"Batter up," she said and sent another light into her batter's box. "I used to do this as a kid, too." And had missed it, she realized. "When I couldn't sleep, or didn't want to. Let's see how he likes a fastball."

Another light, small and blue, shot out from the pitcher's mound. There was a snap of sound, a burst of streaming light. "Yes! Base hit, deep right field. Let's stretch it into a triple."

Forgetting his machines, Mac sat on the foot of the bed and watched, marvelously entertained, as she played through an entire inning.

"Keep it going," he urged. "How old were you when you first recognized and used your gift?"

"I don't know. It just always seemed to be there. Double play, smooth as silk."

"Do you ever play on a terrestrial field?"

"Sure. Hot corner—I've got great hands. You?"

"No. Too clumsy. Divide eighty-four by twelve."

"Struck him out! And the side retires. Divide what? That's math. I hate math." Her brow furrowed. "You didn't say there was going to be a quiz."

"Give it a shot," he told her and rose again to check the readings.

"Twelve's one of the sucky ones. Hanging curveball, low and outside. It's six, no, wait. Damn it. Seven, seven times two is fourteen, and carry the deal to the other deal. Seven. So what?"

Excitement trickled through him, but all that showed in his voice was amusement. "So you strained your left brain a bit, but maintained the pattern."

She breezed through the backward alphabet. He wasn't entirely sure what that said about her mind or her personality, but her readings remained high and steady. "Okay, close the spell."

"But I've got a man out and a man on."

"We'll pick it up later."

"This is starting to feel like school," she complained, but opened her hands again and drew the lights down, extinguished them.

"I need you to relax again. Breathe in through your nose, out gently through your mouth. Slow, deep breaths."

Ready to pout about the game delay, she

looked over at him. And saw what Nell had seen. Cool, calm control. "I'm relaxed enough."

"Breathe, Ripley. Count the beats. Slow, deep, easy."

He sat on the side of the bed with her, checked her pulse with his fingers. "Relax your toes."

"My what?"

"Your toes. Let your toes relax, let all the tension slide out."

"I'm not tense." But he felt her pulse kick. "If this is your prelude to hypnosis, it's not going to work."

"Then it won't work." Watching her face, he trailed his fingers to the pulse in the curve of her elbow, back to her wrist. Soft, steady strokes. "Relax your feet. You've been on them most of the day. Let the tension go out of them. Out of your ankles."

His voice was so quiet, so soothing. His fingers on her skin were a lovely, light connection.

"Relax your calves. It's like warm water flowing up through your body, washing out the tension. Your mind's relaxing, too. Just let it empty out. Your knees are relaxing now, your thighs. Visualize a soft white field.

Nothing on it. It's easy on the eyes. It relaxes them."

He drew the pendant from under his shirt. Wrapped the chain twice around his hand. "Breathe in the calm, expel the tension. It's safe here. You can just drift."

"Aren't you supposed to tell me I'm getting sleepy?"

"Ssh. Breathe. Focus on the pendant."

Her pulse jumped again when he held it up in her line of vision. "That's Mia's."

"Relax. Focus. You're safe. You know you can trust me."

She moistened her lips. "This isn't going to work anyway."

"The pendant's in front of that white wall. It's all you can see, all you need to see. Let your mind clear. Just look at the pendant. Listen to my voice. It's all you need to hear."

He took her down in stages, gently, until her eyelids began to droop. Then slid her deep.

"Subject is unusually susceptible to hypnosis. Vital signs are steady, readings typical for a trance state. Ripley, can you hear me?"

"Yes."

"I want you to remember that you're safe

and that you're not to do anything that you're not willing to do and comfortable doing. If I ask you to do anything that you don't want to do, you're to tell me no. Do you understand?"

"Yes."

"Are you able to stir the air?"

"Yes."

"Will you do so? Gently."

She lifted her arms, as if for an embrace, and the air moved over him like a soft wave of water.

"How does that make you feel?" he asked her.

"I can't explain. Happy, and afraid."

"Afraid of what?"

"I want it too much, want too much of it."

"Close the spell," he ordered. It wasn't fair to ask her questions like that, he reminded himself. She hadn't agreed to it before he'd put her under. "Remember the lights? The baseball lights? Can you bring them back?"

"I'm not supposed to play after bedtime," she said, and her voice had changed subtly, become younger and full of mischief. "But I do."

He stared at her rather than the lights she

threw toward the ceiling. "Subject has regressed, without direct suggestion. The childhood game appears to have triggered the event."

The scientist in him wanted to pursue it, but the man couldn't follow through.

"Ripley, you're not a little girl. I want you to stay in this time and place."

"Mia and I had fun. If I didn't have to grow up, we'd still be friends." It was said sulkily, her mouth in a pout as she played the lights.

"I need you to stay in this time and this place."

She let out a long sigh. "Yes, I'm here."

"Can I touch one of the lights?"

"It won't hurt you. I don't want to hurt you." She brought one down until it hovered above his hands.

He could trace it with his finger, a perfect circle. "It's beautiful. What's inside you is beautiful."

"Some is dark." As she said it, her body arched, and the lights flew around the room like bright stars.

Instinctively Mac ducked. The lights began to whistle shrilly and pulse bloodred.

"Close the spell."

"Something's here. It's come to hunt. To feed." Her hair began to twist into wild curls. "It's come back. One times three."

"Ripley." Lights flew past his face as he rushed back to her. "Close the spell. I want you to close the spell and come back. I'm going to count back from ten."

"She needs you to guide the way."

"I'm bringing her back." Mac gripped shoulders he knew were no longer Ripley's. "You have no right to take her."

"She is mine and I am hers. Show her the way. Show her *her* way. She must not take mine, or we are lost."

"Ripley, focus on my voice. On *my* voice." It took all his control to keep his voice soothing. Firm but calm. "Come back now. When I reach one, you'll wake up."

"He brings death. He craves it."

"He won't get it," Mac snapped. "Ten, nine, eight. You're waking up slowly. Seven, six. You're going to feel relaxed, refreshed. Five, four. You'll remember everything. You're safe. Come back now. Wake up, Ripley. Three, two, one."

As he counted down, he saw her come back, not just to the surface of consciousness but physically. As her eyelids fluttered, the lights vanished, and the room was still.

She breathed out, swallowed. "Holy shit," she managed, then found herself plucked off the bed into his lap and crushed in his arms.

Seventeen

He couldn't let her go, couldn't stop blaming himself for taking chances with her. Nothing he'd seen, experienced, theorized, had ever terrified him the way watching Ripley change in front of him had done.

"It's all right." She stroked his back, patted it. Then realizing they were both trembling, she wrapped her arms around his neck and held tight. "I'm okay."

He shook his head, buried his face in her hair. "I should be shot."

Since gentle soothing wasn't working, she switched tactics into something more natural to her. "Get a grip, Booke," she ordered and shoved at him. "No harm, no foul."

"I took you under, left you open." He pulled back, and she could see it wasn't fear on his face but fury. "It hurt you. I could see it. Then you were gone."

"No, I wasn't." His reaction had given her little time for one of her own. Now her stomach quivered. Something had come into her. No, she thought, that wasn't quite right. Something had come *over* her.

"I was here," she said slowly, as she tried to puzzle it out for herself. "It was like being underwater. Not like drowning or sinking, but just . . . floating. It didn't hurt. More of a quick shock, then the drift."

Her brows drew together as she thought it through. "Can't say I cared for it, though. I don't like the idea of being tucked aside so someone else can have her say."

"How do you feel now?"

"Fine. Actually, I feel great. Stop taking my pulse, Doc."

"Let me get these things off you." But when he started to remove the electrodes, she closed a hand over his wrist.

"Hold on. What did you get out of all that?"

"A reminder." He bit off the words. "To be more cautious."

"No, you don't. Think like a scientist. The

way you were when we started this. You're supposed to be objective, right?"

"Fuck objectivity."

"Come on, Mac. We can't just toss the results out the window. Tell me. I'm interested." When he frowned at her, she sighed. "It's not just your deal now. I have a pretty personal interest in what went on here."

She was right. Because she was right, he dug down for calm. "How much do you remember?"

"All of it, I think. For a minute I was eight years old. It was kind of cool."

"You started to regress, on your own." He pressed his fingers to his temples. Clear the brain, he ordered himself. Bag the emotion. And give her some answers.

"Maybe the game was the trigger," he considered. "If you want a quick analysis, I'd say you went back to a time when you weren't conflicted. Subconsciously you needed to go back to a time when things were simpler and you didn't question yourself. You used to enjoy your gift."

"Yeah. And for a while, the Craft—the learning, the refining, I guess you'd say." Restless now, she moved her shoulders.

"And then you get a little older and you start thinking about the weight. The consequences."

He laid a hand on her cheek. "This, all of this, troubles you."

"Well, things aren't simple now, are they? They haven't been for me for ten years."

He said nothing, watching her patiently. Words trembled on her tongue, then began to spill out in a flood. "I could see, in dreams, how it might be if I took a step too far. If I didn't strap it in, wasn't careful enough. And sometimes, in those dreams, it felt good. Amazingly good to do whatever I wanted, whenever I wanted. Screw the rules."

"But you never did," he said quietly. "Instead you just stopped it all."

"When Sam Logan left Mia, she was a wreck. I kept thinking, why the hell doesn't she *do* something about it? Make him pay, the son of a bitch. Make him suffer the way she's suffering. And I thought of what I'd do. What I could do. Nobody would hurt me that way, because if they tried . . ."

She shuddered. "I imagined it, and almost before I realized, a bolt of light shot out of the sky. A black bolt of light, barbed like an arrow. I sank Zack's boat," she said with a weak smile. "Nobody was in it, but they could have been. He could have been, and I wouldn't have been able to stop it. No control, just anger."

He laid a hand on her leg, rubbed. "How old were you?"

"Not quite twenty. But that doesn't matter," she said fiercely. "You know that doesn't matter. 'And it harm none.' That's vital, and I couldn't be sure I could keep that pledge. God, he'd been in that damn boat not twenty minutes before it happened. I wasn't thinking of him, wasn't concerned about him or anyone. I was just mad."

"So you denied yourself your gift, and your friend."

"I had to. There was no one without the other in this. They're too twined together. She would never have understood or accepted, and damn it, she'd never have stopped nagging at me. Plus, I was pissed at her because . . ."

She knuckled a tear away and said aloud what she'd refused to admit even to herself. "I felt her pain like it was my own, physically felt it. Her grief, her despair. Her desperate love for him. And I couldn't stand it. We were too close, and I couldn't breathe."

"It's been as hard on you as it has on her. Maybe harder."

"I guess. I've never told anybody any of this. I'd appreciate it if we kept it between us."

He nodded, and when his lips brushed hers they were warm. "You'll have to talk to Mia sooner or later."

"I choose later." She sniffled again, rubbed her face briskly. "Let's move on, okay? Or I guess it's back. You got your readings, you got your tape," she said, nodding at his equipment. "I didn't think you'd be able to put me under. I keep underestimating you. It was relaxing, even pleasant." She pushed back her heavy hair. "And then . . ."

"What then?" he prompted. He didn't have to check his machines to know her heart rate and respiration were spiking.

"It was like something was trying to get it. Claw its way in. Something crouched and waiting. Boy, that sounds dramatic." And though she laughed at herself, she drew her knees up protectively. "Not her. It wasn't her. It was something . . . else."

"It hurt you."

"No, but it wanted to. Then I was sliding underwater, and she was the surface. I can't explain it any other way."

"That's good enough."

"I don't see what's good about it. I couldn't control it. Like I couldn't control what happened to Zack's boat. Couldn't control what I started with the lights tonight. Even though she was inside me, some part of her, it didn't seem as if she could control it either. Like the power was caught somewhere between. Up for grabs." She shivered and felt her skin grow icy. "I don't want to do this anymore."

"Okay, we'll stop." He took her hands, soothed. "I'm going to put everything away."

Though she nodded, she knew he didn't understand her. She didn't want any of it any longer. But she was afraid, deeply afraid, that she wasn't going to be given the choice.

Something was coming, she thought. For her.

He tucked her in like a baby, and she let him. When he drew her close to comfort her in the dark, she pretended to sleep. He stroked her hair, and she felt the beginning of tears.

If she was normal, if she was ordinary, her life could be like this, she thought bitterly. She could be held close in the dark by the man she loved.

A simple thing. Everything.

If she'd never met him, she'd have been content to go on as she was. Enjoying a man now and then when he caught her fancy and her interest. Whether or not she would have embraced her powers again she couldn't be sure. But her heart would have remained her own.

Once you gave your heart, you risked more than self. You risked the one who held it.

How could she?

Weary of the worry, she breathed him in, and gave herself to sleep.

The storm was back, cold and bitter. It drove the sea into a frenzy of sound and fury. Lightning blasted over the sky, shattering it like glass.

Black rain gushed from the shards to be hurled like frozen barbs by the wicked wind.

The storm was feral. And she ruled it.

Power fueled her, pumping through muscle and bone with such glorious *strength.* Here was an energy beyond anything she'd known before, had believed possible.

And with this force at her fingertips, she would have vengeance.

No, no. Justice. It wasn't vengeance to seek punishment for wrongs. To *demand* it. To mete it out with a clear mind.

But her mind wasn't clear. Even in the throes of her hunger, she knew it. And feared it.

She was damning herself.

She looked down at the man who cowered at her feet. What was power if it couldn't be used to right wrongs, to stop evil, to punish the wicked?

"If you do this, it ends in violence. In hopelessness."

Her grief-stricken sisters stood in the circle, and she without.

"I have the right!"

"No one does. Do this, and you rip out

the heart of the gift. The soul of what you are."

She was already lost. "I can't stop it."

"You can. Only you can. Come, stand with us. It's he who will destroy you."

She looked down and saw the face of the man change, features over features that slid from terror, to glee, to plea, to hunger.

"No. He ends here."

She threw up a hand. Lightning exploded, arrowed down to her fingertips. And became a silver sword. "With what is mine I take your life. To right the wrong and end the strife. For justice I set my fury free, and take the path of destiny. From this place and from this hour . . ." Thrilled, darkly thrilled, she lifted the sword high as he screamed. "I will taste the ripe fruit of power. Blood for blood I now decree. As I will, so mote it be."

She brought the sword down in one vicious swipe. He smiled as its tip sliced flesh. And he vanished.

The night screamed, the earth trembled. And through the storm, the one she loved came running.

"Stay back!" she shouted. "Stay away!"

But he fought his way through the gale,

reaching for her. From the tip of her sword, lightning erupted, and arrowed into his heart.

"Ripley, come on, honey. Wake up now. It's a bad dream."

She was sobbing with it, and the wrenching grief in the sound worried him more than the trembling.

"I couldn't stop it. I killed him. I couldn't make it stop."

"It's over now." He fumbled for the bedside lamp, but couldn't find the switch. Instead he simply sat up with her, cuddled her, rocked. "It's all over now. You're okay. Wake up." He kissed her damp cheeks, her forehead.

Her arms banded around him like steel. "Mac."

"That's right. I'm here. You had a nightmare. Do you want me to turn on the light, get you some water?"

"No, just . . . no. Hold on to me a minute, okay?"

"Absolutely."

Not a nightmare, she thought as she let

herself cling to him. But a vision, a blend of what had been and what would be. She'd recognized the face—the faces—of the man on the beach. One she had seen in other dreams. He'd died three centuries before. Cursed by the one called Earth.

Another she had first seen in the woods by the yellow cottage. When he'd held a knife to Nell's throat.

And the third she had seen in the café, reading a newspaper and eating soup.

Three parts of one whole? Three steps in one fate? God! How was she to know?

She had killed them. In the end she'd seen herself standing in the storm, with her sword in her hand. She'd killed because she could, because the need had been so huge.

And the payment horribly dear.

It had been Mac she'd seen running through the storm. Mac who'd been struck down, because she couldn't control what was inside her.

"I won't let it happen," she whispered. "I won't."

"Tell me. Tell me about the dream. It'll help."

"No. This will." She lifted her mouth to

his, poured herself into the kiss. "Touch me. God. Make love with me. I need to be with you." Fresh tears spilled as she melted against him. "I need you."

To comfort, to fill, to want. She would take this, and give it. This last time. All that might have been, all that she had let herself wish, would gather together and stream into this perfect act of love.

She could see him in the dark. Every feature, every line, every plane was etched on mind and heart. How could she have fallen so deeply, so hopelessly in love?

She'd never believed herself capable of it, never wanted it. Yet here it was, aching inside her. He was the beginning and the end for her, and she had no words to tell him.

He needed none.

He tumbled into her, the yield and demand. There was a tenderness here, a depth to it that neither had explored before. Swamped by it, he murmured her name. He wanted to give her everything. Heart, mind, body. To warm her with his hands and mouth. To hold her safe forever.

She rose to him, drew him down. Met his

sigh with her own. Love was like a feast, and each supped slowly.

A gentle caress, a melting of lips. A quiet need that stirred souls.

She opened, and he filled. Warmth enclosed in warmth. They moved together in the seamless dark, beat for sustained beat, while pleasure bloomed and ripened.

His lips brushed at her tears, and the taste of them was lovely. In the dark, his hands found hers, linked.

"You're all there is."

She heard him say it, tenderly. And as the wave rose to sweep them both, it was soft as silk.

In the dark, she slept away the rest of the night in his arms. Without dreams.

Morning had to come. She was prepared for it. There were steps to be taken, and she would take them without hesitation and, she promised herself, without regret.

She slipped out of the house early. She took one last glance at Mac, how he looked sleeping peacefully in her bed. For a moment, she allowed herself to imagine what might have been.

Then she closed the door and didn't look back.

She could hear Nell, already up and singing in the kitchen, and knew her brother would be up and starting the day soon. She needed to get a jump on it.

She left by the front door, heading for the village and the station house at a brisk jog.

The wind and rain had died in the night. Under clear skies, the air had turned bitter again.

She could hear the pounding of the sea. The surf would still be high and wild, and the beach littered with whatever the water had cast out.

But there would be no long, freeing run for her that morning.

The village was as still as a painting, captured under a crystalline coating of ice. She imagined it waking, yawning, stretching, and cracking that thin sheath like an eggshell.

Determined that her home, and everyone on it, would wake safe, she unlocked the door of the station house.

It was chilly inside and warned her they

were running on emergency power. Lost power during the night, and the generator kicked on. She imagined that she and Zack would be busy later, dealing with any of the residents who didn't have backup power.

But that was later.

With a check of the time, she booted up the computer. She could run it off the battery long enough to get what she needed.

Jonathan Q. Harding. She rolled her shoulders and began her search.

The basic police work steadied her. It was routine, it was second nature. Her stop at the hotel had garnered her his home address—or the address he'd given, she reminded herself.

Now, she would see just who the hell he was. And with that, begin to piece together the puzzle of what part he played in her personal drama.

She scanned the data as it scrolled onscreen. Harding, Jonathan Quincy. Age forty-eight. Divorced. No children. Los Angeles.

"L.A.," she repeated, and felt the little quiver she'd experienced when she'd gotten his city of residence from the hotel registration.

Evan Remington was from Los Angeles. So were a lot of other people, she reminded herself, as she had the day before. But there wasn't as much conviction in it this time around.

She read his employment information. A magazine writer. Reporter. Son of a bitch.

"Looking for a hot story, Harding? Well, it's not going to happen. You just try getting through me to Nell and . . ."

She broke off, blew out a breath, and deliberately, consciously, tamped down on the instinctive anger.

There had been other reporters, she reminded herself. Gawkers, parasites, and the curious. They'd handled it without any real trouble. They would handle this one the same way.

She went back to the data, noting that Harding had no criminal record. Not even an outstanding parking violation. So he was, by all appearances, a law-abiding sort.

She sat back, considered.

If she were a reporter from L.A. looking for a story, where would she start? Remington's family was a good bet. His sister, then some friends, some associates. Research the key players, who included Nell. From there? Police reports, probably. Interviews with people who had known both Remington and Nell.

But that was all background, wasn't it? You couldn't get to the meat until you'd talked directly to the main characters.

She snatched up the phone, intending to contact the facility where Remington was being held. And heard the line crackle and die. First the power, she thought, now the phones. Muttering complaints, she yanked out her cell phone, hit Power. And ground her teeth when the display announced that her battery was dead.

"Damn it. Goddamn it!" Pushing herself out of the chair, she paced. There was an urgency in her now. Whether it was the cop, the woman, or the witch pushing didn't seem to matter. She *had* to know if Harding had met with Remington.

"All right, then." She steadied herself again. It was imperative to stay calm and controlled.

It had been a long time since she'd attempted a flight. She had no tools with her to help focus her energy. And though she wished, just once, for Mia, she accepted that in this she was on her own.

Struggling not to rush, she cast the circle, and in its center cleared her mind, and opened.

"I call to all who hold the power, unto me your help endower. Rise up the wind to aid my flight, open your eyes to aid my sight. My body remains, but my spirit flies free. As I will, so mote it be."

It was like a drawing up, a tingling that flowed gently through the body. Then a lifting out of what she was from the shell that held it.

She glanced down at her own form—the Ripley who stood, head lifted, eyes closed, in the circle.

Knowing the risks of lingering, of becoming too charmed by the sensation of flight, she centered her thoughts on her target. And let herself soar.

The stream of the wind, the sea beneath. There was such joy in it—and that, she knew, was a dangerous seduction. Before she could be lulled into the glorious silence and motion, she let sounds fill her head.

Voices humming—the thoughts and the speech of an entire city were alive within her. Worries, joys, tempers, passions mixed together in such a wonderfully human music.

As she traveled, sliding downward, she separated them and found what she needed.

"There was no change overnight." One nurse handed a chart to another. Their thoughts sent up a mild interference.

Complaints, fatigue, a remembered fight with a spouse, and one gnawing desire for ice cream.

"Well, he's less trouble in a coma. Strange, though, the way he dropped just a couple of hours after that reporter left. He'd been alert, stable, responsive for days, then this complete turnaround."

As the nurses moved down the corridor, one of them shivered slightly as Ripley passed.

"Wow. Got a chill."

She moved through the closed door and into the room where Remington lay. Machines monitored his vital signs, cameras watched him.

Ripley hovered, studying him. Comatose, restrained, behind lock and key. What harm could he do now?

Even as she thought it, his eyes opened and grinned into hers.

She felt a stab in the heart, the pain unbelievably sharp and completely real. The power in her, around her, wavered. And she felt herself falling.

His thoughts beat at her mind. Bloody, vicious fists that spoke of vengeance, death, destruction. They pinched at her, greedy fingers that were somehow, hideously, arousing. Tempting her to surrender.

And more than surrender, tempting her to take.

No. You won't have me, or mine.

She fought back, struggling to free herself. Little wings of panic fluttered at her throat as she realized the sheer strength of what had come alive in him.

She tore free with a cry of both fury and fear.

And found herself sprawled in the circle she'd cast on the simple wood floor of the station house.

Wincing in pain, she tore open her shirt and stared down in horror at the angry red welts between her breasts.

She struggled to her feet, found the control to close the circle. She was stumbling for the first-aid kit when the door burst open.

Mia flew in the door like a whirlwind. "What the hell do you think you're doing?"

Instinctively Ripley drew her shirt closed. "What're you doing here?"

"Did you think I wouldn't know?" All but shaking with anger, Mia closed the distance between them. "I wouldn't feel? How dare you do such a thing on your own, without proper preparation? Do you know what you risked?"

"It was my risk, and you've got no business spying on me."

"You risked everything, and you know it, just as you know I wasn't spying. You woke me out of a lovely little dream."

Ripley angled her head, took a good look. Mia's hair was in wild disarray, her mouth unpainted and her cheeks pale. "Now that you mention it, you didn't take time to put on your war paint. I don't think I've seen you without makeup since we were fifteen."

"Even without it, I'll always look better than you—particularly now. You're bone white. Sit down. Sit—" she repeated and solved the problem by pushing Ripley into a chair.

"Mind your own business."

"You, unfortunately, are my business. If you wanted to check on Remington, why didn't you just *look*?"

"Don't lecture me, Mia. You know I have less luck with that area than you. Plus, I didn't have a glass or a ball or—"

"A cup of water would do, as you're perfectly aware. It's foolishly dangerous to fly without a partner, someone who can call you back should it be necessary."

"Well, it wasn't necessary. I got back fine."

"You could have asked me for help." Sorrow pierced the frustration. "By the goddess, Ripley, do you hate me that much?"

Simple shock had Ripley dropping her hands, gaping. "I don't hate you. I couldn't—"

"What have you done to yourself?" Temper vanished as Mia saw the welts. Moving quickly, she pulled Ripley's shirt aside. And her soul shuddered. "He did this. How is it possible? You were in the circle. He's just a man. How could he break the protection and do this to your corporal body?"

"He's not just a man," Ripley said flatly. "Not anymore. There's something in him, and it's very strong, and very dark. Part of it's here. There's a man at the hotel."

She told Mia what she knew, as she would tell Nell. They needed to be prepared.

"I need to study," Mia said. "To think. We'll find the answer. In the meantime, do you still have your amulet, any of your protective stones?"

"Mia—"

"Don't be a fool, not now. Wear the amulet. Recharge it first. You have to stay away from this Harding until we know more."

"I know that. I'm not going to let this happen, Mia. I need you to promise you won't stop me, however it has to be done."

"We'll find a way. Let me tend to those burns."

"You'll stop me," Ripley repeated, taking Mia's wrist, squeezing urgently. "You're stronger than I am, and you know just how close I am to the edge to admit that."

"What needs to be done will be done." Impatient, Mia pushed Ripley's hand away. "These are painful. Let me tend to them."

"For a minute, the burn was arousing."

Ripley took a steadying breath. "Seductive. I wanted it, and what it would do to me."

"That's part of its slyness." But fear, cold and clammy, shivered over Mia's skin. "You know that, too."

"Yeah, I know it. And now I've felt it. You and Nell can hold out against it, and Nell stands in front of Zack. But I saw what could happen, and I'm not taking any chances. I can't leave, it won't work. So Mac's going to have to go."

"He won't." Mia soothed the welts with her fingertips.

"I'll make him."

With her hand on Ripley's heart, Mia felt the beat that was love and fear. Her own ached in sympathy. "You can try."

Steps to be taken, Ripley reminded herself as she approached the yellow cottage. This one, most of all, had to be faced. She didn't need second sight or a ball of crystal to foresee that it would be painful. More painful than the raw welts that even Mia hadn't been able to erase completely from her skin.

He might hate her when she was done. But he would be safe.

She didn't hesitate, but knocked, then strolled in.

Dressed in a ragged sweatshirt and rattier jeans, he stood in the crowded bedroom. He was reviewing the tape from the night before. It was a jolt to see him on the monitor—so calm, so unruffled, so *steady*—sitting on the bed beside her, gently taking her pulse while his voice reassured.

A jolt to see him glance over at her now, to see the concentration in his eyes, then the easy pleasure that warmed them.

He stood, blocking the monitor with his body, then switching it off.

"Hi. You snuck off on me this morning."

"Had stuff," she said with a shrug. "Back at work, huh?"

"It can wait. How about some coffee?"

"Yeah, that'd be good." She didn't avoid the kiss, but neither did she respond. She knew he was puzzled, so she breezed by him into the kitchen.

"I wanted to talk to you," she began. "I know we've been hanging out a lot."

"Hanging out?"

"Yeah. We've got a real nice sizzle between us, especially between the sheets." She sat, stretching out her legs, crossing her feet at the ankles. "But the thing is, it's getting a little intense for me. Wow, last night especially really went over the top. I'm going to have to back off."

"Back off?" He caught himself parroting her again, shook his head. "I understand last night's session was rough." He got down two mugs, poured coffee. "You need a break from that."

"You're not following me." Already bleeding inside, she took the mug he offered. "It's not just the work area—I've got to admit, I found it a lot more interesting than I thought I would. Brains are pretty sexy. I've never hung out with a really smart guy before."

She sipped the coffee, burned her tongue, and kept right on talking. "Look, Mac, you're really a nice guy, and I think we both had a good time. You even helped me clear my head about a lot of stuff. I appreciate that."

"Do you?"

There he was, she thought, looking at her as if she were a bug on a slide. "You bet. But I'm starting to feel a little, you know, confined. I need to move on."

"I see." His voice was calm, just a bit detached. "So, you're dumping me."

"That's a little harsh." He wasn't reacting as she'd expected. He didn't look angry, upset, hurt, shocked. He simply looked mildly interested. "Why don't we keep it friendly and just say it's been fun?"

"Okay." He leaned back on the counter, crossing his long legs at the ankles in a move that eerily mirrored hers, then sipped his coffee. "It's been fun."

"Great." A little sliver of resentment worked through, pricking her heart, and her voice. "Figured you for a reasonable type, which is probably why you're not really *my* type. I guess you'll be heading back to New York pretty soon."

"No, not for several more weeks."

"I don't see the point in staying. I don't want to play anymore."

"I guess I have to make sure you're not the center of my universe, then. I still have work to do on the Sisters."

"You won't get any more cooperation from me. Look, I'm just thinking of how you're going to feel. It's a small world here. People are going to know I broke things off. It's going to be embarrassing for you."

"Let me worry about that."

"Fine. Not my problem." She pushed to her feet.

"No, it's not." He spoke pleasantly as he set his mug aside. She never saw it coming. One second he was studying her with that vague curiosity, and the next he'd yanked her against him.

His mouth was like a fever on hers. Hot, angry, draining.

"Why are you lying to me?"

She was out of breath, and her thoughts had scattered like ants. "Hands off!"

"Why are you lying?" he repeated, and backed her up against the refrigerator door.

Detached? she thought wildly. Had she thought he was detached?

"Where did all this bull come from?" He gave her one quick shake. "Why are you trying to hurt me?"

And it did hurt, a deep, throbbing ache in the pit of his stomach, a slow, twisting twinge in the heart.

"I'm not trying to hurt you, but I will if you keep pushing yourself on me. I don't want you."

"You're a liar. You held me when you slept."

"I can't be responsible for what I do in my sleep."

"You turned to me in the dark." His voice was relentless. A part of him felt as if he was fighting for his life. "You gave yourself to me."

"Sex is—"

"It wasn't sex." He remembered how it had been. For both of them. His hands gentled, and his anger became exasperation. "Do you think you can trick me into turning away from you, leaving the island? Why?"

"I don't want you here." She shoved at him, and her voice began to hitch. "I don't want you near me."

"Why?"

"Because, you moron, I'm in love with you."

Eighteen

He ran his hands down her arms, taking hers as he leaned over to touch his lips to her forehead.

"Well, you idiot, I'm in love with you, too. Let's sit down and start there."

"What? What?" She would have pulled her hands free, but he only tightened his grip. "Back off."

"No." He said it gently. "No, Ripley, I won't back off. I won't go away. And I won't stop loving you. You might as well swallow that, then we can work on what's scared you so much you want me gone."

"Mac, if you love me, you'll pack up and go back to New York for a while."

"It doesn't work that way. No," he repeated as she opened her mouth again.

"Don't be so damn—"

" 'Implacable' is a term I've heard applied to me occasionally. It's classier, I think, than 'hardheaded.' In this case, however, I don't think either applies." He angled his head. "You get spooked about something, worried about someone, your instinct is to step away. The way you did with your gift," he continued over her protest. "The way you did with Mia. I won't let you do that with me. With us. Ripley." He lifted their joined hands, kissed her knuckles. "I'm so in love with you."

"Don't." Her heart, she thought, couldn't take it. "Just wait."

"I hate to keep saying no to you. I'll make it up to you later." And he lowered his head and kissed her until her bones went liquid.

"I don't know what to do, how to handle this. I've never had this before."

"Me, either. We'll figure it out. Let's sit down and get started."

"I told Zack I'd be back in twenty minutes. I didn't think it would take that long to . . ."

"To dump me." He grinned at her. "Surprise. You want to call him?"

She shook her head. "I can't think straight. Hell, he knows where I am if he needs me." It seemed as if everything inside her was jumping and twisting around. And yet, at the center of it, her heart was glowing like the moon. "You're in love with me?"

"Completely."

"Well." She sniffled. "How come you never mentioned it before?" she demanded.

"How come you didn't mention you were in love with me?"

"I asked you first."

"Got me there. Maybe I was building up to it. You know . . ." He squeezed her arms before he nudged her into a chair. "Softening you up."

"Maybe I was doing the same thing."

"Really? Telling me you were done with me is an odd way to accomplish that."

"Mac." She leaned forward, and this time she took his hands. "You're the first man I've ever said it to. You have to be careful throwing that word around. If you're careless with it, casual with it, it loses power. You're the first because you're the first. And for me, you'll be the only. That's how it works with the Todds. We mate for life. So you have to marry me."

His system kicked, a quick boot. "I have to marry you?"

"Yeah. So that takes care of that."

"Hold on." Pleasure trickled through him. "Don't I get a ring or something? Then you get down on one knee and ask, and I say yes or no?"

"You're pushing your luck."

"I feel lucky. I'm buying a house."

"Oh." There was a tug. Grief, sorrow. Acceptance. "New York. Yeah, well, that's where your work is. Guess they always need cops there."

"Probably, but I'm buying a house here. Do you think I'd ask you to leave your heart? Don't you know mine's here now, too?"

She stared at him. For one long moment, she could do nothing but stare at him. And saw their lives in his eyes. "Don't make me cry. I hate that."

"I put in an offer on the Logan place."

"The . . ." Big and beautiful and by the sea. "It's not for sale."

"Oh, but it's going to be. I can be very tenacious. I want children."

"So do I." Her fingers tightened on his. "It'll be good with us. Good and solid and real. But you have to do something for me first."

"I'm not going away."

"Can't you trust me enough to do this one thing?"

"That won't work either. Tell me what's frightening you. Start with the dream last night."

She looked away from him. "I killed you."

"How?" he asked, sounding intrigued.

"What, have you got ice in your veins? I ended your life, your existence."

"We'll figure out the solution faster if we don't panic. Tell me about the dream."

She shoved away from the table, paced the room three times in tight little circles trying to burn off her agitation. And told him. And in telling him brought it all back so clearly that fear crawled through her like freshly hatched spiders.

"I killed you, and destroyed everything that matters," she finished. "I can't carry that load, Mac. Can't deal with it. It's why I turned away from what I am. Turned away from Mia. It seemed the right—the only— thing to do. Part of me still thinks that."

"But you know that won't work and that you have to face it."

"You're asking me to risk you, my family, my friends, my home."

"No, I'm not," he said gently. "I'm asking you to protect us."

Emotion totally swamped her. "God, Mac, that was a big button to push."

"I know it. I'll help you, Ripley. I think I was meant to. Meant to love you," he added, taking her fisted hand, smoothing it open. "To be a part of this. I don't think my life's work is a coincidence, or my coming here, or my sitting here with you right now. And I know we're stronger together than we are apart."

She looked down at their joined hands. Everything she wanted, she realized, and hadn't known she was looking for, was right here in her grasp.

"If I kill you, it's really going to piss me off."

His lips twitched. "Me, too."

"Are you wearing Mia's pendant?"

"Yeah."

"Don't go anywhere without it. Or this." She dug in her pocket. She should have known where it was all heading when she felt compelled to bring it with her. The ring was a complex twist of silver, a trio of melded circles, scored with symbols. "It was my grandmother's."

He was humbled, and incredibly moved. Had to clear his throat. "So I get a ring after all."

"Looks like. It's going to be too small for your hand. Wear it on the chain with the pendant."

He took it from her, squinting as he tried to make out the symbols without his glasses. "It looks Celtic."

"It is. The middle circle says 'justice,' the ones on either side say 'compassion' and 'love.' I guess that covers it."

"It's a beautiful piece." He took off the chain, opened it, and slid the ring on. "Thank you."

Before he could slip the chain back over his head, she gripped his wrist. "Hypnotize me again."

"It's too dangerous."

"Don't give me that crap. This is all too dangerous. I want you to take me under, give me some posthypnotic suggestion or whatever it is. Something that will stop me if I start to lose control."

"In the first place, you're too open to other energies when you're in a trance state. You were like a sponge, Ripley, soaking up what others poured into you. And in the second place, I have no idea if any suggestion would hold. When you're conscious and aware, you're too strong-minded, too strong-willed, to be influenced in that way."

"It's another line of defense. We don't know it won't work unless we try. This is something you can do, and I'm trusting you. I'm asking you for help."

"That's a hell of a button, too. Okay, we'll try it. Not now," he added quickly. "I want some time to do a little more research and prepare. And I want Nell and Mia here."

"Why can't this be just between us?"

"Because it's not. I'll try it, but only when you have your circle. Now wait here a minute." He said it in such a no-nonsense, don't-bother-to-argue tone that Ripley wasn't sure if she was irritated, amused, or impressed. But she sat, drumming her fingers on the table, as he left the room.

While she listened to him rummaging around in the bedroom, muttering to himself, she drank the coffee she'd let go cold.

When he came back, he drew her to her feet. "I bought this in Ireland a dozen years ago." Turning her hand over, he placed a silver disk in her palm. Through its center ran a swirling rise of silver, and on either side sat a small, perfectly round stone.

"Rose quartz and moonstone," Ripley said.

"For love, and for compassion. I bought it as a kind of talisman, a good luck piece. I always carry it with me. Can't find it half the time, but it always turns up. So I think it's been pretty lucky. It has a loop in the back, so I imagine it was once worn as a pendant. Or you can just carry it in your pocket. I didn't know it at the time, but I bought it for you."

She rested her head on his shoulder. "This is going to make me mushy."

"I don't mind."

"I have to get back to work, and I can't be all googly-eyed. I really love you," she told him as she turned her mouth up to his. "I really do."

He nudged her along, careful not to behave as if he was nudging her along.

He had a great deal to do.

Mac wasn't foolish enough to believe he couldn't be hurt. Even killed. No, he believed Ripley's dream was a foretelling of what could be. The cycle that had begun three hundred years before was still in play.

But he was also smart enough to know various means to protect himself, and to believe that knowledge is power. He would gather more knowledge and strengthen the shield over both of them.

He wouldn't risk putting her in a vulnerable trance state unless he was certain she would be safe.

He got out the copies of his ancestor's journal entry, and found the page he wanted.

February 17

It is early, before dawn. Cold and deep dark. I have left my husband sleeping warm in bed, and come to my tower room to write this. A restlessness is on me, a worry that nags like a bad tooth.

A mist hangs over the house like a shroud. It presses against the glass. I can hear it scratching—sly little fingers made of bone. How it craves to come in. I have charmed the doors and win-

dows and all the tiny cracks, as my mother taught me before despair swallowed her spirit.

How long ago that was, and yet on a night such as this it was only yesterday. And I pine for her—the comfort, the strength, the beauty of her. With this chill seeping into my bones, I wish for her counsel. But it is barred to me, even through crystal and glass.

It is not for myself I fear, but for my children's children's children. I have seen the world in my dreams, a hundred years times three. Such wonders. Such magic. Such grief.

A cycle spins. I cannot see it clearly. But I know my blood, before and after me, spins with it. Strength, purity, wisdom, and, above all, love will war with what now creeps outside my house.

It is ageless, it is ever. And it is dark.

Blood of mine freed it, and blood of mine will face it. From this place and *time I can do little more than protect what is now and pray for what will come. I will leave what magic I can behind me for these beloved and distant children.*

Evil cannot and will not be vanquished by evil. Dark will only swallow dark and deepen. The good and the light are the keenest weapons. Let those who come after hold them ready, and end this in time.

Beneath was a charm written in Gaelic that Mac had already translated. He studied it again now, hoping that the message from the past would help with the now.

Harding felt better than he had in days. The vague fatigue that had dogged him was put down to recovery from whatever bug had invaded his system. But his mind was clear, and he was certain he'd passed the crisis.

In fact, he felt well enough to be annoyed that a touch of the flu had thrown him off stride and off schedule. He fully intended to rectify that by approaching Nell Todd that very day for his first interview.

In preparation for it, he decided to have a light breakfast and a large pot of coffee in his room so that he could go over his notes, refresh his memory of the details, and plan the best strategy for persuading her to talk to him for his book.

The idea of the book, and the money and glamour he intended to reap from it, filled him with anticipation. For days, it seemed, he hadn't been able to think of it clearly, to imagine it, to remember just what it was that he planned to do.

It was as if his mind had been locked away behind some thick door, and whenever it had fought its way clear again, had been too tired to function.

While he waited for his breakfast, he showered and shaved. Looking at himself in the mirror, he admitted that he didn't look his best. He was pale, a bit gaunt. Not that he couldn't get by without the pounds he could clearly see he'd shed. But the dark circles haunting his eyes offended his vanity.

He considered using a portion of his imagined advance for the book for a little nip and tuck, and a regenerative stay in some posh spa.

After he had completed his initial interview with the former Helen Remington, he would finish putting his book proposal together and send it to the New York agent he'd contacted about the idea.

In the bedroom he considered the choice between tailored suit and the more casual look of slacks and sweater. He opted for the casual—more friendly, approachable. That was the image for Nell Todd, rather than the formal business attire he'd used with Evan Remington.

As he thought of Remington, a wave of dizziness washed over him, forcing him to grip the closet door to steady himself. Not quite a hundred percent yet, he thought. He would feel better, he was certain, after breakfast.

His next shock came when he put on his slacks. They gapped at the waist, bagged at the hips. He realized he'd lost at least ten pounds during his bout with the flu, perhaps more. Though his hands shook a bit as he cinched his belt in the last notch, he told himself he could take advantage of this unexpected development.

He would just keep the weight off, start an exercise program, watch his diet more carefully. He'd look fit and trim for public appearances when his book was published.

By the time he sat down to breakfast at the table that room service had set up by the window, he'd convinced himself he was perfectly fine. In fact, better than ever.

With his first cup of coffee, he gazed out the window. The sun was bright, almost too bright as it bounced off the ice that seemed to slick every surface. He found it odd that the strength of that sun didn't appear to be melting any of the ice. And that the village street seemed so still. As if it was genuinely frozen. A bug in amber.

He hoped the bookstore wasn't closed because of the weather. He preferred to approach Nell Todd there, this first time. She would feel safer, he imagined, and more inclined to listen to his pitch. He might also be able to set up an interview with Mia Devlin.

As the person who'd hired Nell, who'd rented her a house, when she had first come to the island, the Devlin woman would add a great deal to the book.

More, Mia Devlin was reputed to be a witch, not that Harding himself actually believed in such nonsense. But something unusual had gone on in the forest the night Remington had been taken into custody, and the Devlin angle was worth exploring.

Blue lightning, a shining circle. Snakes under the skin.

Harding shuddered despite himself, and began to look over his notes.

He could approach Nell Todd, tempering his request for information with his admiration for her courage and intelligence. And quite sincerely, too, Harding admitted. What she had done had taken guts, skill, and brains.

He would flatter her ego. Tell her how he had followed her trail across the country, interviewed dozens of people she'd worked for, or with. And ah, yes, he mused, flipping a page in his notebook, appeal to her sense of compassion, her duty to others who found themselves in abusive situations.

A beacon of hope, he scribbled down hastily. *A shining example of courage. Female empowerment. For some, escape is an option too terrifying to be considered or too far beyond their crushed spirits. (Confirm latest statistics on spousal abuse, women's shelters, victims of marital homi-*

cides. Select family therapist to interview re: most common causes, effects, results. Interview other survivors? Batterers? Potential comparisons and confirmations.)

Pleased that his thoughts were flowing smoothly again, Harding began to eat.

Conception often cubbyholes victims of this nature as being part of an abuse cycle. Helen Remington—Nell Channing Todd— appears to have no such cycle in her background. (Continue research into childhood. Obtain statistics on what portion of abuse victims have no such activities in their previous home life.) A cycle, however, must have a beginning. From all appearances, this cycle began and ended with Evan Remington.

Harding continued to write, but his concentration began to waver. His fingers dug into the pen, and the pen into the paper.

BITCH! WHORE! BURN THE WITCH! MINEMINEMINEMINEMINEMINE! BLOOD. DEATH. VENGEANCE. VENGEANCE IS MINE, IS MINE, IS MINE.

He flipped pages rapidly, slashing words over them, as his breath quickened. And the writing that was not his own all but scorched the paper.

THEY MUST DIE. THEY ALL MUST DIE. AND I WILL LIVE AGAIN.

When he came back to himself, his notebook was neatly closed, his pen set aside. And he was nonchalantly drinking coffee, gazing out the window, and planning his day.

He thought it might be wise to take a nice long walk, to be out exercising in the fresh air. He could fill in several areas of description of the island, take a closer look at the cottage where Nell had lived when she'd first arrived.

It was certainly time he had a personal look at the woods where Remington had chased her that night.

Feeling comfortably full, Harding tucked away his notebook, secured a fresh one. He slipped it, along with a small tape recorder and a camera, into his pockets and set out to work.

He remembered nothing he'd written, nor the bloodlust that had gushed inside him as he'd done so.

Nineteen

The yellow cottage stood quiet at the edge of the little forest. The trees were bare and black and cast short shadows on the ground. Within them was utter silence.

There were thin, lacy curtains at the windows and the glass sparkled in the bright sunlight.

Nothing stirred. Not a blade of winter grass, not a single crisp brown leaf. There seemed to be no sound at all, though the sea was close and the village just at his back. As he stood, staring at the house by the wood, Harding thought it was like studying a photograph taken by someone else. A frozen moment, given to him for reasons he couldn't explain.

He felt a chill run up his spine. His body shook with it, and his breath came hard and fast. He took one stumbling step back, but it seemed as if he was rammed against a wall. And could not turn and run as he so suddenly wanted to do.

Then, as quickly as the sensation had come, it passed. He was only standing on the roadside, looking at a pretty cottage by a winter wood.

He would definitely get a checkup when he got back to the mainland, he decided, as he took one shaky step forward. Obviously, he was under more stress than he had realized. Once he had all the background data and research for the book organized, he would take that vacation. Just a week or two to recoup and recharge before he got down to the serious work of writing.

Cheered by that thought, he continued toward the woods. Now he could hear the soft and steady heartbeat of the sea, the careless call of birds, the light rustling of wind through naked branches.

He shook his head as he marched into the trees, and glanced around with the suspicious condescension of a confirmed urbanite for the solitude of nature. Why anyone would choose to live in such a place was beyond him.

Yet Helen Remington had done so.

She'd given up great wealth, a privileged lifestyle, a beautiful home, and a gilded social standing—and for what? To cook for strangers, to live on a rocky lump of land, and one day—he imagined—to raise a brood of squalling brats.

Stupid bitch.

His hands clenched and unclenched as he walked. Beneath his feet a dirty fog began to churn, to boil over his shoes. He quickened his pace, nearly running now, though the ground was slick and patched with ice. His breath came out in visible streams.

Ungrateful whore.

She had to be punished. To be hurt. She and all the others had to pay, *would* pay for everything they'd done. They would die. And if they dared challenge his power, dared challenge his rights, they would die in agony.

The fog ate along the ground and spilled at the edges of a circle that pulsed with a soft white glow. His lips peeled back, and a feral growl sounded deep in his throat.

He lunged at the ring—and was repelled. Light rose from the circle, a thin, sparkling curtain of gold. In fury, he threw himself against it, time and time again. It burned, white fire scorching his skin, smoking his clothing.

As rage devoured him, what was inside the body of Jonathan Q. Harding threw itself on the ground, howling and cursing the light.

Nell made up two orders of the day's lunch special. She hummed while she worked and toyed with adjustments to the menu for the wedding she was catering at the end of the month.

Business was good. Sisters Catering had found its feet, and even in the slow winter months kept her busy and content. But not so much so that she hadn't eked out time to work on a proposal for Mia. A cooking club in Café Book and an expanded menu were both very doable. Once she had the details more refined, she would present the idea to Mia—businesswoman to businesswoman.

After she served the orders, she glanced at the time. Another half hour and Peg would relieve her. She had a dozen errands to run and two appointments to discuss other catering jobs.

She'd have to move fast, she thought, to get everything done in time to put dinner together. The simple chaos of housewifely chores and business obligations piled together in overlapping layers made her happy.

But there were serious issues to be faced, she couldn't deny it. Dinner that night wasn't just a social function. She understood Mac's concern, and the need to focus her energies on what was to come. But she had already faced the worst and survived.

Whatever had to be done to protect who and what she loved would be done.

She strolled out to clear a table in the café, pocketed her tip. Tip money went in a special jar and was considered her splurge money. Paychecks were for expenses, catering profits would be plowed back into the business. But tip money was for fun. It jingled cheerfully in her pocket as she turned to carry the plates and bowls back to the kitchen.

She stopped short, then rushed forward when she saw Harding standing by the counter staring blankly at the chalkboard menu.

"Mr. Harding, what happened? Are you all right?"

He stared at her, through her.

"You should sit down." Quickly, she put the dishes on the counter, took his arm. She led him around the counter and back into the kitchen. He sank into the chair she pulled out for him, and she rushed to the sink to get a glass of water.

"What happened?"

"I don't know." He took the glass gratefully, gulped down the cool water. His throat felt scorched and raw, as though it had been scored with hot needles.

"I'm going to fix you some tea, and some chicken soup."

He simply nodded, staring down at his hands. The nails were full of grit, as if he'd clawed at dirt. The knuckles were abraded, the palms scraped.

He saw that his trousers were stained with dirt, his shoes filthy. Bits of twig and briar clung to his sweater.

It embarrassed him, a fastidious man, to find himself in such disarray. "Might I . . . wash my hands?"

"Yes, of course." Nell tossed a worried look over her shoulder. A red streak, like sunburn, covered half his face. It looked vicious, painful and frightening.

She led him to the rest room, waited for him outside the door, and then walked him back to the kitchen. She ladled the soup, brewed the tea while he stood as if in a trance.

"Mr. Harding." She spoke gently now, touching his shoulder. "Please sit down. You're not well."

"No, I . . ." He felt vaguely nauseous. "I must have fallen." He blinked rapidly. Why couldn't he *remember*? He'd taken a walk in the woods on a bright winter afternoon.

And could remember nothing.

He let her tend him the way the very young or the very old allow themselves to be tended. He spooned up the warm, soothing soup, and it comforted his aching throat and uneasy stomach.

He drank her herbal tea sweetened with a generous dollop of honey.

And he basked in the sympathetic silence she gave him.

"I must have fallen," he said again. "I haven't been feeling quite well lately."

The scents of the kitchen were so appealing, her movements as she took and filled more orders so graceful and efficient, that his anxiety receded.

He remembered his research on her, and the admiration he'd felt when he'd followed her path across the country. He would write a very good story—book—about her, he thought. One that spoke of courage and triumph.

Ungrateful whore. The words echoed dimly in his head and made him tremble.

Nell studied him with concern. "You should go to the clinic."

He shook his head. "I prefer seeing my own doctor. I appreciate your concern, Mrs. Todd. Your kindness."

"I have something for that burn."

"Burn?"

"Just a minute." She moved out of the kitchen again, spoke to Peg, who'd just come on for her shift. When she came back in, Nell opened a cabinet and took out a slim green bottle.

"It's mostly aloe," she told him briskly. "It'll help."

He reached a hand to his face, snatched it away again. "I must have . . . the sun's deceptive," he managed. "Mrs. Todd, I should tell you I came to the island for the specific purpose of speaking to you."

"Yes?" She uncapped the bottle.

"I'm a writer," he began. "I've followed your story. First, I want you to know how much I admire you."

"Do you, Mr. Harding?"

"Yes. Yes, indeed." Something wanted to crawl up from his belly to his throat. He forced it down again. "Initially, I was merely interested in the story for a magazine piece, but as I learned more I realized the value of what you experienced, what you did. It speaks to so many people. I'm sure you know how many women are caught in the cycle of abuse," he continued as she dabbed the balm on her fingers. "You're a beacon, Mrs. Todd, a symbol of victory and empowerment."

"No, I'm not, Mr. Harding."

"But you are." He looked deep into her eyes. They were so blue. So calm. The cramps in his gut eased. "I followed your trail across the country."

"Really?" she replied, then her coated fingers slid over his burned cheek.

"I spoke with people you worked with,

stepped in your footprints, so to speak. I know what you did, how hard you worked, how frightened you were. You never gave up."

"And I never will," she said clearly. "You should understand that. Prepare for that. I'll never give up."

"You belong to me. Why do you make me hurt you, Helen?"

It was Evan's voice—that quiet, reasonable voice he used before he punished her. Terror wanted to burst free. But it was terror, she knew, that it wanted.

"You can't hurt me any longer. I will never allow anyone I love to be harmed by you."

His skin rippled under her fingers, as if something crawled there. But she continued to smooth on the balm. He shuddered once, gripped her wrist. "Run," he whispered. "Get away before it's too late."

"This is my home." She fought her fear. "I'll protect it with all that I am. We'll beat you."

He shuddered again. "What did you say?"

"I said you should go rest now, Mr. Harding." She capped the bottle as pity for him

welled up inside her. "I hope you'll feel better soon."

"You let him go?" Ripley paced the station
house, tugging at her hair in frustration.
"Just patted him on the head and told him
to take a nap?"

"Ripley." Zack's voice held a quiet warning, but she shook her head.

"For Christ's sake, Zack, think! The man's
dangerous. She said herself she sensed
something in him."

"It's not his fault," Nell began, but Ripley
whirled to face her.

"This isn't about fault, it's about reality.
Even if he were just some reporter with
delusions of grandeur, that would be bad
enough. He came here looking for you, he
followed your path all across the damn
country, talking to people behind your
back."

"That's his job." Nell held up a hand before Ripley could snap at her again. A year
before, she would have backed away from
the confrontation. Times had changed. "I'm
not going to blame him for doing his job, or

for what's happening to him now. He doesn't know what's happening, and he's sick, he's frightened. You didn't see him, Ripley. I did."

"No, I didn't see him because you didn't call me. You didn't bring me in."

"Is that the real problem? I didn't ask you for advice, for help?" Nell tilted her head. "Tell me, would you have called me? Or Mia?"

Ripley opened her mouth, then shut it again in one hard, thin line. "We're not talking about me."

"Maybe we are. Maybe we're talking about all of this. It's a cycle, after all. What started it is inside us. What's inside us will end it. He was hurt," she said, appealing to Zack now. "Confused, afraid. He doesn't know what's going on."

"Do you know?" Zack asked her.

"I'm not sure. There's a power, and it's dark. It's using him. And I think . . ." It was hard to say it, hard to think it. "I'm afraid, it's using Evan. Like a bridge, from wherever it is through Evan to this poor man. We need to help him."

"We need to get him off the island," Ripley interrupted. "We need to get his ass on the next ferry to the mainland, and it doesn't take magic to do that."

"He hasn't done anything, Rip," Zack reminded her. "He hasn't broken any law, made any threats. We've got no right to order him off the island."

She slapped her palms on his desk, leaned forward. "He'll come after her. He'll have to."

"He won't get near her. I won't let it happen."

She spun back to Nell. "He'll destroy what you love. It's his reason for being now."

Nell shook her head. "I won't let him." She reached for Ripley's hand. "We won't let him."

"I've felt what he is, and what he's capable of. I've felt it in me."

"I know." Nell's fingers linked with hers. "We need Mia."

"You're right," Ripley agreed. "And I hate that."

"You're a fascinating woman, little sister." Mia leaned on the kitchen counter and watched Nell slide pasta into boiling water. "A crisis is upon us, an event that has been brewing for three centuries. Ripley frets and curses. And you cook and serve."

"We all do what we do best." She glanced up as she gave the pasta a quick stir. "What do you do, Mia?"

"I wait."

"No, it's not as simple as that."

"I prepare, then." Mia lifted her wineglass, sipped. "For whatever comes."

"Did you see this? What's coming?"

"Not specifically. Only something strong, something blighted. Something that formed from blood and vengeance. It craves what birthed it," she said. "And grows as it feeds. It uses weakness."

"Then we won't be weak."

"It underestimates us," Mia continued. "We should take care not to underestimate it. Evil doesn't concern itself with rules, with what's right and fair. And it's clever. It can twist itself into the desirable."

"We're together now, the three of us. I have Zack, and Ripley has Mac. I wish—"

"Don't wish for me. I have what I need."

"Mia . . ." Trying to find the right words, Nell got out her colander. "Even if—when—

we face what's here now, there's one more step. Yours."

"Do you think I'll fling myself off my cliffs?" Mia relaxed enough to laugh. "I can promise you, I won't. I enjoy living entirely too much."

There were other ways, Nell thought, to leap into a void. She started to say so, then held her tongue. They had enough to deal with for now.

What was *wrong* with them? Ripley listened to the conversation hum around the table, spiced with the scent of good food well served. Everyday words in easy voices.

Pass the salt.

Jesus.

It felt as if something was simmering inside her, right on the edge of boil, ready to bubble up and spew over the lid. And everyone else kept chatting and eating as if it were just another evening.

A part of her knew it was only a lull, that space of time used to gather forces and brace. But she had no patience with it, with Nell's utter calm, with Mia's cool waiting.

Her own brother helped himself to another serving of pasta as if everything in his life that mattered wasn't teetering on the brink.

And Mac . . .

Observing, absorbing, assessing, she thought with a helpless resentment. A geek to the last.

There was something hungry out there, something that wouldn't be sated with a tidy, home-cooked meal. Couldn't they *feel* it? It wanted blood, blood and bone, death and anguish. It craved sorrow.

And its need clawed at her.

"This blows." She shoved at her plate, and conversation snapped off. "We're just sitting here, slurping up noodles. This isn't a goddamn party."

"There are a lot of ways to prepare for a confrontation," Mac began, and laid a hand on her arm.

She wanted to slap his hand away, and hated herself for it. "Confrontation? This is a battle."

"A lot of ways to prepare," he said again. "Coming together like this, sharing a meal. A symbol of life and unity—"

"It's past time for symbols. We need to do something definite."

"Anger only feeds it," Mia chimed in.

"Then it should be full to bursting," Ripley snapped back and shoved to her feet. "Because I am supremely pissed off."

"Hate, anger, a thirst for violence." Mia brought the glass of wine to her lips. "All those negative emotions strengthen it, weaken you."

"Don't tell me what to feel."

"Could I ever? You want what you've always wanted. A clear answer. When you don't get it, you pound with your fists or turn away."

"Don't," Nell pleaded. "We can't turn on each other now."

"Right. Let's keep the peace." Ripley heard the bite in her own voice, and even while it shamed her she couldn't soften it. "Why don't we have coffee and cake?"

"That's enough, Rip."

"It's not enough." Frustrated beyond bearing, she rounded on Zack. "Nothing's enough until this is dealt with, until it's over. It'll be more than a knife to her throat this time, more than a knife already coated with your blood. I won't lose what I love. I won't just sit here and wait for it to come after us."

"On that we can agree." Mia set down her

glass. "We won't lose. And since arguing is bad for the digestion, why don't we get to work?"

She rose, began to clear the table. "Nell will feel better," she said before Ripley could make some snide comment, "if her house is put in order."

"Fine, great." She snatched up her plate. "Let's be tidy."

She sailed into the kitchen and gave herself points for not simply heaving her plate into the sink. What control. What amazing restraint.

God, she wanted to scream!

It was Mac who came in quietly behind her, alone. He set the dishes on the counter, then just turned her, put his hands on her stiff and rigid shoulders.

"You're afraid." He shook his head before she could speak. "We all are. But you feel that the weight of this, what happens next, is on you. It doesn't have to be."

"Don't placate me, Mac. I know when I'm being a bitch."

"Good. Then I don't have to point that out, do I? We're going to get through this."

"You don't feel what I feel. You can't."

"No, I can't. But I love you, Ripley, with

everything that's in me. So I know, and that's the next thing to feeling."

She let herself give, just for a minute. Let herself go into his arms and be held there. Safe within the circle of him. "It'd be easier if we'd found this after."

His cheek rubbed her hair. "You think?"

"You could've come along when everything was normal again, and we'd've gotten mushy on each other and had a regular life. Cookouts, marital spats, great sex, and dental bills."

"Is that what you want?"

"Right this minute, it sounds aces. I'd rather be mad than scared. I work better that way."

"Just remember, it all comes down to this." He tipped back her head, laid his lips on hers. "Right there is more magic than most people ever know."

"Don't give up on me. Okay?"

"Not a chance."

She tried to curb her impatience as the preparations were made. She refused to lie down on the couch because it made her feel too vulnerable. Instead she sat in a chair in the living room, her hands on the arms, and blocked out the monitors and cameras.

She knew she should have felt comforted by having Mia and Nell standing on either side of her, like sentinels. But she felt foolish.

"Just do it," she told Mac.

"You need to relax." He'd pulled a chair up to face hers, and sat there, almost idly holding the pendant. "Breathe slow. In and out."

He put her under. So effortlessly this time, so swiftly, it brought him a quick ripple of nerves.

"She's tuned to you," Mia said, herself surprised at how completely Ripley had given herself over. "And you to her. That, itself, is a kind of strength."

They would need it, she thought, as she felt something cold shiver along her skin. In response to it, she stretched out her arm and, across Ripley, clasped Nell's hand.

"We are the Three," she said clearly. "And two guard the one. While we are joined, no harm can be done." As warmth seeped back, she nodded to Mac.

"You're safe here, Ripley. Nothing can harm you here."

"It's close," she said with a shudder. "It's cold, and tired of waiting." Her eyes opened, stared blindly into Mac's. "It knows you. Watched you and waited. You share the blood. You'll die through me, that's what it wants. Death to power, and power to destruction. Through my hand."

Grief ground down to her bones. "Stop me."

Her head fell back, her eyes rolled back white. "I am Earth."

She changed, even as they watched, her hair springing into curls, her features subtly rounding. "My sin must be atoned, and the time grows short. Sister to sister, and love to love. The storm is coming, and with it the dark. I am powerless. I am lost."

Great tears spilled down her cheeks.

"Sister." Mia laid her free hand on Ripley's shoulder, and felt the cold again. "What can we do?"

The eyes that focused on Mia weren't Ripley's. They seemed ancient, and unbearably sad. "What you will. What you know. What you believe. Trust is one, justice makes two, and love, without boundaries, makes three. You are the Three. Be stronger than what made you or all is for nothing. Should you live, your heart will break again. Will you face that?"

"I'll live, and guard my heart."

"She thought the same. I loved her, loved them both. Too much or not enough, I've yet to see. May your circle be stronger and hold."

"Tell us how to hold."

"I cannot. If the answers live inside you, the questions won't matter." She turned to Nell then. "You found yours, so there is hope. Blessed be."

Ripley gasped again, and came back. "In the storm," she said as the first flash of lightning burst blue light into the room.

A lamp crashed to the floor. A vase of Nell's flowers spun into the air to hurl itself against the wall. The sofa upended itself, then shot across the room.

Even as Zack whirled toward Nell, a table tumbled into his path. He leaped it, cursing, and gripping her, used his body to shield hers.

"Stop." Mia called into the wind that had gushed into the room. "Nell, stay with me." She tightened her hold on Nell's hand, used her other to take Ripley's limp one. "Still the power and quiet the air. Challenge this circle, he who dares. Here we stand, we are the Three. As we will, so mote it be."

Will pressed against will. Magic thrummed against magic. Then as abruptly as it had begun, the wind died. Books that had been spinning in the air fell to the floor with a thud.

"Ripley." Mac's voice remained utterly calm, in direct opposition to his speeding heart. "I'm going to count back from ten. You're going to wake up when I reach one. Slowly."

He leaned close to her, brushed his lips over her cheeks, and whispered the magic he'd read in the journal.

"You'll remember that," he promised her, hoping it would stay in her mind when she needed it most. "You'll hear that. You'll know that."

She felt herself rising as he brought her back, as if waking from a hill of feathers. The closer she came to the top, the more she began to feel the cold. And the dread.

When her eyes were open, and her vision clear, she saw the blood on Mac's face. It trickled down his forehead, down his cheek.

"God! My God!"

"It's nothing." He hadn't realized he was cut until she touched her hand to his face and brought it back smeared with blood. "Some flying glass. It's nothing," he repeated. "A couple of scratches."

"Your blood." She fisted her hand over it, felt the guilt, the power. The hunger and the fear.

"I've done worse shaving. Look at me. Relax. Nell, maybe you could get Ripley a glass of water. We'll take a little break here before we talk about all this."

"No." Ripley snapped as she rose. "I'll get it. I need a minute." She touched his face lightly. "I'm sorry. I couldn't control it. I'm sorry."

"It's all right."

She nodded as though she agreed with him, but she knew as she walked back toward the kitchen that it wasn't. Wouldn't be. Couldn't be.

She knew what she had to do. What had to be done. His blood was already cool on her fingers as she walked out the back door and into the rising storm.

Twenty

She stepped out into the wind with only one clear purpose. She would get Harding and herself off the island. Away from Mac. Away from Nell and Mia and her brother. After that, she would do whatever came next. But the most immediate danger to those she loved was inside her, and linked to whatever was inside Harding.

She had shed Mac's blood.

She curled her fingers, still damp with it, into a fist again. Blood was power, one of its most elemental sources. The darker magics used it as a conduit, or fed on it.

Everything she was and believed rejected that. Refused it. Refuted it.

Do no harm, she thought. She would try to do no harm. But first, she would see to it, she would ensure, that no harm could or would be done to those she loved.

The murdered innocents.

It was a whisper in her ear, so clear, so urgent, she spun around expecting to see someone standing behind her.

But there was nothing but the night—the dark, and the bright and brutal force of the storm.

The farther she got from the house, the more violent the storm raged, and the more her anger grew. It would use her to hurt Mac, to get to Nell, to destroy Mia.

She would die first, and take it with her.

When she reached the beach, she quickened her pace, then whirled around at the sound behind her.

Lucy bolted out of the dark, ears alert. She nearly sent the dog back home with one abrupt command. But Ripley lowered the arm she had lifted to point and hissed out a breath.

"All right, then, come along. Might as well have a goofy dog as a familiar as none at all." She rested her hand on Lucy's head. "Protect what's mine."

Her hair flew in the wind as she and the dog jogged across the sand. The surf pounded, a wall of black water that slammed relentlessly against the shore.

The sound of it beat in her head.

Her sister was dead. Slain like a lamb for her love, for her heart. For her gift. Where was the justice?

The air itself was full of howls and screams, a thousand tormented voices. Under her feet, a dirty fog began to creep along the ground, rising until it was up to her ankles, then halfway to her knees.

The chill of it seeped into her bones.

Blood for blood. Life for life. Power for power. How could she have believed there was any other way?

Something made her look over her shoulder. Where the house should have been, with its lights glowing against the window, was nothing but a curtain of dirty white.

She'd been cut off from home—and she could see now, as the fog continued to rise and swirl and thicken, from the village as well.

Fine and good, she thought, shoving fear down beneath fury.

"Come on, then, you bastard." She shouted it, and her voice cut through the fog like a scalpel through gauze. "Take me on."

The first punch of power knocked her back a full three steps before she dug in.

Rage curled inside her. As she threw up her arms, embraced it, lightning slashed the sky and sea like red-tipped whips. Ah, here, she thought, here was magic with muscle. She saw herself, and not herself, standing in the gale, gathering forces. Air, Earth, Fire, Water.

Beside her, Lucy lifted her head and let out a long, ululant howl.

Harding, or what had mastered him, stepped out of the fog.

"Rip always did throw a good tantrum," Zack said to try to lighten the mood.

The living room was in shambles, and if he let himself, he could still feel the buzz of what had whipped through it sting along his skin.

"Fear and anger, anger and fear." Mia paced as she spoke. "I couldn't get through it. Ripley's and the one she comes from. It's so strong, so thick."

"Like her skull?" Mac said with a faint grin.

"Precisely. I'd hoped to see what tactic would be taken next, so that we could counter it. That, naturally, would be too simple."

"This hurts her," Nell commented.

"I know it does." Mia patted Nell's arm absently. "And I'm sorry for it. The thing to do now is to sit down and figure out how to use those emotions, their negativity, in what comes next. A protective spell, at this point, is only a stop-gap. As much as I hate to agree with the deputy, we have to take action."

She stopped to gather her thoughts. "You haven't had much experience, Nell, and it wouldn't be an easy matter in any case."

"What wouldn't?" Mac asked. "You're thinking of a casting out?"

"So handy to have a scholar around. Yes," Mia continued. "There are five of us. We'd do better with twelve, but there isn't time to round up recruits. Just as there isn't time to do much in preparation. We'll use what we've got. Once we've . . ."

She trailed off, and her cheeks went deathly pale. "She's gone. She's outside the protective boundary." Fear leaped out of her before she could cage it. "She's broken the circle."

Even as Mac rushed for the door, Mia grabbed his arm. "No, no. *Think.* Feeling's not enough, which is her problem. We go together." Her gaze swept the room. "And we go ready. Do you know how it's done?"

Mac struggled against panic. "In theory."

Mia watched Zack snap on his holster. She wanted to tell him that wasn't the way, but the expression on his face warned her not to bother.

"Tell us what to do," Nell said urgently. "And let's do it quickly."

Ripley planted her feet, legs spread, body braced. It was a dare, and she knew it. Draw him out, she thought. Draw him to her, and save the rest.

And destroy him.

Beside her, Lucy growled low in her throat.

"Harding." She frosted her voice with amused derision. "Middle-aged, paunchy city boy. Not such a keen choice, if you ask me."

"A useful shell." The voice was deeper, and somehow wetter, than it should have been. "We've met before," he told her.

"Have we? I only remember interesting people."

"What's in you remembers what's in me." He circled her, light on his feet. Ripley turned with him, careful to keep face-to-face. She slid her fingers into Lucy's collar to hold her in place as the dog leaped and snapped. "You reached for what I have once, took it into you like a lover. Remember the ecstasy."

It was not, she discovered, a question. But a command. A fast, pulsing thrill pumped through her. Heady and *full.* Glorious. A kind of full-body orgasm that nearly brought her to her knees with its sheer and ferocious pleasure.

She shuddered from it, didn't quite bite back a moan.

Yes, God, yes. She could have *this*? Such a thing would be worth any price. Betrayal, damnation. Death.

As she struggled to clear her head, she caught the flash of movement. She stumbled to counter, and ended up sprawled on her face in the frigid sand.

It felt as though she'd been rammed by a truck.

He was chuckling, a kind of tickled delight as she shoved to her hands and knees. She watched Lucy charge, leap, teeth bared, and slam into a shield of air that went flaming at the edges at impact.

"No! Lucy, no! Hold."

"I can give you what you want, and more. But it won't be free. Not free, yet easy. Why don't you take my hand?"

She had her breath back, barely. Held a hand out for the dog that trembled with each growl. "Why don't you kiss my ass?"

He knocked her flat again. One wicked sweep of wind. "I could crush you. Such a waste. Join your power with mine, and we'd rule."

Liar, she thought. He lies. And he's toying with you. Be smarter, she told herself. Be meaner. "I'm confused," she said weakly. "I can't think. I need to know the people I love are safe."

"Of course." He crooned it. "Whatever you want can be yours. Give me what you are."

She kept her head down as she got slowly to her feet, as if with great effort. It was her mind she shot at him when she tossed her head back. All the fury of it. It was shock she saw on his face, for one gratifying instant. Then his body flew back, hurled by her temper.

The sand where he landed turned black beneath the fog, as if scorched.

"I'm going to send you to Hell," she promised him.

The light was blinding, and heat and cold burst in the air like shrapnel. She went on pure instinct, leaping away, countering, attacking.

She felt pain—bright and stunning—and used it as she would a weapon.

"You and yours will suffer," he told her. "There will be agony, then there will be nothing, which is worse than agony. What you love will cease to be."

"You can't touch what I love. Until you get through me."

"No?"

She could hear his breathing, ragged, strained. He was tiring, she thought darkly. She would win. And even as she gathered herself to end it, he clasped his hands, raised them. Black lightning spewed out of the churning sky, pierced his joined hands and formed a glinting sword.

He sliced it once through the air, then twice. His face was triumphant as he came toward her.

She called to the Earth, felt it tremble lightly. As it began to quake, Lucy leaped to defend her. Even as Ripley screamed, the sword bit.

"Everything you love," he said as the dog lay still on the ground. "Everything dies tonight."

"For that alone—" She threw her hand skyward, and her power with it. "I'll kill you."

She felt the hasp of the sword in her hand. The fit true as a glove, the weight familiar. She swept it down, and the clash of blade to blade rang like doom.

Now it was she who called the storm, a hundred bolts that lanced the sand and water until they circled like fiery bars and caged them. Its rage and violence fueled her, became her.

Her hate grew with an appetite so greedy it swallowed all else. "You killed the innocents."

He was grinning, lips peeled back. "Every one."

"You destroyed my sisters."

"They died weeping."

"You murdered the man I loved."

"Then, and now."

The thirst for his blood burned in her throat, seemed to feed her with impossible strength. She beat him back, back toward those flaming bars.

Dimly she heard someone calling her—in her mind, in her ears. She blocked it out as she continued to hack and thrust, as she felt his sword tremble and give a bit more each time.

She wanted nothing—nothing—so much as the glory of running her blade through his heart. And feeling the power sing through her at that murderous stroke.

It coursed through her, a little deeper, a little truer every moment. Closer, she thought, so much closer. She could taste the promise of it—dark, bitter, seductive.

When his sword spun out of his hand, and he fell at her feet, she felt the thrill of it, like sex.

With the hilt of her sword gripped in both hands, she raised it high over her head.

"Ripley."

Mac's voice was so quiet through the roaring in her head that she barely heard it. But her hands trembled.

"It's what he wants. Don't give him what he wants."

"I want justice," she shouted as her hair flew around her head in coils and snaps.

"You're too weak to kill me." The man at her feet lay back, deliberately exposing his throat. "You haven't the courage."

"Stay with me, Ripley. Look at me."

With the sword gripped in her hands, she stared through the bars. She saw Mac only inches away.

Where did he come from? she thought dully. How did he get here? Beside him stood her brother, and on either side Mia and Nell.

She heard the wheeze and panting of her own breath, felt the cold sweat sliding over her skin. And the pulse of that greed swimming in her veins.

"I love you. Stay with me," Mac said again. "Remember."

"Lower the barrier." Mia's voice was brisk. "And cast the circle. We're stronger."

"They'll die." The thing with Harding's

face taunted her. "I'll kill them slowly, painfully, so you hear them screaming. My death or theirs. Choose."

She turned away from those she loved and met her match. "Oh, yours."

The night exploded with sound as she brought the sword down. A thousand images echoed through her mind. Through them she saw the triumph in his eyes, the sheer glee in them.

An instant later, they were baffled and lost. And Harding's.

She stopped the blade an inch from his throat.

"Help me." He whispered it, and she saw his skin ripple.

"I will. The root of magic is in the heart," she began, repeating the words Mac had put in her subconscious. "From this the gift of power must start. With its light we burn off the dark, with its joy we leave our mark. To protect and defend, to live and to see. As I will, so mote it be."

Beneath her ready blade, Harding began to laugh. "Do you think such weak women's spells will hold me?"

Ripley tilted her head, almost in sympathy. "Yes. As will this." Her mind was clear as glass as she closed her hand over the edge of the blade. It sliced into her palm, already stained with Mac's blood.

Against her heart, the amulet Mac had given her glowed warm and bright.

"His blood," she said. "And my blood. Mixed now and true." She squeezed until drops fell on his skin. And he began to yell. In rage, she thought as she continued. Wonderful rage. "Poured from the heart, they conquer you. This is the power that I set free. As I will, so mote it be."

"Bitch! Whore!" He bellowed as she stepped back, strained to snatch at her, to rise. Snarled when he could do neither.

Her vision was suddenly so incredibly clear. Hope, she realized, was blinding bright. She vanished the bars of light, turned. "We can't leave Harding like this." Pity for him swarmed into her. "Poor bastard."

"We cast it out," Mia said.

They laid out a circle of salt and silver. Inside it Harding spat and howled like an animal, and his curses grew more foul, his threats more hideous.

Faces shivered across his face, as if the bones knit and re-knit themselves.

Thunder rolled across the sky in waves as wild as the surf. The wind cried piercingly.

Harding's pupils rolled as they ringed him and clasped hands.

"We cast you out, dark into dark, from here till ever, you bear our mark." Mia focused. A small white pentagram scored Harding's cheek.

He howled like a wolf.

"Into the void and into the night," Nell continued. "Out of this soul and beyond the light."

"Helen, I love you. You're my wife, my world," he said in Evan's voice. "Have pity."

It was pity she felt. But the single tear that slipped down Nell's cheek was all she could give.

"In this place and in this hour," Ripley chanted. "We cast you out and scorn your power. We are joined, we are the Three. As we will, so mote it be."

"We cast you out," Mia repeated, and each who clasped hands repeated, one by one until the words overlapped into a single voice.

The force of it came like a gale, cold and fetid. It swirled up, a black funnel, then spewed into the air. And into the sea.

On the sand Harding, his face gray but unmarked, groaned.

"He needs tending," Nell said.

"Go ahead and take care of him, then." Ripley stepped back. Immediately the strength went out of her legs and she buckled.

"Okay, baby. Okay." Mac caught her, lowering her gently to her knees. "Catch your breath, clear your head."

"I'm all right. Just a bit wobbly." She managed to lift her head, look at her brother. "Guess you won't have to lock me up for homicide."

"Guess not." He knelt as well, took her face in his hands. "Scared me, Rip."

"Yeah, me, too." She pressed her lips together to keep them from trembling. "We're going to be busy tomorrow. Storm damage."

"We'll handle it. Todds take care of the Sisters."

"Damn right." She breathed in, breathed out, and felt free. "You ought to give Nell a hand with Harding. Poor sap. I'm okay."

"You always were." He kissed both her cheeks, held on for another minute. Then looked at Mac as he got to his feet. "Make sure she stays that way."

She drew in another breath. "Give me a minute, will you?" she asked Mac.

"I can probably spare two, but not much more."

"Okay," she agreed as he helped her up.

Her knees were jelly, but she willed them to hold her, steadied herself, and turned toward Mia. Then she forgot the weakness, the shock, even the echoes of power. Mia stood, smiling just a little, one hand on Lucy's head. The dog's tail was wagging like a madcap metronome.

"Lucy!" In one leap she had her face buried in the dog's fur. "I thought she was gone. I saw . . ." She jerked back and began stroking at Lucy, searching for the wound.

"It wasn't real," Mia said quietly. "His sword was only an illusion, a trick of violence to test you. He used it to push you to repeat the sin. He didn't want your death— not yet. He wanted your soul, and your power."

Ripley squeezed Lucy one last time, then straightened and turned to Mia. "Well, he lost, didn't he?"

"So he did."

"Did you know, all along?"

"Pieces." Mia shook her head. "Not enough to be sure, just enough to doubt and worry." She held out a hand as Nell crossed to them. "In my heart, I knew you wouldn't fail. But in my head, I wasn't sure. You've always been a difficult puzzle for me."

"I might have done it. I was mad enough, frightened enough. But I felt both of you, inside. I never wanted this," she said in a furious whisper. "You know I never wanted this."

"Life's tough," Mia said with a shrug. "You play the cards you're dealt or you fold."

"I knew you'd win." Nell took her injured hand, gently uncurled the fingers. "You need to see to this."

"I will. It's not bad." She pressed her lips together. "I want the scar," she said. "I need it."

"Then . . ." Slowly, Nell curled Ripley's fingers into a loose fist. "Zack and I are going to take Mr. Harding back to the house for now. He needs a hot meal. He's shaken up, confused, but all in all"—she glanced back to where Zack had Harding on his feet—"amazingly unharmed. He remembers little."

"Let's keep it that way," Ripley demanded. "All right, let's go back, clean the rest of this up." She tilted her head up to the sky, saw the clouds dissolving, and the halo of the moon glowing pure and white. "Storm's passing," she murmured.

Mia nodded. "For now."

Ripley opened her mouth, looked toward Harding again. "Maybe the guys could take Harding back, give us another minute here."

"All right. I'll tell Zack."

The wind had gentled to a breeze, and the breeze smelled of night and of water. Ripley waited until the men, and the cheerful dog, turned toward home.

With Mia and Nell she closed the circle they had cast. She took her ritual sword—that had been real enough—and cleansed it. The surf foamed up, tame now and lovely, and dampened her boots.

"When I lifted the sword," she began, knowing her friends were beside her, "I wanted blood. Like a craving. Bringing it down seemed to take hours." She shifted her feet. "I'm not big on this vision crap.

That's your deal, Mia. Usually. But I saw images. I saw Mac, Mac and me. My parents, my brother. I saw the three of us in the forest the way we were last fall. I saw Nell. You had a baby in your arms."

"A baby." Nell's voice went soft, dreamy, as she pressed a hand to her belly. "But I'm not—"

"Not yet, anyway."

"Oh, boy!" Nell let out a thrilled and baffled laugh. "Oh, boy, oh, boy!"

"Anyway," Ripley continued, "I saw those things, and more. The three sisters, in a dark wood, in a circle of light. The one who was Earth on this very beach, in a storm. There were so many, coming so fast they overlapped, but each was perfectly clear.

"And I saw you, Mia. Standing on your cliffs, on the edge of your cliffs. Alone and crying. There was darkness all around you, the kind that came out of Harding tonight. It wanted you. Somehow, I . . . It's always been you, most of all."

Even as the chill crept up her spine, Mia nodded. "Are you telling me to . . . beware?"

"Very ware. I saw something else, at the instant I stopped the sword. One last flash.

The three of us, in a circle. And I knew it was okay. What I'm saying is, I know it *can* be okay. If we do what we're supposed to do, make the right choices."

"You made yours tonight," Mia reminded her. "Trust me to make mine."

"You're the strongest."

"Well, well. Is that a compliment I hear?"

"Can it, okay? In the magic stuff, you're the strongest. What comes at you's going to be the strongest, too."

"None of us is alone now." Nell took Mia's hand, then Ripley's. "We're three."

Ripley took Mia's hand to finish the link. "Yeah. Witches Are Us."

Ripley told herself she was doing what needed to be done, but that didn't mean she would enjoy it. She watched Nell soothe and charm Harding. Bolster him with soup and tea. She let Mia treat and bind her hand. And avoided being alone with Mac until they left to walk to the yellow cottage.

"We can load up your equipment tonight if you want."

"I'll get it tomorrow," he answered. He

didn't touch her. He didn't know why, but he sensed she wasn't ready for that yet.

"I guess Harding's going to write his book after all."

"Not the one he might have had in mind. But, yeah, I think Nell likes the idea of a book that offers hope to people in an abuse cycle. He's barely the worse for wear now that he's . . ."

"Exorcised?"

"In a manner of speaking. Can I ask you a technical question?"

"I guess." It was a beautiful night. Cool and fresh and clear. There was no reason, she told herself, to be so edgy now.

"How did you know the blood would hold him?"

"I don't know exactly."

"Hereditary knowledge?" Mac offered and got a shrug.

"Maybe. That kind of thing's your bag. Magic runs through the blood. Mine," she said, lifting her hand. "Yours, even though it's pretty diluted." She glanced over when he laughed. "That's accurate enough," she said testily. "And blood is a transmitter, a sacrifice, whatever. It's life."

"No argument." He stopped, turned at

the verge of the trees where the shadows were soft and the moonlight dappled through black branches. "Was that all?"

"There's a bond. It's emotional—apart from intellect or logic, even from ritual, I guess."

"Love." He waited a beat. "Why can't you say it now?"

"You've never seen me like that before," she said in a rush. "Everything that's come before has been like kid stuff compared to tonight."

"You were magnificent." He watched her eyes widen. It was going to be fun, he thought, to blindside her with statements like that for the next fifty or sixty years. "Did you think that seeing what I did would change what I feel for you?"

"No. I don't know. Mac, I was nearly seduced. Maybe when I went out it was with the idea that I could sacrifice myself—and don't tell me that's lame. I've already figured that out."

"Then I'll restrain myself."

"Good. But the farther I got from the house, from all of you, the more I wanted blood. There was a moment, more than a moment, when I might have turned, when I might have grabbed what was offered. The power was outrageous—huge, seductive, staggering."

"But you didn't take it."

"No."

"Why?"

"I wanted me more. I wanted you more. And I . . . this sounds hokey."

"Say it anyway."

"I wanted justice more."

He laid his hands on her shoulders, brushed a kiss over her brow. Then he lifted her bandaged palm and kissed that, too. "I said you looked magnificent. That's accurate, too. There was a light, bursting out of you. Nothing could have dimmed it. And now . . . you're just my girl."

"Your girl." She snorted. "Please."

"All mine," he said, and did what he'd wanted to do since he'd seen her with a shining sword gripped in her hands. He lifted her off her feet, nearly crushing her in an embrace as his mouth sought hers. "Marry me. Live with me in the house by the sea."

"Oh, God, Mac, I love you. It's better than everything, more than everything. Hell,

Mac"—she tipped her head back—"it *is* everything."

"And we're just getting started."

She laid her head on his shoulder while he stroked her hair. Brilliant mind, tough body, generous heart. Her lips curved as she thought, All mine.

"When the power was in me, I felt invincible, tremendous. It's like having molten gold running through your veins. Do you know how I feel right now?"

"How?"

"Even better."

She lifted her face to his once more so their lips met, once more. The sound of the sea was a steady heartbeat in the distance, the moon sailed white overhead. Around them the night shimmered with the echoes of magic.

And was enough.